EILEEN RAMSAY OMNIBUS

The Quality of Mercy
Harvest of Courage

By the same author:

THE BROKEN GATE
THE DOMINIE'S LASSIE
BUTTERFLIES IN DECEMBER
WALNUT SHELL DAYS

EILEEN RAMSAY OMNIBUS

The Quality of Mercy
Harvest of Courage

EILEEN RAMSAY

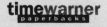
timewarner
paperbacks

A *Time Warner* Paperback

This omnibus edition first published in Great Britain by
Time Warner Paperbacks in 2002
Eileen Ramsay Omnibus Copyright © Eileen Ramsay 2002

Previously published separately:
The Quality of Mercy first published in Great Britain in 1997 by
Little, Brown and Company
Published by Warner Books in 1997
Copyright © Eileen Ramsay 1997

Harvest of Courage first published in Great Britain in 1998 by
Little, Brown and Company
Published by Warner Books in 1999
Copyright © Eileen Ramsay 1998

The moral right of the author has been asserted.

A CIP catalogue record for this book is available from the British Library.

ISBN 0 7515 3299 1

Typeset by Palimpsest Book Production Ltd
Polmont, Stirlingshire
Printed and bound in Great Britain by
Clays Ltd, St Ives plc

Time Warner Paperbacks
An imprint of
Time Warner Books UK
Brettenham House
Lancaster Place
London WC2E 7EN

www.TimeWarnerBooks.co.uk

The Quality of Mercy

For my mother –
another bonnie fechter,
and in memory of my father

Acknowledgements

I would like to thank the following members of the legal profession for all their help while I was researching this book. They may now stop dodging behind the aspidistras when I enter a room, unless, of course, they wish to continue to do so. The Right Honourable Lord Frazer of Carmyllie; The Right Honourable Lord Weir; William Berry W.S.; Sheriff Robin McEwen; Mike McGinley; Graham McNicol; Sandy Ingram; Hugh Annan; Jim Robertson and Fiona Raitt of the Faculty of Law, the University of Dundee; Mrs Maria McGuire; and very special thanks to my friend Marian Gilmour, a wonderful advocate in two languages.

Prologue

1933 Edinburgh

BLAIR KNEW IT was not going to work. Ferelith could exert herself until she was blue in the face. Mother had set her mind, and more importantly her heart, against her. Grimly he kept smiling while his heart crumbled into little bits inside him. What could he do? He loved his mother who, since his father's tragic early death in the Great War, had devoted her whole life to him. And yet, at the same time, and with an even fiercer passion, he loved the girl who was so bravely fighting a losing battle against the tide of inexplicable antagonism that flowed across the room towards her from the tiny, but oh-so-elegant, figure of his mother.

Ferelith soldiered on. He knew her so well: he could see how near to tears she was and her soft west-coast accent got stronger and stronger as she struggled against the clipped vowels of the older woman.

'Do you know, Mother?' Blair was determined to help. 'One of our professors says he wouldn't doubt that one day Ferelith might well be Lord Chancellor.'

'Oh, Lord Advocate would be enough,' laughed Ferelith, but Blair's mother did not smile.

'In my day girls stayed at home to look after their families.'

'But I have no family,' said Ferelith quietly, 'and so I must earn a living.'

'Shall we have lunch?'

In four seemingly neutral little words, Helena Crawford managed to convey her dislike, her distrust, her implacable opposition to this girl. Why? Why? What had Ferelith done? Or was it what Ferelith was?

No, it would never work until Mother was forced to see that unless she accepted this working-class girl from a Glasgow orphanage, she would lose her son too.

I can't give her up, Blair decided, as he sipped a very fine pre-lunch sherry.

Sometimes his feelings for Ferelith frightened him. Since that day two years ago when he had walked into the large lecture hall in the university and seen her standing there like a terrified rabbit caught in the gaze of a headlight, she had been more important than eating or sleeping, and far more important than his studies. She was part of him, and how it had happened he could not understand. Their backgrounds were so different. His was privileged: nannies, governesses, servants who anticipated every wish of the fatherless little boy, Eton but not Oxford. He had never worked hard enough. Why should he? He had inherited an estate and the fortune to support it on his eighteenth birthday. He had never wanted anything enough to work for it, not until Ferelith. And why Ferelith?

She had inherited nothing on her eighteenth birthday. There had been nothing to inherit. She had been brought up in an orphanage in Glasgow where one of the sisters of the religious teaching order had recognized her not inconsiderable brain and had fought for the girl's right to further education. Who her parents were and why she had been in the home Ferelith did not know. Blair did not care. The skinny girl with the badly cut hair, the obviously second-hand clothes and the bitten nails was his future. He was not given to introspection. He marvelled at the kismet that had made Ferelith as familiar to him as the skin on his face and he accepted his fate.

Ferelith did not, at first, approve of his plan, the simple but so obvious little plan that had occurred to him somewhere between the sherry and the port his mother had insisted on offering him, because *Grandpapa always had port, dear.*

'We can't, Blair. It's against everything I've ever been taught to respect. We'll wait: she'll come round when she sees how much we love one another.'

Blair's heart gave a sickening lurch inside him. Dear God, how he wished that were true.

'She doesn't care,' he said quietly, and in saying that and admitting that, he grew up. 'My mother has had her own way all her life. You can't believe how much my grandfather spoiled her. She will never accept you because she has not written a nice, brainy, skinny, working-class Catholic orphan into her life script.'

'When she sees that we mean to continue friends . . .'

'I don't mean to continue friends . . . at least I do, but I want us to continue as husband and wife. During that ghastly lunch I saw so clearly that you mean more to me than she does. I love her. I'm sorry that she has chosen to be as self-centred as she is and maybe that was Grandfather's fault and my father's. I don't think he ever refused her anything either. It's not good for children to get their own way all the time. I shall be very strict with all of ours.'

Ferelith laughed and the ferocious scowl eased from his handsome face. 'We're going to have children, are we?'

'Yes, five.'

'After I become Lord Advocate or before, or are you going to have them?'

'Don't laugh. We can do this, Ferelith. I can support you. We'll get married because I need you so much and you need me. With my money, and my name, it will be easier for you, and with your brains, spacing five children between court cases should be easy.'

She was angry. He had forgotten how very sensitive she was about money. She thought about it, or the lack of it, all the time. He never considered it for a moment. It continued to flow when he wanted it just as the mighty Forth flowed through his fertile acres.

'I did not fall in love with you because of your name.'

'I know. That's why I fell in love with you, though. There you stood in that ghastly frock Mother Superior found in the poor box and you said your name. Ferelith, a fairy princess. You cast a spell on me. It will remain until I die and even after death.'

He was silent and it was her turn to wonder. How sensitive and romantic he was! If her life depended on it, she could not tell him that her love would continue through all time. She would want to say it: she would say it in so many ways but never never with words. But she would not marry him to ease her way through law school.

'You have just been kidnapped, Miss Gallagher. I don't think you noticed that we are now on the road to Gretna Green. I am going to marry you to save your good name because I have absolutely no intention of stopping this car until we reach the border. There I shall take you with or without benefit of clergy or blacksmith or whatever, and please don't get into a Holy Roman snit because you can get things sorted out with your priest when we get back to university. Hell, we'll need to find an apartment. I can't take you into Residence.'

'You're being very childish, Blair. This isn't the Middle Ages.'

'Oh, Ferelith, Ferelith. I aged a hundred years this afternoon. I am older than time. Marry me. You want to, don't you, and really, what does it matter whether you marry me before or after graduation. That's surely academic. And if you marry me, you can keep me at work because if you are in the same room, even better in the same bed, then I won't spend all my studying time writing sonnets to your funny little nose. You owe me a good education.'

'I couldn't hurt Sister Anthony Joseph.'

'You won't. She understands more about life and love than you do.'

Five hours later Mr and Mrs Blair Crawford sat down to dinner in the dining room of the best hotel they could find. Five hours and ten minutes later they were in the hotel's best bedroom strewing clothes feverishly across the floor as they made for the bed. Neither of them was prepared for the intensity of their feelings, for the overpowering wildness of their mutual passion. Amazed, exhausted, satisfied, at last they fell asleep.

It was the last good night's sleep either of them was to have for quite some time.

They woke late the next morning. Ferelith lay on the bed and laughed as her naked husband averted his eyes from the body he had so much enjoyed during the night, and covered her with the sheet before sprinting for the bathroom and his dressing gown. Dear God, how sweet and innocent he was.

If he had grown a hundred years older in one afternoon in his mother's opulent home, my God, the night had made her as old as time itself. At last she knew all the secrets. He had invaded her very body. He had conquered her and by conquering he had been conquered. Modestly she hid herself under the sheet and waited while he shaved.

They went down hand in hand to the dining room. There were two men seated at a table in the corner. They were not eating. They were not speaking. They were just sitting as if they were waiting. They stood up as Ferelith and Blair entered.

Blair stopped. 'Oh, no,' he said, and he blushed a bright red. 'This is totally unacceptable.'

Ferelith felt her stomach contract. A second, a lifetime ago, it had felt light and soft and so fulfilled and now, now . . . Such a feeling of foreboding. Oh, God, no. Don't let it be spoiled.

'Blair?' she asked tremulously.

'Mr Crawford, Blair, please.' The older of the two men held out his hand in supplication.

Blair pushed the hand aside. 'This is really insupportable . . .' he began.

'Will you listen, you bloody young fool?'

Blair stared in embarrassed anger and humiliation at his mother's lawyer. 'How dare you follow us, McAndliss. I can't understand. I don't . . . I mean why would Mother even think I was doing this? We said nothing.'

He thought back to the luncheon. He had been, he decided, very mature, very civilized. He had kissed his mother goodbye with the usual throwaway lines. 'I'll see you soon, darling. I'll pop home for a weekend.' He had been as he always was. She could have suspected nothing. But she had. He turned back to the senior man. 'You will crawl back to my mother and tell her that Ferelith is now my wife and . . .'

Sinclair McAndliss looked at the young couple. It was not his job to spare them, even to wish that he did not have to do this cruel thing. And there was only one way to do it.

'She's your sister, laddie,' said the lawyer baldly. 'My God, Blair, I told Helena a dozen times, a thousand times to warn you, to alert you.'

Blair sat down abruptly and clung to the table top as if it was a lifeline. This could not be happening. He could not look at Ferelith. No, no, it was not true. To what depths would his mother dive to get her own way?

'My mother is insane,' he said. 'My sister? My father was killed in action in 1914. Ferelith . . .'

'Was born in 1914 in Bombay, India, the daughter of one Niamh Gallagher, spinster, of Cork. Niamh had worked for an army family as a nanny but apart from her employer who was blameless, the only man she met alone was one Major Winterton. The birth certificate of Miss Gallagher says 'Father Unknown'. Even in death Niamh Gallagher refused to betray her lover, but there was an investigation and it could not have been anyone else. When the pregnancy was discovered your father shot himself, laddie. He was no hero, dying in battle, but a cold-blooded seducer. Why ever did you think your grandfather insisted that you change your name?'

'My name?' Blair looked at the lawyer. He had no idea what he was talking about.

'You were born Blair Winterton, laddie. Your mother was so ashamed of your father that she had her name and yours legally changed after the war. She said it was for continuity in the estate, a condition of your grandfather's will, that you could only inherit if you had his name. I'm sorry, Blair, but there is no doubt at all in my mind that your father, Major the Honourable Archie Winterton, and Mrs . . . Miss Gallagher's father were one and the same man.'

Mr and Mrs Blair Crawford looked at him in misery and then in horror at one another and then looked away, each embarrassed by the other's presence.

And then with horrifying abruptness, Mrs Crawford was violently sick all over the beautiful starched linen cloth on the hotel's best table. Blair rushed to help her but she threw him off as if she could no longer bear his touch. Last night his hands had inflamed her. Now . . . She turned and ran weeping from the room.

1

1913 Fife

CRITICALLY, HELENA WINTERTON examined her image in the full-length mirror. She was displeased with what she saw. Breasts far too large for fashion and disagreeably full of milk, and no waistline that she could discern, no matter how hard she sucked in the stomach that, to her eyes, looked too soft and round.

Was there nothing that would tighten up this overstretched skin? Baby was a poppet and she absolutely adored every hair on his precious little head, but he had cost her.

Her skin was not the only part of her life that demanded firm treatment. Archie, darling Archie. Helena smiled despite herself and felt that too familiar frisson of excitement in her lower belly. No, really she had been just the teeniest bit dishonest in telling Archie that dear Doctor Ferguson advised against the renewing of . . . how could she put it . . . connubial relations just yet. Archie was so patient and so undemanding. But no, she did not want another baby, at least not for a year or two; and it seemed as if Baby had started on the first day of her honeymoon and she could not, would not, risk another pregnancy immediately after his so stressful and painful birth.

She would, however, manage to *reward* her dearest Archie for his forbearance before he left for India.

There. She had said it. Before *he* left for India. She had made the decision then. When Major the Honourable Archie Winterton sailed with his regiment to Bombay in a few short weeks, Mrs Helena Crawford Winterton would not be with him.

Imperiously Helena rang the bell for her maid.

'Quick, Bessie. Ask Nanny to bring Baby. I want to feed him before I dress for dinner: I must see Sir Gordon before Major Winterton returns.'

Helena ignored the tightening of Bessie's lips. Nanny would fume and fuss at the disruption of her precious charge's schedule and might even have the audacity to defy her mistress. Well, she would see who ruled in this house. Helena wrapped herself in her brocade dressing gown and sat in the wing chair by the fire.

Bessie, without the baby, hurried into the room. She bobbed a curtsey to her mistress.

'Mrs Hendry says as Baby is asleep . . .' She stopped before the glint in her young mistress's eye.

'Go upstairs, Bessie, and bring me Baby before I leak all over this chair. I am dressing for dinner and I have no intention of jumping up after the fish to attend to my son.'

Mrs Hendry herself brought Baby. He had not fretted at being wakened from a sound sleep. Really, he was so like Archie in nature. Even at two months old Helena could see the signs of patience and courtesy exhibited so often by her darling Archie. She smiled sweetly at the discomfited nanny.

'I know how we hate to disrupt Precious's schedule, Nanny, but I must talk to Sir Gordon before dinner, and see, Baby is so greedy and so good-natured: he doesn't at all mind dining early. Do you my precious?' she added to the baby as she pressed his beautiful little head against her full breast.

The baby looked up at her out of one eye. His little rosebud mouth was already fastened on her nipple and he was swallowing noisily. Nanny bent over and inserted a finger between his nose and the full softness of his mother's breast.

'Try to keep his nose clear, Mrs Winterton. Baby has the teeniest little cold.'

Helena smiled. 'Yes, poor lamb,' she said. 'You may go, Mrs Hendry. His grandpapa will want to see him. His papa will return him to the nurseries before he himself dresses for dinner.'

Mrs Hendry frowned but apart from registering strong disapproval there was nothing she could do. At least the Major might remember that what went in one end of a tiny baby almost immediately came out the other.

Helena felt the frost in the atmosphere and she regretted it, because really it was so much more pleasant when everyone was happy; but she was the mistress of this estate and had been since she had persuaded her father to dispense with the services of her governess on her fifteenth birthday. She held her breast away from the baby's nose and Mrs Hendry was forced to remove her finger.

'You won't let him be jiggled about too much, Madame?' Mrs Hendry asked anxiously. 'Sir Gordon has a terrible habit of playing too strenuously with him after his feed.'

'I don't think even the most indulgent of grandpapas will court being vomited over too often, Nanny. Sir Gordon has become a very paragon among grandfathers, hasn't he, my sweet?'

Helena lifted the baby and burped him on her shoulder before transferring him to the other breast.

She said nothing but she could see how annoyed Mrs Hendry was that she was becoming such an expert mother. Really there was absolutely nothing to it. Why the whole business had been wrapped in such a veil of secrecy and old wives' tales, she could not imagine. Babies were just like horses. They needed to be fed, watered, housed, and loved, and when they were old enough, exercised and disciplined. She smiled complacent dismissal and Mrs Hendry was forced to leave.

Helena enjoyed these minutes alone with her son. As soon as he was weaned, and unfortunately he would have to be weaned if she was to enjoy any of the season, Mrs Hendry would rule supreme. There would be fewer excuses to steal him away, fewer moments when she could hold him like this and nuzzle his soft little neck with her face, smelling the milky warm smell of him, watching the little mouth open in an enormous yawn that wrinkled up the tiny little nose.

'Come along, Precious, before I change my mind and decide that you shall have a sister before the year is out. We will wait, Poppet, just for a few years and then we will see.'

Helena laid the baby down on the settee from where he contentedly watched her as she buttoned up her robe. That done she pulled a brush through her red-gold hair and bit her lips to give them a little colour. Then she picked the baby up, wrapped him in the finest of Shetland shawls, and hurried out to her father's rooms.

Sir Gordon Crawford was reading the racing results in the morning's papers. He never bet on any horse he had not seen but enjoyed making and losing paper fortunes with his butler. He looked up when an imperious knock announced his daughter and only child, and when he saw that she carried his precious grandson, he jumped from the chair with even more alacrity than he would have shown had it been only his daughter who stood there.

'Come in my darling girl and give that heavy child to me.'

Helena was quite happy to hand the baby over to his grandfather and to take the chair beside the fire, the chair she had always sat in when she came to this very special room. At first they talked about the baby and how amazingly he seemed to have grown since his grandfather had last seen him – only that morning.

'You are the cleverest of clever little mothers, my darling,' said Sir Gordon, 'and what your dear mamma would have made of this poppet . . .'

'They do grow quickly,' Helena interrupted his fond musings, 'but he's so delicate, Father, and he has a nasty cold in his poor little nose.'

'He is trying to breathe through his mouth, Helena. Damn it, if he don't sound like that ghastly boot boy with his constant catarrh.'

The baby, caring nothing at all for the sensibilities of anyone but his all-important self, looked into the face of Sir Gordon Crawford and rid himself of an almighty belch.

'Your boot boy is a paragon of gentility compared to that, Papa,' said Helena and they gazed in complacent wonder at this precious child.

'I will miss him so,' said Sir Gordon, 'and you too, my dear.'

'Actually, Papa, that's one of the reasons I wanted to see you before Archie comes home.' Helena knew she had to be very careful. Her father adored her but he believed implicitly that a woman's place was with her husband. She could not merely tell him that she was bored to tears with India, where almost every young officer had a lovely young wife and where the conversation was always of bridge, tennis, servants, and babies. Till the arrival of her son, all four subjects had wearied Helena immeasurably.

'I'm so torn, Papa. You see, life has changed in these past few months and now I have Baby to consider. I have two duties and which is the predominant one – my duty as a wife or my duty as a mother? It was so hard to leave you when I married Archie but that was a clear cut decision: my duty lay with my husband and, although it broke my heart, I went.' She stopped and stole a look at her fond father out of her red-gold eyelashes. Yes, he had been affected by thoughts of her broken heart, her bravery. 'I think Baby is too small,' she went on, 'too delicate to sail to India, and then he has this cold. Surely it would be better to let the winter pass before making such a long voyage?'

Half an hour later Helena almost skipped back along the passage to her rooms. Sir Gordon, totally besotted with his male heir, was firmly on her side.

When she reached her bedroom Helena put the baby down in the middle of the pink satin coverlet on her bed, and he watched her as she moved across the room to her wardrobes.

'Now what shall we wear, Precious?' she asked as she pulled dress after dress from the cavernous interiors and piled them on the day bed.

She went back to the dressing table, picked up a heavy silver-backed brush and pulled it through her hair.

There was a tap at the door and there stood Bessie, a pile of the baby's linen in her arms. 'I thought I'd change Baby, Mrs Winterton. The Major is in his bath, Madame. He said as how he wouldn't disturb you while you were with Sir Gordon.'

'Thank you, Bessie,' said Helena. She waited while the girl dealt quickly and surely with the infant. When he was ready she would take him and show him off to Archie. Archie, bless his heart, no matter how seductive he thought her in her satin peignoir, would remain in his bath while they chatted. She would leave the baby in his dressing room: Archie would relish the privilege of returning him to the dragon upstairs.

'You're a good girl,' she said as she picked up her son. 'I'm throwing out all those dresses. I'm sure I can't get into one. Perhaps you and your sisters can find a use for them.'

She smiled and went out, leaving the girl standing there looking from the door to the heaped pile of satins and laces with a dazed expression on her face.

Niamh Gallagher was frightened. She was standing at the quayside in her best, her only, coat, and in the bag she had in her hand was everything she owned. That was not much with which to be travelling halfway across the world. One dress, her best, one nightgown stitched by herself and therefore nothing really to be too proud about, two pairs of drawers – one for wearing, one for keeping in case of an accident, a second pair of knitted stockings, a Sunday petticoat with a fine edging of exquisite Limerick lace, and her extra bodice which she had been told, with some glee, would 'crucify her in the heat' but had still to be worn for decency's sake. She had the shoes she stood up in, a shawl, two linen handkerchiefs, a meagre collection of toilet articles that included her Aunt Maeve's tortoiseshell-backed hairbrush, and a prayer book. Niamh was a decent Catholic girl.

Niamh looked at the ship and then back at the town. No matter how hard she tried she could not force her legs to follow one another up that gangplank.

'May I help you?'

Niamh looked up through a mist of tears and saw a soldier shimmering in the sun. He was so tall that she had to look up into his face. It was a nice face, a kind face, and if only that voice had not issued from that face . . . she would have been reassured. But the voice was the voice of the gentry, of the lords and the landlords, and before this moment Niamh had only ever heard it raised in anger.

The voice soothed Niamh Gallagher's frightened heart and she looked straight into his fine eyes and fell instantly and irrevocably in love, and so Niamh smiled and spoke.

'Oh, I'm that nervous, sir, of getting on that boat, but haven't I a grand job waiting for me at the other side of the ocean.'

'Off to India, are you?'

'Yes, sir. I'm to be a nursemaid, sir.' To her surprise Niamh heard herself rattling on as if she and the officer were social equals and he interested in what she had to say. 'My mistress doesn't want a black person looking after her children, and I'm sure she can't be blamed for that because they can't be the same as us now, sir, can they, or they wouldn't be black. Still and all though, how she thinks I'll be better and me never having touched a babby in all my born days, I do not know.'

He smiled at her prejudices. India would teach her a great deal. 'Oh, well, ladies who have just had babies get strange notions, do they not? Let me take your bag and help you aboard. If this is your first voyage no wonder you are a little hesitant about trusting yourself to a ship.'

'Oh, sure I've no worries about the ship, sir. It's all that water.'

He laughed heartily and Niamh basked in the new and heady sensation of being laughed with and not at. She had not known she was funny.

'It'll be full of sharks and things,' she hazarded a guess. He was a soldier and a gentleman and therefore would know.

'In some parts, but really one is in much more danger from a carriage or one of these ghastly new motor vehicles in the middle of town than from a shark in the middle of the ocean. Ships seldom sink, you know.'

She was aboard the ship and had not felt herself walking up that strange thing called a gangway. There were several people standing there and Niamh felt their looks of displeasure. She flushed with embarrassment. 'You and your tongue, Niamh Gallagher. It'll be the death of you, so it will.' She wanted to hurry away and hide: a nursemaid had no business laughing with a gentleman even though the gentleman had initiated the conversation.

He sensed her panic. 'Don't run off. The Purser here will show you where you are to go, Miss . . . ?'

'Gallagher, sir. Niamh Gallagher.' She curtseyed quickly.

'*Bon voyage*, Miss Gallagher,' he said, and he replaced his cap and half bowed. Almost, Niamh felt, as if I were a lady.

'This way, Miss Gallagher,' ordered a voice that was not pleasant and not at all friendly, and Niamh began to follow the querulous tones away from the gangplank and down into the depths of the ship. At the top of the iron stairs that led to the steerage she turned and saw that the soldier was still standing there. Once more the sun prevented her from seeing him properly. His tall slim figure was surrounded by light.

'Like God,' thought the good Catholic irreverently. 'He's like God.'

Niamh was sharing a cabin with one other girl and an older unmarried woman. They too were in service but *Mrs* McCann was very superior: after all, was she not a nanny and her charge the daughter of an Honourable, who was in turn the daughter of a real live lord. Mary Gibson was, like Niamh, going out as a nursemaid but whereas Niamh was to be in full charge of the three children of Captain and Mrs Butler, Mary was joining a large happy household where there were two other nursemaids under the overall care of a Registered Nanny.

'My madame has money,' Mary whispered to Niamh as they lay in their bunks that night, trying to accustom themselves to the rolling of the ship. 'When I went to the big house for my interview, do you know, the housekeeper told me there were seventeen inside servants and goodness knows how many outside and more hired in from the village when my madame comes home with her children. Can you imagine, Niamh, seventeen people to look after two. What would they find to do all day? You don't think someone holds your drawers for you to step into if you're rich, do you?' At the hilarious picture conjured up by Mary's words the girls choked with laughter. 'The rich aren't like you and me, are they?' continued Mary when she could speak. 'I wonder why.'

'It's not your place to criticize your elders and betters, my girls,' said Mrs McCann. 'What would a lady born and bred know about cleaning fireplaces or blackleading grates or washing and ironing, and aren't they all too delicate to turn a mangle anyway?'

Niamh tried to hear if there was any humour in the voice. Surely Mrs McCann wasn't serious. She, Niamh, couldn't really see dirt as any respecter of any person, rich or poor. She was, however, sensible enough not to argue with Mrs McCann. She fell asleep.

The next few weeks were sheer hell as Mrs McCann and then poor Mary fell victim to seasickness. Niamh could quite cheerfully have abandoned Mrs McCann to welter in her own vomit but Mary was different. She could not abandon Mary.

'You're a good girl, Niamh Gallagher,' whispered Mrs McCann when the ship stopped trying to capsize itself and began to cut a straight furrow through the ocean. The sun, which had dazzled Niamh as she had embarked, having hidden itself for most of their journey down the length of the British Isles and out into the Mediterranean, now blazed out in splendour. Mrs McCann was finally able to sit up a little on that small part of the deck not reserved for the wives and children of the army officers travelling with them out to India. She grasped Niamh's calloused hand in her soft ones. 'Should you ever need help you have only to ask.'

Niamh smiled but said nothing, content just to sit and feel a slight breeze blow around her face. She loved watching the women on the deck. How beautiful their dresses were. She opened the top button at the neck of her dress and rolled up her sleeves.

'Poor things,' she said to Mrs McCann. 'They're dying in this heat and they're too hemmed in by restrictions to make themselves comfortable.'

'Ladies have standards, Niamh, and we would all be the better for adopting some of them.'

'Surely only the ones that make sense,' said Niamh pertly. 'I'm going for a stroll, Mrs McCann. I've paid my fare same as them and God's good clean air belongs to everyone.'

She walked off on to the main deck and leaned over the side of the ship, fascinated by the great surge of water that spread out from the sides of the ship like corn falling at the sweep of the reaper. She was mesmerized by the precision of the great sweeps of the waves, at the way the sun found every separate drop of water and turned them all to liquid silver.

Archie Winterton saw her there as he stood immaculately dressed in tropical kit. He had seen Helena sometimes like that, her neck exposed to the sun, her sleeves rolled up, her hair unbound. Longing for his wife and for his new baby son filled him.

'Miss Gallagher?'

She turned and saw him and he saw her eyes fill with pleasure as she smiled. 'Good day to you, sir,' she said. 'Is this not wonderful after that storm?'

'It is indeed. I hope you were not made unwell by the violent rolling of the ship.'

'Oh, not me, sir, which is just as well since poor Mary and Mrs McCann were unable to lift their heads from their pillows.'

'Mary and Mrs McCann?'

'My roommates, or should I say cabin mates? I am become very knowledgeable about boats, I mean ships, sir. Mary is an Irish girl like myself but unfortunately for me she is to stay in Bombay. There are five children in her family but two other nursemaids and isn't Mrs McCann, who has never

been near an altar with a man in her life, a nanny.
She has been to India before and has just taken her
Master Thomas home to prep school and is now back
for three years. She has told me everything I need to
know.'

'Well, that is good. And what did she feel that you
ought to know, Miss Gallagher?'

'Daft things about protecting my head from the
sun's rays and wearing two bodices to mop up the
sweat. An important thing she taught me is that I
should not talk alone to officers and gentlemen,
sir.' She looked up boldly and laughed into his
eyes. 'But didn't I know that already,' she finished
breathlessly, and turned back to her contemplation
of the ocean. 'There's just something about the ocean
though. Does it not make us and our problems and
our little peculiarities small?'

He looked at her strangely. She really was the
oddest young woman. He could not place her in
society. Her position was menial, her clothes were
poor, but her manner was assured and her accent,
although Irish, was not so strong that he could
not understand it. 'Are you going out as a governess, Miss Gallagher? You have a remarkable turn
of phrase, if you will excuse my boldness, for a
nursemaid.'

'Wasn't my old cousin, Maeve, that brought me
up, not housekeeper to the parish priest, sir. He
was a good man and kept me when my parents
died. I went to school till I was fourteen, would
you believe, and then I stayed at the parish house
because really, wasn't Maeve crippled half the time
with the rheumatism. You read an awful lot of
books, sir, when you are alone with an old man who
spends most of his time on his knees in prayer and
an old woman who can't get on her knees at all.'

'And why have you left them?'

The laughter was gone from her face and he was sad to see it go. It lit up the rather austere thin features and made her almost pretty. With more money, Niamh Gallagher could have been beautiful.

'Maeve is dead and the old man has been retired. Was the Bishop got me this job and I hope I don't disappoint them. I know nothing at all about children.'

'There's not much to know. Feed them and water them, like horses, and keep them clean. I should think that would do it. Oh, yes, and discipline and affection.'

She laughed at his absurdity and he laughed back.

'Affection the least important, is it, sir?'

Suddenly he was serious. 'No, Miss Gallagher, affection is always primary.'

'You have children, sir?'

In his mind he saw Baby and his gummy open-mouthed grin: he could feel the child's small warm body and he could almost breathe in that special clean smell of new baby.

'One. A little boy.'

She looked round. The deck was full of small children and nursemaids. She put her hand up to close the buttons at her throat. 'Are they here then?'

'No. They are not here.' He put out his hand and touched her hair gently. 'We go ashore at Aden, Miss Gallagher. I would advise you, if Mrs McCann has not, to buy a hat at Firpo's.'

He nodded his head and turned and walked away, conscious of the looks of displeasure from the dowagers under their awnings, and he cursed himself for his stupidity.

'Oh God, Helena, how can I bear one year alone. It's not a month yet and I ache for you and for Baby.'

He went down to his cabin where he wrote yet another passionate letter to his wife. He poured out all his love for her and his longing, and his need to see his son grow.

Many children survive admirably in India. The ship echoes to the sounds of their games and their tears. Hire an army of competent nursemaids and join,
Your most loving and most desolate,
Archie

For the rest of the voyage Archie resolved to stay close to those brother officers who were also unaccompanied, in most cases because they were unmarried, and in their company he was able to forget the clinging of soft arms. He took to retiring immediately after dinner before the military band began to play for dancing, and in his cabin he read and studied and wrote to Helena. He did not see Miss Gallagher again until they reached Aden.

Like most of the returning military he wanted to go to Firpo's for new tropicals. He forgot that he had encouraged Niamh to go ashore. There she was, the first of the non-military passengers to disembark, her red hair flying like a standard.

'That saucy madame is about to get sunstroke.'

General McWhirter's wife had come up behind him. Strange how so large a lady could move so quietly.

'If she does, Ma'am, Captain Butler's wife should be ashamed of herself for not warning a simple girl of the strength of a tropical sun.'

'Simple, Archie?' she said coyly. 'Her eyes are too bold and her demeanour not at all what poor Mrs Butler has been led to expect.'

'She has an education,' he said. 'It must gall her to have to suffer fools gladly.'

She laughed, taking no offence. She knew that he was referring to the many empty-headed young socialites on their way out to India to catch a husband. 'So Caroline has hired a governess and a nursemaid in one. How very astute are the Scottish. Now take me ashore. I must guard you for Helena: it really was very naughty of her to abandon such a divinely handsome man.'

He gave her his arm. 'Helena trusts me, Ma'am.'

She looked up at him. 'Helena never was a very clever girl and dreadfully spoiled, of course. You should have been much more stern, Archie. A woman's place is with her husband.'

'Baby was unwell . . .' he said, beginning to make excuses.

'Nonsense. She never did deserve you, Archie, but I shall save you for her.'

He laughed. He had dreamed about Helena and the dream had been so strong that he had almost felt her in his arms: he did not need guarding.

'Your obedient servant, Mrs McWhirter,' he said and gave her his arm.

Niamh saw them go ashore, the tall, handsome young officer with the lovely voice and the fat, raddled-looking old lady who had had half the girls on board crying with vexation and exasperation before they had reached the Mediterranean.

She felt the sun on her head and knew that its rays were turning her head to gold. He admired her hair. She could feel his eyes on her. He was a mystery. He was married and he had a child but why were they not with him? He loved the boy: she knew nothing of parental love but there had been something in his voice, something in his eyes when he had spoken of the child. Was it love, regret?

Suddenly she knew that she wished that he would think of her the way he thought of his son. She wanted to mean something to him but no, stupid Niamh, she told herself, he is as far above you as the stars that shine on this ocean at night, and as untouchable. Don't be misled by a courtesy, a kindness. You mean nothing and can mean nothing to him. Buy your hat and hide your golden hair.

2

IT WAS THE heat. She would never get used to it. No matter how many bodices she wore to sop up all the sweat, her dress was still soaked after the slightest exertion, and running after the three spoiled brats that Mrs Butler fondly called her 'darling little people' could never be classed as slight exertion. Niamh's palms itched to make painful contact with any part of the small solid bodies that daily made her miserable existence even more of a hell. She had absolutely no idea how to interest or control them, and the imps of Satan knew it. They had figured her out accurately within a few hours of her being admitted into their spacious, airy nurseries. To give Mrs Butler her due, she had chosen the most pleasant rooms in the house for her children and any breeze that was to be found in Calcutta found its way into the eyrie on the top floor of the large house on Alexandra Court.

Niamh sighed and buttoned up, right to the very high neck, the third of the dresses she had worn that day. Whether Mrs Butler was kind or whether she could not bear to see her children's nursemaid look unkempt, Niamh did not know, but within twenty-four hours of her being in the house, the durzi had been sent for, and dress after dress had hurried from his clever brown fingers. Because he was kind as well as talented the dresses, though fashioned from the cheapest cottons available, were also very flattering to the young girl. Ibrar would sit cross-legged on the verandah and, although he was paid only to make the simplest summer frock, he would embroider an exquisite flower or an initial, and once, even her name. He had ripped that out though, for its formation and pronunciation made no sense to him at all.

'This does not make sense to my way of thinking, Missy,' he said, as he had tried painstakingly to hide the marks where the strange letters had been set.

'Sure it makes little sense to me either, Mr Ibrar,' Niamh had consoled him, 'but then it's Irish, not English, and aren't we both glad of that.'

'In that case, Miss Neeeeve,' he had laughed, proving to her that even brown men have a sense of humour, 'we will rework the unpronounceable word.'

Niamh often wondered if Mrs Butler was wrong about how to handle the Indian climate. She had wonderful ideas for handling the entire subcontinent, and these, and her modern ideas for the upbringing of children, received no favour from her nursemaid.

'Sure doesn't she say the children are flowers that need to be given space to grow,' she informed Major Archie Winterton when, to her great joy, she encountered him on the Maidan, that great stretch of park through the middle of Calcutta. Calcutta, teeming city of the subcontinent, and yet not one brown or black face showed itself anywhere on the Maidan. The Maidan was for the Raj. Archie Winterton accepted this and Niamh had not yet realized it.

Archie had dismounted and was leading his horse along the path as he and Niamh followed the antics of the children. 'A little judicious pruning seems in order,' he said as he watched these spoiled unruly children and compared them with the spoiled unruly borders of his father-in-law's gardens at home: he did not think of his absent wife in terms of discipline.

'Wasn't it you who said all they needed was affection and food, like horses. Sure your horse here is far more the gentleman than young Tom.'

Archie laughed. 'I did mention discipline, Miss Gallagher, and there is a vast difference between affection and indulgence. The former helps the growth, the latter stunts it.'

'It will be my hand stunts these three I'm telling you, Major.'

She sounded serious and Archie looked at her in alarm. She would lose her place if she attempted physically to discipline Captain Butler's children. 'You need a little space away from the children, Miss Gallagher. You do have some free time?'

'Oh, aye. Wednesday and Sunday afternoons and Wednesday evening until ten, but I put one foot in front of the other and I'm sweating like Father Murphy's pig.'

He laughed. He could never see Helena or girls like her admitting to such human failings. 'There are many beautiful buildings in the town that are cool and quite safe for a European, Miss Gallagher. And what of other girls? There must be some your own age. Your friends from the ship, for instance?'

'Isn't that always the way of friendship, Major? There's Mary now moved to Delhi and Mrs McCann still in Bombay. But in the letter I had from Mary she informs me that she is to go to the Hills at the same time as my family and that will be a joy to me.'

The Hills. Everyone who was able would go to the Hills to escape this appalling heat of the Plains. He was to go to Simla himself.

'Mrs Butler has taken a house called the Deodars. I

think that's poplar trees. Won't it be nice to sit under
the shade of a real tree?'

At that moment, five-year-old Tom gave his four-
year-old sister a violent push and she fell on to the
red gravel with a yell that sent resting birds from
the tops of the trees that lined the walk. Were not
these real trees, Miss Gallagher? he thought, but he
said nothing.

Niamh and Archie started forward and Niamh
picked up the squalling child who rewarded her
with a kick in the stomach. She took a deep con-
trolling breath but said nothing to the little girl. She
turned to the soldier. 'Aren't they the little angels,
Major?' she said. 'Well, it's been nice talking to you.
No, please,' she said in some fear as he reached
for Tom, 'I can handle them myself. We'll just go
home now and do some arithmetic. I shall give Tom
problems to do. If there are three horrible children
and one of them, a boy five years old, is carried off
by a jackal, how many nice little girls are left?'

At this picture of his future Tom too started to
bawl and Archie retreated cowardly leaving Niamh
with her charges.

It was not the first time he had seen her since
their arrival in India. The life of the military, at least
for the officers, in Calcutta was fairly restricted.
Everyone knew and entertained everyone else of
similiar rank or met them at the various dinner
parties, bridge parties, lawn parties, tennis parties.
He had not been surprised to see Niamh with her
charges at Mrs Butler's tennis afternoon, but he
had surprised himself and his host by claiming
the acquaintanceship of the outward voyage and
introducing himself. Niamh herself had handled
the situation better than he had done. She had
been polite but not servile, had stood chatting for

a moment and had even laughed at his reminding
her of her fear of *all that water*, and had moved
away from him as soon as possible and had never
looked his way again. Oh, she knew how to behave
all right, better than her employer who, annoyed
that her nursemaid was on easy terms with one of
her most important guests, had come forward to
make herself better known. For Archie Winterton,
although he had not two pennies of his own to rub
together, was the second son of an Earl and therefore
was Major the Honourable Archie Winterton. Even
better, he was the husband of the beautiful Helena
who would come soon, everyone agreed, with her
beautiful clothes paid for out of her father's vast fortune which grew ever larger as his companies sold
more and more Scotch whisky to an ever-expanding
market.

Mrs McWhirter had assured everyone that the
marriage was not in trouble. The young couple had
taken their first furlough and gone home so that
Helena could give birth to her son in her father's
magnificent Fife home, and unfortunately the baby
had contracted a cold and had been deemed unfit
for the long ocean voyage. Mrs McWhirter, who
had little patience for the Helena Wintertons of this
world and vast sympathy for the Archies, lied like
the proverbial trooper in her attempts to make sure
that Helena's return to Calcutta and her duty would
be an easy one.

'The dear child was devastated,' she told every
cocktail party guest, 'but what is the use of employ-
ing the best and most expensive medical men and
then ignoring what they say?'

No one was left in any doubt that Helena and her
son would join her husband in a few months, after
– although Mrs McWhirter did not tell Calcutta this

– the London season, which was so much more fun than life in Calcutta.

And although Mrs McWhirter had kept her own counsel, Calcutta had decided that since the Honourable Archie Winterton had refused any of the lures cast to him by sophisticated women of his own class, who knew how to play the game of dalliance, he was unlikely to be caught by an Irish servant girl.

Archie remounted and cantered along the Maidan, raising a cloud of brick-red dust as he went. It settled lightly on his polished boots: it seeped into the creases of his immaculate jodhpurs. Later he found it on his very skin under the handmade, skintight shirt, and he laughed, for dust, like the constant smell of evacuated bowels, was an integral part of this great land. And later, as he sat in the hip bath and allowed Aboubakir to sluice him with warm water, he thought not of Helena and her milk-white skin, but of Niamh Gallagher. Her skin, under her clothes, would be soft and white like Helena's, but today it would be covered by a thin mist of powdery red dust and he hoped she had a nice deep bath to sit in while a servant washed it all away.

'I LOVE YOU, Archie. I've loved you since that first moment.'

Archie Winterton opened his eyes and looked at the girl who lay so trustingly beside him and he groaned in self-induced pain.

'Oh dear God, Niamh, this should never have happened. I never meant it to happen.' He started up from the soft bed of mosses and pine needles where they had been lying and turned away from her to straighten his clothes.

Niamh propped herself up on her elbow and pulled at his legs. 'But Archie, dear, it's all right since we love each other.' She saw the look of mingled despair and disgust in his eyes and hurried to her feet, pulling down her skirts and rearranging her bodices. 'Archie, you do love me, don't you? You couldn't do that to me and not . . .'

'We did it to each other, Niamh, but yes, I started it, I suppose and, oh my poor little girl, I am to blame. I am so dreadfully sorry.'

'My Aunt Maeve said this happened when young people were in love, Archie. We should have waited till we were wed but . . .'

She was not a stupid woman. Why did she not understand? How could he make her understand?

He held her arms and forced her to look at him. 'Niamh, I am already married. I told you that.' He could not tell her that when he had entered her he had thought only of Helena, Helena, Helena.

'I know,' she said simply, 'and it's a mortal

sin, sure, but we won't let it happen again till we're married. I wish we didn't have to wait . . .' She blushed. 'I mean wait to get married, Archie, but . . .'

'I am married, Niamh,' he said again as slowly and deliberately as he could. 'I have a son, and my wife and child will join me here soon.'

'Oh, the rich can get divorced and I've never been married before and so it will be all right. Your wife won't mind, Archie. Sure if she minded at all, she'd be here, wouldn't she? Everyone says so.'

He dropped his arms and stepped back as if he had been struck. 'If she minded at all . . .' Was that true? No, Helena loved him. It was just that she had been so spoiled all her life that she could not, no matter how hard she tried, put anyone else first. It was not her fault. Sir Gordon was to blame. Helena was a sweet, pretty little thing who had no idea how much loving her hurt him.

'We have to go back, Niamh. I'm sorry. I was an undisciplined oaf and I should be shot . . .' Another horrifying thought leapt into his overactive mind. 'We must hope there will be no serious repercussions' – except that you have taken an innocent girl's virginity, he accused himself – 'but we must never see one another again.' He turned away and began to walk back towards the settlement and she hurried after him and threw her arms around him. He could not wrest her free without hurting her and they stood there on the path, the world crumbling around them.

Niamh screamed and wailed and wept and threw herself down at his feet begging. Every word, every tear, every moan, pierced his heart and his brain.

Far below them one of the dilapidated buses that daily carried at least one hundred people at a time up the untarred roads that turned into mudslides in the monsoon months of July and August, lurched like an ungainly slug around a hairpin bend. What was the area called, this beautiful country from Simla to Kashmir? Had his bearer said Kulu? Archie looked but did not see dusty, winding hilly land, perfect for ponies, not for battered buses. He saw only Niamh.

My God, how had he let this happen? He had deliberately, yes, deliberately, he could admit it now, sought her out. She needed a friend, he had told himself. The Butlers demanded more than Shylock's pound of flesh: she was worked too hard and she was superior in education to most of the nursemaids with whom she came in contact, and inferior in position to any other girl with whom she might have struck up a friendship. How rigidly we hem ourselves in with rules and regulations, he had thought. Here she is, articulate, intelligent, with more than a smattering of education and yet no girl of her own age will deign to make her a friend. Helena, the same age, and not nearly so well-read, would not even have noticed her. But then, he told himself brutally, were Helena here, you would not have noticed her either.

'I will chat to her at tennis parties as she marshalls her charges,' he had said and then he had found himself telling her that should she find herself in the Army and Navy Stores on Wednesday afternoons, she might also find him there. He would buy her an ice – an ice as if she were a small child. He would not take her to tea as if she were a woman.

He had watched her lick the tart lemon ice and such a feeling of lust had attacked him that he had been unable to rise from the table. He had sent her away. He had been, for him, unbelievably rude.

'You are attacking that like a schoolboy, Miss Gallagher. You should really learn to eat ices like a lady if you want to attract a man.'

She had not been a bit dismayed. 'Sure, isn't this the only way to eat ice cream,' she had said, 'but if it's that fat old lady that's just come in you don't want to see me, Major, you only had to say.'

And she had gone from the table before Mrs McWhirter could come bearing down on them to ask what in the name of heaven he thought he was doing.

'An ice,' he would have laughed. 'Is there anything more innocent than an ice and the child needs at least one friend in Calcutta.'

And he could so assuredly have laughed it off.

But how had that meeting led to this? It had been inevitable, like night following day, like the sun rising morning after morning and painting the tips of the Himalayas with pink and lilac and gold.

He pulled her arms from his legs and forced her to her feet. 'I did not mean to hurt you, Niamh. I will help you to find another position or I will help you return to Ireland, whichever you wish. Oh my poor girl, I cannot ask you to understand, but I love my wife. I never meant to dishonour her or you . . .'

She looked up at him again through her tears and as he stood there the Indian sun filtered through the trees and sent a halo of light around his head. Her knight in shining golden armour. Her knight with feet of clay. A red-hot rage surged through her. He had taken her virginity, the only gift a poor girl could give to the man she loved and he had thrown her sacrifice in her face. She would have preferred that he lie to her. He should be saying that he loved her: he should be making plans to get out of the entanglement of a loveless marriage but

'I love my wife and I have dishonoured her by loving you'
was what he was saying.

'I'll tell her,' she said and wrenched herself free.
'I'll tell your precious Helena.'

For a moment she glared with her lovely eyes into
his troubled ones and then she turned and raced
away from him down the hill. He started after her,
his hand held out in a supplicating gesture and then
he stopped and watched her slip and slide down the
slope. He made as if to go after her. If she stumbled
she would fall and could hurt herself quite badly,
as badly as he had already hurt her. He had ruined
her young life.

'Oh God, Niamh, I never meant to hurt you,'
he yelled down the slope at the slithering, slid-
ing figure.

He had meant only to be her friend: it had never
occurred to him that he would become her lover.
He was Helena's lover, Helena's husband, the father
of Helena's son. He was a swine. And Niamh,
hurt, betrayed, was going to write to Helena. Was
she right? Did Helena really love him? She wrote
wonderful, loving letters, promising that maybe
next month, maybe when Baby had cut this oh-
so-troublesome tooth . . . when Papa had got over
this latest painful bout of the gout that attacked him
no matter how he restricted his appetites . . .

Dear God, it was over. Niamh, his career, his
marriage, his chance to teach the little chap . . . Oh,
God, what about the little chap?

Archie saw very clearly the only decent and
honourable thing to do.

And he did it.

4

1931 Glasgow

FERELITH GALLAGHER LOVED the old Convent. Sometimes she pretended that she lived there alone, apart that is, from the hordes of servants who were needed to keep one young girl in comfort. Her imagination was so strong that, with no trouble at all, she could dress the simple nuns, who scurried around all day, in the black dresses and white aprons that all the maids wore in the B movies she loved to watch every Saturday afternoon. Whenever she had a free moment she would take her notebook or the novel she was reading down to the ruined castle that stood at the farthest edge of the orphanage property, and she would sit there amid the crumbling and overgrown stones and imagine that she was a princess or a missing heiress, and one day soon a handsome knight on a white horse was going to come riding up the path to rescue her. He would need to come soon or the end of this year of 1931 would see her, like all the other orphaned girls, in domestic service, or, if they were like Ferelith and had a brain, working in a shop as a cashier.

Ferelith's knight in shining armour was an old nun in a black serge dress and a starched white wimple. While her princess mooned away the hours in her ruined castle, Sister Anthony Joseph fought for her future.

'We have never put a girl through university

before, Sister. I shudder to think what the Bishop would say.' That was Reverend Mother.

Sister Anthony Joseph, who had known the Bishop since the days when together they had purloined apples from the trees in their neighbour's garden, wished with a sigh that dear Reverend Mother would remember that Tom might be a bishop but he was also a man and perfectly approachable and reasonable.

'Ferelith Gallagher has an unusually gimp brain, Reverend Mother, and the dear Bishop would not want it wasted.'

Reverend Mother, who addressed the Bishop as 'my Lord Bishop' but knew perfectly well that dear Sister Anthony Joseph called him Tom when they were alone together, asserted her authority.

'That unusually gimp brain, as you put it, Sister, makes her spend most of the time when she should be helping with tasks sitting on a cold stone in that ruin we should knock down, and she will no doubt be troubled with piles in later life. Girls marry, if they do not enter religious life and for that certainly Ferelith has no aptitude. It would be scandalous were we to waste our precious resources on a girl who will no doubt marry as soon as she obtains a degree if not before. Besides she has never once mentioned a desire for further education.'

Sister Anthony decided not to attack with 'surely an educated woman makes a better mother than one who has not had the benefit of education' because she wasn't sure that that made any sense.

'Ferelith has not expressed an ambition, Reverend Mother, because girls are not encouraged to do so and that, surely, is wrong. Mr Smith, her English teacher, says that she could be a teacher. We could send her to Craiglockhart.'

'The Sacred Heart?' Reverend Mother emitted a very faint and superior sniff. 'Educated women.' Alas, even the truly religious have their moments of weakness.

'They turn out educated ladies, Reverend Mother. Ferelith is clever and, although she does not realize it, she is very pretty. She will marry. I have absolutely no doubt about that, but she could also teach nice Catholic boys and girls for a few years before she takes her skills to a marriage. A perfect scenario, I think.'

'I think that I do not know how you managed to persuade me to let her do Highers. We had a conversation not unlike this then and you said how your precious Ferelith could get a better job were she better educated, and be a credit to the orphanage.'

'And I meant it, Reverend Mother, but I did not then know how clever she actually is. What a credit a university degree would be to the work you have done all these years.'

Reverend Mother looked at the elderly nun. She was not a fool and she knew she was being flattered but she was not immune to flattery and besides, she did have the best interests of the children, or at least what she considered to be their best interests, very much at heart. 'I will pray for guidance, Sister. We will both pray.'

Sister Anthony Joseph bowed her head and smiled. The game was now 'deuce' and she could get the advantage – if she could get to Tom. And time was running out for Ferelith. She should be applying to universities and so far she had not even thought of further education.

At that very moment Ferelith Gallagher was sitting in her crumbling fortress which, with no trouble at all, she had turned into the warm, dry stately

rooms of Buckingham Palace, and she was promising the King that she would head a coalition
government and that she would work with Ramsay
MacDonald and Mr Baldwin in the best interests of
Britain and the Empire. The King was moved and
invited her to tea. That's when Ferelith's imagination
failed. Did the King have bread and jam sandwiches
for tea as she did or did kings eat more exotic foods?
She remembered the picture of their majesties in the
last Pathé newsreel she had seen. They certainly ate
something, both being exceptionally well padded.
Mind you, Sister Anthony was well padded and as
far as Ferelith could discover, ate nothing at all.

The coldness of the stone on which she was
perched finally got through her heavy skirt and thick
knickers and she rubbed at her backside to warm it
up and get the blood flowing again. She sighed. To
be Prime Minister, surely you needed education and
you needed to be a boy. Mr Smith said she could go
to university. That would take care of the education
bit. But, as Sister Mary Immaculate said every day,
'Pigs might fly and we'd have to shoot bacon.'

'If I was Lady Astor,' Ferelith solemnly told a
ladybird that was crawling along the stone she had
just vacated, 'I would force them to make me Prime
Minister. Why is she content just to be the first
female Member of Parliament?' At the word 'just'
Ferelith laughed at her own nonsense. Just, just a
Member of Parliament. My God, in 1931 that was
wonderful. 'And I'll do it too. I'll, I'll . . . I'll go and
clean the lavatory before Reverend Mother discovers
it isn't done.'

Even her agile imagination balked at turning the
cleaning of a lavatory into a romantic scenario. A
lavatory was a lavatory and this one was particularly well-used, since there were eighteen girls and

twenty-three boys in the home. The nuns, if they *had* human attributes (and Ferelith was unsure of this), used a lavatory in a different part of the sprawling old house. Since, however, this one was cleaned at least once a day, cleaning it was really not too onerous a task.

'How nice to find you on your knees.' The sarcastic voice of Reverend Mother startled her. 'And without a book too, or do you have one hidden under your pinny?'

'No, Reverend Mother,' said Ferelith, jumping to her feet. 'At least, I have one under my apron but it's not hidden, just there for safety.'

'A life of a saint, no doubt,' said Reverend Mother drily. 'I would like to see you in my office. Fifteen minutes and change your frock. You have cleaned more of the floor with that one than with your washcloth.'

Ferelith curtseyed and looked ruefully at the simple cotton dress she had put on to spare her school uniform. How had it got wet? A much greater question, one that set her heart beating fearfully, was what did Reverend Mother want with her? She could not be really angry. Had she been angry her rapier tongue would have been flashing cruelly but she had been, for Reverend Mother, almost friendly, almost human. Oh, if only she could see Sister Anthony Joseph.

Fifteen minutes later, tidy and clean, she stood outside Reverend Mother's office waiting to be admitted, and told herself it was the all-permeating smell of cabbage cooking for the midday dinner that was making her stomach heave.

'Come.'

She opened the door and the smell of beeswax coming out fought with the smell of cabbage coming in. Ferelith loved this room, although she had never yet enjoyed any occasion when she had been in it. Now she tried to take comfort from the heavy, beautifully-polished antique furniture, the shelves of leather-bound books, the delicate painting of an Italian Madonna and child.

'Sit down, Ferelith, and tell me what you would like to do with the rest of your life.'

The bald question startled the girl. She had almost hoped to be taken to task yet again for some contravention of the rules. Only that morning, drawn by the fresh call of the early morning air, she had gone for a walk outside the grounds among the neighbouring fields. Only Sister Glenn had seen her and Ferelith had begged the old nun to keep her secret.

'Don't tell Reverend Mother,' she had said clasping the elderly woman's frail work-worn hands.

Sister Glenn had shrugged her off and turned to her milk churns. 'Reverend Mother? Sure it's God I came to serve.'

No, Sister Glenn had not betrayed her.

'Well, Ferelith. Sister Anthony Joseph says you have some ambition to enter a university?'

'I have? I mean I have.' Until that moment Ferelith had never considered a university education no matter what Mr Smith said. Universities were not for orphans, and certainly not for female ones. 'I love learning, Reverend Mother.'

'For the sake of learning, child, or for the greater glory of God?'

Ça va sans dire, said Ferelith to herself but she dared not say it aloud. It was her favourite French phrase. 'I believe God wants me to make the best use of the brain He has given me, Reverend Mother.'

The nun looked at her sceptically. 'We should make you a lawyer.'

A lawyer. The only lawyer Ferelith had ever read about or heard about was Portia in *The Merchant of Venice* and Shakespeare's heroine had surely only pretended to be a lawyer. But, guessing rightly that Reverend Mother did not really expect an answer, Ferelith said nothing.

'Sister Anthony seems to think that you will not throw away an expensive education on Holy Matrimony, although it is said that if a woman is educated it helps her family. I am also aware that, as far as your future is concerned, I am, one might say, outgunned, since Sister has the ear of the dear Bishop. You are a clever girl, Ferelith, and I will have no objection to helping to finance your education, but I would ask you to consider very carefully what you want to do with the rest of your life. You have no vocation for the religious life. As far as I can see, all you want to do is to sit in that damp old castle and read trashy novels.' She paused to give Ferelith a chance to defend herself but the girl merely blushed furiously and hung her head, and Reverend Mother remembered another young girl a lifetime ago who had lain in the grass on the top of a hill and read what her mother had called trash. It was the spirit of that young girl who now smiled at Ferelith.

'Just don't believe that life is like your books, my dear,' she said with a real and pitying tenderness. 'Now go to the chapel and pray for guidance.'

'Yes, Reverend Mother,' said Ferelith, and fled.

She could not pray. She knelt in the chapel and waited for the peace to wash over her and eventually it did and her stomach stopped heaving and the blood slowed its mad race around her body.

University. What would Mr Smith say and did she want to go and where? She had never been anywhere but this convent. Sometimes she hated it but mostly she loved it and she was well aware of its security. All decisions were taken from her: what to wear, when to eat, when to sleep, when to work, when to pray. Could she go to Glasgow University and come home here to the blessedly familiar every night with her books? Yes, that's what she would do.

She worked it all out and then, with great glee, shared her plans with Sister Anthony Joseph.

'Not a good idea, Ferelith,' said the old nun decisively. 'Far too disturbing for the other children and too restrictive for you. A hostel is what you want, or a university residence, but first we need to get you into a university. What would you like to study?'

And Ferelith had stared at her blankly. 'I don't know,' she had finally admitted.

'Pray for guidance, child, for you must have a compelling reason for the Bishop and for Reverend Mother. Education costs money. Besides, you're a girl, and men will think it's wasted on you.'

Ferelith nodded respectfully at this simple truth but then she thought, no, Mr Smith is a man, and he doesn't think education is wasted on women.

'It's your only way out of the trap of poverty. With a decent education, you can go anywhere, speak to anyone, be anything.'

At school next day Ferelith looked in her favourite teacher's fat unwieldy dictionary.

'Lawyer, member of the legal profession, especially attorney or solicitor.'

Sounds dull, she thought.

'Solicitor. One who solicits (rare); member of the legal profession competent to advise clients and instruct and prepare cases for barristers but not to appear as advocate . . .' I don't like the sound of solicit. I'm never going to ask for anything that a person isn't willing to give me. Besides I'd hate to do all the work and have someone else walk off with the glory.

'Advocate. One who pleads for another. Faculty of Advocates. Scotch Bar. Lord Advocate. Principal law officer of the Crown in Scotland.'

Later she was to tell Sister Anthony that she had enjoyed an experience not unlike that of the blessed Saint Paul on his road to Damascus: she felt rightly that the sister would enjoy the religious parallel.

'It was as if a light went on in my head, Sister, and I knew, suddenly, that I wanted to study law.'

The classroom was empty. She stood up and struck a histrionic pose. 'Well, Reverend Mother, you hit the nail on the head. It is now beautifully crystal clear. I want to be an advocate: I want to plead for others as Sister Anthony Joseph has always pleaded for me. I want to be the top advocate, and I shall fight for the downtrodden, especially women and orphans. Education wasted on me indeed. I shall be hailed as the new Portia in the press but I won't need to pretend to be a man. I shall be beautiful, feminine, and devastating.' She caught a mental picture of her skinny undersized frame and giggled. 'Well, feminine and devastating can't be too bad.'

She argued her first case against Reverend Mother and won. Ferelith Gallagher, orphan, would be allowed to go to university.

'We must try to get you into Glasgow where we can keep an eye on you.'

Ferelith immediately began to pray that Glasgow would not accept her and, at the same time, applied for admittance to the University of Edinburgh. A few anxious months later, she stood with an acceptance in her hand. After the first few moments of euphoria she felt her knees begin to tremble. Why had she not been open and confiding?

Now what do I say to Reverend Mother?

'Why did you apply to Edinburgh, Ferelith?' asked the old voice so gently that Ferelith felt like a criminal. 'Why did you mislead us?' She shook her head as if the weight of disappointment was unbearable.

'I'm sorry, Reverend Mother, but I thought it was time that I became a little independent.'

'And you thought we would not understand?' The gentle voice chided: the calm, sweet unlined face with its straggly white hairs creeping out from the edge of the wimple gazed at her. 'Well, we must see what we can do about Edinburgh. Independence but safety. Ferelith, it is unlikely that you will find anyone like you at the University, not among the girls anyway. You are an orphan. You have spent your entire life in a convent, ordered around by bells. Apart from limited school work, you have never in your life had to think for yourself and now you want to go out into the world and you think you can survive on your own. My dear child, you are a little minnow and the sea is full of sharks. We will find a nice safe bowl in which our own little minnow can swim happily – a hostel, I think, run by a religious order.'

Ferelith left Reverend Mother's study and went to the chapel as she had been bid but she did not pray. She was too angry. A minnow, was she? She wanted out, she wanted to be free, to make mistakes if necessary. What could possibly happen to her that would be so awful?

She had spent her entire life in an institution: she did not want to exchange a Glasgow orphanage for an Edinburgh Catholic hostel. She wanted a

Residence. The fascinating information sheets from the university told her that there were five suitable residences on East Suffolk Road for female students. Each had a common room, a dining room, a library and, holy of holies, separate study bedrooms and all for the (*gulp, gulp*) mere bagatelle of fifty guineas for the session of three terms. In all her life Miss Gallagher had personally handled no more than a shilling. Where was she to find one guinea, let alone fifty?

In October, when she was enjoying her first classes at the University of Edinburgh, she agreed that it was probably just as well that her guardians had decided that she should exchange one convent for another: the shock of finding herself, at seventeen, on her own might have been just too much. At Springhill Gardens she had her own room, an unimagined luxury for someone who had spent every night of her life in a large dormitory with girls of all ages. The room was plain and sparsely furnished but to the young girl it was wonderful. A bed, a small wardrobe that held her spare frock, her coat and her outdoor shoes, a dressing table for her three sets of underwear and her two nightdresses, a chair and a table for her books. There was an electric light hanging from the ceiling and a small lamp on the table. On the bare highly-polished linoleum floor there was a rag rug, but the glory of all glories was the window which looked out over the garden to the street beyond. The hostel was within walking distance of the University and, for economy's sake, Ferelith decided that it was within walking distance of everywhere else in the city she might want to visit. And she resolved to explore everything – castle, parks, museums, old town, new town, everywhere. She walked everywhere and became fitter and stronger as the months passed. She still looked frail but she blessed the fact that from some unknown parent she had inherited an iron constitution. The food at the hostel was plain but substantial and, if her lecture room was full of cold and flu germs, by the time she had walked back home the friendly Edinburgh winds had blown them all away.

The other residents were a pathetic mixture of women who had, for the most part, been badly treated by circumstance. Annie Black had spent almost her entire life, woman and child, in the care of the Sisters. Her mind had been damaged by some early childhood experience and she was only relaxed and at ease when a nun, any nun, in dark dress and starched wimple was within her sight: then she felt safe.

Sister Frances told Ferelith not to speak to Peggy Wilson and, therefore, naturally, if there was any free time at all, Ferelith longed to hear Peggy's stories, of the men she had loved, of the children she had conceived and lost, and even of a king she had met once and who had smiled at her and kissed her hand.

'Don't listen to her blethers, lassie,' screeched old Annie. 'Kissed her hand indeed. Wasn't she in service and didn't she near spill gravy all over the old king and he held the gravy boat and her hand to save his best suit. Kissed her hand, indeed.'

Tears had started in Peggy's eyes and Ferelith had soothed her. 'I'm sure he kissed your hand when he held it, Peggy. Sister Anthony Joseph saw him once and said he was a most gallant old gentleman.'

Dorothy Johnston wanted desperately to enter the religious life and although she appeared to Ferelith to be totally dedicated and even holy, no convent –

for no doubt viable reasons that they did not care to divulge to Miss Gallagher – would take her and so she stayed in the hostel and earned her keep by doing clerical work.

Ferelith looked at them and mourned for them and for the countless others whom life had condemned to live in the shadows. She was living in the shadows a bit herself, getting up in the morning, washing, dressing, running downstairs to eat her breakfast with the other strange residents who, one and all, warned her every morning to look out for the dangers that lurked in the Edinburgh streets waiting to pounce. And then, as she walked along past the castle, she saw only the beautiful skyline of this most lovely of cities and heard only the ghostly murmurings of the long dead. Did they warn her too of danger? No, they welcomed her. She was one of them. She was beginning to love as they had loved and she would fight as they had fought, perhaps with different weapons and for different causes, but always against injustice.

She walked briskly around the ancient city and she dreamed her dreams of yesterday's heroes and vowed to become one of tomorrow's, and perhaps it was the animation in her usually still face that excited and captivated Blair Crawford. He did not reason: he merely accepted that he had met his ideal mate. She was so unlike anyone he had ever known but it was as if he had known her always.

'Hello,' he said. 'Just up?'

'I beg your pardon?' Ferelith thought that he was asking her if she had just got up out of bed. Sister Anthony Joseph had warned her of young men like the one standing gazing down at her so foolishly.

'Up?' he asked again. 'I'm second year. I thought you looked as if you were new: you know, just up.'

Ferelith laughed. 'I thought you were being rude,' she said and he laughed at her consternation. 'The Sisters warned me about boys like you.'

'The Sisters?'

'Nuns. Religious. I was brought up in an orphanage.'

A warning bell tried to ring in his head but he ignored it. 'It must be quite awful not to have parents. My father died in the war but I still have my mother.' As he spoke he thought of his mother who wore only grey or black because she was still in mourning for her husband, his mother who had sent him away when he was seven years old and whom he saw very rarely, his mother whom he adored and wanted desperately to please. He frowned and Ferelith noticed the frown.

'I think it's the not knowing who you are or wondering why no one wanted you that hurts,' she said after much quiet thought.

'And not being loved, surely that hurts?'

Ferelith considered the question and he laughed a little as he saw how seriously she was preparing her answer.

'I have never really felt unloved,' she said at last. 'There are all kinds of love, aren't there?'

Blair remembered his strong tall grandfather: he felt the remembered harshness of his beard as he had hugged the small boy, smelled the oddly lovable smell of horse and leather, tobacco smoke and whisky, and very old tweed.

'My grandfather loved me very much,' he said.

They stood looking at one another, saying nothing.

'Would you like a cup of tea?' he asked, because suddenly he was afraid that if he did not keep her she would fly away like a little bird and he knew that he could not bear never to see her again. And so it began.

*   *   *

Ferelith Gallagher learned almost as much from Blair Crawford as she learned from her books and her lecturers. She learned without knowing that she was learning because her sheltered upbringing had made her like a sponge and she was ready to soak up everything and anything with which she came into contact. It was good that the first man she met was Blair for, although he was expensively educated and widely travelled, he had a quality of innocence and goodness that matched her own. He knew music, art, and books and he opened the world of the arts up to her and she was eager to learn. His taste became her taste. Beethoven was God, his orchestral music the sublimest and *Fidelio* the greatest opera ever written. They sat through *Fidelio*: she understood not a word and was secretly disappointed that there were no beautiful gowns or luxurious sets, but she wept, she knew not why, at Florestan's magnificent aria, and marvelled at the genius of the mind that could write such glorious music and not be able to hear it.

'We have our own musical genius here at the University,' Blair told her. 'Professor Donald Tovey has the Reid seat of music and he is acknowledged everywhere as one of the greatest musicians and composers of the twentieth century. I really can't understand why his concerts aren't packed like sardine tins. We take him too much for granted, I suppose. Now you shall accompany me on Sundays to the Reid Concerts. Students get in for sixpence, and what a sixpennyworth it is. On Mondays we have the Scottish Orchestra at the Usher Hall. You must join the Musical Society. Can you sing?'

'No.'

He looked at her sceptically. His music teachers had told him that the entire human race was born musical; but then there had been a chap at school whom even Ferelith's church St Cecilia would have found a challenge.

'Too bad but never mind, you can appreciate. It's only two and six a year and members get discount tickets for Reid and Scottish Orchestra Concerts. Do you play golf?'

Ferelith laughed, a laugh that made him think of clean clear water tumbling over the white stones in a Highland burn. He could not believe the effect this young woman was having on him.

'Blair Crawford. Orphans don't play golf: rich young men play golf.'

He blushed furiously and at once she felt sorry for him.

'I'll beat your socks off on the tennis courts though.'

'You're on. We have a marvellous athletic union and some of it has come out of the dark ages: I mean we do concede that women can play hockey, tennis, and golf, even boating. Join the tennis club. I'm afraid it's possibly a bit more expensive than hockey.'

It was, but Reverend Mother agreed that physical activity was very good for young bodies that she fondly imagined would otherwise spend too much time sitting at desks studying.

'You will have seven and six for hockey in the winter and spring, Ferelith, and you'll have twelve and six for tennis. Sister Glenn will make your clothes. Department store prices are scandalous.'

Department store prices did not concern Blair Crawford. Nor did study, as far as Ferelith could see. He asked her to join several other societies and he always had tickets for every dance and social, concert and play.

'When do you study?' she asked him innocently one November afternoon as they struggled against the Edinburgh wind down the Mound to the art galleries.

'Oh, I will. I really learn best if I give it a real go just before the exams, otherwise if I waste time studying now, I've forgotten it by the time I sit down trembling in the examination hall.'

Never in her life had she heard such nonsense, thought Ferelith, and she had not yet learned to guard her tongue. 'You're fooling yourself, Blair. You haven't forgotten it: you just haven't learned it.'

'We all learn differently,' he said rather huffily and immediately she changed the subject. She could not bear to hurt him.

'I'm sorry,' she said, tucking her hand into his arm. 'You're quite right. When you swim in a small pool you tend to think you know everything. I think I'm in for some shocks at university.'

Immediately he smiled again. 'No shocks today,' he said. 'Just some awfully nice pictures and then high tea at Crammond.'

'My parents bought some rather nice French impressionist stuff,' he told her as they wandered Saturday after rainy Saturday around the art galleries, 'but I must confess to an admiration for these fellows called the Glasgow School or the Glasgow Boys. They're not all Scots, they didn't even all live in Glasgow, but every single one of them was a frequent visitor to studios near, well I think but I can't be sure, the area around Sauchiehall Street and St Vincent Street. Shall we take the train through some day and see some of it? They're actually almost

completely ignored by the art world, in a sort of
limbo. You know "Limbo", good Catholic that you
are, the place where you just hang around and wait
for delivery. James Guthrie and John Lavery have
both been bought by Mummy and I do wish she was
brave enough to adopt some of the others because
the world will, one day.'

They did go through to Glasgow and she adopted
the paintings of E.A. Hornel, Alexander Davidson,
and Duncan MacKellar: why steep oneself in the
undoubted glories of France or Italy when there
were paintings like these? She was, after all, a Scot,
or was she? For the first time, faced with Blair and
his background of hundreds of years in the same
house on the same plot of land, if 12,000 acres could
be called a plot, she wondered who she was.

'It doesn't matter,' said Blair, 'even if you have
just sprung, as I think you have, from the head of
Zeus, you are you, whole and entire, and I . . .' he
shrank on such short acquaintance from saying the
word that sat on his tongue begging to be allowed
to burst forth into glorious birth, 'and I think you're
just wonderful.'

She laughed at him, which was not nice, but then
no one had ever told her that she was wonderful
before. Quite bright, a daydreamer, woolgatherer,
too smart for your own good, my girl – these phrases
had been hurled at her many times in seventeen
years, but wonderful . . . ?

'Blair Crawford, I am a skinny woolgathering girl
from a Glasgow orphanage. I have no father, no
mother. Did they die or did they just take one look
and say, "Oh no"?'

'No, they did not,' he said intensely, 'and it
doesn't matter and you are the nicest thing that
has ever happened to me.'

He was so intense, so serious. She looked at him. 'Well then, aren't you the nicest thing that has happened to me too?'

But she did not take him to the orphanage where she had grown up: she did not introduce him to Sister Anthony Joseph. Indeed, there was no mention of him at all in her letters home and she made no effort to let anyone know when she was in Glasgow.

There isn't time, she defended herself, to see paintings and to go to the Convent, and anyway, Blair is not a Catholic and he would be amused and possibly unnerved by sister after sister coming to have a look at him.

She did not, of course, spend all her time with Blair Crawford. She had decided to begin her assault on the great Scottish legal system by taking a degree in modern languages. French was to be her first language with Spanish, of which she knew not one word, as her second. As a practising Catholic she felt that her knowledge of church Latin should surely spin over into Spanish which was, after all, an offshoot. She became heady with excitement at the thought of spending her third year abroad at a French-speaking university.

'Time enough to think of being in gay Paree when you have passed a few exams, miss,' said Reverend Mother drily. 'You will find the intellectual level of your peers at the University *un peu* more advanced than that to which you have sadly become accustomed, miss. You have been the pike in the wee pond, Ferelith,' said the old nun, exhibiting once again her preoccupation with fish. 'Now you are about to become the wee guppie in a tank full of big ones.'

There were lectures and tutorials and so much reading: Desgranges, Molière, La Bruyere, Rousseau,

Hugo, La Fontaine's *Fables*, which she had already read both in English and French, Levy, Duruy, Michelet's *Histoire de France*, Brillat-Savarin, and more. She was intoxicated with the whole idea of university education. There were lectures and discussions, dear God, from Professor Sarolea, Mr Moore and Miss Burns who was a *Docteur de L'Université de Paris*, who thought that the opinions and ideas of mere mortals – and Ferelith Gallagher was surely the merest of the mere – mattered. Mattered? They discussed the History of French Literature and the History of French Civilization in its relation to French Literature; there were interpretations of French authors and translations from French into English and vice versa and lectures on philology and grammar.

Ferelith listened and absorbed and wished that she could sound like Blair.

'It's easy,' he said. 'Think French, think of red wine, champagne, croissants and cheese, *et voila*, and for heaven's sake, Ferelith, relax and rrroll your Rs. That's it. That sounds really . . .'

And he could say no more for he had been going to say seductive. What was she doing to him, this skinny little orphan from Glasgow? He could think of nothing but her, so much so that for the first time ever, he failed all his term's exams and had to spend the Christmas vac with a tutor like a schoolboy.

Ferelith, who had passed her first exams as she would pass all her exams – with consummate ease, spent the holidays earning her board and keep at the orphanage where she had been raised. She loved every minute but whenever she could escape to her castle she wrote letters to Blair in first-year French, but she never posted them. Such flowery expressions of love were surely merely exercises in her new skills and not for a moment to be taken seriously.

Reverend Mother and Sister Anthony had been quite pleased with her scholastic achievements and they were, at least Sister Anthony was, delighted that she had become a member of the University hockey team.

'But, what,' they asked, 'did you do for anyone besides Miss Gallagher in the past three months? The word "Catholic" has been singularly absent from all these wonderful tales of the goings-on at the Students' Union. Are we to suppose, Ferelith, that you have not bothered to join the Catholic Students' Union?'

'I go to Mass and the Sacrament every Sunday, Reverend Mother, and Confession . . . some Saturday nights.'

It was impossible to tell Blair, when he was taking her to a party or a dance or a concert, that she really ought to drop in to the Church, and so she had got into the habit of going to Confession only on those weekends when Blair was in Fife seeing his mother.

Now Reverend Mother was looking at her with that look which had instilled unbelievable guilt into generations of Glasgow orphans. Sister Anthony's mild stare was more understanding, but there was a hint there too of disappointment that her chick seemed to care more for the transient delights of the flesh – if holding hands with a young man during a Beethoven symphony could be so called – than for the more lasting delights of a living religious faith. Reverend Mother reached into her cavernous pocket and withdrew a small, worn leather purse. She took out a half-crown.

'This is the annual subscription to the Catholic

Students' Union, Ferelith. I believe it's a shilling entrance fee. It's at twenty-four George Square, young lady, and you will be able to hear Mass daily and also to have the joy of meeting His Grace the Archbishop on many Sunday evenings. I am sure that if you look after the spiritual side of your life, everything else will slot into place quite nicely.'

Ferelith had seen photographs of the Archbishop in the Catholic papers several times and was perfectly sure that such a normal-looking human being would understand that at eighteen she would find Blair Crawford infinitely more attractive than an elderly archbishop, but wisely she did not share this confidence with either of the two sisters on the other side of the table. She promised to mend her wicked ways and to at least join the union.

'A step in the right direction,' conceded Reverend Mother to Sister Anthony Joseph, 'but time will tell how much use your precious chick makes of the facilities.'

5

IN FEBRUARY BLAIR contracted a very heavy cold and his mother sent a car, comfortably equipped with hot-water bottles and several blankets, to convey her son from cold and windy Edinburgh to cold and windy Fife. He went without a murmur. He did not often fight with his mother because he usually lost the war. On the few occasions when he did win Mrs Crawford was so miserably unhappy that for weeks Blair felt that he was undoubtedly the world's most ungrateful son. This time though, he wanted to crawl home. He was quite ill.

'I'll come back as soon as I get over this,' he sneezed at Ferelith, who, never having been allowed to submit to ill-health at any time in her short life, had little sympathy for him.

His absence, therefore, meant that she found herself with some free time which could have been used in study.

The half-crown that Reverend Mother had given her stared at her from the edge of her table and so, feeling exceedingly virtuous, Ferelith wrapped herself up against the rigours of the elements, and set off for George Square. It was not too long a walk, just along Lauriston Place, past George Heriot's School For Boys, and then the Infirmary, down Meadow Walk and there it was, but so unrelenting was the rain that she was completely soaked by the time she was blown up the steps and in the front door.

'Hey, wait a minute,' said a very angry voice

whose owner had received most of the excess rainwater from Ferelith's coat all over his immaculate
blazer.

'I'm sorry,' gasped Ferelith, ineffectively trying to
wipe him dry with her wet hands.

'Stop helping me, please,' he gasped and then
started to laugh. His laughter was so pleasant that
Ferelith had to laugh too. 'I'm so sorry,' she said
again, 'but I didn't see you standing there.'

'The story of my life,' he said ruefully and Ferelith
pushed her hair out of her eyes and looked at him.

'I can't believe that,' she said.

He blushed. 'People look at me once they see me,'
he said, 'but being so short . . .'

He was smaller than Ferelith and could have been
no more than five foot five but he was, there was
no other word for it, exceptionally beautiful. He
reminded her of someone: it was that nose. That
was it! Surely he was like the Italian priest who
had holidayed at the orphanage one summer. But
he was talking.

'Dominic Regent,' he said. 'Since you have just
re-baptized me I feel we can dispense with other
introductions.'

'Ferelith Gallagher.'

'I've never seen you before,' he said. 'May I show
you around? I'm the secretary.'

The union was full of students, steaming clothes,
and laughter. Dominic introduced Ferelith to several
of the other students, showed her the room where
the chaplain celebrated daily Mass, the library, the
other facilities.

'Now a nice hot cup of tea,' he said when the tour
was over. 'You can have one on the house tonight
while you tell me all about yourself.'

He was easy to talk to and very easy indeed to

look at. She was so aware of his physical appearance. No, it was not really Father Coia, although she could almost be sure that he was of Italian extraction. Perhaps he was Greek. Yes, a statue: he must remind her of a statue . . . or did he resemble a holy picture in a book that she had read in the orphanage?

He became self-conscious as Ferelith gazed at him, and stopped talking. 'It's rude to stare,' he said.

It was Ferelith's turn to blush. 'I'm sorry, Dominic. It's just that you remind me of someone or something, an Italian painting, I think.'

'The Regents are proud to be good Glasgow Scots,' he said, and asked her about herself.

Ferelith continued to watch him as she told him the, to her, very dull story of her life and thought rightly that he would not want to know that he reminded her, not of some strong Greek god, but of the beautiful face of a goddess, or even worse, a fairy in one of the illustrated poetry books she had read to the babies during the Christmas holidays. When she had finished her great tale he told her that he was doing a master's degree in English Literature and that he wanted to be a lawyer.

'Snap.'

'You're reading English Lit. and you want to be a lawyer?'

'I'm studying modern languages and I want to be an advocate.'

'An advocate. A real live Portia. Great heavens. Is the world ready for this?'

'It had better be. We are almost one third of the way through the twentieth century and you men want to keep women —'

'Steady, steady,' he interrupted. 'Not *you men*, some men, and some women too, feisty little Ferelith, prefer the status quo.'

'I can't believe that.'

He smiled at her naivety. 'Come with me to the University Settlement . . .' He saw her look of puzzlement. 'You've never heard of it? Tut, tut. It's the University's own charitable foundation. It's in Kirk O' Field College . . . you must have heard of Kirk O' Fields? You know where Mary Queen of Scots – it is supposed or theorized – blew up, or had blown up, or connived at the blowing up of, her husband. Not that one would blame her. The Settlement is run by a wonderful woman called Miss Drysdale, and there you will see sights, Miss Gallagher, that would make that pretty hair of yours curl, if it didn't already do so.'

He proceeded to tell her of the Settlement and the work among the poor and unemployed of Edinburgh that the University tried to do.

'I go one night a week, sometimes a bit of time at the weekend. What do you think I teach, Miss Gallagher, to the disadvantaged, to the so-called dregs of society?'

She looked at him and she saw well-tailored clothes. She listened to him and she heard a cultured voice, not like Blair's but yet educated. She hazarded a guess. 'Literacy skills?'

'I'm teaching a basic cooking class and coaching football.' He saw her smile and said angrily, 'Now which of those do you find amusing, Miss Gallagher?'

Ferelith blushed when she saw how annoyed he was. 'Actually I didn't find either funny. I was wondering what you would say if I enrolled in your cookery class.'

'I can't believe you weren't taught to cook in an orphanage.'

'I didn't have time: I did my share of scrubbing lavatories but, for some reason, probably because I was always swotting, or as Reverend Mother would say hiding in the ruins, reading rubbish, I have never learned to cook.'

'Then you won't be able to help with my classes, but there's much that needs to be done and if you are going to be an advocate you might as well get to know the people you will be representing one day.'

Blair was not pleased to return to Edinburgh and to find Ferelith immersed, as he called it, in dirt and disease, and on first name terms with people whom he would never, in the course of a day, notice. It was not that he was unsympathetic to the poor and disadvantaged, it was just that he preferred to write a cheque in the calm and beauty of his home and to feel vaguely that he was doing good. Hands-on goodness was not something that he had ever encountered and he very much disliked this weedy effeminate-looking fellow who seemed to be becoming so important to Ferelith. He was furiously angry, and could not really understand why, when Ferelith told him that he and Dominic were very much alike.

'He is so like you, Blair. Well educated, well brought up – his father has a huge business in Glasgow – and he's passionately interested in the arts: music, the theatre, painting.'

'I am not passionately interested in anything, except, perhaps, keeping you away from somewhere where you will encounter depravity.'

'The people at the Settlement want to get away from depravity, Blair. They are poor and jobless and some of them drink and beat their wives and their children but they are trying to make things better and I want to help.'

'Because of your precious Dominic?'

'He introduced me to the Settlement.'

'Decent women don't go there.'

Oh Lord, whether he liked it or not, he was going to have to be dragged screaming and yelling into the twentieth century.

'Oh, Blair, what a prejudiced and muddleheaded thing to say. Come for yourself and see these people. I am so ashamed of all my advantages when I see girls the same age and look at their lives.'

Her advantages? He looked at her and again his heart swelled with love. She had had no advantages but she felt rich compared with others. He was ashamed of himself, and to make amends he promised to go with her on her next visit. It was his first visit and his last. He was unnerved at first by the familiarity with which Ferelith and Dominic were greeted. There was no tugging of forelocks here.

'Dominic! Ferelith! Hey weans, look who's here!'

'Dominic, ye gaun tae play fitba wi' us?'

'Ferelith, show us how tae dae wir hair like that?'

Ferelith introduced him to someone called 'Maggie Broon', a thin pasty-faced girl in a too-big blouse and skirt whose probable good looks were marred by the hunger in her face and the ugly bruise under her eye.

'It wis me dad,' she explained to Blair who was looking at her, dismay and horror written all over his handsome young face. She turned to Ferelith and her own gaunt face lit up. 'I'm walkin' oot, Ferelith. I've a lad, Bert Sturrock. He wis that mad when he saw this bruise. I wis near pleased I got it fer maybe he wouldnae hae spoke.'

Nothing in Blair's sheltered life had equipped him to cope at first hand with poverty and despair. He saw this as a weakness in himself and, to give him credit, never again tried to persuade Ferelith to stop going. He could not imagine his mother in such a setting. She was very good at visiting the poor and destitute on their own estate but was quite sure that the poor would do better if they would just, in her words, *get down to it*. Ferelith, and her friend Dominic, of whom he found himself more and more jealous, would not agree.

'Many of them would like to work, Blair,' argued Dominic, 'but there are no jobs and if there is a job, usually they are too untrained or too unskilled. If they are apathetic it is life that has made them apathetic. You're a good Presbyterian. You read your Bible much more than we Catholics do. You should know my favourite quote. *Without vision the people perish*. The Settlement will give them a little vision.'

'I'm quite happy to give them some money.'

'Gratefully received, I'm sure, but education is better.'

'Then they should have stayed at school,' argued Blair hotly. 'That Maggie Broon . . .' he began and was furious when Ferelith and Dominic laughed at him. 'What's so funny?'

'Your toffy tones saying Broon, you idiot,' said Dominic. 'It's "Brown". Don't you ever speak to the peasants on your boundless acres?'

'Where did you find your friend?' asked Dominic of Ferelith later and was so scorched by her blistering answer that it was some time before he mentioned Blair again.

Ferelith too decided to keep the two young men apart as much as possible. She could not understand what her feelings for Dominic were: friendship, yes, respect, most definitely, affection? What was affection? She knew two young men and each time she saw either one she felt good, but seeing Dominic or thinking about Dominic did not make her go hot and cold all over. It was a warm, pleasant feeling. She could not decide whether the feelings she had for Blair were pleasant or disturbing. As the days and weeks and months passed she even began to wonder if the feelings were this strange thing that the latest films called Love.

The first time he kissed her she felt in no doubt. It had to be love. Nothing else could make her heart do these amazing somersaults, could make the blood rush through her veins so strongly that she felt it must burst out through her skin.

'If music be the food of love, play on,' they demanded of Donald Tovey, and he and the Reid Orchestra unwittingly obliged. Ferelith and Blair, like every other couple discovering the delights of young love, knew that they alone were experiencing these emotions, and that no one anywhere had ever loved and felt quite as they did.

Sometimes Ferelith feared that she was too happy. Perhaps it was an inheritance from her Celtic past but she found it so difficult to accept her life and her love. She would sit in the lovely library at Edinburgh University and, instead of studying her books, she would study the head of Blair Crawford as he struggled to assimilate what she found so easy.

Sometimes he would feel her wide blue gaze and he would look up and they would look at one another as if they had just met and a slow smile of recognition would cross Blair's face.

'Hello, friend of my heart,' he would say, and she would blush and look down at her books again for she, in her turn, could not say the things that came so easily to Blair.

She could love him though, with her eyes and her lips, and by the end of Ferelith's first year everyone, including Dominic, knew *Blair and that funny wee girl from the orphanage are a pair. Inseparable, my darlings, like Siamese twins.*

Everyone knew but the two people who mattered most: Sister Anthony Joseph and Blair's widowed mother, Mrs Helena Crawford. Blair had tried to tell his mother: he had tried to bring the two of them together but Ferelith was afraid and Helena Crawford was . . . difficult.

'Nonsense, darling,' she would say when Blair tried tentatively to tell her that he felt he had met the one woman whom he could really love. 'Now do send Penelope a wire to tell her about the Ball.'

And so it went on until in the summer of 1933, Blair Crawford decided that it was time for him to assert himself and to tell his mother that he loved Ferelith Gallagher. The results, of course, of his decision were disastrous, both for him and for Ferelith, his love, his sweetheart – his sister.

Ferelith had run from Gretna Green to the orphanage in Glasgow and had been welcomed, not with scolding for her wickedness in celebrating a clandestine and unblessed marriage, but with loving arms and countless cups of hot sweet tea.

'I suppose part of the fault is ours,' the old nun had told the heartbroken girl, 'but Reverend Mother thought it best at the time not to tell you what we knew.'

Ferelith heard again the bald statements of the dry-as-dust lawyer. 'Well, for God's sake tell me now,' she had begged.

'You came to us when you were only a few months old, Ferelith. You were supposed to go to Ireland

where, we think, there might have been someone
who had known your mother: there might have
been relatives even. We never did trace anyone.
Anyway, because of the outbreak of the Great War,
the sister who was charged with taking you back,
never got to Ireland at all but stayed in Scotland
and you with her. She knew nothing of your history,
only that you were an orphan and might have Irish
relatives. We knew that you were born in a convent
in Bombay. Sister told us that your mother was a
nursemaid to a British officer's family and,' the nun
hung her head to save Ferelith embarrassment, 'she
got into trouble. The father, your father, was already
married, and there's some talk of a suicide . . . we
were never really told.'

She stood up and, on safer ground now, went to
the window. 'Your mother's employers took a very
un-Christlike attitude and threw her out when it was
discovered that you were on the way. Thanks be to
God she was able to take refuge with an English
nanny she had befriended on the ship out.' She
laughed a little. 'They're not all bad, the English.
The nanny got Miss Gallagher into the Convent but
Niamh, your mother, made no real effort to keep
well. She blamed herself, you see, for the soldier's
death. We believe that he shot himself rather than
face up to the consequences of his actions, well,
their actions. It was all hushed up for his wife's
sake, you see. Apparently, Niamh Gallagher kept
saying, "I told him I'd tell but I never would. I
only said it because I was angry and scared." She
died a few hours after you were born: she wanted
to die, Ferelith. I doubt she even saw you or she
would have made an effort, I'm sure she would.'

'I'm sure,' said Ferelith drily. 'Who decided to
send me back to Ireland?'

'The Mother Superior in Bombay. She could hardly send you to the Major's wife and you were white, you see, all white. The other babies were half-castes. She thought there might be a chance of adoption for you, but who had thoughts of adoption during the war? We kept you and we loved you and when we saw you had a brain we decided that there had to be more than domestic service for you.'

Ferelith smiled at her warmly. Well, she knew who had spent hours fighting for her, fighting that she be singled out. 'You mean *you* saw that I had a brain. I wasn't going to throw it all away, Sister. I love Blair, loved him . . .'

She began to cry again and the old nun rocked her in her arms and soothed her.

'You love him. Of course you still love him and it will be a long time before that love changes itself into a more acceptable and manageable form of love, but don't turn it into hate, Ferelith. Blair is a victim too and he is suffering as you are suffering and we must pray that he too recovers.'

Ferelith had not thought of Blair as another victim of the tragedy and thinking about him and his unhappiness helped her recovery. Then too, this was to be her third year, and the third year of an honours course in language meant a continuous year of study abroad.

Dominic was the only other person in whom Ferelith confided her secret.

'Dearie me, as my old nanny would have said. You poor old thing.' He stopped and then began again. 'And Blair, of course. He must be devastated. Dear God what a shocker. I do feel for you both but it's not the end of the world, little one. Actually, if you had to do something as drastic as marrying less than halfway through your education I suppose

this was the year to do it. You must get away from
Edinburgh, from all the memories. There's a chap,
keeper of the register, a Mr Lyford-Pike. He can
give you a card of introduction abroad. You should
go to Paris, or Rouen, or even Marseilles for a year.
The Honorary Academic Consul there, with whom
Mr L-P will put you in touch, will introduce you
to university circles. You'll have a marvellous time
and I shall miss you unbelievably. I've quite got
used to having you around.'

'Perhaps I should have married you, Dominic.'

'I don't think I'm quite cut out for holy matrimony: couldn't bear howling babies. Who knows
though. I certainly like you better than anyone
else I know and I'm quite sure we're not related.
Oh God, what an insensitive thing to say,' he said
as Ferelith dissolved into tears. Awkwardly he put
his arms around her and she sobbed into another of
his immaculate blazers as she had sobbed into Sister
Anthony's serge front.

'I'm sorry, Ferelith,' he said as she grew calmer.
'I just have no idea what to say and so should have
said nothing. Here.' He handed her his freshly-
laundered handkerchief and she blew her nose
soundly.

'It's not lesson one, is it? How to deal with someone who marries her own brother. Oh, Dominic.
It's a bloody awful nightmare and I wish I could
wake up.'

Who was the first person to work out that working hard is a positive antidote to heartbreak? But
Dominic was right in believing that an even better
way to deal with loss is to get as far away from
the memories as possible. So October 1933 found
Ferelith Gallagher, for so unbelievably beautiful a
moment, Ferelith Crawford, living in France and

studying at the Université de Paris. *Paris is a city for lovers*. Trite. Any city, anywhere, is a city for lovers when the lovers are together. But Paris does have a charm and for Ferelith it had its newness, its excitement, its foreignness . . . The smells and sounds of Paris were not the smells and sounds of Glasgow or Edinburgh. She wandered the streets of Paris as she had wandered the streets of Scotland's beautiful capital and she found that once more she was able to breathe and to feel and even to smile. She smiled at the unbelievable beauty of the huge tulips the *concierge* put in all her rooms. She even smiled on the morning that she found herself hungry and, for the first time, really tasted the hot sweet chocolate and the freshly-baked croissants that Madame had prepared for *le petit déjeuner*.

Sister Anthony and Dominic were right again, thought Ferelith as she savoured the textures and aromas. I am coming back to life: nothing will be the same. I am not the same but I am alive. I feel, and oh, dear God, I feel so absolutely awful, so full of despair. Bring it out and look at what has happened, Ferelith, and then put it behind you.

She sat on a park bench and watched Paris going past her: people hurrying to work, to school, to the markets, each with his own secrets, his own desires, fears, loves, hates. All her life she had wondered about her parents. Why had they abandoned her? Had her mother wanted her, had she looked forward to the birth of a child with joy or with fear? And her father? Who was this shadowy person who was responsible for her very existence? She had wondered if he had begot her with love. He must have loved her mother: he had to have loved her mother. Too awful, too awful to be the result of some casual encounter, of rape.

Oh, how she had prayed that it had not been rape.

She had often sat in classrooms, marked out by her orphanage uniform, and thought of the other boys and girls, running home to tea with brothers and sisters, loving, squabbling, sharing secrets, and she had wished that there was one, even just one person to whom she belonged. And all the time there had been Blair. Blair in his privileged, gilded home. Son of the same father, her brother, her half-brother. In his body there were the same genes; in his character there were the same traits. No wonder that when they had met she had loved him. Was he not part of herself? Had she loved the husband, the brother, or herself that she had found in him?

Ferelith Gallagher cried in Paris. She wept for the young Ferelith and for Blair and for that Irish nursemaid. I'm Irish. I'm Scottish. I'm Celtic. At least now I know something. Was she loose, this Irish mother? Was she blindly in love with an unprincipled man? He killed himself. Because of me? Dear blessed God, what a legacy to leave me, Father dear. And my mother, like Monsieur Le Dauphin, turned her head to the wall – and died. No. No. No. I refuse to accept the blame.

She stood up and blew her nose loudly. She wiped her eyes with a dry corner of her handkerchief and she began to walk into her future.

'You loved Blair Crawford, Blair Winterton, whatever his name was,' she said to herself. 'You married him and . . . you slept with him and it was . . . beautiful but it's crazy, crazy, insane for he was . . . is . . . your brother, your brother, the son of your father, Major the Honourable Archie Winterton. You have other family out there somewhere, Wintertons all over the place. Don't cry, don't cry but hide here in Paris and learn to rrroll your Rs and forget about love. Why the hell couldn't you fall in love with Dominic or Dominic with you?'

Because she was still so badly bruised she did not allow love or even friendship to get close to her in Paris. She sat in a class full of students from all over Europe and she was alone, for she shied away from every approach and after a while fellow students gave up on the prickly Scot with the prickly pride and she was left alone and, she told herself, that was how she wanted it. She filled the year with study and research, very occasional letters to Dominic and more frequent letters to Sister Anthony. To her great sorrow she also missed out on the greatest of France's cultural joys for she could afford to do no more than live quietly.

'I'll come back and go to the opera,' she said each time she passed the beautiful opera house. 'I'll come back and I will tour the chateaux of the Loire valley. But this year is for work, this year is for Sister Anthony and Reverend Mother. I owe them so much and I have to repay it for some other girl.'

'You have learned the French language well, Ferelith,' her tutor, Mireille Lefèvre, told her when she was leaving, 'but of France I think you have learned very little. That is a great regret.'

'I have learned what I needed to know, madame,' said Ferelith. 'It would be good to stay longer, to learn more, to travel, explore a little, but for me it is not the right time.'

'But France has healed a wound, *ma petite*, no?'

'Healed? I don't know. Covered it over so that I no longer wince, madame.'

She returned to Edinburgh for her final year. Dominic had graduated and had gone to study law in

Glasgow and she knew that she would miss him, that the Settlement would miss him. At first she was afraid that she might run into Blair. The cold legal communications from his family's lawyers had said nothing of where he was, how he was, what he was doing. She assumed that, if he had stayed at the University, he had graduated. But although, in Paris, he was constantly in her thoughts, she never mentioned him in her letters to Dominic who, in turn, had written only of his work at the Settlement and of his studies, nothing at all of his personal life, and he had asked no questions about hers.

From Paris she had submitted satisfactory reports on the work covered and had attended lectures on French history. That gave her a head start for her final course in French history. She had sent too a draft of her thesis for the approval of the professor and now she had two full terms to deliver it in its final form. She had decided to study four stages in the development of French medieval prose and was reading Villehardouin, Joinville, Froissart, and Commines, and wished heartily that she did not have to read the old French text, *Chanson de Roland*, as another obligatory part of the final year. France and the French were too romantic.

She kept to her strict regime and the Ferelith Gallagher who graduated in the summer of 1935 was a very changed girl from the naive trusting student who had entered the hallowed halls with such expectation and excitement four years before.

'You're twenty-one now, my child,' reminded Reverend Mother, who had greatly surprised her by turning up to the graduation ceremony with several other sisters including Sister Anthony Joseph, 'and the time has definitely come to sever some of the ties. We will continue to pay for your education until you have received your law degree but this Convent is no longer your home.' She saw the stunned look on Ferelith's face and smiled. 'That's what you wanted, my dear, remember. We are becoming a habit, if you will excuse the unpardonable pun, and it is not a good one. You are on your own, Ferelith. We will watch and we will pray and we will never turn you away from our doors but you must fly the nest, to use an overworked poetic phrase.'

'I don't quite know what to do, to say.'

'Go away again. Take a summer job. Sister Anthony has been writing letters for weeks. Go and see what she has contrived, and good luck and more importantly, God be with you.'

Ferelith fled to Sister Anthony. 'I've been thrown out. I have wanted to be out from under for ever and now that it's come, I'm terrified. Where will I live? I mean how does one go about finding somewhere to live? I can't stay in hostels all my life.'

'Well, you haven't lost your taste for melodrama. You are not being thrown out as you put it: you are being set —'

'Adrift without a paddle,' Ferelith interrupted.

'On your own two feet,' Sister Anthony finished her own sentence. 'I think it is more than time that you left the umbrella of the Church. Next session you must go into a residence and Ferelith, you must put the episode of your marriage behind you. There are other nice men . . .' She saw the mulish look on the young woman's face. 'Ferelith, there are other nice men out there,' she said again. 'You have no friends at all, girls or boys . . . well, except this Dominic. You must allow yourself to open like a flower.'

'No more, Sister. I will never marry: I will devote my whole life to my career,' said Ferelith grandly.

'Oh my, how dreadfully dull. Perhaps you will never marry but don't let it be because you hid away from the chance. Let someone else into your heart, Ferelith. Joy is all the greater when there has been some pain before, believe me.'

Ferelith looked at the nun. The old face smiled with serenity and inner peace. I wish I was like that, she thought, so accepting, not wanting to fight all the time. 'Very well, Sister. How do you want me to start?'

'Join something else: the choir,' she said, then laughed. 'Well, maybe not. Or the debating society. That would be good experience for an advocate. Don't sit alone or always with the lost souls. As an advocate you will deal with lost souls all the time. I should imagine one might go crazy if there was nothing around but human misery.'

'I'll try something but right now I have to do something with the summer. Reverend Mother hasn't even let me unpack.'

'How about a job where you will have to meet lots of different people, some nice some nasty?'

Ferelith sighed. 'You don't give up easily, do you?'

'No,' said Sister Anthony. 'I never give up – ever.'

And so the summer of 1935 found Miss Ferelith Gallagher, M.A. working in a hotel in Rome. There were advantages, she had to admit, in having been brought up by Roman Catholic nuns. Sister Anthony Joseph had a friend at the mother house in Rome, Sister Aquinus, who had a friend who knew someone, who owned a really nice guesthouse and who would be delighted to have cheap, for the entire summer, a law student who spoke good English, satisfactory Spanish, excellent French and who was prepared to learn Italian. Needless to say, the said student was also supposed to work very hard at everything from cleaning rooms to waiting tables.

In Rome she found to her surprise that she was not miserable. The *pensione*, which was within sight of St Peter's, had been a private house, then a convent and then a private house again. The family who owned it had lost their money in the Great War, but not their pride and self-respect, and they had decided to turn their beautiful home into a hotel. All surviving family members who were fit to work did so. The furniture in the rooms was the remaining treasure of a once rich dynasty: the china, glassware, linens, silver were all beautiful and valuable. Guests who had never been accustomed to such treasures in their own homes wrote glowing reports to their friends.

There isn't much furniture but what there is, is magnificent. The bathtubs are medieval but the water is hot and the food, served on translucent porcelain plates, is superb. You must see it before they realize how crazy they are.

And their friends came and they told their friends, and Ferelith worked almost until she dropped. By the end of the summer she found that she had learned passable Italian, she had absorbed an incredible amount of knowledge of Italian painting and music, and she had been adopted by an eccentric group of Italian aristocrats. Pietro Angelosanti, the younger son of the house, did not, however, want her for a sister but for a lover and that was a complication she would have been happy to do without.

'Why are you so cold, Ferelith?' he asked her.

Ferelith looked at him and felt separated from him

by light years. One day he wanted to be a priest; the next day he was going to audition for the Teatro San Carlo in Naples where his godfather, a Cardinal, was a friend of the Director of Music; the next he – like most Italian boys (and that, thought Ferelith, was all he was, a boy) – wanted to play football.

They stood together in the central courtyard of his family home. If she looked up through the intertwining branches of the huge grapevines she could see the top of St Peter's Basilica and above that the stars twinkling in a sky that looked fashioned from a luscious deep-blue velvet. She looked at him and he was good to look at. He was much shorter than Blair and not much taller than Ferelith herself but he had the muscled body of an athlete and the classic Roman profile that would look very good on the stage. She felt nothing and she sighed.

'I'm not cold, Pietro. I'm merely a hundred years older than you.'

He looked at her, a puzzled expression on his handsome face. 'You are a little older, yes.'

'I have been married . . .' she began.

He started back from her. 'You have a husband?'

She shook her head. 'I had a husband, Pietro.' She hesitated. How much should she tell him? How much did he have the right to know? 'I was married but . . . there was a problem, and the marriage had to be annulled. But you have to understand that I loved my husband. I still love him and I can't just jump from one relationship to another.'

He smiled at her. 'I am a Roman, Ferelith and therefore have all the time in the world to wait. You will let me keep in touch? You are part of our family now, yes? You will come back to see us, to help maybe?'

'I promise to come back if you make your debut

at the Teatro San Carlo. I promise to come back when you are ordained, if you are ordained. I do not promise to come back when you start playing football.'

'It is gone,' he said. 'No more football. I will come to Scotland to the University. You will learn to love me.'

Ferelith sighed. A lovesick Italian nobleman she did not need or want. 'Please, Pietro. I have years of university ahead of me. I don't just want to become a lawyer. My sights are set much higher. I intend to read for the Bar: I'm going to be a barrister and try cases, usually a male prerogative, and I may even become a judge. Who knows? Maybe I'll be the first ever female Lord Advocate.'

He laughed at this obvious nonsense. A woman, and a pretty woman at that, wasting her time in a man's world when she could do so well in her own. 'Why do you want to be a lawyer? It is so unfeminine.'

Ferelith laughed. 'And you are so typically male and typically Latin.'

Pietro flushed but said nothing. He walked away from her across the courtyard and then turned and smiled. 'There is nothing wrong in believing that a woman is best suited to gracing the house of the man who loves her. It is God's perfect plan and we should not throw defiance in the face of the Almighty, but I do not want to fight with you, Ferelith. I want to know what draws you to this so masculine profession.'

She decided to ignore his last adjective.

'I need a career that will use the talents God has given me. I also want to help other people, especially . . . well, frankly, I want to help poor people, people who have had it hard. Then, I find that I have an extremely good memory, I think clearly and logically and I have a very analytical mind. My teachers tell me I'm good at sifting through masses of information to find the small nuggets in it that are important: I don't get sidetracked by poetic prose or misplaced sentiment. My thinking is precise and, I believe, accurate, and I have the ability to absorb and understand all kinds of information. I hope I'm good at interviewing others, so I should turn this question and answer session on to you, Pietro.'

He looked at her sadly. 'You make yourself sound like a machine and you are not. You are warm and lovely and soft and oh, so desirable. These are God-given talents too. You are throwing away your chances of fulfilment as a woman, Ferelith, for a dream of a cold, lonely office. This dream takes years and what is there at the end when you become this Lord Advocate?'

'Fulfilment as a human being.'

'A barren woman. A barren life, and you must feel the same way yourself or you would not have already married. Or is it that you wish to punish men now that your first dream is over?'

Ferelith tried not to be offended. She looked up at the sky and again she saw the beauty of this eternal city and she smelled the good smells of grapes hanging heavy just above her head. 'He was part of the dream, Pietro, and through no fault of his own, his dream too is shattered.' She turned away from him and walked across the courtyard to the door from where lights and soft music and the mingled smells of wine and garlic and sun-dried tomatoes were creeping through the still night air. At the door she turned again. 'I wanted it all, Pietro, and I will let nothing and no one stand in the way of my chance of getting the part that's left.'

When the door had closed behind her he took out his silver cigarette case and looked sadly at the engraving of his family crest. Then he took out a cigarette and rapped it smartly on the head of the little dragon. 'And what of me, my Lady Advocate?' He lit the cigarette and inhaled deeply and blew the smoke up into the grapes hanging above his head. Never had he been more thankful that he had been born an Italian. It was easy to decide that his best course of action was to pray – for both of them.

ON THE TRAIN back across Europe to the Channel ports, Ferelith mused on the fact that a woman's road to worldly success seemed to be like a hurdle race. She, Ferelith Gallagher, wanted to be Lord Advocate. Was this a totally unrealistic aim? She pushed that unworthy thought deep down inside. But still she had to deal with the realities: she was penniless and had no family to support her. To do well in law did one need both family and financial support? As yet she knew little of the august body she hoped to join but the members of it she had seen did seem to be rather special people, all of whom spoke with the same voice and had been to the same schools. Once, and only for a few moments, she had allowed herself to wonder what would have happened had she become pregnant on that one beautiful night; and after she had found from books that the dangers to the baby's mental and physical health were negligible she had, for one second, allowed herself to daydream, and then she had pushed the thought away and had never let it return. There was to be a clean break. She would never see Blair or think of him ever again.

She would keep instead the shadowy figure of a female Lord Advocate before her as something at which to aim. The first hurdle was to get into law school. In 1935, the year in which one Stanley Baldwin formed a National Government, Edinburgh University Law School admitted twenty-seven female students: Ferelith Gallagher was one of them. She stopped humming last year's popular song, 'Blue Moon', and sang either 'Just One of Those Things', or 'I Got Plenty of Nothin' which seemed to sum it all up.

She had enough money saved from her time in Italy to buy her books, which included the *Introduction to the Law of Scotland* by Gloag and Henderson which she carried around for days as if it was as precious as her Bible. This was not because at £2 and two shillings it was the most expensive book she had ever had to buy but because she felt that, like the Bible, the answers to so many questions would be inside if she could but ferret them out. She went from Green and Son, carrying her brown-paper parcel of books, to Patrick Thomson's on the Bridges where she bought a very smart, grey suit and a white blouse which told the world that she was a practising lawyer's clerk, and with her last five and six a knit-wool muffler in the University colours which, thrown nonchalantly around her neck, perfectly completed this grown-up ensemble. Nothing she was now wearing had been stitched by the patient hands of Sister Glenn and, perversely, as soon as she had discarded her home-made cotton knickers she missed them and retrieved them from her wastebasket. Washed and folded up, they were put at the bottom of a drawer against one of Sister Glenn's proverbial rainy days.

The law degree was a part-time course. Ferelith, like all the other prospective law students, had had to find a solicitor who was willing to hire her on a part-time basis and who would teach her the day-to-day running of a legal practice in the hours around her class times. Her professors gave her a good reference and she was hired by an old friend of Docteur Burns, Graham Lord. The work was not well paid but it was certainly not onerous. Mr Lord wondered gently how a knowledge of three European languages would help a solicitor in a firm that dealt mainly with conveyancing and mercantile law. Even so, he promised to instruct her in all parts of the business and profession of procurators of Court and conveyancers in order that she might learn the same – *so far as he knew himself and the said apprentice shall be capable of learning* – but he clearly felt that women were tender flowers to be protected from all the nastiness of life and he found it difficult actually to ask Ferelith to do anything. He even made his junior partner, his great nephew, James, make the morning tea. Ferelith was allowed to keep the stamps which meant that she bought stamps every few months at the Post Office, stamped all Mr Lord's letters and made neat notes of how many stamps she used each day. Little by little, however, she managed to persuade him to allow her at least to read his mail and to do research for him and, since she was not tall and had learned to remain very quiet, he eventually forgot that she was there at all and she was able finally to watch a very conscientious solicitor at work.

Sometimes visiting clients assumed that she was Mr Lord's secretary and made remarks like, 'Mak sure the lassie taks a' this doon, Maister Lord,' and she smiled at them sweetly and did exactly what they wanted.

She heard from Pietro, who wrote her an almost hysterical letter reminding her that Adolph Hitler had polluted the air of glorious Venice by meeting Benito Mussolini there.

Now he has invaded Abyssinia. Did he discuss this action in the shadow of the Frari, whose austere Franciscan interior houses some of Titian's major works? Did they talk casually about the Nuremberg laws against the Jews in the church of San Giovanni where the immortal Vivaldi was baptized? Why did the very buildings not disappear for ever under the Lagoon in protest? But why should simple stone and paint cry out against injustice when man does not? I have been accepted at the Conservatory. Shall I learn to sing of the glory of God or man?

All her classes, apart from forensic medicine which she had to take with real medical students, were in the Old College, and her first class was at 9 a.m. on Wednesday the 16th of October 1935. The lecturer was Professor Annan and the subject was accounting. The second day was more interesting. Professor James Mackintosh introduced his students to civil law. He promised them practising lawyers as guest lecturers and the first one was an ancient – to Ferelith – lawyer called Angus Webster.

'He'll be Lord Advocate one of these days,' other students said or, 'Wait for it. He's already a K.C.'

'King's Council,' agreed the first student. 'He's got everything: a fantastic record, a great brain, impeccable antecedents and bags of money.'

'That's awful,' said Ferelith. 'You mean he's buying his advancement?'

'No, not really, but if you are going to be a judge, with all that it entails, it doesn't hurt to know the right people and to have some money. Face it, Ferelith, law is a closed shop. Every judge just happens to have a daddy who was a judge, or a godfather, or his wife's great-uncle.'

Ferelith watched and listened to her first guest lecturer and wanted to dislike him because he was one of the men like Blair who seemed to get everything they wanted because of who they were. But she could not. Angus Webster, forty if he was a day, was . . . nice. He was tall, and would be even taller if he stood up straight. He seemed to be one of those gentlemen who had so often bent over to deal with the problems of someone smaller that he had developed a stoop. He was grey and that was to be expected at his age but he was thin, too thin. She wondered if he ate properly and thought of what Sister Glenn at the Convent would have done about fattening him up. His voice, although definitely Scottish public school, was, she had to admit, charming, not at all dry and colourless, and what he had to say, at this first lecture and every other time she heard him, was fascinating.

'You want to leave this university with a degree, Bachelor of Laws – plural, laws, civil and common,' he began. 'You want . . . *Baccalaureus utriusque juris* . . .' Several students began to look rather uncomfortable and he smiled at their consternation – a lecture in Latin, oh, please, no! That's when Ferelith decided that she liked him – and he went back to the King's English, 'Bachelor of both laws. LL.B. As you all *know*' – did he say this with sarcasm or humour? Humour, Ferelith decided – 'it is the Latin convention when abbreviating plural words to repeat the initial letter. We will begin with Civil Law, the laws governing private rights, those rights which belong to every man, woman, and child, whether they be rich or poor.'

I like it, thought Ferelith. He's saying the right words, every woman, every child, poor.

'Since fourteen hundred and twenty-four, gentlemen – sorry, ladies and gentlemen, I will not make that mistake again – five hundred and ten

years, think of it, there has been a law in this country
of ours that allows free legal aid to the poor among
us. Perhaps one or two of you may go on to become
advocates' – did he look directly at Ferelith? She
thought he did – 'and you will become directly
involved with that elderly but still powerful law.'

Ferelith scribbled and scribbled and then, when
she realized that her writing was becoming so
untidy that she could no longer read it, she sat
back and tried to really listen and to absorb. 'I'll
read it up later. I'll go over my notes later. Oh, dear
God, I am in the right place. At last, at last, I am in
the right place.'

It was not all work. She had moved out of the
hostel in Springhill Gardens and had taken a room in
a student hostel. Again it would have been perfectly
simple to keep herself away from everyone and just
to work but she was beginning to find that she no
longer wanted to be isolated from human contact.
Pietro had helped her more than either of them
realized. She was still deeply in love with Blair
and it was no use to tell herself over and over
that he was her brother and that her feelings for
him were wrong, even sinful. But she had to admit
that she had been stirred ever so slightly by Pietro's
admiration. No matter what she said to herself, she
was a young woman and she wanted the company,
the conversation, the fun of being with other young
people.

She decided to continue to attend the Reid Concerts, although the first one clashed with the showing of *The Brothers Karamazov* at the Caley picture
house, but she went to the concert, not really for
the music but because at a concert one could speak
to other concert-goers. She was unlikely to speak to
anyone at the pictures.

In 1935 the famous Dr Albert Schweitzer came to the faculty of the University of Edinburgh and even though the title of his first lecture – Problems of Natural Theology and Natural Ethics – did not sound too terribly exciting she decided correctly that everyone who could possibly get into Rainy Hall would be there, and she joined them.

Simon Osborne, also a law student, saw her there but lost her in the press of students and faculty who had come to hear and see the great man. To his delight he saw her again at his next class.

'Well hello, sweetness.' What an odd way to greet a perfect stranger. Sweetness. She smiled: she liked it. 'Come sit beside me,' he continued, 'and tell me why you always look like a startled rabbit.'

Ferelith looked in some surprise at the only other student in the lecture hall. This was going too far. 'I beg your pardon,' she said frostily.

He jumped to his feet and came over to her and she saw that he was about her age and, although by no stretch of the imagination could he be called pretty, he reminded her immediately of Dominic. They were about the same height. This man was slightly taller and broader but there was something about the eyes, the set of the head.

'You have been well brought up,' he said. 'I can tell, and your mother told you never to speak to strange men and I, my love, am very strange. Allow me to introduce myself. My name is Simon Osborne. How do you do? There, we have been formally introduced and now you have to tell me who you are.'

'Ferelith Gallagher,' said Ferelith, holding out her hand.

'Ferelith. But what a totally adorable name. Perfect. I have never heard it before and I'm so pleased because it's obviously a name for a goddess who . . .'

'Looks like a startled rabbit.'

'I was going to say looks like a wood sprite.'

'Really, you can't have it both ways. I can't look like a rabbit and a sprite at the same time.'

He laughed. 'You are going to become a lady advocate, aren't you, I can tell. I shall tell my father to expect you. He is not ready for you but then the poor darling wasn't ready for me either and he coped. Amazing how some class of Scot always manages to cope, isn't it?'

'Do you always talk like this?'

'Only when I am fearfully nervous.'

'There's no need to be nervous around me.'

He looked at her and understood that that was so. He smiled. 'Ferelith Gallagher, I shall adore you for ever. Come and sit beside me and protect me from all the hulking rugby players in this class.'

'Why do you need protecting?'

He looked at her measuringly. 'What an innocent we are. Never mind, sweetness. We shall help one another. Come and tell me where you have been all my life and then after this terribly boring lecture – I can say that because my own dear daddy is the lecturer – I shall take you away for lunch.'

'You are a very strange young man.'

'And you are repeating yourself.'

Ferelith sat beside him during the lecture, which was an introduction to conveyancing, and was surprised to see that he took not one note. She scribbled furiously. Her practice was to make notes as clearly as she could and then to write them up more fully when she got to the library. Only when she was sure that she had a textbook that covered the lecture almost verbatim did she allow herself to relax and just listen and even then she made heading notes. She said nothing however but allowed herself, at the end of the lecture, to be led from the benches.

'Come and meet my pa and then we'll have lunch.'

She hung back, not quite sure if she wanted to be introduced to a lecturer, but Simon propelled her forward and she found herself shaking hands with the lecturer. George Osborne did not look in the least like his son and was also much more reserved. He was very kind though and wished them both luck with their law degrees and invited them to join him for lunch.

'Sorry Dad, Ferelith and I are having lunch together.'

His father smiled. 'That's wonderful, Simon. I do hope I meet you again soon, Miss Gallagher.'

'What a nice man,' she said to Simon later as they walked along George IV Bridge. 'I thought you said he didn't approve of women lawyers.'

'He doesn't but then he has never met a lady lawyer or at least never allowed one near him. Frightfully prejudiced, my pa. But I could see that he most certainly approved of you. Come on, I shall buy you a steak.'

'A steak. You're out of your mind.'

'Don't you like steak?'

Ferelith tried to cast her mind back to a time when she had actually eaten steak. Rome, oh yes, she had eaten steak in Rome.

'Of course I like steak.'

'Then stop complaining. We'll munch away and you can tell me what you thought of the great Schweitzer.'

She turned to him animatedly. 'Oh, were you there? I couldn't believe I was actually in the same room.'

'I feel the same way about being at a concert when Barbirolli conducts but then perhaps that's really because I'm terrified that he's going to be carried away by his enthusiasm and fall off his podium into my waiting arms. What would one do with him?'

'He does beat the air a bit, doesn't he?'

'Philistine.'

Ferelith spent a lot of time with Simon that term. He was as well read and as interested in the arts as Blair but, unlike Blair, he was also very serious about his studies. After their first few meetings he dropped what she called his very jolly pose and was calm and natural. She liked the calm Simon better than the one she felt wore a defensive shell, and became very much at ease with him. She liked especially that, like Dominic, he made no move to touch her: it was like having a friend who just happened to be male, like having, she hated to say it, a brother. This should have been her relationship with Blair. She began to find that it did not hurt so much to think of Blair, to wonder where he was and what had happened to him. She even began to hope that he had met someone else, one of the *correct* young women his mother had picked out for him, and that he had married. She did not mention him to Simon, not that first year or the second.

She enjoyed the freedom of her relationship with Simon, a relationship she could not quite fathom but which she deliberately decided not to try to understand. She spent as much time with him as she had with Dominic and almost as much time as she had with Blair, but her heart did not race as it had when she had been with Blair, she did not find herself yearning for his touch, his kiss. But she was just a little annoyed that he seemed to feel exactly the same about her. She wondered why he never made any effort to touch her. He helped her on with her coat: he pulled her on to moving trams, but his hands never lingered and his eyes never caressed.

'He's like me,' she told herself. 'He works too hard to want to complicate life with love.'

At least once a term she attended a lecture given by Angus Webster and she thought that he definitely was the ideal lawyer. She was, she decided, going to be just like him, knowledgeable, caring and compassionate. He had also a droll sense of humour and sometimes she had the feeling that he was speaking just to her for she understood his humour and would laugh before, as the children in the orphanage had said years before, 'the penny drapped', or realization dawned on her peers.

In her third year, having saved almost every penny she had earned, she left the university residence and moved into a tiny flat in Newington. It was hardly big enough for her and contained a poky living room with a fold-down bed and a table that doubled as a desk, or really a desk that doubled as a table since she spent far more time studying than eating. There was also a pocket-sized kitchen and a lavatory. Ferelith, scrubbing herself nightly in the kitchen sink with water hot from a kettle, thought she was in paradise. For the first time in her life she had a home of her own and she could entertain. She invited Simon to supper and he came bringing flowers, a bottle of wine, and a gilt-framed oil painting.

'Simon, I can't accept that.'

'Don't be silly, sweetness. It's a house-warming present.'

'This isn't a house. It's a minuscule flat.'

'What a good advocate we are practising to be.'

'Don't be facetious.'

'Ferelith my love, you must learn to accept nicely. Giving is easy especially when you have it to give but to accept is an art. I hope this little picture will be the first of many gifts that I will have the pleasure of giving you.'

She turned away from him, troubled. He was her friend. Was he now going to want more than friendship? The painting was obviously valuable.

'I love the flowers, Simon, and we'll share the wine. I've made spaghetti the way I learned to make it in Rome. It's very simple.'

'It's very pungent: the whole of Newington is sharing it with us by default. Now you open the wine and tell me where to hang your present.'

'Simon, please, I can't. It's too much. You must see that.'

He ignored her and went into the kitchenette and began to look through the drawers.

'Well, I shall have to use the heel of my shoe as a hammer. I brought my own nail. On that wall, I think, above the table, and then you will be able to see it all the time. You do like it, don't you? I should hate to think that you loathed it. Pour the wine, sweetness, and Uncle Simon will tell you something about life that your Sister Anthony never told you.'

She did as she was bid and stood watching him take as much time and trouble over hanging the little painting as he did over everything else. He was such an intense person under that silly veneer he affected.

'There.' He stepped off the chair and stood back to admire the effect. 'Entrancing. Brings this . . . charming little nest to life, don't you think?'

'If it was mine, Simon, I should never tire of looking at it.'

'What a perfectly lovely thing to say. Come, some wine. I need some courage for the next part. It's not usually something I have to explain.'

She poured the wine and he moved the room's only other chair around so that they were both looking at the painting.

'Ferelith, you do like me, don't you?'

'Of course, Simon, but . . .'

'I like you too, but that's as far as it goes. No, that's a lie. I think I love you . . .' he felt her tense beside him and laughed, '. . . as much as I can love any woman, sweetness.'

The words sat in the air beside them and Ferelith absorbed them and then coloured furiously. 'Oh, how stupid. It never occurred . . .' She stopped talking, unable to cope with his revelation.

'I hope it's not going to make any difference to us except that I'm a *wee thing* worried about your lack of interest in the male body and yet you're not like me.'

She looked at him. 'No, no I'm not.'

'I cold-bloodedly decided to use you, you know, Ferelith, as a buffer. I used to be beaten up quite regularly by *real* men. Spare me from real men who have to beat the hell out of everything they don't understand or that frightens them. I'm not a threat to anyone. Do and let do, is my motto, but when I saw you at that lecture I recognized you as an answer to a prayer, a prayer for peace. Who hurt you, sweetness? Why are you avoiding any kind of emotion? Why aren't you falling in love with a good, kind, solid man and leaving the pursuit of the law to chase small children all over the place?'

'I did fall in love,' she said simply and told him the whole story.

'Poor you,' he said when she had finished. 'Poor

Blair. Now can you warm up that congealed garlic or shall I run out for fish suppers?'

And that was the only time for several years that they talked about Blair but it was the first of many discussions they had about Ferelith's love life.

'You should meet other people, make other friends, male and female.'

'So should you.'

'Ferelith, I'm not you. I'm not even really sure who I am. Night after night I tell myself that I would be supremely happy if I could love you, I mean really love you, or if I could feel that kind of love for anyone, even for another man. I'm so frightened sometimes. Perhaps I should have been born three hundred years ago.'

'Why on earth would that make a difference?'

'I wouldn't be out of place as someone who worships beauty.'

Again she was reminded of Dominic. Was he like Simon?

'Surely a lover of beauty isn't out of place in this society especially with what is happening in Europe. You do have a strong social conscience too.'

'Perhaps that's my problem.'

'Oh Simon, don't ever regret caring about people.'

There was so much caring to do in the next few years. Pietro wrote despairing letters from Italy about the worsening situation in Europe.

Doesn't the rest of the civilized world see what is happening here, the Jews who disappear over-night, the old men beaten up in the streets? This German is a mad creature and he will not be satisfied until Europe drowns under a sea of blood. I study Cavaradossi and Florestan and I say Verdi and Beethoven have been dead for many years but the social injustice and political intrigue of which they wrote is even more alive in Europe than it ever was.

Ferelith spent three years studying for her law degree. She had classes at 9 a.m. almost every day of the week including Saturday, lectures at 2 p.m., at 4 p.m. and at 5 p.m. She learned about the ownership of inheritable property and about obligations and contracts. She studied palaeography so that one day, if necessary, she could help clients decipher the Scots of ancient documents. Words like competency, burden of proof, evidence and procedure, conveyancing, became a natural part of her vocabulary. At Professor Sydney Smith's classes in forensic medicine she learned a great deal that she would rather, at first, not have known, and she made another of her lifelong friends, this time a woman.

Elspeth Baxter was a medical student and held Ferelith's head for her as she vomited up the contents of her stomach after a particularly graphic lecture on death from violence which included the examination of blood and seminal stains.

'I hate to tell you that the professor was sparing your maidenly blushes a bit,' Elspeth said matter-of-factly as she handed over her handkerchief which she had thoughtfully dipped in cold water.

'I didn't mind "Death in its Medico-legal Relations" or even "Lunacy Certificates", "Toxicology". In fact, they were extremely interesting lectures but this . . . and those pictures.'

'Not a patch on the real thing, my dear,' said Elspeth as she carefully held Ferelith's hair away from the rim of the toilet bowl. 'Why are you taking this class?'

'I want to be an advocate.'

'Then, face up to it. Try to think of the poor person who was on the receiving end of the violence. Our job, yours and mine, is to at least try to make it better for them, or to at the very least get them some justice. I would imagine advocates only ever get to see the pictures, if that's any consolation. It's the poor police on the beat and the doctor who get the glorious technicolour. My name's Elspeth, by the way, Elspeth Baxter.'

'Ferelith Gallagher.'

'Come on, a walk through the meadows to the Union and a nice hot cup of sweet tea – doctor's orders.'

Ferelith stood up rather shakily. 'I'm sorry about this. It's years since I vomited. I do seem to do it rather suddenly and well.'

'I rather enjoyed it, especially the doctor's orders bit. I've never actually said that to anyone before.'

They laughed together and went out into the courtyard and Elspeth, a naturally gregarious and affectionate person, put her arm into Ferelith's as they fought together against the wind. It was a completely new experience for Ferelith to have a female friend. She had never had a close friend at school in Glasgow mainly because her institution-alized home life had made after-school friendships difficult. Blair, Simon, Pietro, and Dominic, were all men and she was fond of each of them in a different way, but having a woman as a friend was a completely different and special relationship. From Elspeth she learned to laugh. She met her for coffee as often as possible that term and, to her great joy, was invited home with her for Christmas. It was a revelation to find herself, for the first time, in a large happy family circle.

'It's true, Elspeth,' she said as they took the train

back to Edinburgh in the middle of January. 'You really don't know you're missing something until you find it.'

'Feel free to borrow any one of our lot at any time. That's one negative side of being part of a large family, even a very loving and happy one – there is absolutely no privacy. The first time I was ever alone was when I went up the first year: I didn't know how to handle it, used to talk to myself for company, but then I began to relish it. When I marry I plan to have only two kids. What about you?'

It was too early. She could not tell everything, not yet. 'I don't think I want to marry,' she said lightly. 'I'm wedded to the Law.'

'I hope he's good in bed,' said Elspeth. 'You'll change your mind, you know. We modern women are learning to expect everything out of life as a right. You wanted to take our Flora's baby back with you didn't you?'

'For one mad moment. He was an awfully sweet baby.'

'They all are when they're full and dry.'

Ferelith could not imagine having such conversations with anyone else and treasured her growing friendship with Elspeth and the warmth and continuing welcome of her family. The term, however, was very full and, apart from occasional concerts and snatched meetings for coffee, she saw little of Elspeth or Simon until after the March exams. She did well and attributed her success, at least to Mr Lord, as a result of the bouquet of flowers that he had sent her from the firm.

At the Christmas of 1937, when she was halfway through her law course, she realized that she had not heard in some time from Pietro. She sent a Christmas card to his family but there was no reply. Was it the situation in Europe or just the fact that it was years since they had seen one another? It had seemed as if the friendship was meant to last but perhaps it was natural that a relationship would fade and die if it was not nourished.

'Maybe I'll hear of him at Covent Garden one day and I can go round to the stage door and say, Remember me? I worked for your family in 1935.'

'He's not a Jew, is he?' asked Elspeth.

'No, Roman Catholic.'

'Don't think our friend Hitler cares much for you lot either,' added Simon, 'and he certainly doesn't like boys like me.'

'Do you think . . . ?' began Ferelith but then stopped because she could hardly bear to hear the words she had been about to say voiced out loud.

'Of course there's going to be a war,' said Simon. 'If not this year, then next year but there's certainly going to be a war. Hurry up and qualify, Elspeth my pet. Your first patients may well be half the male students at this university.'

'Oh, don't joke, Simon. War doesn't bear thinking about.'

'Start thinking, sweetness, and praying.'

7

EARLY IN DECEMBER of 1937 Dominic came to Edinburgh to take Ferelith to dinner and a recital of Verdi and Puccini duets. The programme had originally been German *lieder* but it was obvious that the organisers felt that no one in Edinburgh, no one anywhere outside Germany, wanted to hear German songs. The tenor had a German-sounding name and a notice appeared in the newspapers a few days before the recital announcing that J.K. had left Germany in 1914 as a small boy because his parents hated the then regime and that he had been naturalized in 1927 and was a most loyal subject of King George VI. Many notices of the same kind, written by grocers and restaurateurs, were appearing daily in newspapers up and down the land.

'How long are we going to be able to listen to Beethoven or Mozart? Or, for God's sake, Verdi? Surely that will become subversive too.'

'I think it's only German music, Dominic, and really only Wagner since Hitler likes him so much.'

'Because he's anti-Semitic and Hitler is anti-everything decent and is going to involve us all in a war.'

Ferelith looked at him sharply. War. Even Pietro had spoken of war as if it were the natural culmination of all that was going on in Europe. 'There mustn't be a war, Dominic. We must talk to one another.'

He hugged her spontaneously and planted a delicate kiss on her forehead and again she wondered, as she had wondered so often before, if he was another like Simon.

'What a little innocent,' he said lightly. 'Peace through negotiation.'

He saw her back to her flat. 'Not quite the same ambience as the Convent, my sweet,' he said, 'but better for you.'

'I feel guilty that I haven't gone back to see them. There were some poor souls there, Dominic.'

'You can't nurse everybody,' he said matter-of-factly. 'What about the Settlement? I hope you're managing to go there.'

'Still doing my one evening. Maggie married Sturrock, you know. She had to, as is politely said, but he's even worse than her father.'

'Physical abuse?'

'All kinds, I would think, but she believes it's coming to her, her fault or something. Her father, by virtue of the fact that he was her father, had the right to thump her and now Sturrock does, especially since she was – well, what she calls easy. I am giving all manner of legal advice.'

'And you not even qualified. Shame on you. I miss the Settlement, you know, and the people. It's strange but it's the one place I feel really at home. I'm useful and I'm liked and I don't have to think if what I am doing is right or wrong – I just know. When we're qualified, Ferelith, let's work for the downtrodden, the refugees . . . so many of us Scots are the children of people who struggled . . . and the Maggies. Let's help the Maggies.'

He kissed her, something he had never done before. 'I must come through and see you more often, Ferelith, and you must come to Glasgow. The trains are so convenient and I do miss you.

Letters aren't quite the same as a cup of coffee and a blether in the Union.'

'After Christmas. I'll make you a New Year resolution. See Dominic more in 1938.'

She never saw him alive again. On the 10th of December in a snowstorm, the Edinburgh to Glasgow express hit the Dundee to Glasgow express at Castlecary near Glasgow. One hundred and seventy-nine people were injured and thirty-five passengers were killed, among them Dominic Regent.

It was the worst thing that had happened to Ferelith since her annulment and she travelled through to Glasgow to Dominic's funeral at the Roman Catholic Cathedral. At the graveside Dominic's father clung to her and it was obvious that he could not come to terms with the tragedy that had hit his family.

'He was such a good boy,' he said over and over again. 'Such a good boy.'

The voice was guttural, heavily accented. Ferelith thought immediately of Pietro.

'They're Italians,' she said to herself. 'Why did I never suspect? Dominic was so proud of being a Scot. His father must have been an immigrant. Goodness, it wouldn't have mattered to me. I didn't even know what I was until . . .' But she did not want to think about that again.

Now, at his son's funeral, Ferelith could do nothing but leave Mr Regent surrounded by family and friends. Dominic's oldest sister, Mary di Rollo, took Ferelith back to the station.

'Such a waste,' she said. 'My father hoped Dominic would marry you, you know, and he came close to loving you. I think going through to see you was the beginning of his campaign to at last make up his mind about what he was and what he wanted.'

'What he was?'

'He was such a beautiful baby. My mother died giving birth to him. Maybe it would have been different, well, of course it would have been different if she had lived. He was talking lately about the priesthood. That was probably what he was fighting? An inclination towards a vocation and a fear of it at the same time. Did he tell you?'

'No.'

'Don't lose touch, Ferelith. There's a bed for you in Glasgow any time you want to come through. We Italians have huge extended families, you know, and you're part of the di Rollo's if you want to be, or if you ever need us.'

'If he hadn't come through . . .' Ferelith began.

'Don't do that,' Mary said harshly. 'You make yourself unnecessarily important in the scheme of things and we can all do without extra burdens. He could have been hit by a tram in Sauchichall Street; he could have fallen down the stairs at his flat. He was never at rest, since he was a tiny baby, rush, rush, rush everywhere.' She looked up the platform and grabbed Ferelith's arm. 'Quick, there's your train. You're not afraid?'

'No. I'm too numb.'

Mary smiled. 'You did love him.'

'Oh, yes, I loved him.' She would not say that it was sisterly love and not the special love between a man and a woman but Mary seemed pleased and she smiled.

'Come and see us. Make a New Year resolution. My Mauro's Nono makes the best pasta. You'd sell your soul.'

'I'll come . . . to see you, not just for grandfather's pasta. I never knew Dominic had an Italian background. Did he tell you I worked in Italy for a summer? I even speak a little Italian and I certainly eat like an Italian and I have other Italian friends, from Rome. I'm worried about them.'

'Yes. We all have family over there and we worry and we pray. Don't stay away, Ferelith. Come back.'

Ferelith promised again and she sat in the train back to Edinburgh thinking of Dominic whom she would never see again and Pietro whom she might not. She would not make a New Year's resolution to visit the di Rollos . . . Resolutions to love people and to see them and to let them know that they were important should be made all the time – not just at the beginning of the year, along with the resolution not to eat so much chocolate.

Christmas was a gloomy affair, no matter how Mr Lord and his family tried to make it merry. One joy was in the form of a Christmas card from Pietro saying that all his family were well and that he hoped 1938 would be better for everyone. It was not better for Anthony Eden who resigned from the Government on the 21st of February because he was angry over the policies of appeasement towards Italy and its annexation of Abyssinia. No wonder Pietro's card had been so terse. He was unhappy with it too and he was an Italian.

In May Ferelith went back to Glasgow to Mary di Rollo's rambling house in Hillhead, not just to see the family but to watch the King and Queen open the Empire Exhibition. Dominic's death and war in Europe seemed so far away from the glittering crowds and the fun of the huge family party, not attended by old Mr Regent.

'I watch him die a little bit every day, Ferelith. I tell him a new baby is coming and if this one's a boy I say it will be another Dominic for him and he smiles at me and says "that's nice". It *will* be another

Dominic: he was conceived the night of Dominic's funeral. Four kids are enough, I told Mauro, even for an Italian, but it happened, and who'll notice in this family?'

Ferelith laughed. 'Everyone will notice. You and your sister have seven girls between you. A boy will be noticed, believe me.'

Mary laughed. 'Oh, you're good for me, Ferelith. I can see why Dominic liked you.'

Ferelith returned to Edinburgh for her last few weeks as a law student, having promised to become the new baby's godmother. Scottish, Italian and a sprinkling of Irish: that should make a happy combination, she thought.

Ferelith Gallagher M.A. added a Bachelor of Laws degree to her name and title in the summer of 1938. With other students she had waited nervously for the results of the June examinations and was among those delighted to be told that in the opinion of the Department of Law at the University of Edinburgh, she knew enough about Scots law, international law, mercantile law, forensic medicine, private law, conveyancing, civil law and a hundred and one other laws, to be admitted to the select body of Scottish lawyers. But Ferelith, of course, was not finished with education. She had her precious LL.B. At the same time as she had studied for her degree she had done her three years in Mr Lord's firm and her 'master' had granted her a discharge which stated that she had *properly and faithfully served him during the period of her indenture.*

Now she had to do some serious thinking about the way ahead.

If she still intended to become an advocate she had to take her year away from formal education. This was a requirement of the regulations of the

Faculty of Advocates and was irreverently known
as the 'year of idleness'. In England it was termed
devilling but in Scotland the system of having an
aspirant admitted as a pupil to a junior counsel
could not work because advocates worked, not from
Chambers, but from their homes. The year was for
study and in the past was often spent abroad visiting
the famous seats of learning in the Netherlands.
Ferelith could not do this: for one thing, she had
already lived in France for a year and did not feel
that a year spent sightseeing would be productive,
and secondly she was now *on her own* and therefore,
penniless.

If she found an advocate willing to allow her to
attach herself informally to him, to, perhaps, look
up authorities, digest papers, even, if she was bold
enough, formulate opinions, she still had to eat
and pay rent. Simon wanted her to go with him
to Glasgow. He fully intended to be one of her
instructing solicitors when she was called to the Bar.
He felt that although advocates lived and worked in
Edinburgh and travelled through to Glasgow once
or twice a week to plead cases, she herself, as the
first female advocate in Glasgow, could make a very
nice living once she was started. He felt strongly that
she should begin to make herself known in the circle
where she would eventually practise.

'Strike out, Ferelith. You're breaking new ground
all the time. There is only one woman advocate in
the country – Margaret Kydd. You be the second
one and the first one in Glasgow. It's a wonderful
opportunity. Dad has all the contacts: his firm is the
biggest in the city and you'll be proud to *belong* to
Glasgow. Solicitors in Glasgow will be glad to have
an advocate there all week instead of at the other
end of a railway line.'

She considered it carefully. She could see more of Dominic's family, especially her godchild whose advent she awaited with a strange mixture of pleasure and pain, and Simon who had been accepted into his father's firm. But first she had to be accepted somewhere and she had to be able to live. Simon had no need to worry about finance and did not even realize that for her, the year, or even two years, when fees would not be coming in but when books and wigs and gown and rooms and more would all have to be financed, presumably from the pot at the end of the rainbow. This presented something of a nightmare. She could, too, see more of her beloved Sister Anthony, but just before her graduation the old nun wrote to tell her that she was being transferred to their house near London.

London, I believe, is a very exciting city and should definitely be visited by brilliant lady lawyers. You know you are always sure of a clean bed and a decent meal and you can't beat the price . . .

When would she find time to get to London? It went on the list which included opera in Paris and a second visit to the Eternal City.

'I have to find a junior advocate who'll let me follow him around, Simon, and I'll have to do some part-time work too.'

'What about Mr Lord?'

'Not fair to ask him. He isn't an advocate, and he doesn't need another solicitor. I'll go around with my begging bowl.'

She did and was not surprised to find a certain hostility among senior male colleagues. Law had been a strictly male playing field for so long that many solicitors, advocates, eminent and not so eminent but, unfortunately, still important law lords, faced the future of a life surrounded by competent female practitioners, with something approaching horror.

'Not while I live and breathe,' said more than one when the twenty odd applicants from Edinburgh University applied for training or places.

'Old stick in the muds,' said Simon, safe in his promise of a junior partnership. 'Don't fret, Ferelith, something will turn up and in a few years you'll have such a splendid reputation that all the old fogeys will be on their knees before you.'

If I don't starve to death first, Ferelith thought to herself but she could not say anything to Simon.

'I think I want, eventually, to move back to Glasgow because I feel as if I belong: I mean I spent most of my childhood there and see my future there. Apart from Elspeth who plans to go back to Dumfries to practise medicine, everyone I care about lives in Glasgow.'

'Then that's settled.'

'No. I must stay in Edinburgh for one more year. I shall send applications to everyone . . .'

'Including the Lord Advocate?' Simon interrupted.

'*Ca va sans dire*,' she teased. 'Of course, Philistine. I think he's watching the post for my letter.'

She did not, as it happened, have to send one letter of application because, one afternoon just before the end of term and completely out of the blue, a visitor arrived at Mr Lord's offices who had been encouraged to watch Ferelith's progress by a fellow advocate and who was now prepared to give her a helping hand.

'But for goodness sake, Oliver, let her think the idea was all yours because she's as prickly as a hedgehog and would just get her dander up. No free lunches for the Ferelith Gallaghers of this world: wants to do everything for herself and hasn't faced the fact that for any aspiring advocate with no family backing, it's impossible.'

'Miss Gallagher,' said Mr Oliver Belanger, 'I have a bit of a problem and I am hoping that you can see your way to helping ease the situation.'

Mr Belanger K.C. was a practising advocate with a large and lucrative practice. He was also a man with strong political views and very definite political aims. He intended, in fact, to stand for Parliament.

'As a general rule, Miss Gallagher, I would have no time to have you shadow me. Over the past twenty years I have allowed enough beardless young wonders under my wings to more than repay any debt I might have to the advocates who set my own feet on the proper path. Now, however, I feel that if I had a depute, not legally you understand, just someone like yourself, with excellent academic qualifications, to do . . . well, shall we call it the dirty work, the day to day work, the reading, the piles of note making . . . Sheriffs and senior law lords like to see me in court, Miss Gallagher, because I do them the courtesy of always being well prepared. Have you any idea of how many hours of work that entails? We are talking of a way of life here, a commitment that would not suit everyone. We are talking twenty-four hours a day every day, including Sunday if I need information on precedents . . . if I need facts, references, opinions. For a year, while I prepare my parliamentary campaign I would like someone whom I could trust implicitly to help prepare my cases. We would meet every morning to discuss what was to be done and then we would meet every evening when I was in Edinburgh to discuss

what has been done. I should expect you to come to
court with me to listen to me plead, in other words,
Miss Gallagher, to be as familiar with my cases as I
am myself. My practice is large and varied and you
would learn a great deal and because I am buying
you body and soul, Miss Gallagher, I should expect
to pay you a living wage.'

He stopped for breath and she looked at him
squarely. He could have and indeed must have
had a dozen requests for a place from the top of
the graduating class. 'Why me, Mr Belanger?'

He smiled. 'Perhaps because you graduated with
distinction. Perhaps because we both speak excellent
French. Perhaps, Miss Gallagher, because I see the
way the wind is blowing.'

And with that enigmatic remark she had to be
satisfied. She would have loved to have been able
to ask him if he meant only that it was obvious
that women were going to take their rightful place
at the Bar. He could not have meant – oh, what a
stupid and conceited thought, Ferelith Gallagher –
that she was being watched over by a very senior
member of the Scottish Bar. He could not possibly
have meant that.

'If you think I can be of use, Mr Belanger . . .'
she began.

'If you are not, my dear,' he said in tones that
assured her that he meant exactly what he said, 'I
will throw you out.'

Ferelith accepted the offer nervously but with
gratitude. She could never have hoped to be associ-
ated with him, believing this successful advocate
to be unapproachable, but in July, shortly after she
graduated, she began a year's work at his lovely
home in Heriot Row in the New Town of Edinburgh.
He insisted that she join him for breakfast which

saved him, he said, time. It also saved her money for which she was grateful. He discussed the case or cases with her, and then she left to sit in the Advocates' Library reading and making notes. She loved this place with its hundreds of years of history. It was the main library in the country with an unparalleled collection of books that the Faculty of Advocates, at considerable private and personal hardship, maintained for the free use of anyone who wanted to consult a text. For years the Faculty had been trying to have the Government take over the expense of the library which was one of a handful of libraries entitled to receive a free copy of every book printed and entered at the Stationers' Hall. Alexander Grant, the President of the biscuit company, McVitie's, had given a free donation of £100,000 to Lord Macmillan, who was one of those instrumental in trying to establish a National Library of Scotland from the nucleus of the Advocates' Library and then had doubled his gift for the building of a suitable repository. All his life this great benefactor had bemoaned the lack of leisure to indulge in the enjoyment of books and, very sadly, never lived to see his dream of a National Library fulfilled.

'We're almost there, Sir Alexander,' whispered Ferelith every time she entered the law library.

An expense that she had not accounted for was transportation. It was unthinkable for an advocate to travel by tram or bus and he – the Faculty had not foreseen women when it made the guidelines – could travel by train only if he went first class; otherwise he might conceivably mix with the proletariat and what? Be contaminated, hear words unsuitable for his gentlemanly ears? Unthinkable. As a student Ferelith had often travelled in the third-class section

of any train. Those days were over. Mr Belanger had,
of course, his own transportation or he hired a taxi.
When she could get away with it, Ferelith walked
and remembered often her first lovely learning days
in Edinburgh when she had walked miles each day
to save a few pence. Now she walked to save her
reputation. The idiosyncratic Miss Gallagher who
believed in a healthy mind in a healthy body.

Two or three days a week she sat in Court listening
to Mr Belanger argue, often from notes that she
herself had prepared for him, and several times a
week she attended consultations in his luxuriously
furnished office. Almost every evening she worked
in his study and his housekeeper prepared a supper
for her which she, at first, attempted to refuse.

'His nibs says as how a labourer is worthy of
his hire, Miss Gallagher. He says as how you're
thinner than when you started working for him
and he doesn't want to grind you into the dirt.
He works like a dog hisself, you know, and he
sometimes forgets as others are made of flesh and
blood.'

Mr Belanger gave a Christmas party to which
Ferelith was invited.

'Do you have a beau, Miss Gallagher, or have I
worked you so hard that a social life is a thing of
the past?'

'I enjoy my work, Mr Belanger,' said Ferelith
diplomatically.

'Good. Now your only job at the party is to enjoy
yourself, but I should be grateful if you would help
Nancy decorate the tree. I like hundreds of candles.'

The tree was the tallest tree Ferelith had ever seen.
It stood in the drawing room, a room she very rarely
entered, and she could quite see how Mrs Dimmock
would need help.

'This room is too pretty for tawdry paper deco-
rations, Miss Gallagher,' she said, 'although Mr
Belanger is like a child over Christmas and would
have streamers everywhere. I like greenery myself
and will ask you to go to the greengrocer's for
me. We'll put streamers, as will keep him happy,
in his study, but in here . . . nothing as is not in
good taste.'

It was a delightful way for Ferelith to spend a
day and she wondered where Mrs Dimmock had
developed her taste, for when everything was ready
for the party the house looked, to Ferelith, like a
wonderland.

'What his nibs needs is a wife and kids to enjoy
all this,' the housekeeper said archly and Ferelith
blushed. She had never thought of Mr Belanger as
a man. He was her employer, her teacher, and he
had always treated her with the most professional
courtesy, just as she had treated him. Poor Mrs
Dimmock, determined to seek and find romance
everywhere and anywhere.

Ferelith smiled to herself as she hurried away. Probably Mrs Dimmock, her undoubted talents greatly
underused if not undervalued by her employer, saw
every professional woman who came into his orbit as
a possible romantic liaison.

The first guests began to arrive and were welcomed with silver cups of hot, mulled wine. Ferelith
wandered among the public rooms, rather in awe of
her surroundings, and reflected that she had never
seen so many important people under one roof at
any one time.

The bell rang again just before eleven when Mrs
Dimmock was busy with the late supper and the
butler was refilling the punchbowl.

'I'll go,' she said to no one in particular and

opened the door to a tall thin man who was vaguely familiar.

She was disconcerted to find herself kissed heartily and she stepped back in surprise to see his laughing face looking up at a bunch of mistletoe under which she had been standing.

'A happy Christmas to you, Miss Gallagher,' said Lord Angus Webster. 'Did I frighten you? I'm sorry but if you must stand under the kissing bough looking absolutely delectable, what is a poor over-worked lawyer to do? Absolutely the most enjoyable experience I have had in some time. I heard my clerk tell a caller today, "Oh, don't disturb his Lordship: he's doing lewd and libidinous." You are still, Miss Gallagher, standing under the mistletoe.'

Ferelith almost jumped backwards and he laughed. 'You took me by surprise,' she said.

'And you me. Just think. Gallantry would have forced me to treat Mrs Dimmock in exactly the same way. That is why Oliver, the crafty beg-gar, always hangs the wretched thing right over the door.'

'Let me take your coat, Lord Webster.'

He refused and hung his heavy coat in the cloak-room himself. 'And how are you enjoying beastying for Oliver?'

'Oh, it's wonderful. I'm learning so much.'

'Good. I shall look forward to meeting you in Court soon and remember, you will have an advan-tage over many a beginning advocate. You will see me up there on the Bench looking so pre-posterous in my antediluvian wig and you will say, "The last time I saw that man, he kissed me, and he enjoyed it," and I did, Miss Ferelith Gallagher, I did.'

Before Ferelith could think of an answer Mr

Belanger bore down on them and led his friend away. Ferelith stood in the hall for a moment and put her hand against her lips.

'And so did I, Lord Angus Webster,' she said.

BETWEEN JANUARY AND June of 1939 Miss Gallagher shadowed Oliver Belanger on several cases that were heard by the Right Honourable Lord Webster of Dalmarnock.

At the first one, when she looked up to find his rather alarming gaze fixed on her she had found herself blushing like a witless girl instead of behaving like a sophisticated and well-educated woman. She had been unable to look up at all after that and had spent the rest of the afternoon scribbling furious notes.

Later she and Oliver had met Lord Webster in the Great Hall and, like Scottish advocates since time immemorial, had walked up and down, hands behind their backs, gowns billowing around them.

'You remember Miss Gallagher, Angus?' said Oliver as they began their perambulation.

'Indeed,' agreed Lord Webster remembering with great delight the last time he had seen and spoken to Miss Gallagher. 'How are you, Miss Gallagher? I thought you handled yourself very well in there.'

That enigmatic remark had left Ferelith blushing more furiously than ever and she was grateful that advocates did not look at one another as they paced the Hall but instead seemed to examine the floor searching, perhaps, for signs of the progress of the past's brilliant minds. She had to stop this immature nonsense. Not for the first time she relived the Christmas party. She had jumped from under the mistletoe as if she feared that Mr Belanger's late-coming guest might kiss her again: he had had, for an establishment figure of such eminence and reputation, quite a gleam of mischief in his eyes. She had blamed his fall from grace on the festive season. She must not let a simple kiss and a few sweet Christmas moments colour her professional association with him.

Perhaps it was because he himself always behaved towards her – after that one lapse – with impeccable propriety, that after that first case she was able to dismiss her nervousness and just enjoy listening to him work. He was, she decided, absolutely perfect: kind, gentle, wise, humorous but also quite ruthless in his pursuit of justice. He had some tolerance for petty criminals but none at all for the hardened felon.

He spoke to her once or twice out of Court and when that happened she found herself tingling with happiness. She would, she decided, miss him most when she left Edinburgh for she had come to the conclusion that she had to do so. Each morning she looked out of the tall windows of Oliver Belanger's town house and saw Edinburgh and all its glories. She walked up from the New Town to Princes Street and crossed over at the Art Galleries. Then with Princes Street Gardens laid out below her and the imposing presence of the Castle to her right, she walked up the Mound into Edinburgh's past. One morning in May she stopped at the Heart of Midlothian outside St Giles's Cathedral. After looking around furtively to make sure a pillar of the Law did not see her she had spat right into the Heart and whispered the old charm: 'I have to leave: I cannot afford to stay. My heart is here and I will, I must come back.'

The decision to abandon her plans or at least to set

them aside for a while had not been easily reached. So often during her studies she had felt that life was treating her too easily. The Religious Order had paid her expenses to the end of her formal education. Then Mr Belanger had sought her out, an unheard-of action. It had been too easy, too pat. Even men were having difficulty in getting work in Edinburgh where there was very much an old-school-tie feeling about the legal profession. She knew of at least one brilliant west-coast student, also, as it happened, a Catholic, who was having a frustrating time trying to establish himself in a club where everyone knew everyone else and where advocates were often sons or nephews of advocates or judges. He had had to borrow his wig and gown from a friendly classmate and lived in terror that he and the other young man – who, obviously had the prior claim – might have to appear in Court at the same time. Ferelith was not so badly off and had managed to buy a second-hand gown and wig which fitted fairly well.

For the first six months of 1939 she had worried and wondered about her future. Once her year of devilling was up, she could not stay on with Mr Belanger and there was absolutely no way that she could afford the type of residence that was expected of the Edinburgh Advocate. She had fought with her conscience and she had finally won. She would not be beholden to anyone: she, Ferelith Gallagher, was now twenty-five years old and must take full charge of her own life. She had rehearsed her speech in the security of her rooms but it had not come out quite so well when she was face to face with her mentor. His reaction had surprised her.

'My dear girl, you can't do that. You must stay in Edinburgh. I'll see to it that you get instructions and you can do some free legal work which will get your name known to solicitors.'

Ferelith had looked around his beautiful breakfast room, a room that spoke of inherited wealth, and she had shaken her head in disappointment and despair. She could not, would not, tell him that if she did only free work she would starve to death and if she became his protégée she would lose her self-respect. He seemed to have known what she was thinking for he argued with her.

'If I could keep you on a retainer, an unprecedented step in Scottish legal circles, sensible but unprecedented, I would do so, but I have enough influence to get you some work. Oh don't bristle. That's how the system works, Ferelith. I can help you get started. There are too many instructing solicitors out there who will ignore you simply because you are a woman. I'll call in a few favours and then once you have established yourself, you will be on your own. You must go to the Bar. Lord . . . everyone says you have a future.'

What had he been going to say? Lord Webster? No, that was too bizarre. Lord Webster was very kind every time they met but he was a kind man, everyone said so.

'I have decided to work as a solicitor, Mr Belanger, in Glasgow. I can get adequate accommodation on the outskirts and Charles Smythe is part of the biggest firm in the city. It'll be wonderful experience. In a year or two I will come back to the Bar.'

'I shall hold you to that promise, young lady. You must remember, Ferelith, that you are the pathfinder. Don't forget your duty, not just to those who have taught you and watched over you, but to those hundreds of women who will read of your work and wish to emulate you.'

The pathfinder. There were just too many tangles in the way. She went to Glasgow and stayed with Mary di Rollo while she looked for digs. These were found, to everyone's horror, in Clydebank.

'You can't live there, Ferelith. Those are slums.'

'Mrs Thomson is as clean as Sister Anthony Joseph. The office is solid, Mary, and that's where clients will see me, and remember for me this is just a stepping stone but I must do it, or lose my self-respect.'

And she loved her work. She saw Simon, who was in the same building, every day, and she had Sunday dinner with the di Rollos. She worked hard and had the satisfaction of watching her Bar fund grow. One afternoon she had worked steadily on the reams of papers that dealt with the last will and testament of one Sydney Smallwood when the door of her office opened . . .

'Miss Gallagher.'

Ferelith recognized the voice and, for some absurd nonsensical reason her heart started to pound, and she found it difficult to look up from the brief she was studying.

'Lord Webster,' she said at last. 'May I help you? Are you looking for Mr Smythe? He is, unfortunately, in Edinburgh today.'

'Yes, I know. I had dinner with him last night and I told him I was on my way here to try to get you back where you belong. All fair and above board.'

She could hardly believe she had heard him correctly.

'Get me back . . .?'

He looked around as if for a chair and she blushed and showed him to the comfortable chair kept for special clients.

'Yes,' he said as he sat down. 'I helped educate you, Miss Gallagher, and therefore have a proprietory interest. I don't like to fail just as you don't. If you are not at the Bar after all these years of expensive education then the Bar and the legal system are losers.'

'I'm very flattered, Lord Webster, but I have strong and compelling and deeply personal reasons for not being called to the Bar.'

He dismissed her reasons with a wave of an immaculately manicured hand. 'You are not the only poor person who has made it, Miss Gallagher. I know at least one senior judge who started out with less than two halfpennies to rub together. I'm angry that I was in London when you decided to run away . . .'

'I did not run away,' Ferelith, as angry as she had ever been, interrupted. 'I made a very difficult but perfectly rational decision and I have no intention of telling you or anyone else my reasons.'

'The status quo is the reason, Ferelith,' he said in a calm voice that effectively took the wind from her sails, 'but things will change and you can change them and I want to help. Will you at least talk to me?'

She looked at him and part of her brain told her that she was dreaming and that this conversation had to be a figment of her imagination. She could not possibly be arguing with the next Lord Advocate, not in Court but in her office. At her audacity there should be a thunderclap which would effectively silence her impertinence.

'Why?' she asked, looking at him candidly. 'I'm sorry. It's a tremendous compliment, your interest in my legal career, but why? There are many, many struggling advocates in Edinburgh.'

'There is only one Ferelith Gallagher and she is not in Edinburgh where she should be . . .' He leaned

over the desk and his index finger poked her papers.
'What's that? A will? You don't want to spend the
rest of your life among wills and conveyancing?'

'No, and I won't. I'll return to Edinburgh in a few
years . . .'

'Oh, Ferelith, don't be too proud. Allow me to
help.'

Ferelith looked at him, taking in the well-cut
clothes, the well-groomed greying hair on the lean,
sensitive face. Should she take him at face value?
His interest was altruistic: he was a crusader for
women's rights? He liked her?

'Why on earth should you help me, Lord Webster?
Frankly, I can't understand why you even remember
my name. Oh, I don't want to be rude and —'

'I remember kissing a girl under the mistletoe. I
remember a very lovely face under a rather ill-fitting
wig. I remember someone smiling at me in approval
when I was lecturing. You look surprised. Surprised
that I remember you or surprised that I should
confess to having as many nerves as the next man?
Not allowed for Law Lords?'

'You always look so . . . well, serene and at ease.'
How easy it was to talk to him, not senior law lord
and very junior solicitor but man to woman, woman
to man.

'Easy when one is hiding under a wig. You'll find
that too, if and when you come home.'

Home? Glasgow was home but suddenly she was
homesick for the Law Courts of the capital.

'I return to Edinburgh tomorrow, Miss Gallagher,
and I don't know when I'll be back. Will you have
dinner with me and we'll discuss the future of the
woman's place in the Scottish legal system in general
and Miss Gallagher's future in particular?'

Dinner with Angus Webster? No, she could not.

She might have to ask herself why he affected her so much. This nervous tension was much more than just because he was so senior and she was a mere parvenue. It was the hardest and yet easiest decision she had so far had to make.

'I can't . . .' she began.

'You can't eat. If you don't want to discuss law we could discuss music, art, books . . .' He stopped for a second and leaned very slightly towards her and then immediately straightened up. 'How very, very lovely you are.'

It was obvious that he had not meant to say that. He blushed furiously and at once it was she who felt older, calmer, more in control.

'I'm very interested in the Glasgow Boys,' she said primly.

'The only Glasgow boys I know are those whom I have sent to jail.' So he had a sense of humour too. Well, she had seen that humour in his court appearances, hadn't she? 'There, Miss Gallagher,' he went on, 'you have a duty to educate me. May I pick you up at seven?'

Clydebank. She thought of the tiny room in a tenement where she lived because it was cheaper than anywhere else. Her salary did not cover high living plus the strict regime that she had set herself of saving and paying back the Convent. Her appearance was important, and she had to spend money on clothes which she hid under a huge wraparound coat that she pulled off and bundled up as soon as she reached the offices on Vincent Street. She was not ashamed of living frugally: in fact she was quite pleased with herself, but suddenly she could not bear the thought of Angus Webster seeing her there.

'Could I meet you somewhere?' she asked. 'I . . . I have so much work to do.'

He smiled. 'Rogano's, on Exchange Place. Do you know it? It's almost just around the corner.'

Rogano's. Quite new but already becoming *the place* to see and be seen.

'No,' said Ferelith, 'but I've heard of it.'

'As an artist *manqué* you will appreciate the Art Deco interior. I, on the other hand, merely enjoy a good meal. I must go and make a reservation. See you at seven.'

She watched the door close behind him and pinched herself. She had just made a date with an institution.

'He thinks I'm lovely. Am I lovely? Oh, God, what am I going to wear? I can't go to dinner at Rogano's in this suit. It will look like a business dinner. It is a business dinner. No, it isn't.'

She buzzed the intercom for Sarah.

'I have to go out, Sarah, just for a half-an-hour or so. Tell Mr Sommerville for me.'

'Forgive me, Reverend Mother,' she said to herself later as she took a tram back along Argyle Street. 'I meant this money for the Convent but I just had to have a pretty blouse. I hope he appreciates it.'

If Lord Webster appreciated the blouse in particular he gave no indication but was a perfect, unfrightening host. In fact, Ferelith felt a little silly that she had made too much of that remark in the office. Better to ignore it, to forget for a moment that she had seen interest, even admiration in his eyes. Meanwhile he was not nearly so ignorant of the Glasgow art world as he had pretended to be, though much of the evening was spent discussing the latest books, *Rebecca* by Daphne du Maurier and *Brighton Rock* by Graham Greene.

'What do you mean, you don't have time to read

novels,' he said as he poured her a second, no a third, glass of the most incredibly delicate white wine. 'You must feed the civilized part of your mind too, Ferelith. You cannot possibly read nothing but legal tomes. You will soon become as dusty and dry as they are. If you think novels are too frivolous try George Santayana's latest, *The Realm of Truth*.'

If I can remember a word of this conversation when I get to the library tomorrow I'll borrow it, Ferelith thought to herself and wondered whether admitting to a taste for the cinema would be a plus or a minus.

'If I have time I like the cinema,' she said desperately. 'I saw *Pygmalion*.'

'Oh, the new Leslie Howard film. I missed that. What about Hitchcock? I believe he has a new film this year.'

'*The Lady Vanishes*.'

'Have you seen it?'

'No.'

'Then perhaps when it comes to Glasgow or Edinburgh we could see it together.' He leaned back in his chair and she had the feeling that he was as surprised by what he had just said as she was herself.

That had to be a date, a real date, not a meeting to discuss law or anything else.

'I'd like that,' she said, a little too relaxed to be on her guard.

He smiled gently. 'Me too,' he said and gestured for the waiter.

At her insistence that he should not escort her home he had put her in a taxi.

'You modern young women,' he said half-laughing, half-serious. 'Not the done thing, you know, and I shall bring my own motor when next I come through and will accept no excuses. You live alone, I take it, no worried mother waiting up?'

'It's only ten-thirty, Angus' – when had he become Angus? – 'and besides, I'm an orphan.'

'You are an amazing young woman, Ferelith Gallagher. I salute you,' he said, and as the taxi pulled her away she watched him standing, his hat in his hand, looking after her.

Much later that same evening Ferelith was startled by a strange noise and looked at her watch. It was already two in the morning. She looked at the fireplace to see if the dull thud had been a log falling but the embers in the grate were simply sighing. She listened intently and was just about to throw another log on the fire when she heard a scrabbling at the door.

She stood up, went to the fireplace and picked up one of the heavy andirons. What she thought she might have to do with it, she did not consider. Its cold weight made her feel better and she shuffled to the door with it.

'Who's there?' she asked, her mouth against the wood.

'Sweetness,' she heard very faintly.

She put down the andiron and, with hands that were beginning to shake, struggled with the key and the bolt and opened the door. Simon, his face and hair covered in blood, almost fell into the room.

'I'm so sorry, sweetness,' he breathed, 'couldn't go home, couldn't think.'

She was on her knees on the floor beside him. 'I'll phone for an ambulance, Simon, and the police.'

With a surprisingly strong hand he pulled her back. 'No, please, my father . . . just help me clean myself up. Brandy? Whisky?'

'Oh, God, I don't have anything like that. I'll
make tea.'

He almost snorted. 'Yes, tea, and a wet cloth and
a towel, please.' Even in his state he remembered
his carefully-taught manners.

'You must let me go, Simon, and I'll look at
your head first and then make some tea. Here, lie
on this.'

'I'm so sorry, sweetness, but I think I'm going to
be sick.'

And he was.

Ferelith ran to the sink for a wet cloth and wiped
his face. Then she covered the vomit with a towel
while she rinsed the cloth and bathed his face again.
He had been badly beaten but she was relieved
to see that there seemed to be no really serious
wound: even the head injury, from which he had
lost so much blood, did not appear to be too deep.

'Simon, I do think you should see a doctor,' she
said later when he was drinking hot sweet tea, his
thin hands clasped around the bowl of the cup for
warmth, for stability?

He looked up at her, his eyes shadowed with
pain. 'Have you any idea what this would do to
my father? I can't go to hospital, Ferelith. I want
to stay here until the bruising dies down. May I?
Here on the settee? You could go to my flat if you're
worried about your reputation.'

He had obviously forgotten in his distress that
the settee was her bed but she did not remind him.
'No, my dear friend, I am not worried about my
reputation but I am worried about you.'

'If you can tell my father that I have a shocking
cold he won't come near me for a few days. Then
I will tell him that I fell down the stairs when I got
drunk.'

'But you never get drunk: your father knows that.'

'He will be thrilled to believe that I got drunk, Ferelith. He's not blind, you know, or stupid. He is desperately seeking signs of what he sees as a real man in his only son. I can't bear disappointing him again and again. Maybe that's what I was doing tonight, trying to find out for sure, but I can't be what he wants and I can't be what I thought I was either. I'm a nothing, sweetness, an absolute nothing.'

She put her arms around him and he sighed and relaxed and eventually fell asleep. She sat there holding him until the early signs of dawn began to struggle through the smoke-grimed windows.

'I don't understand, Simon,' she whispered into his hair, 'and I don't think you do either. I wish I knew who had done this to you.'

She looked down at him again. He was, according to the world, one of the winners. He had everything – looks, education, position, family. He could not be put into the same list as one of her first clients, Maggie Sturrock – oh, God, she had not thought about Maggie for such a long time and she had promised Dominic – but he was still a victim. He still needed to be helped and protected. Very carefully she stood up and lowered him on to the sofa. Then she went to the cupboard, took out a blanket and covered him with it.

She set her alarm clock for seven and curled up in the armchair for two hours sleep. Simon was still asleep when she woke and before she went out to the communal lavatory to wash, she checked that his breathing was peaceful and regular. His bruising, in the cruel morning light, was horrifying.

'We have to get you out of this slum dwelling,

Ferelith my sweet,' he tried to tease her later through lips that were swollen and painful. 'I ache from head to toe and I thought, Ah, while Ferelith is out earning our daily bread I will soak in a nice hot tub. Where do you bathe?'

'At the public baths or in a bucket in front of the fire.'

'How quaint. I looked around and realized that my bed was *the* bed. Where did you sleep?'

'I was fine, Simon. I'll scramble some eggs. Will you manage that?'

'Sounds divine, and my pa?'

'Wants you to drink hot water, lemon juice, honey, and whisky.'

'What a frightfully good idea. Can I ask you to go to my flat for some stuff and then when it's dark I'll go home, Ferelith, if you'll help me.'

There was no point in arguing with him about reporting his beating to the police, no point in begging him to go a doctor. Several times during the day she had found herself on the point of telephoning the police surgeon but she kept hearing Simon's anguished voice pleading for his father's serenity. She could so easily imagine the headlines.

TOP LAWYER'S SON IN VICE BRAWL
GLASGOW SOLICITOR BEATEN UP IN VICE DEN

If he had been in a vice den. Where had it happened? Why had it happened? What other life did Simon live, Simon who loved paintings and music and everything that was lovely? She would not now or ever ask him anything but she would try, to the best of her ability, to help him, and that started with scrambling him some eggs. After that she went across town to his flat and got him clean clothes, washing things, a bottle of brandy, and a bottle of whisky. She had honey and lemon juice in her kitchen, if he really wanted the hot drink his father had recommended as a cure for his non-existent cold.

'I will never forget your kindness, sweetness,' he said later as she was leaving his flat having seen him safely installed.

She tried to speak lightly. 'What are friends for?'

'It will never happen again, Ferelith, and I'll never speak of it.'

'It's finished, over.'

'It will be when you new carpet comes. Oh, don't fuss: I know you cleaned up beautifully but I'll never be able to look at your carpet again and it was quite hideous anyway, wasn't it?'

Ferelith, who had quite liked the carpet, agreed. 'It would remind us.'

It was several weeks before Simon was well enough or mentally strong enough to return to her apartment and then only to show her brochures for a new development at the West End.

'You can't live here, Ferelith. When the war comes, it's going to be more and more difficult to travel and there'll be unsalubrious characters in plenty around. Far better that you stay closer to the offices.'

'I can't afford the rent on a place like this, Simon.'

'Uncle Charles has paid it for one year: it's to be a "now Ferelith is a fully qualified solicitor and can be worked even harder" present. Please don't argue. He knows, you see, and he's grateful for anything that spares my mother.'

'I didn't help you for gain, Simon.'

'He'd spend the same money on a watch or a

brooch or something for you. He's about the only solicitor who has made any money in the last few years but you're getting qualified just in time for the upsurge in legal business. Accept graciously. You can buy a few bits of fairly good furniture at auction and then just add a bit here and there as you begin to get your financial head above water.'

Ferelith accepted. Living in town actually saved her money. For a year she would have no rent to pay, thanks to Mr Smythe's generosity, and because it was near the offices, transportation costs and time spent travelling were cut substantially. At the back of her mind too was the hope that maybe, just maybe, Angus Webster had meant it when he had said they would go to a film together.

But he never telephoned. And then it was September 1939.

In Rome on Friday the 1st of September Mussolini declared to an interested world that Italy would remain neutral in any forthcoming confrontations. Pietro Angelosanti left the Conservatory where he was studying voice and conducting and disappeared.

In London on Sunday the 3rd of September Britain declared war on Germany. After the King's evening broadcast Ferelith Gallagher switched on her gramophone and turned up the volume. Beethoven's *Fidelio* streamed down Byres Road and earned her angry telephone calls from two of her neighbours.

'It's not because it's German, Miss Gallagher, it's because it's too loud. I'm trying to get my baby to sleep.'

'I know, Mrs Burns, and I'm sorry. It was thoughtless to play it so loud but I just wanted to defy Hitler somehow.'

'You won't do that by keeping my baby awake,' said Mrs Burns angrily and slammed down the receiver.

Simon, for one, was relieved that war had actually come.

'I know it's going to be terrible, Ferelith, maybe more horrible than anything we could ever imagine, but we've crept along for years trying to pretend that if we didn't look, it would all go away. My father fought in the Trenches, so did Uncle Charles and so did the Honourable Lord Webster . . .'

'He can't have,' she interrupted. 'He's not nearly so old as your father.'

Simon laughed. 'So he is ringing your bells, sweetness, you wicked thing you.'

'Stop it, Simon. I hate you when you're vulgar.'

'I'm vulgar only when I'm scared,' he began but she had rushed from the room and slammed the door behind her.

The letter was lying on her desk. She could not believe it. She recognized the writing, of course, even though it was years since she had seen it. Ferelith dropped the letter from suddenly nerveless fingers.

Blair. Six years and here was a letter, or some sort of communication, from him. Memories, so bitter, so painful, so beautiful, so unbearably tender, flooded back.

'Oh dear God, when will you let me be rid of him?'

She picked up the letter, slit it open carefully with the silver letter-opener Simon had given her for Christmas, and read . . .

Dear Ferelith,

I won't ask how you are because I know. I have always known.

This morning I decided two things. One is that I can no longer live here in luxury while my friends, my tenants, go off to . . . what? Shall I be clever and say, 'do their bit'? I shall wait a few days in hope and then I will enlist in the Air Force.

And why do I wait, Ferelith? Why don't I rush immediately to take the modern equivalent of the King's shilling? It's you. I would like to see you before I go. I love you still: I think I always will love you and time, if I am granted any, will tell whether it is the love of a brother or a lover. From what I have heard, I believe that shooting himself was the only shabby thing our father ever did, if that makes you feel any better. Perhaps it doesn't. Perhaps you say like my mother that fathering you was a pretty shabby thing to do but I cannot sit in judgement. May I see you just once before I go, not to whine or beg, just to see you and to know that you are all right?

I have made my will. You, my closest relative, are my sole heir. It would be poetic justice, would it not, if you were to inherit my shoes, much too big for your little feet.

On Saturday I will be in Glasgow at Rogano's . . . I believe they do a fair meal. Meet me, please.

Blair Winterton

Winterton. So he has taken his father's name back again. Our father's name. God. I don't want his estate. I want nothing. I'm the result of one of the shabby things he did in his uncheckered life, am I? Ferelith Gallagher burst into tears and when she had stopped she telephoned Simon and read him the letter.

'Go, sweetness. How can you resist such a *cri de coeur*? Sounds rather nice, your big brother. Well he would, wouldn't he? He's your brother.'

'I wanted him as a husband.'

'And why not? Stop replaying the old record, Ferelith. You have not committed a mortal sin.'

Was that what she thought? Was it?

'He has no right to storm back into my life like this.'

'He's a victim too, my sweet.'

A victim. Of course he was a victim. That's what Sister Anthony had said all those years ago.

'Go and see him and lay the ghosts, Ferelith. Then maybe you'll be able to decide whether it's lust or daughterly affection you have for old Angus.'

At once she was angry. 'He's not old.'

'It's lust then,' he said and hung up.

On Saturday she was at the restaurant.

She was greeted by the maître d'. 'Good afternoon, madame. Are you lunching alone? I have a very nice table.'

'No, I'm meeting a . . . friend. Mr Winterton?'

'Ah yes. Mr Winterton is already here. We have not had the pleasure of his company . . .' Ferelith could hear him talking as he walked along beside her between the potted palms and the tables but she could not distinguish the words. She made no effort to make them out. Her whole energy was focused on this meeting.

'Ferelith.'

'Hello, Blair.'

The years had not treated him as well as they should have done. His hair was receding and his eyes were dull and looked as if shadowed by pain.

His skin was weather-beaten, a farmer's complexion, the skin of a man who spent a great deal of time out of doors. Well, of course, he was a landowner after all.

'You look wonderful,' he said as she sat down. 'I am so unbelievably proud of you. I know I shouldn't feel the right to . . .'

'Please, Blair. I don't know why I am here. What I did want to say, and I could have written it, should have written it, is that I cannot bear to be mentioned in your will. The idea makes my flesh creep. It's a macabre thought, to contemplate inheriting the estate of a man who shot himself rather than face my birth.'

'I love you,' he said simply and the wine waiter hovering at his tweed elbow saved her from having to say anything. 'I looked while I was waiting,' he explained. 'Shall I order some claret and we'll drink it with fish and defy the establishment?'

She smiled and he muttered to the waiter and she sat back and felt herself begin to breathe naturally. It was not so frightening: it was Blair, a little older, a little bruised but still Blair.

'Why Winterton?' she asked eventually.

'I'm his son. I can't enter his head, Ferelith, but I won't judge him.' He was quiet for a moment as if he was seeing something she could not see or hearing something she did not hear. 'I've lived with my mother for a long time,' he finished eloquently.

'Why join up, really? Isn't there a more useful role for a farmer?'

'I'm twenty-six and I'm not a farmer. I'm nothing useful at all. I lost heart and failed all my exams at the varsity and there was even less need to struggle without you to impress or to bully me into working. I do nothing but ride and fish and shoot. Managers run the estate. My mother wouldn't even leave me that much dignity, but at least I had the guts to take back my identity.'

She had met his mother once. She could remember how formidable she had been. Blair must have found that defiant act very difficult.

He seemed to read her mind or to have heard a question that she would never ask. 'She was furious, of course. It was the embarrassment, not just to her but to his family.'

'Then you do have other relatives?'

He looked surprised. 'Of course I must have, but my estate doesn't belong to the Winterton side: it was my maternal grandfather's.'

'As a lawyer let me give you some free advice. Make peace with the Wintertons and, if you are going to join up, and probably you won't have any choice in a month or two, make another will. I don't want anything from your family, Blair. I don't want to hurt you any more but I have managed well enough without your . . . our family. The Catholic Church, especially a very determined old nun, helped me and so if you want to please me, send them a donation, but don't burden me with this, please.'

He stared into the depths of his glass and eventually smiled as if he had seen something in the reddish-violet liquid that pleased him.

'Let's have a good lunch and I'll meet you here again as soon as this nonsense in Europe is sorted out and we'll talk again.'

She smiled. 'That's more positive, and now let me tell you, Mr Winterton, that I've developed extremely expensive tastes.'

Nearly two hours later, feeling very content and just a shade light-headed, she walked in front of

Blair out of the restaurant. Her way was barred by a tall, stooping figure.

'Miss Gallagher, how very nice to see you.'

It was Angus Webster. For some reason Ferelith blushed. It was a Saturday. She had every right to have a good lunch with a personable young man.

'Lord Webster. Nice to meet you again too.' Oh, she was being too friendly: she should not have had that third glass of wine. 'This is Blair Winterton, my . . .' Had she been about to say, brother? No, she would not admit the relationship. It was an accident, nothing more. 'My friend,' she ended weakly and the two men shook hands.

'Well, you have moved into higher circles, Ferelith,' said Blair as they waited for the taxi he had ordered for her. 'Webster is definitely the right kind of legal brain to cultivate.'

'That was a nasty thing to say. I'm not cultivating him.'

'Just as well. No doubt he thinks that, at the very least, I'm important and, at the very worst, that I'm an immoral liaison.'

Ferelith looked distressed.

'Gosh, he is important to you, isn't he?'

'Oh, I don't know.'

'If you can't bring yourself to say, "my brother", just introduce me as Blair Winterton.'

'I don't intend to introduce you as anyone at all,' she said angrily.

He laughed and taking her hands turned her around lightly to face him. He looked into her face and it was Blair, the old Blair, the man she had had no right to love.

'You won't have a chance, Ferelith. I'm a soldier off to war, remember.'

The spring day seemed suddenly to grow cold and she shivered.

'I'll write,' he said as he ushered her into the taxi, 'and please answer – just friendly letters between friends.'

She said nothing because if she had tried to she would have started to cry. As the taxi pulled away she looked back and saw him still standing there, so alone, on the pavement.

'Oh, God, keep him safe,' she prayed and then, emotionally exhausted, she lay back against the nicotine-smelling seat and began to cry.

'It's madness, Ferelith, sheer madness. You must help.' Dominic's sister Mary, now calling herself Maria was desperate. 'He came from Aulla nearly forty years ago. He's as Scottish as you are.'

For months the country had been in the grip of fear. Men and women who had known one another for years and had eaten and played and talked and worked together in friendship now watched one another furtively, looking for signs of they knew not what. 'Alien' was the swear word. Men who had lived ten, twenty, thirty, years as Britons, who had changed their names from German or, as in the case of Mary's father, from Italian, now found themselves classed as aliens.

'Dominic would have been an alien. Dominic Regent, born Domenico Regente. If it wasn't so tragic, it would be funny, Ferelith. There won't be a fish and chip shop open if they round up all the Italians who own them. London won't have a decent West End restaurant. It's insane. We must join together to fight the common enemies, Hitler and Mussolini, not people we went to school with.'

'Mr Smythe is working on it, Mary.'

'Maria. I'm Italian, Italian.' She broke down and burst into tears and Ferelith bent over to comfort her. Her father, Dominic's father, had had to register as an alien. He had to report to his local police station every day. If that indignity was not enough, there was now talk of interning aliens. Some, with no doubt many among them who were subversive,

had already been interned for their protection as
well as the safety of the realm. But to intern an
elderly man who had spent most of his life working
hard, paying taxes, improving his community, was
surely an obscenity.

'The Lord Advocate is asking for Scots aliens to
be released, Maria. The Regional Commissioner for
Scotland is working day and night on these cases.
All I can say is please be patient.'

'Are you going to give me that crap about the
wheels of justice grinding slow?' snarled Maria,
'because if you are, don't bother. My father has been
half-dead since Dominic's death. To be interned,
away from me and the children, will kill him.'

She stood up, pushing off Ferelith's comforting
hand.

'I told him we could depend on you but I see we
can't.' She swept out slamming the door behind
her, and Ferelith, feeling more than slightly sick,
sat down and looked at the empty chair where the
vibrant dark-haired young mother had sat just a few
minutes before.

'She didn't mean that last bit,' said Simon who
had come in just in time to see the door slam.

'Oh, I know but they've been so good to me and
now the first time they ask me for help . . .'

'You chose the job, sweetness, and this is just
the first time you're going to, well I won't say fail
because you have no chance to fight, but you're not
going to win. If the Lord Advocate can't do it, a
barely qualified advocate who isn't even at the Bar
isn't going to fare any better.'

'It's so ludicrous, so stupid, so . . . unjust.'

'Maybe internment won't be too dreadful. It's not
prison: it's somewhere to be safe.' Simon wondered
if even he believed what he was saying.

Ferelith was angry. 'Won't be too dreadful, for him, away from a baby grandson who is his soul reason for living.'

Simon looked at her and wanted to comfort her and, as usual when he felt inadequate, he joked. 'Have you heard about this local defence thing? I'd better join. I'll look sweet in uniform, don't you think?'

'What local defence?'

'Our esteemed Secretary of State for War, Anthony Eden, has asked for local defence volunteers. He wants about a quarter of a million men between fifteen and sixty to well, patrol, and look out for fires and lights at windows and all manner of things . . .'

Simon's joining of what came to be called the Home Guard was knocked into the shade later that month by the evacuation of the French town of Dunkirk. For two weeks, a few hundred warships, and several hundred small boats of every description, helped by the ceaseless vigilance of the Royal Air Force, took two thousand Belgian soldiers, one hundred and ten thousand French soldiers and two hundred and twenty-five thousand British soldiers off the beaches of France and ferried them to safety in Britain. It was an unimaginable feat of heroism and filled the hearts and minds of the world with praise and thanksgiving.

Funny things happened too. Simon went off to the weekly meeting of the Home Guard. His platoon was an odd assembly of men, of all ages, all types, solicitors, bankers, bakers, shopkeepers. In charge was a fresh-faced former public-schoolboy with the ink scarcely dry on his commissioning papers. He took his job very seriously.

'Gentlemen,' he said, 'it is likely that the enemy

is about to land. Scotland is faced with invasion. It
is up to us to do our bit for king and country.'

Simon tried to stand to attention: he tried to be like
the others who appeared to be listening attentively.
Instead he found himself wondering if their leader
had shaved yet. There was such a delicate bloom to
the young cheeks.

'I have come up with a plan which will give us a
little time . . .' The boy soldier blushed and Simon
knew that he had been about to say 'until the real
army gets here'.

'It's no more than a delaying tactic but I think it
will work.'

The boy stopped and looked at the, in most
cases, much older eyes of the men in front of
him. He sighed. He wanted to be somewhere else,
somewhere where he might do great things, be
noticed, make a difference to the course of the
war.

'I assure you that this will work, give us the time
we'll need. When you hear that the invasion has
started I want you all to go into your butler's
pantry' – he blushed again at this faux pas – 'or
your kitchen and take all the soup plates out and
turn them upside down on to the roads. I appreciate
that you may find this' – and he glared at Simon –
'quite ludicrous but if you look you will see that
upturned soup plates resemble landmines.'

Simon had to bite his tongue to stop his wicked
sense of humour from asking if his mother's Spode
would be better than her Minton or did it matter?
He could hardly wait to share it with Ferelith. But
Ferelith had no time for Simon's juvenile sense of
humour.

Maria di Rollo had telephoned Ferelith during
the evacuation of Dunkirk. 'They have interned him,

an old man whose only crime is that he was born in Italy.'

What could she say to the sobbing person on the other end of the telephone. 'I'm sorry' sounded so inadequate, and it was, but it was all the words she knew.

'It'll take time, Maria, but once the mass hysteria is over, commonsense will prevail. I promise you we'll get him out. I'll petition the Lord Advocate. I know a law lord . . . slightly. I'll get in touch with him.'

She had given Maria her scraps of hope and she was left to wonder why she had mentioned her law lord. It would take time to release the detainees who should not have been detained. Many of them, like Vincent Regent, or Vincenzo Regente as he now insisted on being called, were quite wealthy and knew many members of the legal establishment. That would not help. War. They were at war. Things that would have taken a telephone call, a wink, a quick handshake in peacetime waited for the mills of justice.

Still, she had promised to do everything she could and, she had to admit it, she wanted to contact Angus. He had half-promised to take her to the pictures. He had meant it when he said it, she knew that as she knew the sun came up every morning. Was he shy of her? When he was alone did he think about the age difference? More likely a wealthy, sophisticated and busy man had no time to think of anything but his job.

'Face it, Ferelith,' she said to herself. 'That dinner meant too much to you and meant nothing to him. But this call is work, it's to do with the Law.'

'Lord Webster, please.'

She sat gripping the receiver, her stomach churning with nerves and embarrassment. It's work, she told herself over and over.

'May I ask who is calling?' The voice was educated, well modulated, of indeterminate age.

'Ferelith Gallagher.'

'One moment, please.'

Her knuckles were white. She tried to relax.

'Miss Gallagher?' It was the same woman, his secretary. 'Lord Webster is engaged all day, but if you are going to be in your office he will try to ring you back sometime this afternoon.'

Disappointment dropped in her stomach like a stone.

'Yes, I'll be here. I'm rather busy.'

Why had she said that? Because she was not going to move from the office in case he called but she did not want him to know that.

'I am busy. I am busy,' she told herself and proved it. The telephone rang three times during the afternoon but Sarah did not announce Lord Webster. Finally at a quarter-past seven, Ferelith decided to go home and to get something to eat. She had had nothing but Sarah's stewed tea and a digestive biscuit all day. The telephone rang in her office as she turned out the light.

'Ferelith,' said that unforgettable voice in relief. 'I just knew that I would find you still at your desk. It was nice of you to call and I'm sorry I couldn't speak to you.'

He thought it was a personal call, that she had got tired of waiting. She was glad that the light was out to hide her embarrassment, if only from herself.

'It's the internment policy, Lord Webster,' she said stiffly. 'I have a client, a friend really . . .'

She told him the story, at first haltingly but as her

embarrassment faded she became more articulate. He listened attentively.

'I'm afraid government policy is very clear and the first priority is the safety of the realm. Nineteen thousand Italian fish-and-chip shop owners or West End restaurateurs have been interned and will be deported . . .'

'He's an old man, a good tax-paying businessman who built up a thriving business that employed several hundred Scots. He's not a threat to the King's peace.'

'I'm quite sure that applies to many of them. Ferelith, I will do what I can. I will certainly get his documentation but every lawyer in the country is flooding us with these requests. If I investigate and find myself in total agreement with you, and I'm sure I shall, I will do everything I can to expedite his return to his family.'

She could ask no more. He could not wave a magic wand and it would be childish to expect him to do so.

'Thank you sir.'

'Sir, because this is a business conversation? May we have a personal conversation now? I thought we were beginning to be friends. Are we friends, Ferelith?'

'Sometimes I thought we were and then I remember that I am a very junior solicitor and that you are . . . you.'

'I think only that I am a man and that you are a woman and that when we're together I'm not the man I thought I was, but become the man I hoped to be. Does that make sense or am I moving too quickly?'

'Yes.' It was all she could say because forces were at work in her that had blazed brightly once and which she had damped down and tried to smother.

'I wish you would come and work in Edinburgh. Then we could see one another and we could go so slowly, wherever it is that we are going.'

'I can't leave Mr Smythe.'

'I know and I can't get to Glasgow, not because I don't want to, but because of the pressure of work. Have you seen that film with a nice young man yet?'

'No.'

'I'm glad. I'll ring and let you know about your client.'

On the 1st of July the *Arandora Star* sailed into exile from Liverpool with a cargo of aliens, mainly German and Italian nationals or of German or Italian descent. Off the north-west of Ireland, a country of awesome beauty that Vincenzo Regente had particularly liked, the ship was torpedoed by a German submarine, and it sank with an incredible loss of life: nearly two hundred with German surnames, nearly five hundred Italians. Mr Regent died in the cold waters of the Atlantic while his baby grandson staggered across the drawing room carpet of his parents' lovely Glasgow home, and perhaps wondered why such an amazing feat of creativity was not met with the acclaim that young Dominic, now called Domenico, felt it merited.

And Ferelith Gallagher closed the door of her office and sat at her desk and cried. There had been one terse phone call. Yes, it would seem that Vincenzo Regente's only crime was that he had not become naturalized. Lord Webster would take his case up with the Home Secretary. There was a second call.

'He went down with the *Arandora Star*. I am so sorry, Ferelith.'

'I'm sure you did everything you could,' she said quietly.

He was silent and she could hear the hummming down the wires between Edinburgh and Glasgow.

'This isn't the time,' he said. 'I'll call later.'

But Christmas of 1940 came and went and the receptionist did not announce Lord Webster; and then it was early 1941 and the telephone finally rang.

What a nuisance. She had waited for months to hear from him, and now that he was indeed asking her to see a film with him, she was right in the middle of the most important work that she had yet been given. The feeling of abject disappointment was surprisingly intense.

'I can't,' she said. 'I just can't see that I have the right to take the time.'

He could hear the disappointment in her voice: it mirrored the regret he felt.

'If we ever do manage to woo you away from Charles, you'll be well worth it,' he tried to say lightly. 'May I ring you in a week or two?'

Total honesty at all times, in all relationships. She could hear Sister Anthony's voice.

'I should like that very much,' Ferelith said.

'Good, me too,' he said. 'I shall ring soon.'

She put the receiver down but still held her hand caressingly on the receiver. What a lovely voice he had, warm and gentle but strong and . . . Ferelith Gallagher, you sound just like the poorest of women's magazines. Strong and gentle. What a cliché. Get to work.

She picked up her pen, shook her head to rid it of all lingering thoughts of Angus Webster, and got to work, steadily, conscientiously.

Hours later, she had just made up her mind to leave the office so as to catch a late tram when the telephone rang again.

'Ferelith?'

She recognized the voice at once and her heart began its emotional seesawing.

'Ferelith. Oh, thank God you are still there. I hoped and prayed that I would catch you.'

'Blair, we said when the war was over.' It was almost two years since she had spoken to him: she had almost forgotten him.

'I'm going off tomorrow. I have to see you, just one more time.'

'Oh Blair, what is the point of this?'

'I want to be able to think of you as my sister . . .'

'Your father's second greatest mistake,' she interrupted bitterly. How that still rankled.

'Please. If we can be friends as we were in those early days. Do you remember? Walking up and down the Royal Mile: strolling in Princes St Gardens while it was growing, this love we . . . I still have.'

'Blair. It would be better that we did not think of one another at all, put that whole sorry episode behind us.'

'It wasn't a sorry episode and I regret only the way it turned out. Please, Ferelith. I have stayed away doing all the sensible things I should have done. I've dated pretty Waacs and Wrens and anybody else who could help me stay sane in the hell of the last two years, but I can't go out to it again without seeing you. You're my sister, for God's sake. We share the same blood.'

She had never before thought of it like that: the same blood. She could never get rid of him because he was a part of her. He was her brother and he was going off somewhere . . . destination unknown.

'I can see you for a quick cup of coffee, no more. I have important work to do tomorrow.'

'I'm at Central Station. We could have coffee in the bar.'

Damn, damn, damn: another complication she did not need when she was trying to keep her mind clear. All that was missing now was an air raid. Please God, please God, get me to the station and back to Hillhead in one piece.

Funny that she had not thought of a uniform. The bar was full of them, blue ones, olive ones, khaki ones. It was full of cigarette smoke too, desperate laughter and quiet, strained voices. She peered through the tobacco-induced peasouper, looking for expensively cut but well-aged tweed. Blair, in the uniform of an Air Force officer, was at the bar and she pushed her way through to him without seeing the tall, distinguished man with a briefcase and an overnight bag who balanced a whisky glass and a sandwich.

She could not deny her love for him. It swelled in her and she smiled at him in real affection. He bent and kissed her cheek, a brother's kiss, light as a feather.

For a moment she leaned against him and felt the pent-up feelings drain out of her. She felt relief and a quality she could only describe as peace.

'A drink, little sister? Whisky?'

'I'm developing a taste for white wine.'

'Shouldn't think they'd have a decent wine.'

'I really don't want anything to drink, Blair. Can't we sit down somewhere for a few minutes?'

'The floor?'

They laughed.

'We would have done that years ago,' she said.

'I'm not only a gentleman but an officer now,' he said with mock seriousness. 'Must keep my dignity.'

'You haven't lost your sense of humour.'

'I lost everything else that counts,' he said matter of factly but so, so sadly.

'Blair, I am prepared to think about you, to deal with you, to build up a relationship with you . . . a brother and sister relationship.'

'I'll settle for that. Just don't cut me out of your life, Ferelith.'

'I won't do that. You are very important to me too.'

'You two going to gaze into each other's eyes all night or are you going to order a drink? If not, give someone else the bar space.'

'I must go anyway, Blair. I have so much work to do.'

He pulled her to him and held her hard against his greatcoat. She put her arms around his neck and nestled for a moment against him. Then she broke away.

'I have to go. Write to me. You know my address?'

She turned quickly and struggled through the press of people to the door. There were tears in her eyes and she did not recognize the man who, with sadness etched on his face, opened the door for her.

'Thank you,' she said with a sob.

'Good night, Miss Gallagher,' said Lord Webster of Dalmarnock and closed the door quietly behind her.

Outside she stopped, the voice finally having penetrated the core of misery. It was Angus Webster. Oh, God. She had told him that she was too busy to see him and then she had immediately gone, it would seem, to meet someone else, someone whom he had met two years before. She thought of what Blair had said then. 'You make me sound important. At the very least, an immoral liaison.'

She groaned aloud. Why was life so difficult? Did it ever get easier? It seemed that no matter how sophisticated her outer shell became the inside was still this seething mass of doubts. Why had she not told Angus two years ago that Blair was her half-brother? Now he thought she had lied to him. Well, if you think that, my dear Lord Webster of Dalmarnock, I really don't care.

But he never called to invite her to see a film. Still she found herself hoping that on one occasion Sarah would answer the telephone, turn to her archly and say, 'It's his Lordship. No doubt a very serious legal question. I'll leave you alone to answer it.'

She waited in vain.

She had her first letter from Blair, a letter that was too destroyed by censors to be enjoyed. She did not know where he was, but gathered that he was not in Britain, was on almost constant alert, and had flown several sorties. He gave her an address which told her nothing, but to which she replied telling him as much as she thought he would find amusing about her work. How, although it was at times terribly stressful because she was now being asked to instruct a practising advocate on criminal cases, it could also be very funny.

Not that there was anything funny about the Reid case. Billy Reid had deliberately stalked the man whom the police, no matter how they tried, could not convict of raping Reid's fifteen-year-old daughter. One night he had waited outside the pub where his intended victim, Tom Kay, spent most of

his waking hours and when Kay had emerged in an
alcoholic haze, Billy Reid had proceeded to kick him
into unconsciousness. It had taken three inebriated
chums of Kay, plus a perfectly sober large barman
to get him off his punching bag while there was
still some life in it. It certainly looked as if the
rapist, if so he was, would be unlikely to repeat
his crime for some time to come, if at all. Billy
Reid had not run away. He had waited quite calmly
beside the unconscious Kay until someone had run
to the nearest unvandalized phonebox and put in
an emergency call.

Charles Smythe convinced Billy that the young
female solicitor in his office was really the member
of the firm best able to find him a good advocate.

'The thing is, Mrs,' Billy said to Ferelith, 'they
polis didnae really care whether my wean got
raped or no. Wan of them said she was asking
for it, the way she dresses and the build she his
on her. Well, whit am saying is a lassie of fifteen
disnae ken whit she's asking fer and she should be
able to, well, be a wee bit, ye ken. They're saying
she had experience: ah didnae ken that, but gettin
shugged by a sixteen-year-old boyfriend is no the
same thing as gettin raped by a man older than her
faither and wi a build on him lik a bull. An if yer law
says different then ah don't gie a fuck fer yer law.'

'The last of the vigilantes,' said Simon when
Ferelith discussed the case with him.

'He really thinks he should get off and possibly
with a commendation for gallantry.'

'I can't help a sneaking feeling of admiration.'

'Simon, Tom Kay may be the dregs of humanity
and he may well have raped that girl, but it is
possible that he will never walk again, never mind
any other activity. I'm desperately sorry for Sheila:

she certainly was not treated with the sympathy and understanding she should have received, but, sweet Jesus, imagine the chaos if each of us was to take the law into our own hands or, worse, to totally disregard the law. Where would we be then? We are better than animals, even Tom Kay, even, God forgive him, Billy Reid. Sheila has not been fairly treated, not by the man who raped her, or, God forgive us all, by the law, but we have to work to change the law, not to cut it down and throw it away.'

'Don't you wish you yourself were defending Billy?'

'Oh yes, partly because I think I might just feel as he does had I been in the same position, but I have the education and the training to help me discipline my instincts, something the Billy Reids of this world have never learned. Nigel Watson will probably try to get him off. I would fight the case from the standpoint of "Guilty as hell, but driven to it in a moment of passion". I only wish the moment had not gone on so long,' she finished drily.

'And if Kay dies?'

'Then I will probably be instructing my first case where our client is, as the book says, "hanged by the neck until he is dead". Charming thought. I shall leave you to think about it.'

He left and Ferelith looked at the door which he had closed quite firmly behind him. Yes, the solicitor could go away: she would now ring Nigel to see if he was willing to hear about the case. Then there would be a trip into Edinburgh for consultations and then she would more or less fade into the background. Someone else would do the job that every fibre of her being told her she could do as well if not better.

Damn it, damn it, why should an advocate have

to live in a specific area of a specific city? she
thought. Why shouldn't I be allowed to defend
Billy Reid right from this office in Glasgow? I may
be right up to date but my profession is still stuck
in the Middle Ages. It still thinks that advocates are
gentlemen who don't have to concern themselves
with anything so tawdry as earning enough money
to pay their bills. She thought of Lord Webster's
gown. She had seen it several times when she had
been a student and it had been months before she
had realised that it was slightly different from the
gowns of men like Mr Belanger. Lord Webster's
gown appeared to be the usual full gown of the
Scottish advocate but there was a small flap sewn
onto one of the sleeves. This showed the Scottish
bar that this advocate had, in fact, appeared in
a Scottish case in the great London Law Courts.
All English barristers wore flaps on their sleeves,
a leftover from the days when money for a defence
was never openly discussed between gentlemen but
the little pocket was there so that the client might
surreptitiously insert a generous donation.

'Some day, somehow, I will be an advocate,'
Ferelith promised herself as she asked the operator
to connect her with Nigel Watson in his correct
upper-middle-class home in the New Town of
Edinburgh.

On Thursday, the 13th of March 1941 Ferelith was
in her flat for once. Sometimes she wondered why
she bothered to pay for electricity and heating –
she was never there. Suddenly the sirens went off,
a strange, screaming, wailing noise. Gas masks
had been issued in 1938 and her gas mask, which
bumped against her legs causing bruises every time
she was forced to carry it, was at the door of the

flat with her bag containing her ration book, a few photographs, her birth certificate, her degrees, her passport, and the treasured little gold brooch that Dominic had given her when she had graduated. She turned off the lamp, picked up the bag, and left the flat. She should go to the shelter.

Outside the noise was even worse and the confusion was frightening. She could already hear fire bells and police horns. Her hope that it might have been no more than ARP practice melted. Great swords of light were arching across the sky and she stood transfixed by the strange, frightening beauty of the grey metal of the planes caught in a sudden beam. She could hear what she assumed to be the ack-ack battery at Duntochar. In the Clyde a warship was firing back. On the devastated Clydeside, stricken gas mains erupted and fires exploded into life. Singer's timber yard and the Toker Distillery were very flammable and, in a few terrifying minutes, the entire area was transformed into a raging inferno of fire and annihilation. German bombers were using these fires as flight paths to wreak ever more destruction.

They'll destroy the whole city, everything. There's no chance of survival. The thoughts were very clear and she was very cold but very very calm. She found herself turning away from the shelter and walking on and on, farther and farther westwards. She did not know how far she walked or how long. Then there was a huge whoosh right in front of her and she found herself sucked into a vortex and still her mind remained calm.

'I would have expected to be blown out, not sucked in,' she announced quite clearly but there was no one alive to hear. She had lost her bag . . . her birth certificate . . . Dominic's brooch. She had lost her contact with Dominic and then she remembered Domenico's toothy, slobbery grin and she laughed and cried at the same time. She could never lose him. She picked herself up from the very edge of a bomb crater and screamed as she looked into the shattered window of a car with its dead driver grotesquely staring at her as if he objected to the condition in which he found both himself and the road. And the road was a mess. Tram rails were corkscrewed like the most bizarre exhibits from the most avant garde art group. Ferelith caught what was left of her coat on broken steel and yelped a bit with the pain as it also scraped her legs.

'My God.' Her legs. What had happened to them? They were covered in dirt and blood and yet until now she had felt nothing. She stumbled on, still unsure of where she was going but glad only that her limbs functioned.

'Is there any part of Glasgow left standing?' Ferelith looked through red-rimmed eyes but all she could see was the glow of fires all over the city. 'It's the end of the world. I can't believe we can go on from here. Doesn't the Bible say it will be a fire . . . It's today and I'm too tired to care.'

She was standing in the middle of what had been a street, looking at what had been the orphanage in which she grew up. There was a huge crater in the ground. Part of her mind tried to remind her that the Mother Vicar General had moved the orphans and most of the community to Ireland at the start of the Blitz. Sister Anthony is safe. Sister Glenn is safe. I have lost only a few possessions, nothing that counts. She looked down at her feet. They were bloodied now like her legs and she saw to her surprise that somehow she had lost her shoes.

The wind changed and the smoke drifted away

and Ferelith began to laugh and then to cry. Her castle, her ruined castle, that had withstood everything man and the elements had thrown at it for almost one thousand years, still stood there defiantly at the end of what had been the driveway.

'Up yours, Adolf,' she shouted.

She turned and hobbled away from what had once been her home, the place where she had dreamed her first dreams. 'I'm leaving you the way I came to you,' she said. 'No shoes, no clothes, nothing, but I'm like that castle – indestructible.'

She wondered if tram conductors would let her on without money. 'Stupid worry, Ferelith. Are there any trams? Dear God, am I the only person in Glasgow left alive?'

An ambulance, its siren screaming, raced past her and answered her question and she decided to head for the offices, if she was not too disorientated. She limped on and did not see the car that screamed to a halt beside her.

'Ferelith, dear God, I've been looking for you all night and I've used about all my petrol.'

'Simon.' She fell into his arms with heartfelt thankfulness and he lifted her up and carried her to the car.

'Thank God you're a light weight,' he said. 'I never saw myself as Clark Gable.'

'Your father?'

'Fine. He wants me to bring you there.' He looked at her in puzzlement. 'You do know your building got one of the last raspberries from Jerry: not too bad but you can't go back there tonight . . . this morning. He has plenty of room. You can't stay with me. Look there's a thermos of tea with lots of sugar, and there's a blanket. Wrap yourself up.'

'What brought you out to the Convent?' she said.

'I knew you were too tough to kill and so I went to all the places you might be. None of them are there and I thought: wounded rabbits run home.'

'I'm not a wounded rabbit.'

He took his hand off the wheel and pressed her knee. It was the first intimate gesture he had ever made towards her. 'No, sweetness,' he said, 'you are a lion.'

10

SIMON ENLISTED IN the Royal Scots Fusiliers.

'Damn it, Ferelith, Bevin has just announced the registration of a hundred thousand women. All the young unmarried women, twenty and twenty-one-year-olds and he's even asking married women who can do war work locally to volunteer. He's promising an expansion in nursery facilities, day and night. God knows what I'm capable of doing. I'm hardly keen on the sight of blood, as you well know, but they'll find something for me to do that's useful.'

'You'll look quite pretty in a kilt,' teased Ferelith to stop herself from clutching him hysterically and begging him not to go.

'We're in trews actually,' he said grandly. 'Probably better: I'm a wee thing skinny for a kilt,' he finished in a dreadful parody of a Highland accent.

'What does your father say?'

Simon struck a pose. 'Damn proud, my boy, damn proud,' Simon quoted. 'His cook discovered a *thing* called a rissole yesterday, by the way. Eightpence the pound. Dad's going to eat them while I'm away as an offering to Mars in exchange for the life of his son and heir.'

'A rissole?' asked Ferelith as if her life depended on the answer. 'What's that?'

'It's some kind of sausage without meat, all veggies. He'll loathe them,' he said and stood up to go.

'Oh, Simon, Simon, please, can't you list yourself as a conscientious objector? Even the BBC is going to hire them.'

'Ah but, sweetness, a conscientious objector knows to what he has a conscientious objection. I'm not in that category and especially not after this shelling. I object strongly to the strong exploiting the weak. I object to the systematic destruction of beautiful buildings and paintings and yes, I object very strongly to useless blood shedding, especially my own, but I just can't take any more and the fact that we are killing women and children in Germany doesn't really fill me with enthusiasm, but maybe if I can do something to help stop this . . . this lunacy . . . You know I realized the other day why I went into law and it's not because my father wanted it or because there was an easy place into which I could slot myself. It's because I believe in reason, in reasoned argument. It's the only way for civilized people to behave. Maybe if I was to go and see Hitler and put the case to him *reasonably*. I say Hitler, old chap, you really must see reason. It's so obvious to the rest of us. Trouble is, sweetness, no matter how well couched the argument, if you're arguing with someone who refuses to see the other fellow's position or who is unable to see it then you're up the Clyde without a paddle. The only other thing, Ferelith, is my flat. I would be so grateful if you would stay in it and look after Traviata, my cat, for me. You can't stay with Maria for ever and God knows when your own flat will be fixed. If I leave my place empty it'll be vandalized or squatted in, or whatever. I've told Dad and the dragon lady: she'll be wickedly excited at the thought of you lying in my bed waiting for me to return. I must go. I'll send you an address as soon as I get one and you must write regularly. I shall pretend to the other chaps that you are my pin-up, and you are, my sweet, you are.'

He dropped his keys on the desk, hugged her quickly and was gone. She waited without moving until the sound of his hurrying feet had died away before turning off the lamp by her desk. She moved to the window and pulled the edge of the blind back a millimetre but she could see nothing. He had disappeared into the fog.

First Blair. Now Simon.

Work, as always, was the antidote and there was plenty of work. On the night of the first blitz of Clydebank, the night in which her own flat had been damaged, she had asked Simon to take her, not to his father's home but to Maria and Mauro. Mauro, with a frightened Maria behind him, had answered the doorbell, a golf club clutched in his hand. Maria had taken one look over her husband's massive shoulders, seen the grimy blood-stained girl and had pushed Mauro aside and rushed to Ferelith.

'Wine,' she had ordered her husband, 'then a hot bath and sleep. Food too. You too, Simon.' She had stopped and looked closely at him. 'Why are you still immaculate?'

'I didn't get blitzed,' explained Simon meekly but she had not waited for an answer to her question.

Hours later he had wakened up on the sofa of the di Rollo's sitting room to find a small boy using his handmade shoes as cars and to be told by Maria that Ferelith was well, was still asleep, and would remain with them.

'I have plenty of clothes for her,' she had laughed. 'I get fatter with each baby but I never throw anything out because I kid myself, one day I'll be a sylph again. She will be the best-dressed, bombed-out refugee in Glasgow.'

And so Ferelith had stayed on and for the first time in her life, if she didn't count her one lovely holiday all those years ago with Elspeth Baxter's people, found herself living as a member of a family and she loved it. She drove into Glasgow every morning with Mauro and then went home with a briefcase full of papers, but before she could deal with them she had Domenico to bathe or Alicia to help with her homework, or she had to listen to Gaia, who was in love. There were huge Italian meals to help cook and to eat, but she was pushed away while Mauro and Maria washed the dishes because, 'Ferelith is a career woman: she has real work to do, not dishes to wash like any peasant.' And no matter how much Ferelith protested that she would be perfectly happy to wash dishes, she found herself alone in her room, her briefcase open on the table, while she listened to the muted sounds of love and laughter from the kitchen.

Yes, better for the di Rollo's and for Ferelith herself that she take up Simon's offer of his flat.

Ferelith heard about Blair in a letter from one Jamie Winterton, who was, he said, both her cousin and Blair's. The letter put the phone call she had received earlier that morning completely out of her head.

I'm so sorry to have to tell you that the injuries are quite horrific and it is unlikely that Blair will survive. He came to see me before he went off this last time and told me the whole story and, of course, each of you has the family's sincerest sympathy. Blair listed me as his nearest relative because he did not want you to receive the telegram that I have just received, but he did ask me to let you know if he was killed. I felt that you would want to know about this mess too. I will stay here in London as long as need be and if you would like to come, we can find a bed for you. My wife joins me in this invitation.

Lord Winterton, Jamie, finished by giving her the telephone number of the house in London where he was staying while Blair was being treated in hospital. She could not telephone until the morning and she spent the night packing and praying. She had to go to him. How like him not to want to bother her – as he would see it – with injuries. A clean death was all right but no complications, no pity. She was at her office as soon as the blackout was lifted and asked the operator for the number.

Lord Winterton was at the hospital but his wife spoke to Ferelith.

'He was shot down, my dear. Blair managed to limp back to their field and they crashlanded. Blair, and Graham Smith the navigator survived, but only just. It looks really bad.'

'I want to see him.'

'Of course. We're bunking at a friend's flat and you're most welcome. I'll stay for a few more days but I must get back to my children. God knows why we're worried about propriety at a time like this. If you let me know what time your train gets in I'll try to arrange to meet you. You don't mind a bus, do you?'

A bus. Ferelith laughed. How like the British aristocracy to worry about inconveniencing guests.

Two days later, after a journey that she did not look forward to repeating, she found herself in London.

There was a Naafi canteen open and she went in. The thought of a cup of hot, sweet tea drew her irresistibly. She managed to get to the counter and to count out the few coppers asked for the tea and then tried to find somewhere to sit to drink it. She intended then to find her way to Jane Winterton's without bothering her hostess.

The appearance of the tall young man who approached her gave her a start. Blair. It was Blair, uninjured, unhurt.

'Lord Winterton?' she asked shakily.

'Jamie,' he said, 'and you must be Ferelith. I've been trotting back and forth from the hospital just in case your train arrived before the end of the war.' He smiled at her with Blair's smile and handed her the canteen cup and saucer she had put down on the bare table. 'Come on, there's a good girl, finish your tea – you look dead on your feet – and I'll either take you home for a nice hot bath or we'll go to the hospital.'

'The hospital, please.'

'Of course. Now, I'll try to ring Jane so she'll save hot water for you and then we'll buzz along. There's no change today I'm afraid, but at least he's no worse.'

Where had he managed to find a car and one with petrol? It was joy to sink back against the cushions – she had stood from Glasgow to York and then taken turns sitting from York to London – and to relax. As they turned in to St Thomas's she realized with a further sinking of her spirits that she had never been in a hospital before and she hoped that she would cope. Everything was forgotten, however, as soon as she entered the corridors and smelled that strange hospital smell of carbolic.

Jamie led her unerringly to the ward where Blair

and too many other hurt and battered bodies lay as testament to man's savagery. She would not have recognized him. She had known him intimately but under the swathes of bandages he looked hardly different from any of the others.

The nurse who was standing by his side checking the monitoring equipment looked up at their arrival and smiled with pleasure. Lord Winterton was obviously a favourite.

'Hello, Nurse,' he smiled in return. 'I've brought Squadron Leader Winterton's sister, Miss Gallagher.'

'The cage?' Ferelith's voice when she did force it out of her mouth was a squeak.

'I'm sorry,' Jamie whispered. 'I should have told you about his legs. If he lives, he'll never walk again.'

Grief almost suffocated her. Blair who loved to ride, to walk his land, never to walk again.

She put out her hand to touch him, to hold him. Where was there skin uncovered by bandages?

'He's been badly burned, Miss Gallagher,' said the nurse in a soft Irish voice, 'but I sometimes hold this hand here and I like to think he feels my presence.'

Ferelith went to the other side of the bed and the nurse relinquished her place. Blair's left hand lay quietly on the starched white sheet.

'Hold him, Miss Gallagher,' ordered the nurse. 'Sure maybe he knows you're here. Sometimes faith and love do more than medicine.'

Ferelith sat down and held Blair's hand and watched the nurse move away to the next bed.

'She's a marvel that girl,' said Jamie. 'If I hadn't Janie I'd steal her away from all this. She seems to be on duty every time I come. I'm sure she does more than her share.'

'Probably all of them are doing that, Jamie. I'll

stay for a while. I'm not tired now. Why don't you go home to Jane and I'll find my way there later.'

'If you're sure. I'll come back to fetch you though: I'll want to visit him again.'

He left, but fifteen minutes later was back with a mug of hot, black tea and a roll spread with some kind of fish paste. 'Sorry, it's all the canteen could find,' he said, and left again.

Nothing had ever tasted so good.

She ate the sandwich and drank the tea and looked at Blair, at the bandages that covered everything but his left hand, at the tubes and machines.

'A victim too.' And now he was a victim or a casualty of this war.

'I wish I could make it up to you,' she whispered. 'I wish I could make it all better.'

She was sound asleep, her head resting on his hand when the doctor came. He apologized for waking her.

'Sorry, Mrs Winterton,' he said.

She looked at him in surprise. Mrs Winterton. She had been Mrs Winterton for such a short time. Then she realized that the tired doctor had merely assumed that she was Blair's wife. Probably most of the women who sat by the beds were wives or mothers or sweethearts.

'I'm Ferelith Gallagher, his sister,' she said.

'You'll have to leave for a while, Mrs Gallagher,' he said dispassionately and pulled the curtains around the bed.

'Why don't you pop down to the café,' said a nurse. 'We'll be a while and there might just be some soup or some nice meat-paste sandwiches.'

'I'll just wait here, if you don't mind.'

The nurse shrugged and disappeared behind the curtains and Ferelith walked slowly up and down the ward. What were they doing to him? Was there any change? Would he live?

It seemed an age before the curtains were opened again. Nothing looked different but one nurse had a large bag of soiled dressings. She smiled at Ferelith.

'He's quite a fighter,' she said.

'There's nothing you can do here, Mrs Gallagher,' said the doctor. 'We have done all we can. It's now up to your brother and his God. Go home and come back tomorrow. If he gets through the night he has a chance.'

'I'll stay.'

He shrugged much in the same way as the nurse had done and moved on to his next patient and Ferelith resumed her vigil.

'Hello, I'm Jane,' said a voice beside her.

Ferelith smiled tiredly and held out her hand to the elegant and immaculate young woman who stood beside her.

'Oh, poor lamb, you're exhausted,' said Lady Winterton, giving her a quick hug. 'How is he?'

'They say if he comes through the night he has a chance. Jane, I'm sorry if you came especially for me but I have to stay.'

'I thought you might say that. I couldn't bring the hot bath but I have a little picnic for you.' She reached into her capacious handbag and drew out some newspaper parcels. 'There's some tough old pheasant: the sauce made it edible but I hate cold sauce, don't you? The claret in this beaker is fearfully good and we only decanted it because you were coming so you must have your share. This salady thing is something we ate in the States. My dear, it's the most divine way of eating boring old cabbage, and there's a wodge of cheese and some oatcakes. Nurse Thomson will bring you some cocoa later when she's having some. Jamie thinks she fancies him, the silly man, but it's Blair. He was conscious when he came in and he grabbed her hand and said, "Don't leave me." I think she's afraid he'll give up if she's not there and who knows? There now, you're quite exhausted listening to me and so I'll toodle off. Tomorrow I must go home to my babes but I'll see you before I go. You won't mind staying in the flat with Jamie? He's the soul of honour and besides my grandmother is doing voluntary nursing, would you believe, and she'll pop in and out all the time. *Au revoir*.' She kissed Ferelith and turned to leave, and Ferelith, already sipping the glorious wine, watched her stop and chat to other invalids who were conscious and alone. When she did reach the doors she turned and waved.

'Ray of sunshine that,' said a nurse, 'but I don't need to tell you that.'

'She is lovely, isn't she,' said Ferelith and opened her parcel of 'tough old pheasant'.

Perhaps it was the wine but the pheasant, the cabbage salad, the cheese and biscuits were delicious and gave her an almost immediate feeling of wellbeing.

'That's the wine,' she told herself and settled down beside Blair, holding his hand and talking to him until her mouth was dry and her throat ached. Nurse Thomson, the nurse she had met when she first came in, brought her some hot cocoa. The nurse too sat for a moment and Ferelith sympathized with the fatigue so obvious in her face and body.

'You really shouldn't do more than your shift, Nurse,' she said. 'You'll be no good to any of them if you collapse with exhaustion.'

'I'm a professional, Mrs Gallagher: I don't do any more than my hours unless I'm caught up in an emergency, and God knows there have been enough of those lately.'

'I'm sorry. I had no right to speak at all. It's just that Jamie . . . Lord Winterton said that you always seemed to be here.'

'He looks like him, doesn't he? I've been trying to make a face for him and thought he must have had that same pleasant face.'

'Must have had . . .' Oh God, was Blair to be disfigured as well as crippled? The nurse saw her look of horror.

'I'm sorry. You hadn't realized. He was terribly badly burned. We'll be taking those bandages off to let air in to aid in healing. Then we'll see how bad it is going to be. Certainly some scarring but his eyes are fine. Once the awful swelling goes down the doctors say he'll see perfectly.'

'Jane did tell me. I just didn't take it in.'

'No, you don't, do you,' said the girl sadly and was silent for a minute remembering her own experiences.

'He came in just after . . . just after I lost my husband and my little girl,' she said. 'Jim had leave. He hadn't seen Fiona for a year. "I'll fetch her from the baby sitter," he said, and got there just in time to start digging her out of the rubble of the house. They told him to wait for the fire brigade but he scrabbled with his hands, calling her name. A wall fell in on him. They brought them out together. He had been almost on top of her. I buried them together too. In Daddy's arms for eternity. And then I came back to work and he came. "Don't leave me," he said and I want badly to be here when he comes round.'

'When he comes round? The doctor . . .'

The nurse laughed and stood up. 'Doctors? What

do they know? Haven't I lit a candle every day since
he came in?'

'He isn't a Catholic.'

'It's only people who care about labels, Mrs
Gallagher. Now I must get back to work. It's been
a lovely break.'

She picked up Ferelith's empty mug and walked
off down the ward.

'Nurse Thomson.' Ferelith's joyous cry stopped
her. 'He moved. His hand moved. I'm sure of it.'

The heartbroken girl of a few minutes before
was gone. Nurse Thomson was the consummate
professional. She hurried back to Blair, bent over
him for a few minutes and then straightened up.
'I'll get Doctor Ellison,' she said.

Dr Ellison was a woman in her early thirties,
tall, slender, and attractive. She was also extremely
efficient and once more Ferelith found herself on
the wrong side of the curtains waiting with baited
breath for the professionals to do their jobs. It
seemed hours. Other personnel came back and
forth, some wheeling trolleys in, others wheeling
trolleys out. Each and every one passed Ferelith as
if she did not exist.

At last the curtains were pulled back.

'Are you the next of kin?' asked Dr Ellison.

Ferelith's heart plummeted with fear and she felt
herself grow cold and begin to tremble. 'I'm his
half-sister. Lord Winterton, his cousin, is officially
listed as next-of-kin.'

'Then I'd get in touch with him. We're going to
operate. He's putting up such a fight, we think
he's strong enough for us to go in and give him
a hand.'

Ferelith looked at her watch, although she knew
perfectly well that neither Jane nor Jamie Winterton

would object to being telephoned in the middle of the night. 'I'll ring now,' she said but Ellison had already forgotten her.

The Wintertons joined her nearly two hours later but Blair was still in surgery.

'Did you think we weren't coming?' asked Jane. 'We ended up parking the car – I hope it'll be there in the morning – and walking the last few miles. The streets are abysmal.'

'Don't chatter, Janie. Have you heard anything, Ferelith?'

'No, just that he seemed to have decided to breathe for himself and so they thought they could operate to help relieve some of the pressure.'

'That's wonderful news. Now we wait and pray, I suppose.'

They waited until the early light of dawn began to filter through the blackout curtains of the waiting room. Sometime later a porter came and lifted the blinds altogether but still there was no word from the operating theatre.

'I would kill for a cup of tea,' said Jane just as the door of the operating room opened and Dr Ellison, looking so different in a grey suit with a pink blouse, came out.

'You can see him, just two of you, for one minute.' She smiled and suddenly she was a human being sharing their joy. 'My husband always said the Scots were as tough as old boots.'

Ferelith and Jamie went into the special recovery room, where those patients still too seriously ill to be returned to a large ward were being monitored on an individual basis. The cage was still in place over Blair's legs but there were fewer tubes disappearing into various parts of his poor shattered body.

Nurse Thomson was there. 'It's still touch and go,' she said, 'but he's breathing on his own.'

'When do you expect him to regain consciousness, Nurse?' asked Jamie.

'That's what we're waiting for, Lord Winterton. He seems to know I'm here because there's faint pressure – that's what you felt, Mrs Gallagher, isn't it? – but he's heavily sedated. I really think you should persuade Mrs Gallagher to get some proper rest in a real bed.'

'I'd like to stay.'

Jamie put his arms around her and gently pushed her from the room. 'Head of the family,' he said. 'I'm ordering you to rest.'

Ferelith went with him willingly. Until he had put his arms around her she had not known just how exhausted she was. Even the relief of seeing Blair without the breathing apparatus had added to her fatigue. She contributed nothing to the next several hours, had no real knowledge of how she got from the hospital to the luxurious flat where they were staying. She half-felt Janie and an elderly woman, whom she later found out to be Jane's grandmother, undress her and get her into a bed with crisp clean white sheets and then she slept and slept. She slept without moving for eighteen and a half hours and woke feeling happy and relaxed and unbelievably refreshed. She lay for a moment wondering where she was and how she had got into the most enormous, most beautiful four-poster bed. Then she remembered and jumped up. Blair. She was in London with Blair's cousin and Blair was going to be all right. She just knew he was. Perhaps it was Dr Ellison and her cool skill or Nurse Thomson's candles or a mixture of the two.

'Good morning, you must be absolutely famished.' It was the elderly lady she vaguely remembered and Ferelith rushed to take the tray that she was carrying.

'I'm tougher than I look, my dear. I'm Merry Price, Janie's granny. The poor darling has had to get back to her children. She does hope either that you can get down to Surrey before you go back to Glasgow or that she'll be back in town before you leave. Eat up, eat up, you must be famished.'

'I don't believe that's a boiled egg,' said Ferelith looking at the exquisitely-appointed tray.

'No, it isn't. It's an hallucination,' laughed Mrs Price, 'and so I shall tell any inspectors who call. Enjoy it, my dear. When you're finished, have a lovely hot bath and then join me downstairs. I'm going into the hospital myself this afternoon and you can come with me. Jamie carried straight on from the station after he'd put Jane on the train. He'll be back in an hour or so with the latest news.'

How old was she? Ferelith wondered as she sat down to enjoy the egg that supposedly wasn't there, the toast soldiers, and the delicious pot of coffee. She had to be in her seventies and yet, here she was doing voluntary war work. What indomitable spirit. Later Ferelith was to find out that in 1916 Mrs Price had been left a widow with two daughters – the older of whom, Jane's mother, had just married – and a huge estate to run. She had not buckled under the weight of grief but had decided to get on with the job that had to be done and she was, over thirty years later, still doing it.

Much later she drove Ferelith in an ambulance to the hospital.

'Do you know I have never really had a driving lesson.'

As Ferelith hung on for dear life she felt that she could well believe it, but she smiled with closed teeth and tightened her grip on the seat.

Jamie was at Blair's bedside and he greeted his grandmother-in-law with real affection.

'She's quite remarkable,' he told Ferelith when the old lady had gone off to do her shift. 'She bullies people into getting well: she says that they become so fed up with her that they get well in sheer self-defence.'

'Perhaps she'll bully Blair for us,' said Ferelith softly as she looked down at the bandaged body. 'Do you know, Jamie, that I'm finally coming to terms with the fact that he is my brother. I would have loved to have had a brother, any relative at all, growing up.'

'Now you have lots of us,' said Jamie and proceeded to tell her all about his own two quite remarkable children, his sisters and their husbands and children, and Jane's younger sister who was not yet married but was cutting a path strewn with broken hearts through Society. 'She also does hours of ghastly work with Granny, something I won't let Janie do, and so we forgive her everything and try to comfort her rejected swains as best we can.'

They stayed in the hospital until desperate hunger drove them to try to find something to eat. Blair had not yet moved and Nurse Thomson was back on duty.

'I'll ring you at your flat, Lord Winterton,' she promised, 'if there's the slightest change.'

Ferelith and Jamie hurried out of the hospital. 'If we're lucky, we'll get home before Granny, who does everything beautifully except cooking.'

Ferelith laughed and tucked her hand into his arm to keep up with him as he playfully raced across the almost empty parking lot. They almost bumped into several men who were coming in the hospital gates as they were leaving. The men all raised their hats to one another as they avoided the collision and Ferelith's laugh caught in her throat.

'Why, Mr Belanger,' she said, 'how unexpected to see you in London.'

'Ferelith, but why are you not in Glasgow? Angus Webster, I'm sure told me that you had an engagement. We must fly. It's these interminable War Aid commissions.'

He raised his hat again and before she could introduce him to Jamie, had rushed off after the others.

'An old friend?'

'Yes. No. In a way.' Ferelith was nonplussed. 'I shadowed him at the Scottish Bar. He's a very good friend of . . . a friend.'

Jamie tucked her arm back into his. 'London is just a big village,' he said consolingly. 'I always meet everyone I know here – and usually when I don't want to.'

11

JAMIE DIPLOMATICALLY SAID no more about the encounter as they fought their way home through London's blitzed streets. Ferelith felt that he deserved some kind of explanation but first she gave herself time to marshal her thoughts. She was distressed to realize that she had remembered nothing and nobody after Jamie had written with the news of Blair. She had been looking forward with a singing heart to a hastily-arranged dinner engagement with Angus Webster. 'I'm deputizing for Cameron in a lewd and libidinous,' he had said. 'Can you possibly dine with me at such short notice?' And although he would definitely have understood if she had telephoned and explained or even left a message at the Court, she had rushed off without a thought of anyone.

Her mind had been so full of Blair that until she had met Oliver Belanger she had forgotten everyone and everything else. Mr Belanger had been surprised and would, no doubt, tell Angus that he had seen her in London. Would he say that she had been arm in arm with a very attractive man? No, and he probably would not even mention the encounter. Angus had every right to be furious and hurt. Still, the important thing, the only point that really mattered at this precise moment in the great scheme of things, was that Blair was going to get well. She could explain to Lord Webster: she could tell him everything and if he refused to accept her apology then he would be the loser. She said this to herself very bravely but a teeny-weeny feeling inside told her that she too would be a loser if he did not retain his confidence in her integrity.

Jamie had some sausages and some powdered eggs. He also had a bottle of very good champagne.

'Rather decadent, champagne and sausages, or will this become the *in* thing to have for a post-bombing supper?' He was joking as Jane would have done, sensing that Ferelith was still rather ill at ease in his company as well as being distressed by her meeting.

'I'm afraid I've rather blotted my copybook with Lord Webster of Dalmarnock,' she said. 'I had a date with him and I forgot completely. Very flattering to him. Mr Belanger is perhaps his closest friend and I wouldn't like Angus, Lord Webster, to get the wrong idea.'

'I'm your cousin, Ferelith, and Blair is your brother. Your friend will understand and besides, it's unlikely that your Mr Belanger will mention that he met you. Good friends don't do that sort of thing.'

'It might slip out if Angus is worried.' Would he be worried? Only if she meant something to him and why should she? And here Ferelith found herself telling someone she barely knew what she had been unable to formulate for Maria or Elspeth or even Simon, who knew her better than anyone. 'I quite like Angus, and we have seen one another once or twice and I had agreed to a real . . . date I suppose and then your letter came and all I could think of was Blair. I phoned my office and got them to deal with all business for me, and with Simon's cat too. People are becoming so used to handling one another's tragedies but I completely forgot Angus and then to bump into dear old Oliver . . .'

'He'll understand,' said Jamie handing her a glass of champagne and wondering who Simon was and why his cat was a tragedy, if indeed it was. 'And your Mr Belanger will be discreet. I caught only a quick glimpse but I saw a kind face.'

'It doesn't matter. It's just that one hates being rude,' explained Ferelith gulping the champagne as if it was water.

'Of course,' agreed Jamie and refilled her glass. 'You go and sit down. Put your feet up for a minute and I'll see if I can remember what Nanny told me to do with powdered egg. Supper will be an adventure.'

Mrs Price arrived back just as they were about to eat. They were looking at the mixture that Jamie persisted in calling an omelette and which Ferelith, after three glasses of champagne, called something quite unladylike, and wondering if they were either brave enough or hungry enough to eat.

'No, no darlings, don't eat,' she said. 'We're going out for real food. I met an old beau this afternoon: he's something frightfully grand at the War Office and he asked me to dinner and I told him that I had my grandson-in-law and his cousin here and he said 'bring them too'.'

'I can't, Mrs Price,' said Ferelith. 'It sounds wonderful but I would like to go back to see Blair and if he is doing well I will really have to start thinking about going back to Glasgow. Other people are doing my work for me, you see.'

'Heavens, the conscience of the Scottish Calvinist. But you must of course do what is right for you, my dear.'

Jamie elected to eat his sausage omelette too and to drive Ferelith back to the hospital. 'After all, Granny, there is meat in a sausage . . .'

'I wouldn't count on that, darling boy,' laughed the elderly Mrs Price, who had too much experience of the recipes for sausages through two world wars.

'And we can't afford to waste food,' went on Jamie. 'But you go out with your old flame and behave yourself.'

'Absolutely not. Don't wait up. Use my car, if you like. There's just enough petrol to get you to and from the hospital.'

Ferelith was delighted to avail herself of this offer. One day, she thought, one day she would be able to do something in return for all the nice things these lovely people were doing for her. She tried to express some of this as Jamie drove her back to the hospital. He looked at her in total surprise.

'But Ferelith, you're family,' he said as if that explained everything.

Family. She had never been part of a family. The Sisters at the Convent had tried to make the orphaned or abandoned children feel that they were part of a family. Each was a viable and important member of God's family and that was nice, especially when the world was very dark and troubled, but a family, a real family, that was different. And now these amazing people, Jamie and the lovely Jane and eccentric Mrs Price, were saying that she was a part of this family. But she was the illegitimate daughter of Jamie's uncle, his second biggest mistake. Would she have been acceptable if Sister Anthony had not fought for her right to advanced education, if Sister Anthony had not had some pull with an old school friend who just happened to be the Bishop? Did Jane and Jamie even think of these things? Were they even important at a time like this?

You must learn to accept, Ferelith, she told herself

and thought of Simon whom surely she loved more than any other human being but not with the kind of love that she had once had for Blair. Her love of Simon was surely a maternal love. She wanted to protect him, to shield him, but thinking of their relationship she realized that he had always been strong, that perhaps she had needed him as much as he had needed her. Have we used one another, Simon? she asked him across the miles, and is that necessarily wrong?

Blair opened his eyes that night as Ferelith sat holding his unbandaged hand and Jamie sat dozing into his coat collar.

'Blair,' said Ferelith very softly as if she could not believe it. 'Blair.'

He looked at her for a full moment, trying to focus his eyes, and then he seemed to smile very gently and closed his eyes again. She was terrified and gripped his hand hard.

'Blair,' she almost called his name and Jamie sat up with a start. 'He opened his eyes, just for a second, but I'm . . .'

Jamie, affected by Ferelith's obvious fear, stood up, came close to the bed, and leaned over his cousin.

'Dear God, Ferelith, you scared me,' he said. 'He's sleeping. You must have imagined it.'

'Imagined what?' It was Nurse Thomson.

'He looked at me,' Ferelith almost sobbed. 'He opened his eyes and smiled, I'm sure that he smiled.'

The nurse bent over her patient and then straightened up. She turned and smiled at Blair's family. 'His breathing has changed,' she said. 'He's breathing very easily now. I'm sure he'll be more alert later.'

The relief was palpable. Jamie felt it too. His

uncle's suicide had separated him from this member of his family for too many years and he had been horrified that he would lose Blair just a few years after having found him again. Now his horrifically and permanently injured cousin was being restored to him and with him this other cousin whom he accepted at face value, never having given any thought to the unfortunate accident of her birth.

'Aren't you glad we had champagne with our sausage omelette?'

'I shall never drink anything but, with sausage omelettes,' she said.

'Let's make a pact,' he said. 'Champagne and sausage omelettes at all times of crisis.'

'Sounds wonderful,' said Nurse Thomson whom they had not noticed return to her patient's bedside.

'Especially the champagne,' joked Jamie.

'Oh no, your lordship,' she said seriously. 'Especially the sausages. Real British bangers. My mother has these awful rissoles. They look like a sausage and you can't wait for your teeth to sink in but then you taste the vegetables. Ghastly.'

Ferelith thought of Simon's father eating his rissoles happily as he waited for news of his son. She had to get back to Scotland, to work. But she could not leave until she knew that Blair was out of danger, that he would live.

She stayed in London for eight days and refused Lady Winterton's offer to meet the rest of the family in Surrey. Life's decisions were awfully difficult. She would like to know the Winterton children; she would like to stay at Blair's side until he was ready to leave hospital. But at the same time, she had to be in Glasgow to look after her growing career, to care for Simon's ghastly cat, to touch base with his lonely father and his rissoles and, yes, she had to admit it, to try to mend her fences with Angus Webster.

The day she left was also the day that Jamie returned to his regiment. It had never occurred to her to wonder why a young able-bodied man was not in uniform; but he had been recuperating from an injury himself when Blair had first been shot down and had had his leave extended on compassionate grounds. Now he felt that it was time to 'get back to work' as he called it. Blair would stay in London until he was completely out of danger and then he would be transferred to a hospital in Scotland.

'I'll visit as often as I can,' Ferelith promised the now conscious Blair. 'I'll come back down to London and you'll be tired of seeing me when you come home.'

He merely smiled, since talking was still an almost insurmountable strain.

'Does he have any idea of the extent of his injuries?' Ferelith asked Jamie the night before she left.

'He thought he had no legs at all but apart from knowing that they're still there he's not really assimilating much. He has taken it for granted that you and I are here together. In a day or two he'll wonder.'

'I wish we could move him to Scotland now.'

'He'd never survive the journey. Don't worry, Ferelith, he's in excellent hands here.'

They looked together at Nurse Thomson who was by Blair's bed as often as duty allowed.

'He has established a rapport with her. He won't really begin to fret for visitors for quite a while.'

Again they were silent, thinking of the many operations that Blair still had to undergo.

'I wish I could be here all the time.'

'I know,' said Jamie, 'but it's much more important to be with him when he really knows what's going on. We, you, have got him through the worst . . .'

'Oh, not me, Jamie, all of us and especially, I think, Nurse Thomson, and her part in his recovery will remain constant. And there will be lots of visits from the amazing Mrs Price.'

And so Ferelith consoled herself on the nightmare return journey to Scotland with thinking of her newly-met family and she looked forward with delight to meeting them all again soon.

First she had to speak to Lord Webster and this seemed to be very difficult to arrange. He was not in Edinburgh. No one knew where he was and Ferelith found herself asking Miss McBride, his secretary, if his lordship had possibly gone to London on business.

She was to wish she had not.

'I am not at liberty to discuss his lordship's whereabouts with anyone, Miss Gallagher,' said Angus's very firm secretary. 'His lordship usually lets his particular friends know where he is himself.'

And that's put my gas at a peep, thought Ferelith to herself, in the old language of the children of a Glasgow orphanage. Miss McBride has me down as a not particular friend and I suppose that is exactly what I am, a not particular friend of Angus Webster.

'You will tell him that I phoned,' she said and then hung up. She had the feeling that Miss McBride had enjoyed dismissing her. Should I write but what if the dragon-like Miss McBride opens his personal mail when he is out of town? I couldn't bear to have her witness my apology.

She decided to swallow her pride when Angus had not contacted her after three months. *It's too late to apologize now. I should have done it at once. It's never too late to apologize. If you have done something wrong you must make an effort to set things straight.* So she argued with herself. She wrote several times and tore the letters up and then one afternoon the telephone rang in her office and the Gorgon, as she had taken to calling Miss McBride, was on the other end.

'I have Lord Webster for you, Miss Gallagher, if you are free.'

She felt like a schoolgirl about to come face to face with the hero of the school football team. *Why? It was an absolutely ridiculous reaction.*

'Yes, of course,' she said as easily as she could manage and hoped that when Angus came on the telephone her voice would not sound quite so strangled.

'Could we meet?' he asked without even saying hello. 'I feel I owe you an apology and they're better handled face to face.'

'Yes, of course . . . we can meet, I mean. You don't owe me an apology. It's the other way round and I've been trying to pluck up, no, to handle it the right way.'

'Are you free for dinner? There are one or two places that can still manage to do a decent plate, not pre-war standards but better than Spam, I think.'

'I'd like that.'

'Shall we say Rogano's or would you like to try somewhere else?'

'No, that would be fine.'

'Can you possibly meet me at eight? I have so much work while I'm in Glasgow but I'll see you home. You're at Simon's flat?'

'Yes.'

'Very sensible. See you at eight.'

She had to get home. She would boil a kettle and wash her hair. If she practically sat on the gas fire her hair would be dry in half-an-hour. The black dress, supposedly very flattering to red hair and green eyes, that she had bought for the date she had not kept, would be perfect. If she pinned her hair back with the tortoiseshell comb Simon had given her for her last birthday and wore her very last pair of nylons she would look all right. A memory from the past came mocking her. She was in the Convent deciding to become an advocate. She was going to be brilliant, stunning, and sophisticated or words to that effect. She used to worry about being beautiful, she remembered. Well, she was quite bright and she was sophisticated, at least on the outside. 'Two out of three isn't bad,' she said just as she had said it all those years ago.

War had done away with so many pretensions. One no longer thought of the right time to arrive for a party, if there was a party. Getting across the city at whatever time trams were running was of paramount importance. The tram drivers were threatening to stop their trams after eight if they were not allowed to use more lights, saying reasonably enough that it was dangerous to drive the huge machines if the driver could not see hazards on the lines. That German planes could see the lights too was obvious.

'Six o' one, half a dozen o' the other,' said the tram drivers. 'If we put on the lights the Jerries'll see us. If we drive in the dark we'll crash or run over things.'

'Please don't strike tonight,' Ferelith begged and decided to make her way to the restaurant as soon as

her hair was dry. Better to wander around or hide in
the ladies than to be late or not to get there at all.

She arrived at seven-thirty and went straight
to the ladies room. Angus, who had also been
faced with a similar dilemma, saw her and smiled.
Impossible to follow her and so he decided to hide
behind his evening paper until she emerged.

When she did he pretended that he had only just
spotted her, although he had spent a delightful
thirty-five minutes deciding that her hair was less
red and more golden than he had remembered, and
that her legs were longer and that she was quite the
nicest thing he had seen in some time.

'Let's get everything straight before we go into
dinner, Ferelith,' he said when he had taken her
coat and given it to an attendant to hang up. 'We'll
have a drink of something . . . there was only rum
the last time I was in, very interesting stuff . . . and
then we'll have whatever they offer.'

'Lord Webster, Angus, please, I have to apologize. I forgot all about you. That sounds dreadful
but —'

'I know, my dear, but it puts me perfectly in my
place and I deserved the set-down. The fault is mine.
I should have realized that only something terribly
important would make you just not turn up. You
see, it's just that . . . and at my age I should know
better but I couldn't . . . God this is difficult. I find,
Miss Ferelith Gallagher, that you have become very
important to me. I used to tell myself that my interest was purely academic: that I hated to see the waste
of a fine mind, but it's more. And then, you see, you
are so much younger and I feel I have no right, have
no chance but if we could be friends . . .'

'Oh Angus,' said Ferelith. 'I don't want to be
friends.' Heavens, what was she saying? Logical

thinking, Ferelith, reason. 'I mean I do, of course I do, but I don't think of you as older and I do think of you . . . rather a lot.'

When had he taken possession of her hand? He looked at it as if he wanted to remember every vein, every line. The barman coughed.

'You don't have champagne, I suppose?' asked Angus and the waiter went off to try to do the impossible.

'It's terribly complicated, Angus. I don't know where to start.'

'Your cousin, Lord Winterton, wrote to me, a short little letter and just to say that he had told you that your brother, the young man I saw you with here, had been terribly injured.'

'It's much more complicated than that,' said Ferelith. 'Blair is not my brother, not the way you mean. He is my half-brother. I am his illegitimate half-sister.' There, she had said it.

'Poor you.'

'No . . . Oh I suppose yes, but I never thought of life as having dealt me a hard hand until I met Blair. You see we didn't know about one another. We met at Edinburgh University. We were married, Angus, for all of three and a half weeks. I spent one night with him, slept with my own brother.' She looked at him as she said the words and saw distaste on his finely-featured face. She had expected it. She would leave. She picked up her gloves and he covered her hands again with his and she felt his warmth and sympathy and felt the tension drain away.

'Poor you,' he said again. 'How could your parents have allowed it to happen?'

'Our father shot himself when he realized that I was on the way. My mother lived only a few hours after my birth and Blair's mother tried to cover up

the blot on the family honour. She even changed
her name and Blair's back to her maiden name, told
him his grandfather wanted his family name to be
carried on. Blair didn't know he was a Winterton
until after our horrible débâcle and he promptly
had his name changed back again. I was given my
mother's name because only one old nanny in India
really knew anything about me and, of course, she's
been dead for years and my dreadful secret really
died with her, but Mrs Crawford, Blair's mother,
knew something, and she had me investigated when
Blair and I became friends. She did the same with
all the riffraff he met at school and university,' she
said lightly, trying to show that it didn't really hurt
although it did, terribly.

'Has it never occurred to you that you look alike?
I noticed it when I saw you with Blair Winterton.
The hair is different but the green eyes and the fine
features are similar.'

Ferelith did not answer the question. 'I don't think
Jamie – Lord Winterton – has really figured out my
place in things.'

'His letter proves that he doesn't really care
about such things. He likes you and he obviously
loves Blair.'

'He's a nice man and his wife is a dear and she has
this wonderful granny who flies around London in a
dreadful old ambulance bullying wounded soldiers
into getting better. You can easily imagine her
saying things like, "Eat up all this mush and you'll
grow big and strong."'

'We had better go into the dining room and eat
up all our dinner too.'

Ferelith could never remember what they had
eaten. It could have been old carpet. She was conscious only of her happiness that Angus was there

and that he was the most interesting man she had ever met. He was kind and gentle and clever and sophisticated and he made her feel sophisticated too.

He had a car and he took her home. She knew that with every fibre of her being she wanted to invite him into Simon's flat.

He stopped at the door and turned her to face him.

'I thought I would ask you to make me a nightcap but I daren't. If you say no my heart will break and if you say yes I won't be able to control myself and I feel so so strongly that control is needed. I think something very wonderful is happening and I want it to grow slowly so that its roots will be deep and strong, so that it won't break with the winds that life will throw at it. Do you feel anything like that?'

With tears of pure happiness in her eyes she looked at him and nodded slowly. He put his arms down by his side and leaned forward and kissed her very lightly on her mouth. She had closed her eyes and she felt his lips, soft and undemanding like the weight of the petals of a rose and just as perfect. When she opened her eyes he had gone.

She drifted upstairs like the selfsame petals and spoke nicely to Traviata, who smirked as if to say that she could not be got round so easily. A woman with a philistine's taste in music was no substitute for a man who knew his Wagner and who fed his cat on fresh chicken. Traviata refused to make allowances for the shortages caused by war and would continue to blame Ferelith for her uninteresting diet. Ferelith ignored her and went to Simon's desk and sat down to write letters, to Simon, to Jamie, to Blair, and to Angus Webster.

She did not post the last one: it was too early.

12

ANGUS ASKED FERELITH to marry him on Christmas Eve, 1942. She wished desperately that he had not chosen such a lovely happy night. She did not want to spoil Christmas for either of them.

'I can't,' she said.

'May I ask why? It seems to me, Ferelith, that we love one another very much. Is it because I am so much older?'

'Oh Angus, how can you think such a thing? I have never, since I was a student, considered your age.'

'Then why, my darling? I do love you so. Are you afraid that I don't? Am I perhaps not passionate enough?' He took her roughly in his arms and kissed her eyes, her lips, and then he buried his face in her hair. She could feel him trembling and the passion in her rose to meet his. He pushed her away. 'Oh, Ferelith, if I were to give way to my passions.'

'I love you Angus and, if you will wait, I will marry you one day.'

'One day,' he burst out. 'Ferelith, I am forty-seven years old, nearly twenty years older than you. I want a wife and children and . . . Is that it? Is it your career? Oh, darling, I would never stand in your way and, I know you want to be independent and to make a success of the Law on your own but if you marry me, you can come to Edinburgh immediately and go to the Bar.'

'I know and I don't want to marry you to have you finance my career. Oh Angus please, there are so many thoughts going around in my head. Blair.

Simon and Jamie, still out there somewhere. I feel I have no right to be so happy while they are living in danger and fear . . .'

'They would not . . .'

'Oh please don't say that,' she begged. 'I have to be quite honest, Angus. I want you but I have worked so hard. I owe it to Sister Anthony and Reverend Mother and the Bishop who allowed the use of funds even though I was a mere female. I owe it to them to be the best I can be. I want to get to the Bar. I have saved and saved these past few years and I'm almost ready, but there's Simon and Traviata and besides, I want to take silk.' There it was out. She had said it. The dreams were still there.

She could not tell what he was thinking. His face was calm, the eyes cold and distant. 'There are no women K.C.s.'

'Isn't it about time there were?'

He thought carefully. He always would try to see both sides. 'Yes,' he said finally.

'You want me to marry you and you want children. How could I possibly combine the two? Each job would require all my energy.'

'I will never force you to have a child. I will never ask you. I will never mention the attractiveness of all our friends' children. I will never look in prams parked outside restaurants or shops.'

She put her arms around his neck and leaned against him.

'Oh, not fair, Ferelith,' he said.

'I would like to sleep with you, Angus.'

He pushed her from him almost roughly. 'I have spent my life telling undisciplined males that if they want to do so they can control their desires. I love you, Ferelith, and I want you, all of you, but I want it all and that means marriage.'

'And I can't marry you just yet.'

'When? When you have become the first female King's Council, or will I have to wait until you become Lord Advocate, or why not Lord Chancellor? Will you stagger up the aisle with senile old me then?'

Ferelith took refuge in tears and Angus stamped out slamming the door behind him.

Traviata came over and insinuated herself on to her lap.

'Oh God, Traviata, what have I done? I love him. Why did I drive him away? I don't want to spend the rest of my life with someone else's cat.'

At that the cat stood up, stretched and stalked proudly from her lap. She had merely been offering a little comfort. Her heart, if she had one, belonged to Simon, if it belonged to anyone.

Ferelith laughed through her tears: rejected by a man and now by a cat. Was there any more humiliation in store? She had hoped, really hoped, that Angus would stay with her for Christmas and she had therefore refused Maria's offer of an Italian family Christmas. Was it too late to change her mind?

'We are on our way to Midnight Mass,' said Maria when she answered the telephone. 'Meet us there, bring your toothbrush and prepare to be awakened as soon as you have fallen asleep.'

'I'm feeling absolutely miserable, Maria, even the cat hates me.'

'Then you should definitely be with us. You won't have time to feel sorry for yourself. It's all systems go in a big family on Christmas Day and even worse if they're Italians.'

She knew she should not have telephoned as soon as she had hung up. It was futile to hope that

watching the joy of Maria and Mauro and their
large family would make her feel better. It would
only make her realize what she had thrown away
and for what? Was she doomed to spend the rest
of her life with law books and a cat? She thought
of Pietro. He had believed that her dream of high
office was somehow unfeminine. Poor Pietro. Where
was he now? Was he even alive? Again there had
been no correspondence from him or his family. She
thought of Blair, still in hospital but oh so much
better. He said he had accepted that he would never
walk again.

'Of course I'll be able to ride, Ferelith. Americans
control their horses through the reins: legs are
better but since mine don't function I'll work something out.'

She pictured some of the powerful animals he had
owned before the war. He could never control them.
She hoped he would not try.

Now her tears were for Blair and his lost dreams.
Was he replacing old dreams with new ones?

My dreams are the same as they always were,
Blair, she sent the thought through the air to him.
A happy marriage, a career. Only the man has
changed. Do I always demand too much of life?
Am I greedy to want everything?

There was a beautifully-wrapped gift from Jane
under the tiny tree she had decorated with red
bows and a few white candles. A little angel she
had bought in Rome sat lopsidedly among the
top branches. She cried for Jane alone with her
children and worrying about her husband *somewhere
out there*.

Where do tears come from? Where is the bottom-
less well?

'Oh, pull yourself together, Ferelith, go to the

di Rollo's and be happy if it kills you,' she said to herself.

And she thought, and almost prayed, that it just might. The love in the di Rollo family was almost tangible: the way they spoke to one another, the way Mauro and Maria touched one another as they passed, doing the million and one things that needed to be done in a large family, the way the older girls rallied around to help their mother and their elderly aunts prepare the gargantuan meal, the gratitude everyone showed for even the humblest of presents. This is family, thought Ferelith, and no matter how they try to make me part of it I'm still on the outside looking in.

The doorbell rang as Aunt Sophie was serving the soup and when Mauro returned from answering it, he pulled with him a very embarrassed and dishevelled looking senior law lord. No need for talk, no need for explanations. Ferelith ran to him and Mauro pushed them back into the hall for a few minutes of privacy.

'And don't let the soup get cold,' he ordered, very much the paterfamilias.

'I'm sorry,' said Ferelith and Angus together.

'I should have . . .' they began again and stopped and looked at one another and then Angus bent his head and kissed Ferelith Gallagher as she had not been kissed for a very long time. She felt all her doubts melt away at his touch.

She could feel the words *I'll marry you tomorrow* forming on her tongue but before she had a chance to utter them he was speaking against her hair. 'I love you, Ferelith, but I respect your hard work, your grit, your determination. I won't change my mind about wanting to marry you, about loving you, but I won't ask you again until you let me know that you are ready and if I have to wait until I'm senile then I'll wait.'

'Aunt Katia says the pasta is getting soft,' said Alicia from the dining-room door. 'Mummy has set a place for your friend, Aunt Ferelith.'

Ferelith was never able to decide whether she welcomed or resented the interruption. The rest of the day was pure joy, with Angus joining in as soon as Mauro and Maria could be made to relax and forget that he was a lord. The children, especially Domenico, who fell asleep on his new friend's lap, had no problem dealing with Ferelith's friend. Had not Alicia caught them kissing in the hall?

'Where did you spend last night?' Ferelith asked him as they washed the dishes together in blissful companionship.

'In my car, in terror that either a policeman or a reporter would find me and think me a vagrant. Can you imagine "Senior Law Lord found asleep in car". Ferelith, it isn't that I'm a law lord? You're not afraid of a nepotism thing?'

'An unsubstantiated and totally unjust accusation of nepotism? No. I honestly haven't thought of that. Maybe when they make you Lord Advocate, I'll worry a little.'

'We must see you a K.C. before that but it will take some time, darling. A man would expect to wait at least ten years.'

'Women have been waiting hundreds and so I warn you, Lord Webster of Dalmarnock, that at least one of them will be beating on your door before ten years is up.'

Ignoring his soapy hands, he put his arms around her and kissed her long and hard. 'I am tempted to say something provocative about which door I hope

to find you beating on but if I do one of those delightful girls is bound to come in and hear me and rush
off to tell everyone about Aunt Ferelith's sex-mad
friend. Now, let's finish the dishes because I must
get back to Edinburgh. I usually spend Christmas
with my sister and her family and although she
is absolutely thrilled at the idea that I might be
spending Christmas in the arms of a goddess, I
would like to get back to wish them joy. You could
come with me and meet them, officially presented
as it were.'

Memories of her official meeting with Blair's
mother came unbidden into her head.

'I'm not ready.'

He kissed her again. 'Blast this war. I won't be
back in Glasgow for some time. I'm doing a bit of
work in London as you know and so if you don't
hear, don't worry. I'll be thinking of you every
minute of the day.'

'When you're not thinking of work.'

'Every minute of every night then.'

'Me too.'

'Think of me at midnight on New Year's Eve
and I'll think of you. Say I love you, Angus, and
wherever I am, I'll hear it.'

'You say, I love you, Ferelith.'

There was an explosion of laughter, a smothered
'Soppy' from the door, the sounds of running feet,
furious Italian scolding from Maria and then silence.
They looked at one another ruefully and then leaned
together for a few minutes. Ferelith could feel his
heart beating.

'I'll tell them to behave next time you come or we
won't have them as bridesmaids.'

'Bridesmaids?' His face was joyful.

'Yes, and a solemn little page boy.'

'He'll still be little or is it the one who is on the way?'

'Men aren't supposed to notice such things.'

'I notice everything when I'm with you.' He noticed that she had not answered his question but he said nothing and, instead, dried his hands, rolled down his sleeves, and reached for his cufflinks. 'I brought my mother's engagement ring . . . ?'

She shook her head gently.

'I never give up,' he said lightly. 'You should have seen me on the rugby field, bloodied and battered but unbowed.'

He said his goodbyes to Maria and Mauro, and Ferelith stood alone in the dark on the doorstep and watched him drive away. There were no streetlights and the houses were dark and shuttered. Inside though, surely in almost every one, parties were going on, tired children were being put to bed, exhausted parents were cleaning up the detritus of Christmas revelries.

'A few more years, Angus,' she whispered as the dark bulk of his car turned the corner and disappeared out of her vision, out of her life, 'to get somewhere on my own. Is that too much to ask?'

In the New Year Ferelith went to London again, to visit Blair, and to see Angus who was doing *something* in a government office. She took Angus to meet Blair at the hospital and while they were there Jane too came to visit. It was a family reunion of a sort and reminded Angus that the woman he loved had not as yet met any member of his own family.

'I hope Nurse Thomson plucks up courage before Blair goes back to Scotland,' he said later that evening as they had supper after seeing the heart-throb, Lesley Howard, in *Pimpernel Smith*. Finally they had managed to see a film together.

Ferelith looked at him, her fork halfway to her
mouth. 'What are you talking about?' Then her
face was flooded with joy as the realization of
what he had been saying struck her. 'Oh, you don't
mean . . .?'

'Of course I do. She loves him. I know enough
about being in love with someone to tell.'

'But enough to spend her life with him, the
way he is?'

'If he hadn't been your brother and this had
happened, wouldn't you have stayed with him?'

'Of course, but that would be an easy decision. I
knew him when he was . . .'

'He's still the same, I believe.'

'Yes, even stronger as a person, but he was such
a fine athlete and he loved his horses, great huge
brutes with rolling eyes and tossing heads.'

'I can see you share the family love of horseflesh,'
he said laughing.

'I do, but only if they are in one field and I am
outside it. But, Angus, if it's true, if she loves him
as he is and wants to spend her life with him, what
can we do to help?'

'Help the romance along, you mean? Nothing,
darling, it's disastrous to interfere. They must work
it out for themselves. She has two months to make
him realize that she, the woman and not the nurse,
is indispensable to him.'

When, a few days after her return to Scotland, a
tearful Ferelith telephoned his hotel, Angus thought
that something had happened to Simon or to Jamie.

'No, I feel stupid, but it's Leslie Howard. The Germans shot down the civilian plane he was in: somehow I felt he was very special to us. I just loved him
in *Gone With the Wind* and *Pimpernel Smith*, our film.'

'I don't believe I am hearing this from a rational,

intellectual woman who is preparing to take the legal world by storm.'

'It's not allowable to mourn for someone if I put K.C. after my name?'

'Of course it is, but Ferelith you didn't know him. Are you shedding tears for everyone killed in this war?'

'Yes, I am. Do you know that Goebbels has just declared Berlin a Jew-free city? Do you know what that means? And I am also very angry with landlords who don't repair their properties and illegally evict people who complain and oh, I wish . . .'

He held his breath but she stopped her declaration, if she had been going to make it.

'. . . I wish this war was over and that you were back in Edinburgh and Jamie was back with Jane and the children and that Simon was here because then I could come to Edinburgh . . .'

She stopped and she could almost hear him wanting to ask the question that he had promised not to ask.

'Germany can't hold out much longer,' he said instead.

But it could and it did. Mussolini and Hitler met again in Northern Italy to discuss the worsening situation and, in a daylight raid, five hundred American bombers rained tons of bombs on the Italian capital, destroying railyards and airfields but avoiding the historical buildings. Later martial law was declared in an attempt to prevent civil war. In the same month, the anti-Fascist Marshal Pietro Badoglio asked the Allies for peace terms to celebrate Mussolini's downfall, and the Fascist party was abolished. But still Hitler refused to bow to what the rest of the world was beginning to see as inevitable.

In Glasgow Ferelith worked as hard as she could in an attempt to stop thinking of how much she missed Angus and how much she wished she had agreed to marry him.

'How could I keep up this pace if I had to consider a husband?' she asked herself, 'and if I had a child?'

Ruthlessly she abolished such thoughts. Angus loved her and she loved him. Marriage would come in time. First there was Blair to worry about.

Nurse Thomson resigned from the hospital and travelled with Squadron Leader Winterton as his private nurse back to his home in Fife. Jane and her two children travelled with them. Jamie would be happier if his family was far from the dangers of bombing. It seemed a perfect opportunity for the parts of the family to get to know one another. Ferelith promised to make the long trek to Fife as often as she could and in the meantime she taxed Jane with keeping her informed of the progress of the love affair.

'She'll have to ask him,' Jane whispered into the telephone one cold winter evening. 'He is Winterton all over: the soul of honour.' Luckily she could not see how an illegitimate and unwanted Winterton took that remark. 'He gazes after her if she so much as crosses the room, and he asks the children constantly about her whereabouts. They're turning into perfect little spies. They'll say: "She's talking to the gardeners about raising chickens, Uncle Blair, to help the war effort." Or: "She's asking the keepers about raising trout in the duck pond." And even: "She's having a bath." How much they saw of that activity I really do not want to know. But when she is in the room with him he behaves as if he hadn't even known she was gone.'

'He's in love,' said Ferelith, 'and you have no idea how happy that makes me,' and to Jane's consternation, she burst into tears.

Wisely Jane said nothing but made soothing murmurs. The embarrassed Ferelith hung up and went to moan about the Court of Appeal ruling that savings from housekeeping money belong to the husband.

'It's appalling,' she told all her fellow solicitors who would listen to her. 'With supposedly extinct dodos on the Bench, women need women advocates more than ever.'

She discussed the Appeal court ruling with Charles Smythe. 'You can't possibly agree, Charles,' she argued. 'If a woman scrimps and saves to put a few pence aside for her rainy day, surely it belongs to her and should be spent just as she wants it to be spent.'

'A man, in this case, the breadwinner and provider of the houshold finance, could quite justifiably argue that he must have given her too much housekeeping in the first place.'

'But if she feeds the family well and still has a shilling or two left over then surely she is entitled to keep it?'

'If she feeds the family well on his income and has money over, then obviously he gave her too much in the first place.'

Ferelith almost literally gritted her teeth. She was appalled at how the most rational and logical of thinkers could suddenly find herself wanting to clout someone who could not be made to agree with her. She breathed deeply and continued, 'Not if she has worked really hard to learn new ways of economizing and making a little go a long way.'

'The difficulty would not arise in a happy home

in the first place, Ferelith. A man doesn't pay his wife a wage.'

'Then he damn well should,' snapped Ferelith and flounced out while his shout of 'You should be arguing at the Bar' followed her down the corridor.

He was right, of course. She would only be really happy when she could do the work she had been trained to do. And to be supremely happy she would be married to Angus too. Why, why, why, was it virtually impossible for a woman to have everything? Men seemed to do it quite easily. Where was it written – Thou shalt not have a man and a career?

She took some comfort from looking at her growing bank balance. Soon, please God, the war would be over and she could leave the luxury of Simon's flat and the dubious comfort of Traviata for whatever she could find in Edinburgh.

She phoned Angus. 'I need you,' was all she said.

'As soon as I can, darling. Just wait for me. I'll come as soon as I break the back of this work that somehow keeps coming.'

'We'll eat here. I'll make something with pasta. I learned a few delicious things while I was in Italy.'

'Italian food. My favourite. I'll bring the wine. Just wait for me. That's as definite as I can be. One evening soon I will knock on your door.'

'And Simon's dragon lady will think lascivious thoughts.'

'So will I, my darling,' he said and hung up.

She worked and she waited and she kept the ingredients for her easiest but tastiest sauce in the flat so that she could make dinner the moment he arrived. She thought of how lovely it would be to be in Edinburgh and to see him, to talk to him, every day. Soon. There was almost enough money in the savings bank to ensure a dignified existence until she could secure cases and then they would marry and, and . . . She pushed away the enticing thoughts and scolded herself for her romantic fantasies. Ferelith Gallagher K.C. or Mrs, no Lady Webster? Both, please God, both, but when I am ready.

And then one evening he was there and she opened the door and forgot all her good intentions – and so did he. He kissed her and they stood for a minute just inside the door while he whispered words that meant everything and nothing, sweet words, loving words, and then he laughed and moved away from her, set the bottle of wine down on the table in the hall and reached for her again. She went into his arms and – did one push and did the other guide? – but they went into the bedroom and not into the little living room where the tiny dining table was set for two. They fell together on to the bed and before he entered her she had a feeling of *déjà vu* – I have been here before but this time it's right, it's complete – and she surrendered to him as he surrendered to her and together they cried out in exquisite joy.

Hours later she woke to find him sound asleep beside her, his arm across her breasts, and she turned and gazed into his face. She had never before seen him asleep and she followed his jaw line with the tip of a finger and smoothed the lines on his forehead and her heart ached with love for the whole man, this wonderful man who had given her himself. He felt her touch and his eyes opened and he smiled, not in surprise but in delight that he was where he had always dreamed of being, and he began to kiss her, and again she responded passionately.

At last they lay back exhausted, fulfilled, but in each other's arms.

'Ferelith,' he asked after they had lain there contentedly for some time, 'did you make dinner? I'm perfectly happy to lie here with you for the rest of my life but I'm absolutely starving.'

She snuggled even closer to him, enjoying this companionable closeness almost as much as she enjoyed the passionate intimacy of the hours before. But she laughed, got up and pulled on her dressing gown and went to the kitchen. The smells of garlic and onion and tomatoes soon brought him in after her. He opened the wine, poured it and toasted her, and then stood with his arms around her while she stirred the sauce.

'What are you making?' he asked. 'That smell is tantalizing.'

'It's the poor Scot's equivalent of an Italian sauce. One onion and one carrot, twopence. A powdered egg omelette plus sauce and *Mama Mia.*'

'This is perfect,' he said, his lips against her hair. 'I can handle anything with you to come home to . . . marriage will be so wonderful . . .'

She turned and looked at him. 'Angus, it will be wonderful but I won't always be at home.'

'I know. I meant only that when you are at home it will be wonderful. Shall I ring my sister or do you want to let Blair know first?'

Ferelith turned back to the burning onions and turned the flames down under the pot. She felt as cold as she had felt happy a moment before. 'Tell him what?'

She felt him stiffening behind her but his arms

stayed around her waist. She could feel their warmth on her skin.

'Ferelith, you are going to marry me now, aren't you?' He dropped his hands and she felt alone, confused.

'No, Angus, not now. We made a bargain . . .'

'But after . . . Ferelith, I am a very disciplined man. I never meant . . . damn, what a trite thing to say but it's true. I never meant, or did I? Did I come, hoping to seduce you?'

'For God's sake, Angus, you didn't seduce me. If anything we seduced each other. It hasn't changed anything except perhaps to show us how well suited we are, how wonderful that side of our marriage will be. This is the middle of the twentieth century: you don't have to marry me to save my honour.'

'Am I supposed to congratulate you on your modern thinking, Ferelith? I'm an old fogey, I suppose, but I happen to believe in old-fashioned virtues like abstinence. I can't say that I wish we hadn't made love . . .' He looked at her and she could not doubt his sincerity. 'I have never had so much pleasure or happiness in my life . . . but it's not the way I operate. I want to marry you.'

She looked at him. Why had it all gone wrong? They had shared some magic. Why couldn't he accept that? Lovemaking before marriage wasn't really in her life script either but it had happened and . . . was it wrong? A few minutes ago he had been strong and virile and in command and now he was beset with guilt. Surely it wasn't wrong. They loved one another: they were going to marry. It could not be wrong to give each other such happiness.

'I told you before about how severe I am with rapists,' he began.

'For God's sake you didn't rape me. Perhaps it was the other way round. All right we pre-empted marriage by a few months. We're not loose people, Angus. I haven't been with anyone since Blair. I love you . . .'

'Not enough to marry me, Ferelith.' He turned and went back to the bedroom and she left the sauce and hurried after him. He was pulling his clothes on and he turned from her to hide his body.

'I'm going and I won't be back.'

What could she say? What could she do? Give in? Say, as she had almost said on the previous Christmas Day, *I'll marry you tomorrow*? Let him finance her career?

'I'll leave you to let yourself out,' she said stonily and walked like an old woman into the kitchen where she stood, stirring the sauce that could not cook because she had turned off the burner, while tears of desolation followed one another down her cheeks.

Simon's cat leapt from the counter-top where she had been sitting and rubbed against her ankles in a gesture of comfort.

'We're in the soup together Traviata,' she said. 'Two fallen women with no prospect of getting out of the mess we got ourselves into.'

Traviata smirked. She, at least, had the hope that Simon would return to her.

Christmas of 1943 was miserable for Ferelith. She spent the holiday season alone with Traviata. She had lied to Maria and had said that she was going to spend Christmas with Elspeth Baxter now happily married to another general practitioner and living in Ayr. She ate a cheese sandwich for Christmas dinner, having no heart at all to cook for herself or Traviata, who turned her nose up at the fish heads

begged for from the local fish man, and whined to
be let out.

She apologized mentally, not to the cat, but to
Simon who trusted her to look after his pet in the
style to which he had accustomed the animal.

'Blair has sent me a pheasant, Simon,' she whispered across the miles, 'and I'll cook it and give her
some tomorrow. I just can't bear the thought of "Tis
the Season" and Ho, Ho, Ho.'

On New Year's Eve she sat before the fire and
listened to music, Beethoven's *Fidelio*. Leonora had
stayed faithful to her love and eventually had managed to be reunited with him.

'Please, please, please,' Ferelith whispered but to
whom she did not know, and then just as her clock
struck twelve she whispered *I love you* across the
miles to Angus and fell asleep weeping and hoping
that he was thinking of her too.

Worldly success can cost too much. Had her pride
cost her everything she really wanted? She argued
with herself constantly. Why is it wrong to want
a home and a family and a useful career at the
same time, a career for which her academic and
dramatic ability and not the name of her husband
was responsible?

13

IT WAS GOING to be a good year. The war was nearly over, or was it? All the signs in London were that peace was just around the corner. People began to look forward to normal life, to doing things like going to the theatre. The Old Vic company which had been bombed out of its theatre in Waterloo Road reopened at the New Theatre in the West End. Ralph Richardson and Laurence Olivier starred in *Peer Gynt* and *Richard III* respectively and, true to Old Vic tradition, took small roles in one another's plays. John Gielgud, another splendid young actor, played Hamlet and a fellow called Donald Wolfit acted the finest King Lear that several of the critics covering first nights had ever seen. A note of sadness in that otherwise reawakening year was the death of Sir Henry Wood, founder of the Promenade Concerts.

Pre-fabricated houses that could be erected in a few hours by a few workmen were designed for demobolized servicemen and bombed-out families. The prefabs, which sprang up like mushrooms after rain, were to stand for a few years until 'proper' rebuilding of Britain could proceed.

But the war refused to end.

The Benedictine Monastery at Monte Cassino, from where Hermann Goering had stolen millions of pounds' worth of art treasures, was finally taken and thus the way was cleared for the Allied advance on Rome. A few weeks later Rome itself fell to the Allies. Ferelith felt some solace at the news of the relief of the Eternal City and sat down once more

to write to Pietro. Maybe now there would be some
communication from him. She could not believe
that it had simply been a case of out of sight out
of mind.

In August 1944 she went through to Fife to see
Blair. She had not told Nurse Thomson that she
was coming and decided to take a taxi from the
station. A game of cricket was being played on the
great lawn that swept up to the house. A sturdy
little boy wielding an enormous bat was obviously
the batsman. The fielder was a pretty young woman
in a spotted dress, whom Ferelith at first did not
recognize, and the crowd consisted of a solemn little
girl and two dollies. The bowler who was making
more noise than everyone else put together was in
a wheelchair.

'Stop, stop,' screamed Ferelith to the startled
driver.

He screeched to a halt. She paid him, threw her
overnight bag down on the edge of the driveway,
and sped across the lawn.

'Blair, oh Blair,' she sobbed while the tears rushed
unchecked down her cheeks.

The bowler saw her and held out his arms and
she ran into them.

'Hello, little sister,' he said. 'Good heavens, my
bowling's not that bad: good enough for young
Jeremy here.'

It was not the first time that Ferelith had met
Jamie's two children and she soon walked up to the
house with them to see Jane while Nurse Thomson,
the young girl in the spotted dress, pushed the
wheelchair along beside them. The change in everybody was evident. In the few months since she had
seen them the children had grown as all children do

and were almost unrecognizable. Nurse Thomson, obviously familiarly now known as Emma, was plumper and softer, her face rosy and unstrained, but the most incredible difference was in Blair himself.

'I'll make a horseman of this young man before his daddy comes home,' he said, watching Jeremy playing with toy soldiers at his feet, and Jeremy looked up, smiled at his cousin, and toppled Napoleon.

'You should see them, Ferelith,' said Jane. 'Blair sits in the middle of the paddock holding the lunging rein, poor Emma whirls him around like a dervish, and Jeremy trots around on his pony.'

'Daddy will be pleased when he comes home, Auntie Ferelith,' said Jeremy, 'and Uncle Blair is going to start Constanza just as soon as Mummy agrees.'

'Now.' Constanza removed her thumb from her mouth long enough to express her opinion.

'You look so wonderful, Blair. Nurse, I mean Emma, you have done wonders with him.'

Emma smiled. 'He did it himself.'

'So I did,' agreed Blair. 'At home with almost all of my favourite people waiting on me hand and foot, it would have been uncivil not to get well and strong.'

'What do the doctors say?'

He looked straight at her but she could not read the enigmatic look. 'I'm as good as I'll ever be,' he said lightly. 'Some bits, including the legs, will never work again, but the bits in working order are superb,' he finished with an evil, leering laugh at Jeremy. 'Feel my muscles.'

Jeremy got up with the air of someone who had done this often before but who was prepared to humor the patient. Obligingly he felt the biceps

held out for his inspection. 'Very good,' he said.
'Bigger than yesterday.'

'Bowling does that,' Blair informed Ferelith, 'and
beating horrid little boys.'

Ferelith watched the two of them together, and
then caught the look of anguish on Emma Thomson's
face and the one of compassion for both of them
on Jane's.

'Could he, well, I mean . . .' She and Jane were
alone after dinner in the great bedroom that Blair
had deemed suitable for his cousin's wife. The
children were in bed and Emma was getting Blair
ready for the night

'Father a child? I don't know. That information
is a little too intimate for me but surely marriage
isn't just about sex and children. I would love to
have Jamie here to know he's safe. Just to hold him
would be so wonderful. I know I've had it all and it's
easy for me to pass judgements but I do think that
marriage would be good for both of them. She lost
everything in this senseless war too: it would be nice
if they could salvage a little happiness.' She turned
away and began brushing her hair vigorously. She
kept her face away from Ferelith but she could
see her reflection in the mirror. 'What about you,
Ferelith? Don't you ever long to throw away your
unused barrister's wig and jump into bed with some
nice young man?'

'No, I want more than anything to wear that wig,
and yes, I want to jump into bed with, not a nice
young man but a very nice older man. He loves me
still . . . oh, I blew it, Jane, and I can't bring myself
to talk about it, even to you, but I do love him.
I said no when he first asked me and he's never
going to ask me again. I have to ask him and I'm
afraid.'

'Of rejection?'

'No, in a way I'm afraid of the power I seem to have over him and I believe he still loves me, I know he does, but I'm afraid that having come so far but not quite far enough . . . Blast. It's stupidly melodramatic and complicated but I suppose I'm a little afraid of . . . losing my identity, I suppose, being compelled to give up my work before I break all the bounds imposed on it.'

'Would he expect you to give up your career? I suppose being older he's . . .'

'Wonderful and understanding. I love Angus Webster and he wouldn't ask me to give up the Law but I might feel there were things I would have to do as his wife . . .'

'God, you're not afraid of sex are you? It's great fun, but as Charles the Second said, "There's more to marriage than four legs in a bed."'

'I'm not afraid.' She blushed furiously as she remembered her total abandonment to Angus. 'It's the "more" that's in marriage that scares me. I dreamed as a child of having Angus's next job and as an old nun at the orphanage used to say "there's more chance that pigs might fly and we'd have to shoot bacon."'

'What is his next job?' Jane, looking not much older than Constanza in her dressing gown and slippers, curled up in the middle of the bed and prepared herself for a good gossip. 'Come on, I'm family and I won't tell a soul.'

'Lord Advocate.'

'How splendid, I'm terribly impressed, but doesn't someone like that die in harness?'

'Oh, no. He could resign when he's older or if he was offered a different post, with the Government for instance. He's spending a lot of time in London doing hush hush stuff just now, but the higher up the ladder he gets, the less I feel that I want to marry him. It's so complicated. Blair wanted to marry me and I knew quite well that marriage to him would finance my career. Look at the trouble that decision got us both into. I couldn't bear it if people thought I was being given cases or privileges because of patronage.'

Jane, whose entire existence had been guided and controlled by position and patronage, looked at her shrewdly. 'They will anyway, Ferelith, and if you want my advice you will believe that a marriage is made between two people and they are the only two people who count in it, and they must ignore innuendos and raised eyebrows and all the other nonsense that jealousy carries with it. Now, enough about you. What are we going to do about Cousin Blair?'

Ferelith laughed and remembered ruefully that Angus too had thought one should not interfere. 'I thought marriage was between two people.'

'We have to get them married first and then we'll leave them alone.'

But Emma had been more able to take care of her personal life and her future than they had given her credit for, and the next morning a beaming Blair told the family at breakfast that Emma had agreed to become his wife.

'I think he means, that after much arm twisting, he has agreed to become my husband.'

'Gosh, Emma,' said young Jeremy as he moved his meatless sausage round and round his plate looking for a hole into which it might, with luck, disappear for ever, 'you must be strong if you can arm wrestle Uncle Blair.'

'She is indeed, young Jeremy,' said Blair, 'and now we must pray that this damn war ends quickly because Emma wants your daddy to give her away.'

'I have decided to come to Edinburgh. The war will soon be over and Simon will come back to look after Traviata. In the meantime his father says the cat can live with him. She has been there often with Simon and there are enough of his things there for her to recognize. Can we at least see one another occasionally?'

Ferelith had thought constantly about her decision since the night Angus had walked out. She had heard nothing personal from him and had seen him only once when he was on business in Glasgow. They had not spoken: he had nodded to her as he passed, no warmth at all in his stern face. Now she had decided to contact him, to see if there was to be any future for them. She had telephoned his house late at night and if he was surprised he had given nothing away.

Now he spoke to her. 'I can't believe you don't understand how difficult it would be for me to be in the same room with you remembering the last time we were together.'

'Of course I understand. I was there, remember. My feelings were the same. But I have to ask you if we still have a chance.'

'Oh, Ferelith, if it was anyone else I would think you were playing games with an old fool. You know how I feel about you. My God, I dream about having you . . . and I wake up and you're not there. But I can't sustain one of these terribly modern relationships or, if we are to believe what is said of our Victorian parents, these terribly old-fashioned relationships.'

'Could we meet on neutral territory, just to talk about my chances . . . of succeeding at the Bar?'

'On your own?'

She nodded and, even though he could not see her, he seemed to know. 'All right. I was to dine with my sister on Tuesday. I'll come through instead and we'll go out . . . immediately.'

She looked at herself in the mirror as she prepared for bed. She had lost weight she could ill afford to lose. Her skin seemed to have lost its glow and her hair was dull. Being unhappy in love did nothing for one's overall charm. But if he noticed when he arrived he said nothing. She took his coat and hung it up and then they sat on opposite sides of the room and tried to chat. Abruptly Angus stood up.

'Let's go out to dinner before I start eating that very charming lamp shade . . . or you, Miss Gallagher,' he said with a rather heavy attempt at humour. He held her coat for her and could not prevent his hands resting for a moment on her shoulders and at his touch she sighed.

I love this man: I want this man. Don't let me say the wrong thing.

They went to their favourite restaurant where they were welcomed as old and valued customers.

'The war can last only a few months' longer,' said Angus as they drank their after-dinner coffee, or whatever was masquerading under that name. 'Simon will be back soon, and Jamie, and life will get back to normal. Am I foolish to hope that you are going to change your mind about marriage?'

'Dear God, Angus, when I am with you I hear myself saying, "yes, tomorrow", but I can't Angus, not until I've had a little time at the Bar to prove myself.' She laughed drily. 'Once I know I'm good I won't care how much patronage I get.'

He grasped her hand so tightly that it hurt. 'Ferelith, I'm almost fifty. I always wanted children but until you I never met a woman whom I wanted to marry. I'll give up any rights to becoming a father, if you will only come back to Edinburgh with me now. I can get you a flat, a few cases and then you will be on your way.'

'But too many good advocates are in the forces, Angus. They're coming back and they'll want my cases . . .'

'And some of them will get them because they are men, and some because they are better.'

She accepted this. She had little or no experience. 'I have to be fulfilled as an advocate, Angus, and I have to know that I am where I am because of my ability, not because all the good male advocates my age were fighting a war or because everyone knew that my patron was the Lord Advocate. I want to get started and then, when the war is over, to fight for my career on equal terms. I don't want special treatment, just equality.'

'For God's sake, Ferelith, there will always be doubts. We all have them, men too. Are you in danger of becoming over-sensitive about this man versus woman thing?'

She looked at him sadly. 'I hope not, my darling, but if you will just give me a little more time to fight the male establishment on its own ground.'

'A little time? What is a little time? A month, a year, five years?'

'A year,' she said desperately. 'Give me a year.'

He drove her home to Simon's flat and Traviata. He kissed her gently on the lips. It could have been a kiss from little Jeremy so sexless was it.

'If you change your mind, telephone at any time, day or night, but I will never approach you again, Ferelith. I cannot drive from Edinburgh to Glasgow time after time with my heart pounding and then back again and again with my hopes blitzed. Come to Edinburgh and practise but this is goodbye.'

'Goodbye?'

'Yes. No one will be able to hint at nepotism, no one will say, oh she's only got where she is because of her lover, because her lover is bowing out.'

'Angus, no, wait.'

'Everything, Ferelith. I won't have a part-time wife. I've waited too long as it is.'

'You promised that I could still work.'

'You can, but every night or almost every night I want you in my bed which is where you belong. You think about it.'

'You're bullying me.'

'My darling, you have bullied me for years.' He turned and she could hear him running lightly down the stairs.

Mrs McGillivray, Simon's iron lady, had been an interested spectator. 'Well, and what is my Mr Osborne going to think when he comes back?' she said.

Not for the first time in the years she had lived in the flat Ferelith wanted to shout, 'Shut up, you horrid old trout', but she reminded herself that she was a brilliant advocate and trained to stifle her emotions. She stifled them successfully until the door was closed against the old woman's knowing face and then she fled to the safety of the bedroom and cried her eyes out.

Angus was a beast. No, she was. Angus was unreasonable. No, she was.

At last she fell into an exhausted sleep and woke

up next morning with a blinding headache and mascara all over Simon's silk bed cover.

A perfect reason for moving: she would have everything dry-cleaned for his return. She took a few days off and went into Edinburgh to see Oliver Belanger.

'Things are changing, Ferelith. Soon advocates will live anywhere, where there's hot and cold running water and telephone lines, of course. See your solicitors at Parliament House. It's merely a question of letting solicitors know you are here. After all, you are fully qualified. Take some free cases while you're waiting for some fees to come in: that way you will become known and, naturally, if I can help in any way . . .' He laughed as he saw her body tense. 'Touchy, touchy, no more than one would do for a young man, my dear. You really cannot fight the entire system, Ferelith. Save your energy for fighting for your clients rather than against the status quo. You'll get awfully bruised doing your Don Quixote impersonation. You did study Spanish didn't you?'

She nodded.

'Good. Facility with foreign languages, besides Latin, is going to be invaluable after this war. Now, go back to Glasgow when you have found a *pied-à-terre* and tie up all the knots. Let me know when to expect you and I will put the word around.'

She had to be grateful and to realize that she could not manage without someone's help. Being sponsored by Oliver Belanger was somehow more acceptable than being beholden to Angus to whom she wrote at great length to explain what she was doing. He wrote back from London where he was working. It was a letter that could have been written by one's former university professor.

The dying war monster is, like most monsters, even more bitter in defeat and has unleashed a secret weapon on London, a pilotless, jet-propelled aircraft that travels at an unheard of speed of 400 mph and which is capable of carrying a ton of high explosives. We call them doodlebugs. They have a strange horrifying tell-tale engine noise which scares everyone but what is more frightening is when everyone stands, panic stricken, listening for it to stop.

She telephoned. 'Can't you come home? It's safer here.'

'If I was a young strapping fellow, I'd be in Italy, or God help me, in the Far East. Try to think of it that way.'

And Ferelith, who had no one but herself to blame for the fact that she was not with him permanently, had to agree. Eventually though, he did return to Edinburgh where he found Ferelith furiously angry at the constant snide remarks of many solicitors.

'I don't know who told them that we were . . . friends, but I am so angry that many males seem to feel I'm getting some instructions because of you. Have you told any of your colleagues about me?'

'Of course I have. I'm not ashamed of being in love with you, Ferelith.'

Immediately she softened. 'And I'm not ashamed of being in love with you but for anyone to hint that cases come to me because of whom I know . . . it makes me want to scream. And I have had only two sets of instructions. I'm going to be in my dotage before I get anything decent.'

'Apply to become Advocate Depute. You won't make a great deal of money, and I know you want defence work, but do your bit for the Law and get yourself known at the same time. The word "patronage" will stop, believe me.'

'I know, but I saw doing my bit as coming later. I want to help people, to right wrongs, to make a stand for weaker members of society, women, children. Oh, God, I want to scream.'

'Go ahead. I had hoped that you might murmur tender endearments but if you need to scream or throw something, do so.'

She laughed and threw her arms around him. 'I don't care who comes in. I love you Angus Webster because you are, *sans doute*, the world's nicest man.'

He accepted the accolade graciously and then said, 'I had forgotten that you were a linguist.'

'Oliver said something like that a few months ago.'

'He's very Churchillian: foresees a United States of Europe, a European Court, Parliament.'

'Oliver is definitely in his dotage.'

On the 14th of February 1945, St Valentine's Day, the exquisite baroque and rococo architecture of Dresden, its Dutch and Flemish paintings, were all reduced to a pile of smoking rubble by a day and night of relentless bombardment, and in Fife Squadron Leader Blair Winterton married Mrs Emma Thomson. The bride was given away by the groom's cousin, Colonel Lord James Winterton, and was attended by the Honourable Constanza Winterton and Miss Ferelith Gallagher, the well-known advocate. The groom's man was the Honourable Jeremy Winterton. That the groom was in a wheelchair and the father of the bride on crutches was, at the groom's request, not reported in the newspapers.

Ferelith wept with happiness for Blair, for the peace and joy on his face, for the serenity emanating from Emma and with grief for herself.

I want Angus to look at me the way Blair is looking at Emma, she thaught. I want to look at Angus the way Emma is looking at Blair, and all I have to do is to pick up a telephone.

But she did not.

The war in Europe ended finally in May and Ferelith forgot her heartbreak and joined the millions of people all over the country who surged into the streets to welcome peace. At 3 p.m. she listened to the Prime Minister's broadcast. 'Advance Brittania. Long live the King.'

It was wonderful and like every other woman in the crowd she kissed complete strangers and shook hands with any hand that reached for her, but at midnight when the war officially ended she was completely alone wondering where Simon was and if he was even alive. Where was Pietro? Where were countless of others who had probably disappeared from the face of the earth with nothing to show their passing? 'No more, dear God, no more,' she prayed with Christians and Jews, Muslims and Buddhists, with everyone who was sane.

The blackout ended in July and almost a month later Japan surrendered unconditionally. The war, which had lasted almost six solid years, was over. It was time to change her career pattern again. The fighting men would soon be coming home. Advocates would be returning to the Bar. Would they receive preferential treatment? It did not matter. She would fight for her chances. Surely she was now well enough known to become a defending advocate. She decided to telephone Angus.

'I thought you would know, Miss Gallagher, but he has gone to London again. I think we know why, don't we?' she finished archly.

So it had come as she had always known it would. He was to be made Lord Advocate, Senior Law Officer for the whole of Scotland.

He'll be Lord Chancellor one day. I can't be married to the Lord Chancellor. What am I going to do? Ferelith's mind was in a turmoil.

'Shall I ask him to call, Miss Gallagher?'

'No, no thank you. It isn't important.'

The announcement of Angus's advancement was in all the papers the next day and Ferelith resigned from her office as Advocate Depute. She should have stayed in the post for some months but since, as an Advocate Depute, she was actually deputizing for *the* Advocate, in other words, Angus Webster, she was quietly allowed to return to her almost non-existent private practice.

She sent Angus a terse note to congratulate him but she did not telephone his office and he, in turn, did not try to contact her.

'He's too busy,' she consoled herself. 'And my note was hardly flowery. When things settle down . . .'

She defended a man who was accused of injuring his milkman by hitting him in the face with the milk bottle he had just been handed. The milkman said the defendant had been building up to it, never happy with where the bottles were put on the step, always complaining about the noise they made being set down.

'He jist went crazy and hit me wi' them.'

Ferelith was deeply sorry for the milkman who had had his nose broken but she was able to prove that her client had hit his milkman in the course of an epileptic seizure. It had been an involuntary movement, and he was not, therefore, responsible for his actions.

Her next case also involved the subtle difference between what the Law termed 'wicked reckless-ness to consequences' and 'involuntary action'. Her client, Joe Butcher, was accused of wilfully and maliciously wounding a man who had tried to rob the till in his small garage. Joe had been working on a car at 2 a.m. when he had become aware that someone was creeping up behind him. He had swung round, with the spanner he had been using in his hand and had hit the housebreaker with it, fracturing his jaw. The prosecution claimed that Joe had no right to take the Law into his own hands and that the force behind the blow was excessive and therefore wickedly reckless. Ferelith maintained that Joe, a man wounded in the defence of his country and now working all out at all hours to keep his family fed and his business in the black, had acted by instinct, almost unaware that he had a spanner in his hand, when he had hit out at the person who had set out to rob him of what little money he had earned that day. The jury of fifteen men agreed with her. Joe Butcher was found 'Not Guilty'.

'Yer a star, Mrs,' said Joe as he left the Court. 'Onything needs doin' in yer car, you jist leave it tae me.'

She wanted to share her triumphs with Angus, to tell him that although she had no car, she had her own personal mechanic, but he did not approach her and she could not approach him.

And then one day, Simon turned up at the Court of Session in Edinburgh. He was in uniform and was thinner than ever but he was still the same Simon.

'Hello, sweetness,' he said, 'what a dreadful class of person you are defending. Can't you get a nice corporate swindle where everybody goes to the opera after their day in Court?'

She could not speak. She looked at him, at the lines etched into his face, at the scar – why had he never told them he had been hurt? – running down his cheek.

'Simon,' she breathed, 'oh my dearest Simon,' and she threw her arms around him and hugged him to her as if she would never let him go.

They stood there holding one another, laughing, talking. At last the war was over. Simon was home in one piece. Only Pietro to worry about still. Ferelith hugged Simon, again unaware of the man who had just entered the Great Hall from the courtrooms. Simon saw him as he looked up from Ferelith's shoulder.

It was the Lord Advocate. His face was a picture of anguish and acceptance, and yes, of unbelievable hurt. He moved across the polished floor to the library and left the Hall quickly, the doors swinging furiously and then quite gently behind him.

Simon pushed Ferelith violently from him. She looked at him in stunned surprise.

'Run like hell, Ferelith. That was Angus,' he said.

She looked at the swinging doors. 'Angus?' she questioned again.

'Don't think, just act, for God's sake, Ferelith, for once just do.'

She reached up and touched him very gently on his scarred face and then she turned and ran from the room. She pushed past several eminent men who were not used to being so rudely handled, and by a member of the gentler and weaker sex at that.

'Angus,' she screamed. 'Angus.'

The word fled before her as she ran down the stairs, her leather shoes beating out a tattoo on the marble stairs. The sound was so full of a primeval anguish that at the door, a servant of the crown, who would never normally have been so bold, put out his hand and stopped the way of the Lord Advocate of all Scotland.

'The lady, my Lord,' he said anxiously. 'It's Miss Gallagher.'

Angus made as if to push past him and then he turned, looked up, and saw her resting at a bend in the grand staircase, her hand holding her aching side, her breath coming in short gasps. There was no more room, for either of them, for the sin of pride.

'Angus, oh, Angus my darling, it was Simon.'

She held out her arms and Lord Webster of Dalmarnock, Lord Advocate, ran up the stairs and, to the obvious delight of several advocates, solicitors, policemen, court officials and, no doubt, several petty and not so petty criminals, stopped her explanations with his lips.

'I am so tired, Miss Gallagher,' he said, 'I am so tired of finding you wrapped around various young men,' and then to the accompaniment of hearty cheers, he kissed her fiercely again.

When she could breathe Ferelith looked up. 'Angus Webster,' she said humbly, 'please will you marry me?'

'With so many witnesses to your discomfiture should I say no, Miss Gallagher,' he said smiling down at her in a way that made her heart behave as it had never ever done, even in the giddy happy days of youth, 'how can I say no?'

There was a second enormous cheer but when
the Lord Advocate looked up from kissing his
fiancée, every legal head was looking firmly somewhere else.

MISS FERELITH GALLAGHER and Lord Webster of Dalmarnock were married quietly, at least as quietly as they were allowed to be married, in December 1945. Blair gave his half-sister away and the bridal couple were surrounded by children of all ages. Ferelith kept her promise to Maria's daughters, and Constanza Winterton too was a bridesmaid, Domenico was the ring bearer and Jeremy an extremely officious and efficient usher. The service was conducted by a Catholic Priest. The couple stood in the aisle near the front of the small chapel and not on the altar, because Angus was a Presbyterian and had neither the intention of changing nor even any inclination to change his allegiance. After the wedding Lord and Lady Webster went to Italy, to the eternal city, Rome.

Ferelith wanted to find Pietro or at least to see how the war had treated the family.

Angus had hoped to see the fabled city of Venice.

'The Venetian Republic has rather an amazing history. I would quite like to see some of their ideas transmitted to the Scottish legal system.'

'Like incarcerating someone in a cell below the water line?' Ferelith teased.

'Have an immediate effect on lost memory. Can't you just see some of our worthies as the water rises . . . noo that ye . . . glug, glug, mention it, yer lordship, glug, glug, I dae kinda remember breaking intae that hoos, glug, glug.'

Ferelith laughed. 'I can't think that any other man

would contemplate looking for an old male friend of his wife on his honeymoon. You are very special, Angus Webster.'

'I know,' said Angus taking her into his arms, 'and I shall expect to be suitably rewarded.'

They decided to devote the first few days of their honeymoon to discovering one another and then, without calling, they would visit the *pensione*. It had rained almost non-stop since they arrived but the weather had not ruined their enjoyment of the city.

'This would have been miserable in Venice, darling. Don't you agree?'

Ferelith did not wait for an answer but looked out at the rain. A man, extremely handsome and well built walked quickly past the window. He saw as no threat to his masculinity the frilly pink parasol he held over his expensively-cut suit.

'I love Italians, don't you, Angus? I bet he's a judge: he's perfectly secure in his masculinity and so he picks up the only thing that's to hand when he steps out into the rain, possibly from his mistress's frilly little apartment. Can you imagine some of our legal friends with pink umbrellas? I shall buy one for you as a souvenir.'

'I'm not nearly secure enough in my masculinity to carry it. If, on the other hand, instead of going to look up the Angelosantis, we were to stay here in the hotel while you reassured me . . .'

Ferelith frowned at him in mock horror. 'Shame on you, Angus Webster. You have been married for five days and still all you can think of is . . .'

'Cappuccino,' said Angus to save the non-English speaking maid's possible blushes.

After their continental breakfast, which was more than adequate for Angus and not nearly enough for Ferelith, they stepped out, *sans* pink brolly but adequately protected by the big black umbrella, into the rain.

They were on the street that leads to St Peter's and although they had been in Rome for four days they had never yet toured the building.

'Let's see St Peter's first.'

'If you weren't a veritable tiger, Lady Webster . . .' Angus stopped and gazed down into his wife's wide green eyes. 'Dear God, how I love to hear that name. Lady Webster, Ferelith Webster, Mrs Webster.'

'You were saying?' Ferelith knew exactly what was going through his head and she loved it.

'I would say you were procrastinating.'

'No. I just feel that there is all the time in the world. Let's go to St Peter's. I need to buy a souvenir for Sister Anthony . . .'

'We should have brought her with us. Sister Anthony would have loved this . . . Sister Anthony said to look at that.'

They walked up the street and into the massive square that fronts the Vatican. They stood for a few minutes in the rain admiring the grandeur of the buildings and then went in.

'Can't you feel it?' Ferelith whispered.

'What?'

'Peace. Serenity. Holiness. It's tangible.'

'It's very dark.'

'Oh, Angus. Have you no soul? Just think of all the holy people who have worshipped in here for hundreds of years.'

They wandered around admiring the marble statues, the magnificent paintings, the signs that showed where St Paul's or St Patrick's Cathedral would have disappeared into the vastness that is St Peter's. Ferelith went to light candles at an

altar, an activity that Angus always found faintly
embarrassing, and a moment later Angus saw his
wife of five days being exuberantly hugged by a
man who had approached from the other side. She
was squealing not with fear but with pleasure and
was hugging her assailant as vigorously as she was
being hugged.

'You did say you loved Italians, Ferelith,' said
Angus drily.

She could not speak. Tears of joy were washing down her cheeks and she could not release
her hold of the young old man who seemed to
be having difficulty in letting go of her too. He
recovered first and stood up and held out his hand
to Angus.

'Pietro Angelosanti at your service, signor.'

'Angus Webster,' he said while his heart pounded
unpleasantly in his breast. 'I am Ferelith's husband.'

'Her husband? *Cara*, you have another husband.
Oh, I am so happy for you.'

Ferelith looked up at Angus and took pity on
him. 'Let's go outside. We can't talk here. We'll
have lunch. Pietro, we were actually on our way
to visit your family.'

'*Cara*. They will be overjoyed. I too, I am full of
happiness.' He looked at Angus and smiled and his
smile was that of a man a thousand years older than
Ferelith's husband. 'Signor, you are confuse. Come.
My home is near and my parents will be with great
happiness to see you. It is a time of great joy for my
family.'

They went outside and once more Ferelith and
Pietro looked at one another and hugged and
laughed and cried.

'Is this Italian or Catholic or what?' asked Angus,

who was feeling slightly jealous. Pietro had known Ferelith before he had known her and well enough to embrace her like a . . . a sister.

'Oh, Angus.' Ferelith threw aside the umbrella and almost danced in the rain. She was dizzy with relief that Pietro was not one more casualty of the war. She was married to Angus and she had found Pietro. She felt that she could touch her own happiness.

'Come, signor,' said Pietro. 'You have captured the bird of paradise. Be generous, for her heart is big enough to have a corner for me and I am no threat. Look, we will go to a trattoria until we have talked and then you must come to drink coffee with my parents.'

He took them to a small restaurant hidden from the street and they ate and drank and talked until late afternoon. At last Ferelith leaned back contentedly.

'We have told you everything about us, Pietro, *mi amico*, but you have told us nothing about your life, and I cannot begin to tell you how much your silence worried me these past few years.'

'Well, we were on the wrong side during this war, *cara*, but I could not write. I was a partisan, in the hills. It would not have been safe.'

'And your parents?'

'All well. Rome was spared, you know. Such a civilized war. "Oh, General, bomb that area but not that area and if you move this battle a few miles you will miss the great wine cellars. Don't mention it. You're welcome."'

'I can't believe it was so cold-blooded.'

'Your wife is still naive, Lord Webster, after two husbands and a legal career, she believes in human goodness.'

'Don't you, Pietro?' Tears had started into Ferelith's eyes. She could not bear to have her day spoiled.

'Of course I do, *cara mia*. And now will you come to visit my family? They will insist you stay for dinner, Angus.' He laughed at Angus's look of horror. 'That is all we do in Italy, signor. Eat and talk and make love . . . and music sometimes.' He turned to Ferelith. 'They speak of you often and with affection.'

Pietro smiled and went on, 'There is to be no debut, *cara*, and no great football career either. The war has changed my plans.'

'You're going to work with your parents? How wonderful. We'll come and stay. You'll love it, Angus.'

'Yes, come, Angus, and stay. I think you are almost an Italian, so much you like the food and the wine . . .'

'And Verdi,' smiled Angus, 'but I think there is more you wish to say if my wife would stop speaking for you.'

'You are definitely the right man for her, Angus. Once I thought it might be me but I will baptize the bambinos, no?'

'I hope so,' smiled Angus while Ferelith looked at Pietro with incredulity.

'Baptize? Oh, how wonderful. You're a priest?'

Pietro shook his head. 'I have been hiding in the hills for five years, Ferelith. After Christmas I start in the seminary and you will come back to Rome for my ordination, but now we must go.'

They went back in time to the hotel where the wounded Ferelith had hidden and where she had begun to feel alive again. Pietro's parents welcomed them enthusiastically, insisted that they stay for dinner, were furious that they had gone somewhere else for lunch and demanded to know why they were not staying in the family hotel. Angus used all the diplomacy that had taken him to his position to placate them. That night Ferelith cried all the way back to their hotel but they were tears of joy, and after she and Angus had made love she wept again and the tears were tears of peace and fulfilment.

'I never knew such a woman for crying,' said Angus. 'What do you do when you're unhappy?'

'Get angry and fight,' said Ferelith and kissed him again.

The next day Angus bought her one of a pair of glass candlesticks – 'so that we will come back for its mate' – and she bought him a frilly pink parasol which they carefully carried back to Edinburgh and put in an umbrella stand in their bedroom.

For the next five years Ferelith devoted her not inconsiderable energies to her marriage and to her work. She was blissfully happy, sometimes so happy in her personal life that she felt something had to go wrong. But nothing did. Angus kept to his promise. He did not mention other people's children and he did not peer into prams parked outside shops. Ferelith wrote often to Pietro and each time she did she remembered his offer to baptize her children and sometimes she felt that it might be nice to have a child.

But she did not. Because there always seemed to be just one more person who needed her help, just one more person who felt rightly or wrongly that 'a man wouldnae understand. They're no made the way we are'.

As well as her growing and lucrative private practice she offered her services to the solicitors who found advocates for those unable to pay. Scotland had had some kind of legal aid for the needy for nearly five centuries. It was a system of which Ferelith and her peers were justifiably proud. Legal aid was not usually available in criminal actions and sometimes Ferelith refused to take cases that she knew she would lose.

One such was the heartbreaking story of Martha McPhaill.

Ferelith read the account of the accident that had befallen the McPhaill children in the *Scotsman*. The children were part of a gang of children who constantly played in a quarry that was being worked by a local builder. There were fences around the quarry but they had not been maintained. Children and often adults bent on some purpose other than play had enlarged the holes in the fences until any small child could climb through into the working area. The huge machines that clawed at the sides of the hill during the working day stood silent and still at night but their very size made them dangerous. The children had been with a gang who had sat on one of the earthmovers that was itself on ground heavily undermined by last century's digging. Their game, their constant rocking and bouncing, had caused the machine to tilt and the already-weakened earth had caved in taking the machine and such children as could not jump off in time with it. The McPhaill children had been swallowed up by the quarry and it had taken the police and the fire brigade hours to find their bodies.

And now Ferelith's nightmare had come true. The mother of the children she did not want to represent sat in her office.

'It was the woman up our close. She said as how we could get some money.'

Ferelith looked at the woman sitting or, to be

accurate, crouching on the edge of the chair as if
she were afraid that her work- and life-stained coat
would sully the perfection of this advocate's office.
An attempt had obviously been made to remove
the worst of the stains and the outline of a hot iron
was visible on the almost threadbare material. The
shoes, which were scuffed and down-at-heel, had
been polished, as had the plastic, masquerading as
leather, handbag.

Ferelith sighed inwardly and her whole being
flooded with sympathy which she immediately banished. She said nothing and the woman went on.
Ferelith appeared to listen although she had already
heard it so many times before and had carefully
sorted out the gold from the dross. Unfortunately
there was mostly dross.

She could not take this case to court and that, as
Angus had taught her and the other students all
those years ago, was the main part of an advocate's
brief, knowing which cases to try and which to
abandon.

*Much of your work will be in staying out of court, not
rushing pell-mell in to it . . . Knowing what music to
play in particular circumstances is a large part of the
advocate's skill . . . he, or she, has to, shall we say,
appreciate, yes, appreciate the minor susceptibilities of
any given judge.*

But there was no point in taking this case any
further. The Law was quite clear. There was no
fault to find with the quarry owners.

'They shouldnae huv had them machines where
the bairns could get at them,' Mrs McPhaill went on
dejectedly. She had lost horribly two of her children
and she was trying desperately to blame somebody,
to make someone responsible, someone who could
perhaps give her – Mrs Thomson had said – as much

as £1000. 'It wouldnae bring the weans back but it might make the pain a little less for them that were left behind.'

Ferelith rose and her slender elegant figure in its beautifully-cut grey suit seemed to make Mrs McPhaill shrink even farther back into herself. Ferelith saw her withdraw and she sat again on her own side of the desk and folded her ringless hands, with their beautifully-manicured nails, on the blotter in front of her.

'Mrs McPhaill, I have read everything very carefully and I have listened to everyone. The children were trespassing . . .'

'They were weans, jist weans.'

'I know, but they had been warned repeatedly. There were huge notices all over the fences . . .'

She was interrupted again. 'There wis holes in the fences: they shoulda fixed their fences.'

'The Law does not demand that the owners maintain the fences on their own property, Mrs McPhaill. The machines were parked on their own land next to their quarry and there were notices all over the perimeters . . . the outside fences. Because of the heavy amount of trespassing that goes on in that area, the owners had repeatedly telephoned the local police, they had put a notice in the local newspaper . . .'

'My bairns dinnae . . . oh, God, missus, my bairns didnae read the papers.'

She began to sob loudly and horribly with her mouth open. Her nose was running and she did nothing to stop the flow. Ferelith looked around desperately and then handed her her own immaculate white-linen handkerchief with the discreet F embroidered in one corner. Mrs McPhaill snatched it but instead of wiping her eyes or her nose, she stuffed it into her open mouth and went on sobbing, now holding her frail body with both arms and rocking herself backwards and forwards. Ferelith rose and fetched her a glass of water. She steeled herself to remove the soggy linen from the woman's mucous-covered mouth and dropped it into the wastebasket.

'Drink this,' she ordered and Mrs McPhaill did as she was bid, noisily gulping the water and then wiping the back of her hand across her mouth.

'I'm dreadfully sorry, Mrs McPhaill, but there is nothing I can do.'

'Fucking bitch.' The venom with which the words were uttered disconcerted Ferelith and she started back from the hatred in the wild eyes that stared up at her.

'You've nae bairns huv ye?' She looked at Ferelith's hands again and saw no wedding ring. 'Naw, nae men's fancied ye, huv they, and that's why ye sit here in Buckingham fucking Palace telling the likes of me ah cannae get money for a deid bairn, twa deid bairns. Well their faither's ootside and he's no much but he'll comfort me fer your wickedness and whas gone tae comfort you, ye stuck-up bitch. Dae ye think ah cannae hear Glasgow under that posh voice? How dare ye tell me ah cannae get money for them. They said you was the best. They didnae tell us ye were a stuck-up bitch. Well, ah can get legal aid for another lawyer as clever as you, maybe wan wi a hert.'

She jumped up, pushed past Ferelith and rushed out of the office.

'I take it Mrs McPhaill was none too pleased?' Simon had come in as noiselessly as Mrs McPhaill had exited noisily.

'Oh don't Simon. I can't bear it. The poor woman

thinks if she goes round and round the offices she'll
find someone to take the case.'

'Well, she will, sweetness.'

'But not to win it. Poor woman, not to win it.'

He closed the door swiftly and reached her just as
her unsteady legs gave way and she threatened to
fall to the floor.

'Ferelith *mon ange*, my reputation should anyone
come in and find us in a clinch.'

She laughed as he had known she would and sat
up in her chair.

'I think a healing restorative. Come along, be a
good girl and Uncle Simon will take you to lunch.'

'I haven't time.' She gestured to the pile of files
on her desk.

He moved over and tipped them into the wastebasket on top of the handkerchief and she squawked
angrily and rescued them.

'Come and eat a nice big lunch, Ferelith, or I shall
bring my work in here and be dubiously sweet all
afternoon.'

'I've already had enough to bear today,' she said
and reached for her coat. 'I'm going home.'

'Home?' he asked, 'or home home?'

'Home home. I want Angus. I want his sense and
his calmness . . . and other things I won't bother
you with.'

'Doesn't bother me the teeniest bit, sweetness, but
Ferelith, have you counted the number of times you
have run home to daddy in the past few months?'

'If you call him that again . . .'

'Ferelith,' he interrupted. 'I would call him that if
he was thirty, never mind fifty: it's just a word. The
point is, you have to restrict your work.'

'I don't want to cut down.'

'You can't have a marriage where each half of the

couple spends most of its time in a different house, in a different city, for heaven's sake.'

'But the work I really care about is here.'

'Cases like Mrs McPhaill are everywhere, sweetness. You adore Uncle Charles but you can't abide smarmy George. I've had an idea. What would you think about my opening my own offices in Edinburgh, a kind of expansion of my father's office, and if anyone needs to make the ghastly journey from Edinburgh to Glasgow twice or three times a week, it will be me, with only my poor old Traviata to worry about?'

'The road will get better.'

'Just think, a hundred years ago we would have gone on the canal. Progress is slow but sure. In twenty years we will fly between the coasts but in the meantime, for the sake of your marriage and your sanity, restrict your practice. And you'll be nearer Blair and Emma,' he added as a final inducement.

'You'd actually move to Edinburgh to be with me?'

'I spent too many miserable years away from you already. Besides I want to be godfather to all your children when you get around to having them,' he finished lightly and wondered why she stiffened, but then he had never tried to understand her or any other woman.

Ferelith now had her own car as well as the mechanic to go with it, and she drove home to Edinburgh thinking about Mrs McPhaill and her hopeless struggle for compensation. How do you compensate anyone for the loss of a child? That made her think of Blair and his useless legs. He had asked for no compensation for his loss: he had borne it as the price he was prepared to pay to save democracy. He would have been prepared to pay with his life if that sacrifice had been asked of him. At least he had won Emma who had made her own sacrifices.

And now there was Simon who was prepared to give up his home so that she might be a little more comfortable. And what had he hinted at, perhaps unwittingly or unknowingly: that he might be a godfather to her children?

'Should I tell him that I do not intend to have children? Is that what I intend? I'm still only in my mid-thirties. Plenty of time, and meanwhile there are Mrs McPhaills out there. Almost time for us to hear from Maggie Sturrock again, or Jean or Elsie or . . . or . . . or.'

There was her home. The lights were on in every front room. Ferelith's heart leapt as she saw Angus, dear, kind, loving, gentle Angus standing in the doorway waiting for her.

FATHER PIETRO ANGELOSANTI was ordained in 1950, just in time to offer up his first Mass for a swift end to the conflict in Korea. Ferelith and Angus flew to Rome for the ordination, and Angus found the pomp and magnificence of the ceremony, combined with its innate simplicity and veneration, quite breathtaking.

'Perhaps it's the man-made glories of the Church, darling, or the magnificence of the music but I am quite overwhelmed.'

Ferelith thought of that solemn moment when the men presented for ordination had prostrated themselves on the floor before the altar. Their bodies had expressed acceptance of sacrifice but also whole-hearted belief in the existence of God. Their exulta-tion had been almost palpable: they were where they wanted to be after years of inner and outer struggle. She had felt like that to a smaller, but no less real, degree when she had married Angus. Again she felt the stirrings of conscience. Had she obeyed all her marriage vows? These young – yes, and some not so young – priests now being hugged and kissed and photographed by loving families had made solemn, binding vows that morning. Each one intended to keep them.

'It's a great privilege to have been here,' she whispered to Angus. 'It's so easy to believe in God in a setting like this.'

He looked down at her and smiled. 'God is just as present on the Scottish hills, or is that a dreadful thing for a good Scots Presbyterian to say in this centre of the Roman Catholic faith?'

She smiled but said nothing. How could she tell him that the ceremony had left her with a slight feeling of sadness, not for the priests who were going to keep their vows against almost insurmountable odds, but for the ones who would fail in small or large measure.

I'm getting old, she thought. It's not that I think that I haven't kept my own unspoken vows.

After two days spent trying to absorb a little of the glories of the city they flew back to Edinburgh and Ferelith drowned herself in her work.

She talked to Simon, now happily esconced with Traviata in a lovely flat near the Dean Bridge, and asked him to find her cases dealing with injustice to women. He knew of several, mainly dealing with evictions.

'It seems that certain landlords have taken advantage of the fact that men were at the Front and their womenfolk were at home unprotected. Some men didn't come back at all and not all were casualties of the war. The marriages were the casualties. Landlords are still letting houses run down, they're refusing to carry out proper repairs, they're putting rents up and they're evicting families who can't pay,' Simon said.

Ferelith stood up and walked to the windows that looked out on to the peace and urban tranquillity outside Simon's flat. The trees were wearing their glorious autumn colours. She could see the beauty of the room behind her reflected in the long Georgian windows. She would fight tooth and nail for this. Those women who had so much less had no weapons with which to fight.

She turned from the window decisively. 'Let's

take the bastards to Court. We'll swamp the Courts with cases. Judges will become very aware of this problem: they'll get fed up dealing with the same spivs all the time and maybe they'll lock some of them away. At the same time landlords who're a bit iffy will see that we mean business.'

There was no trouble in finding cases. The trouble was that there were not enough hours in the day to deal with them, but Ferelith and Simon worked day and night. Angus, if he worried that his wife was spreading herself too thin, said nothing, but supported her quietly with his love.

And then the threatening phone calls began. The number was unlisted but several times when Ferelith was alone, except for her daily help, in the house, the telephone would ring and she would pick it up expecting to hear the voice of a friend or a colleague and a harsh guttural voice would speak.

'Yer a bit too busy, Miss Gallagher. I suggest you tone down yer attitude a wee bitty or else. Do you understand me, Miss Gallagher, or will I need tae make myself clearer?'

'Who is this?' But the phone was dead and Ferelith would take herself to task for asking such a stupid question. Call yourself an advocate? He is going to tell you his name, isn't he?

She did not tell Angus until the windows were broken.

'I'm not backing off, Angus.'

'I wouldn't expect you to back off but we'll have to take better care of you.'

'Can you keep this out of the papers?'

Angus tried, but naturally, since Ferelith was the wife of the Lord Advocate, threatening phone calls and broken windows engendered a great deal of press coverage. Ferelith had the windows replaced

– twice – and tried to avoid photographers. She had worked very hard to remain, in her professional life, plain Ferelith Gallagher. It was very painful to see luridly headlined pictures of herself walking across the cobblestones between St Giles's Cathedral and the Law Courts in all the newspapers.

'So much for anonymity,' she said to Simon.

'It's good in a way, sweetness. Now they know they're taking on the big guns. A wee lady lawyer is easy meat: the wife of the Lord Advocate is not.'

'The wee lady lawyer will throw you right out on your *derrière* if you say anything like that again.' Ferelith glared at him. She should have known better.

'Ooh, I just love it when you talk French at me,' he leered at her, and left the room followed by a very heavy legal tome.

Angus was not so sanguine as Simon. Ferelith had been so distressed by her inability to help Mrs McPhaill receive compensation for the loss of her children that she had rushed straight into finding clients she could help. She cared nothing for the fact that her fight with slum landlords would bring her into direct battle with organized crime. Who really owned these slum properties? Angus had been a lawyer long enough to know that the names on the title deeds meant little. He was also quite sure that the people who were harassing Ferelith had always known that he was her husband and that the knowledge did not worry them. They believed themselves to be above the law. He could not ask Ferelith to restrict her campaign: he could only worry.

His worst moment came when she was accosted on the road right outside their house. She had been working late in the Advocates' Library and had taken a taxi home. The porch light was on to welcome her and she could even see the low light from Angus's study as she stooped to pick up the briefcase she had put on the ground while she had been paying her fare. The taxi drew away as she gathered up her things and turned to climb the stairs.

There was the sound of running feet and a heavy body cannoned into her, sending her and her briefcase flying, to land with painful abruptness on the stone steps. 'See this, fuckin' bitch: it's a knife,' snarled a low voice and then abruptly she was released.

A policeman had appeared from nowhere and Ferelith's assailant took to his heels and fled.

'Go after him, go after him,' Ferelith yelled as she scrambled around in the dark picking up her papers, but the constable stopped to help her up.

'He's well away, missus.'

'Did you get a good look? Where were you when he attacked me?' Ferelith was dreading the door opening and Angus appearing at the top of the stairs.

'I was checking some basement windows, Lady Webster.'

Later Ferelith, still considerably shaken, had tried to joke with Angus who had, as she had dreaded, heard their voices and came out to investigate. 'Checking basement windows: he was having a fag, more like.'

Angus looked at her white face and her pale shaking hands, now wearing his rings. Even upset and in pain she had put her rings on again as soon as she had been able to get to her bedroom. She was no longer Ferelith Gallagher, the advocate: she was his wife. 'Ferelith . . .' he began.

'Oh, I couldn't bare it if you told me to stop, Angus.'

'I wouldn't dream of it. You are quite right to fight but I reserve the right to worry and to do what any husband would do in the circumstances.'

'Angus Webster. How many husbands can provide a six-foot policeman outside the door? I don't want special treatment.'

'For God's sake, Ferelith. You are my wife. Am I supposed to sit back and not interfere because of your ridiculous notion that you fight all your own battles?'

'It's not ridiculous.'

'Who gave a certain editor an earful because he, so she said, treated the Lord Advocate unkindly?'

'That's different. You're my husband. You're not allowed by your position to fight back.' She saw that he was about to blow unpatchable holes in her defence and so retreated, wisely.

'Anyway, darling, all it needs is for some judge to put one of these rotten landlords behind bars for a considerable period and for more of the legal profession to back me.'

'That would help and that will happen but it's not so simple as that. You are sitting on a hornets' nest, Ferelith, and hornets mean business.'

'What do property owners plagued by hornets do, Angus?'

'Burn them out, I suppose.'

'Exactly. We shall burn them out and we'll start by redoubling our campaign to find out who really owns all these slum properties with creative tax accounting.'

Angus was not the only person worried about Ferelith's activities. His worries were, of course, wholly altruistic. The same could not be said for others in the legal fraternity.

'Women in the Law are bad news,' Matthew Robertson, a junior advocate, complained at a lunch eon where several senior advocates were also present. 'And this aggressive woman is bringing the wrong publicity to the office of Lord Advocate,' put in another.

'Move with the times, laddie,' said an older and wiser head. 'Women lawyers are part of the twentieth century whether you like it or not.'

'But even criminals don't accept them,' argued the first young man. 'Did you hear Jimmy Taylor in court today? "Mak shair the lassie gets this doon richt." He thought she was a clerk.'

'Jimmy Taylor is an illiterate oaf and totally unfit to clean her shoes. We should be applauding her work, not setting obstacles in her way. She's a damn fine advocate and has won most of her cases.'

'Cases she gets because of her husband,' a rather disgruntled and unsuccessful member of the Bar complained.

'Really? He sends her riffraff, the dregs of society, child molesters, wife beaters, and now these slum landlords? I would have thought he could guide some nice fat money-earners her way. He should encourage her to keep her hands clean and to work only with the huge corporations who cheat the Government and each other, but who are supposedly model citizens who appear at every benefit and give huge cheques to every conceivable charity.'

Since these were the only clients that several of the lawyers had some were ashamed and others annoyed.

'That was unnecessary. All crime is dirty; we all agree on that.'

'Let's make sure we do and let's make sure that we back our female colleague to the limit. It won't hurt us, you know. Remember that the Lord Advocate thinks the sun rises and sets on her head. Oliver Belanger is also rather fond of her. For a while there it was thought that he too had his eyes on the delectable Miss Gallagher.'

'Wasn't there some scandal in her past, some sexual hanky panky which one can easily believe in with looks like hers – all well hushed up, of course?'

But here the jealous young lawyer had gone too far.

'I wouldn't play with that one, laddie. It could be the end of your career.'

'Or hers,' thought Matthew Robertson, but he said nothing of this and set himself to placating his senior colleagues.

'I wonder what Shaw would have had to say about this one, Angus?' asked Ferelith one morning several months later as they sat in their lovely break-fast room, with the remains of a very hearty breakfast before them.

The great writer, who had died the previous November, would certainly have had some witty comment to make on the news item.

'Well, go on. Tell me,' said Angus. 'You have, as always, my undivided attention.'

'It seems,' said Ferelith folding her newspaper in a way that told him that she was incensed, 'that the great British public does not want to hear of momentous events like war or disaster from mere women. There are, therefore, to be no female news announcers on the wireless. There are to be no males with dialects either. I suppose *they* do know

the difference between a dialect and an accent?'
She moved her teapot, which was now empty, and
half-filled her cup with the coffee left in Angus's
coffeepot, a habit which had alternately delighted
and exasperated him now for nearly five years, and
went on, 'Were you asked if you would like bad
news served up over your bacon and eggs by a man
or a woman?'

'The question must have slipped by me: a busy
day, perhaps.'

'I never cease to be amazed at a man's inability to
deal with more than one thing at a time. That's what
happened, of course. They asked men who were
all doing something and therefore were unable to
decide rationally on the answer to the question.'

'What about the women who answered?'

'Mere feeble-minded little women were not asked
such an important question. Go to work, M'Lord,
and send lots of nasty men to jail.'

'Yes dear,' said the Lord Advocate meekly and
went upstairs to dress.

Left alone with his coffee Ferelith cleared a space
and took her diary out of the briefcase which sat
beside her chair. No court appearances today. A
meeting at 9 a.m. with Simon, a committee meeting
of the Edinburgh University Settlement Group at
11 a.m. and lunch with Maria di Rollo who was
coming through from Glasgow because she was,
she said, tired of waiting for Ferelith to visit her.
This, of course, was complete nonsense since Ferelith
was in Glasgow several times a month and saw the
di Rollos on most visits. After lunch with Maria
there was a meeting with Oliver Belanger who
wanted to lead her on a rather nasty rape case he
was defending. She would go from that to a cocktail
party at the City Chambers and then just maybe, she

and Angus could have a quiet dinner together. He
would be in London for the next few weeks and they
liked to stock up their memories of time together to
warm them when they were apart.

She had cleared away her personal mail by the
time Simon arrived. He was a happy man.

'The Fiscal said "yes", sweetness,' was how he
greeted her.

'Yahoo.' Ferelith threw her arms around him and
hugged his thin frame until he winced. 'How super.
I wish Angus was here, and I can't let him know
until that party for the Provost.'

'Rogers will probably be at that too – he's a big
contributor to Festival funds – so watch no one
spikes your drinks.'

'He won't come. Not even Tom Rogers has that
much brass neck.'

'As we speak,' said Simon looking around for
a clean coffee cup, 'lawyers and accountants are
doing incredible things to prove that he is not in
fact aware that he owns all those slums.'

For months Ferelith had been defending families
who had been sued for non-payment of rent and
she had been winning her cases. Slum landlords
were being persuaded to upgrade their properties
and to carry out running repairs. Evicted families
were being rehoused, either in council houses which
were springing up everywhere, or in privately
owned buildings, but the biggest problem for the
Law was to find the owners of the said properties. Lawyers waded through forests converted into
paper covered in legalese, trying to find the small
print that led to revealing the actual owners of the
properties. Address A would seem to be owned
by John Doe, who was in fact merely a front man
for X Industries, which were in turn owned by

L Enterprises, which were in turn found to be allied to an offshore firm called Lifeline Properties with a banking address in Jersey or Switzerland or even in one case, Brazil. Now the Procurator Fiscal had agreed that the creative accounting of one Tom Rogers, honoured business tycoon from Glasgow, could be investigated.

According to numerous reports in the press, Rogers knew nothing of L Enterprises and as for Lifeline Properties, he had never even heard of the company. Perhaps, he made bold enough to say, the Lord Advocate's wife should stay at home and have babies which would surely be a more suitable outlet for her undoubted talents than harassing a hardworking businessman who had devoted his working life to bettering the lot of his fellow man.

Ferelith, who had had several of these articles pointed out to her by *soi-disant* well-meaning friends, tried, in turn, not to let her personal animosity interfere with her investigation. She remembered Jane's conviction that marriage was a matter for the two people involved and no one else, and certainly not Tom Rogers, had the right to interfere.

Angus and I together decided not to have children, she consoled herself.

'It would be so nice to see someone like Rogers take the rap instead of the usual fall guys, Simon,' she said as Karen came in with a tray of fresh coffee.

'Don't hold your breath. His affairs are so convoluted that it will be impossible to unravel all the ends but I'm sure he was the one who told his underlings to lay off last winter.'

After the frightening incident on her very doorstep, Ferelith had been surprised that there were no further episodes. The anonymous caller had evidently decided that intimidation would get him nowhere and had stopped pestering Ferelith by telephone. Her windows had remained unbroken. No thug waited for her as she stepped from a taxi. By Christmas of 1950 she had begun to relax and now in the spring of '51 she hardly ever thought of the possibility of reprisals for her campaign against the slum landlords. It must have been obvious to the underworld that the judicial system was working and was backing Ferelith's efforts. One slum landlord had been convicted and was serving a prison sentence, and five more, whose abuses of their tenants were not quite so obscene, had been fined heavily and forced to modernize their properties.

Simon put another document on the table in front of her. 'The difficulty will be getting evidence gathered in the lead time given us.' He had gone on to another impending trial, and during the rest of their meeting they spoke no more about Tom Rogers and by the time she reached the City Chambers Ferelith had dismissed him completely from her mind.

She joined Angus, who had managed to get there before her, and they were having a discussion with several businessmen about the possibility of visits to the forthcoming Festival by both the Carl Rosa Opera Company and the Teatro San Carlo from Naples, when Rogers appeared. He had no compunction about joining the group around the advocate who would possibly be prosecuting him.

Angus withdrew from the group immediately, pleading a prior arrangement to speak with a newspaperman. Ferelith made as if to follow him.

'Oh, don't leave us, Lady Webster,' smiled Rogers. 'I know that you, like myself, have been deeply fond of grand opera for many years. We must persuade Travers here and Sir James, of course, to try for both companies. I've brought along a little cheque, Sir James, to help the Festival funds. What do you think, Lady Webster? Don't you agree that Edinburgh needs a purpose-built theatre? We should be doing some fund raising for a building fund. Maybe I'll start the ball rolling. You would love to see a new theatre especially built for large-scale productions of grand opera, wouldn't you, Travers?' He smiled at one of the men in the group who was known to be completely tone deaf, and who had admitted on more than one occasion that he thought sitting through any operatic performance should come under the heading of *cruel and unusual punishment*.

There was no way that Ferelith could leave the group without being rude and so she stayed talking and listening to the discussion for some time, admiring both Rogers's gall in trapping her and his obvious knowledge. She also felt sorry for poor Travers who, with the Director of the Festival Committee standing beside him, had had no choice but to agree that a new theatre would be a good thing.

Eventually she was able to make an excuse and she and Angus thanked the Provost for his hospitality and left the room. She was unaware of the look of venomous dislike thrown after her by Tom Rogers and she did not hear him ask a senior member of the Bar for Matthew Robertson's telephone number. She would not have been unduly concerned. She had little respect for Robertson's abilities, and no time at all for the man himself, but she had no reason to suspect that he actively disliked her.

In July a study told interested observers that women in Britain worked fifteen hours each working day and even more at the weekends. Ferelith, who was a perfect example of the study's findings, was too busy working to see the publicity on the findings or she would certainly have brought them to Simon's attention. She would not have told Angus, who was seriously disturbed by the amount of time his wife spent away from home.

'One might almost think you were unhappy at home,' he teased Ferelith on one of the rare occasions that found them curled up together on the same sofa reading and listening to music. Ferelith loved these times because they always ended in lovemaking. Classical music seemed to be a tremendous aphrodisiac: they always made love after concerts or operas, not after plays.

'I'm terribly unhappy,' she said, teasing him. 'Anyone can see that.'

'Then let's see what we can do to cheer you up,' said Angus, and did.

16

THERE WERE CASES that Ferelith took knowing that she was bound to lose. Losing is usually taken to mean that the advocate's client is found guilty and receives the full weight of the penalty of the Law. But if the client gets less than he might have received if he had been represented by another advocate, and perhaps less than he probably deserves, then the defending advocate can be taken as having won at least in a small measure.

Advocates do take cases where they know that their client is guilty and still they try to get them off. They also take cases where they know their clients are guilty and they do not want them to be found innocent but they believe very sincerely that everyone is entitled to a defence. Angus Webster and others like him had impressed this fact of the judicial system into Ferelith and her classmates. Everyone is entitled to a defence and to have someone represent him or her impartially.

One such case was the case of Harry Russell. Harry was one of the world's serious losers. Nothing had ever gone well for him. He had, like Ferelith herself, been brought up in an orphanage but his treatment there had not endeared authority to him or, it must be said, Harry to authority. After leaving school at the age of fourteen he had drifted in and out of prison for petty crimes and had spent the war years incarcerated for his part in an abortive bank robbery. Harry, it has to be said, was always the one left holding the baby – that is, the incriminating evidence.

In October of 1951 he was arrested for receiving and fencing stolen goods.

'Why on earth are you going to waste time on Harry Russell, Ferelith, with everything else we're doing just now?'

'Simon, come on, someone's got to help him.'

'He's guilty as hell. There isn't an honest bone in his body. Look at his record. Birching, birching, borstal, jail, jail, jail.'

'And jail again, I have no doubt, but that's not a record, that's a list of punishments, and doesn't it occur to you, Simon, that something goes drastically wrong with our penal system when it's dealing with the Harry Russells of this world?'

Simon poured himself another cup of coffee. 'Oh, spare me, Ferelith. He likes being dishonest.'

Ferelith held the sugar basin and watched with awe as he ladled sugar into his coffee. 'Perhaps he doesn't know how to be anything else, Simon. Has anyone ever taught him to be different, shown him that there is satisfaction in working for a living?'

Simon looked at her shrewdly. 'Are you all right, sweetness?'

'Yes, I am,' said Ferelith angrily. She knew exactly how Simon's mind was working. 'I'm sorry for Harry Russell. I don't think he's ever had a chance. I would like to represent him, maybe my high profile will encourage more people to think about reform. He needs rehabilitation, not punishment.'

Ferelith duly represented Harry Russell. She did not try to present him to the Court as an innocent man but eloquently tried to paint an honest picture of someone who had been born without a chance, and whose inherent weakness of character had led to his life of crime.

'But perhaps if he had been met by understanding, if he had been brought up to trust authority and not to fear it . . .' she began.

'Is my learned friend really trying to tell us that all children brought up in institutions are victims?' interrupted the Depute Procurator Fiscal. 'That they develop a propensity for crime? I'm sure you will agree, M'Lud, that that supposition is quite intriguing.'

Ferelith was furious with herself. She had laid herself open for such a silly remark. 'I am saying, as my learned friend well knows, that not all institutions have the highest standards. Not all guardians of orphaned children have the ability to spot potential. Children perhaps not academically talented' – poor Harry, everyone knew, was not the brightest of men – 'cannot possibly develop any potential they might have if their guardians are too pressured by sheer weight of numbers to give each and every developing child some individual attention.'

'I grows nice cabbages,' volunteered Harry, and was slapped down by the Judge for his impertinence in speaking out of turn.

Harry got three months penal servitude. 'Perhaps there will be a garden where you can develop your cabbage growing talents, Mr Russell,' said the Judge kindly as he sent him off to prison.

Ferelith was quite pleased with the result. She had felt sure that her client had been heading for at least six months and she thought too that the Judge's remarks about gardening might well be taken seriously.

On the 6th of January 1952, King George VI died and the Princess Elizabeth, a young wife and mother, became Queen.

'Another working mother,' said Ferelith to herself.

'If she can handle it, surely I should be able to do the same.'

'Poor girl,' said Angus as he watched the funeral procession, but why he was calling the slight figure in mourning a 'poor girl', Ferelith decided not to ask.

She was busy preparing a defence for a woman who had been accused by her employer of stealing a valuable piece of jewellery. Miss 'J' maintained that the jewellery had been given to her by her employer's husband in return for certain sexual favours, that her mistress knew this and was punishing her for her own husband's bad behaviour.

'I know what I did with Charlie, Mr Fairweather, wasn't right, Miss Gallagher, but he said he loved me and I couldn't resist him. I knew there wouldn't be a divorce – I mean nice people don't do that kind of thing – but I was sure he would take care of me.'

'Mr Fairweather denies both giving you the brooch and having a personal relationship with you.'

'Well he would, wouldn't he? She's the one with the money and he's terrified that she'll dump him.'

It was a sad, ugly story and not one of the three main protagonists came off well.

'I'll have to try to get Mrs Fairweather to drop the charges, Simon,' said Ferelith when she and Simon were discussing strategy. 'I think our client is telling the truth. He gave her the brooch, paid for with his wife's money – that's another example of creative accounting allowing one to believe what one wants. I paid for it. Ergo it is mine. Ergo, if she has it, she has stolen it.'

'Charlie sounds a right bastard.'

'Both women would be better off without him,' began Ferelith.

'Don't tell me a good Catholic is advocating divorce.'

'I'm not going down that path with you, Simon. Have you got the sales slip from the jeweller?'

He handed it over. 'Fairweather paid for it with cash. Didn't want his wife to see a cheque written for jewellery when she had not herself received it. He's a smart one.'

'But, of course it doesn't tell us who the piece was for and if we can't prove that we're nowhere with a defence. Mrs F asserts that her husband bought her the brooch and he says he did.'

'Their bed must be an uncomfortable place right now.'

'According to Miss J he was very rarely in his wife's bed: he was in hers.'

Together they peered at the newspaper photograph of Charles Fairweather.

'Hardly a Jimmy Stewart, is he?' said Simon.

'No, it amazes me that either woman fancies him, never mind both of them.'

Simon looked at her and laughed. 'Listen to us. Isn't it one of the wonders of the human personality that A appeals to B but not to C. I mean if we all fancied the same guy there'd be a right old mess.' He straightened up from the newspaper and looked at her ruefully. 'That isn't what I meant to say.'

Ferelith was saved from trying to find a suitable response by the strident ringing of the telephone. She picked up the receiver and Simon saw her face pale under her light make-up. 'I have nothing to say,' she said with as firm a voice as she could muster and hung up.

She almost fell into the chair beside the table. 'Simon, try to get Angus for me, please.'

Simon wasted no time in asking her questions but

proceeded to ring the Lord Advocate's office. Angus was unavailable. Just as Simon hung up, the telephone rang again and this time Simon answered it.

'Tom Hardy. *The News*. Could Lady Webster confirm or deny this story for us, Mr Osborne. We have been told that there is evidence to prove that Lady Webster entered into an incestuous relationship with her brother while they were at university together in the early thirties.'

'I have known Lady Webster since the thirties and there is absolutely no truth in this scandalous tale. We will make a statement later,' said Simon and hung up.

'Oh God, Simon. Who . . . ?'

'Rogers obviously, sweetness. He knows he's going to jail but he'll make you and Angus as miserable as he is going to be.'

Ferelith started up from the chair. 'Blair,' she cried. 'He's had a dreadful year, Simon. I must let Emma know so that she can shield him, if possible, and . . . there's Jamie and Jane and Angus. This horrible mistake will cost all the people I love.'

Angus was the next person to telephone. He had also been approached by a newspaperman. 'Don't worry, darling, and don't panic. The tabloids will have fun with it and your tragedy will make a few people gloat for a while but the decent papers will print the story accurately and you'll get a sympathy vote. Poor old Blair will be the main sufferer. You know how he hates figuring as the wounded hero, and now this.'

'Is there any way we can suppress it, Angus, for Blair's sake? His lungs have been so bad this year and I can't bear to cause him any more distress.'

'Ferelith, you did not knowingly enter an incestuous relationship with your half-brother. It was the most appalling and heartbreaking tragedy and I could kill Rogers. He's at the bottom of this: I can smell him, but we are not going to let him beat us. Now, I am not coming home. There is no need for me to fly to your side before the end of my working day: that will look as if we have something to hide. You go ahead with your own work and my office will issue a statement to responsible newspapers.'

More than anything Ferelith wanted to feel her husband's comforting arms around her. Even after six years she was surprised by the intensity of her feelings for him, her need for him, but she knew that it would be wrong for Angus to come home. Still, she felt that she could not face the blaze of publicity on her own. She would cancel all her engagements.

'And they'll wait until tomorrow or the next day or the next, sweetness. Chin up. Ring Emma and warn her and I'll get in touch with the Wintertons, but then we are going out together, as usual, and you are going to do a good day's work.'

Ferelith spoke at length to her brother and her sister-in-law and then went upstairs to put on her wedding ring. She never wore it during a working day but today she felt she needed to feel some contact with her husband. She looked out of the windows of the second-floor library and wilted. Already the street was full of newspapermen.

Well, get it over with, Ferelith, she thought to herself. Maybe Sister Anthony was wrong and mud thrown doesn't really stick. Eventually it can all be washed off. And in the meantime there are people depending on you to help them. Would their cases be helped by the notoriety of their advocate?

The worst headline was even worse than Ferelith had foreseen.

WAR HERO SEDUCES OWN SISTER

That came with some nice pictures of a very young
Blair and a rather stiff graduation picture of her.
On the same page was a picture of Blair in his
wheelchair at Buckingham Palace and several shots
of her with Angus.

'They'll wonder what he saw in me, looking
at that graduation picture,' she said and wanted
desperately to break down in tears, but she tried
to smile at Angus who was suffering quietly but
deeply, not for himself but for her. She could see
the muscles in his jaw working, a sure sign that a
usually quiet man was very angry.

'We will issue no further statements, darling.
Everything has been explained simply, without hysteria. You and Blair were caught up in a tragedy, not
of your own making. That, of course, is usually the
way of tragedies. It's the innocent who suffer.'

Ferelith looked at the newspaper before her which
had a picture of Jane taking Constanza to a children's
party. Dirty tentacles were even creeping out to
touch that lovely child. Furiously Ferelith crumpled
up the paper and threw it into the fireplace. She
watched it unfold in its deaththrows and saw little
Constanza's face disappear in a burst of flame.

'And all because Helena Winterton wouldn't join
her husband in India,' she said.

'You can't know that, darling, but if it's true then
I'm glad that she didn't go because you are here.'
He reached out and pulled her down onto his lap.
'I waited a long time for you, Mrs Webster, and I
cannot begin to tell you what you mean to me.'

'Try,' she said, and he did.

There were other appalling headlines.

PROMINENT ADVOCATE AND BROTHER IN LOVE TRYST.
LORD ADVOCATE'S WIFE IN LOVE AFFAIR WITH BROTHER

These were the ones that really hurt and annoyed
Ferelith, especially when it was hinted that Angus
should resign. Some colleagues advised Ferelith to
withdraw from the public view for a while but she,
Angus and the members of their family besmirched
by the scandal, went gamely on behaving decently
and trying to return some decency to the lives
of those around them. She refused to give any
interviews.

'It's a classic damned if you do and damned if
you don't scenario,' said Angus, 'but although I
hate every moment of this, for your sake, Ferelith,
I think we are better to ride out the storm.'

'You must feel awful,' Ferelith said and tried
to smile.

'Of course I do. Why do you . . .'

'It's all your clichés, darling.'

'That's why they got to be clichéd: sometimes
they're the only words that work. Now come on,
business and life as usual.'

Ferelith managed to get the Fairweathers to drop
the charge against Miss J and she also persuaded
Mrs Fairweather to give her erstwhile employee a
decent if not glowing testimonial and a little nest
egg to tide her over until she could find a new job.

'Told you Fairweather was guilty as hell, Simon.
He and his wife deserve one another.'

'Frankly, I wouldn't put any one of the three on
my visiting list.'

'But you're such a snob,' laughed Ferelith.

'Someone has spent a great deal of money digging
up the past, Simon.'

Ferelith and Simon were taking a much-needed break from work and were having lunch together down at Gullane. When her mind was too full of her own and other people's trials and tribulations, Ferelith found that a brisk walk along a windy and, preferably, deserted beach was the best antidote. Simon had waited, snug and warm, in the lovely drawing room of their favourite hotel. He had made a point, after the war, of never getting wet unless he was in his bath and therefore he preferred to sit watching his old friend fight the wind, from the security of four tastefully-decorated walls. The fact that the hotel boasted an internationally acclaimed chef was an added inducement.

Now Ferelith came in, her hair wind-blown, her cheeks as pink as he had ever seen them. She looked, he thought, about twenty years old, but with an added serenity since her marriage that was extremely attractive. She smiled at him.

'There's nothing like a sea breeze for blowing away problems.'

He shivered. 'That's more a gale. Why didn't Angus come? I always feel he's a bit Spartan too: lots of ghastly vitamins washed down by exercise.'

She sat down beside him. 'I love you dearly, Simon, but if you think for one moment that you would be here if Angus was available . . .'

'Nasty,' he said and leered at her. 'It wasn't your undoubted charms that brought me galloping down here, sweetness.'

'I know. The chef. Well, let's order because I'm starving.'

'I do adore women who admit to enjoying their food but I must confess to believing that half the time you have no idea what you are putting in your mouth.'

'True, but today, I want to enjoy everything. No nasty snide remarks in this morning's papers: no letters saying, "Stuck-up hussy, nae better than me". Who helped him, Simon, if it was Rogers?'

'Your annulment is on record and you have to admit that even though you had no idea that you were brother and sister, your one-day marriage does make juicy reading. Decent people are heartily sorry for both of you and I think decent people make up the majority.'

'Oh yes, can you believe I even had a letter from Harry Russell to my office. It's barely literate but he says he knows I'm a decent woman and that he'll come and do the garden for me when he gets out of clink.'

'Great, your gardener with a checkered past can keep your mechanic, with a less than salubrious past, company.'

'Not if he only grows cabbages. Have you any idea how many cabbages are consumed in orphanages? Still, to be serious, we have had lots of supportive mail. Blair too.'

'How is he?'

'Remarkably well. He was like Angus, just dying to get out there and slay a few dragons, but he's calmed down and dear Emma has been so brave and supportive. It was a particularly nasty thing to do to us, Simon. Apart from Rogers, I really would like to know who hates me that much.'

Simon said nothing. He had an idea that certain disgruntled and unsuccessful members of their profession had been delighted to see Ferelith Gallagher's name being dragged through mud and would have been only too happy to see her retire.

'I'll never give up, Simon,' she said as if she could read his thoughts. 'I may never be the first female

Lord Advocate but I'll certainly be putting my good name forward for every advancement possible. I've worked too hard to be scared off by the Tom Rogers of this world.'

Brave words but sometimes Ferelith found herself thinking that it would be quite nice to have a good reason for staying at home out of the spotlight. What better reason than a child? Would having a baby not be the perfect fulfilment of her love and passion for Angus and his for her? No. Having a baby as an excuse for staying at home was no good reason.

I don't want a child, Ferelith told herself night after night as she lay beside her sleeping husband. Young people should have children. Angus and I are both too old, too set in our ways. I don't need a child. I need only Angus and I want all his love: I don't want to share him with anyone.

The love of a child adds a new depth to married love.

I can't give up my work. I just plain love being an advocate and I want to succeed. A child would get in the way. I wouldn't be a good mother. I have no experience.

Night after night Ferelith argued with herself and then punched her pillow irritably and went to sleep.

The scandal of 1952 went the way of all other scandals. By November no photographer was sufficiently interested in Lord and Lady Webster to photograph them as they went to Sadler's Wells to hear the new soprano sensation, Maria Callas, sing Bellini's *Norma*. After the performance they went to their favourite London hotel for a romantic late supper and to discuss the evening.

'How can you say she's wonderful, Angus? The top notes in that Casta Diva aria were so shrill they hurt my ears.'

'You have no musical soul, Ferelith.'

'I have no hearing either after that. I'll give you her dramatic power, darling, but nothing beats a decent tenor.'

'We'll have to agree to differ on that. I'm not going to fight about it when there are so many other nice things we could be discussing.'

'Like this Bentley-Craig case. I am so glad you don't have that to prosecute.'

'Would you want to defend them?'

Ferelith thought about what she knew about the notorious case that was gripping the public. Christopher Craig, aged sixteen, and Derek Bentley, nineteen, were accused of shooting a policeman.

'I think I would do everything I could to make sure Bentley doesn't receive a death sentence.'

'The Law states that everyone involved in a murder is responsible.'

'So you wouldn't mind prosecuting them?'

'Every prosecutor has to face uncomfortable decisions, Ferelith: every judge, every barrister. You know that. We don't do the job because it's pleasant. We do it because we believe in law and order. The policeman is dead. Nothing can change that.'

'But Bentley didn't shoot him.'

'He was heard to say, "Let him have it."'

'Isn't it possible he meant, let him have the gun?'

'Of course it's possible, but surely one would say, "Give him the gun, Chris," not, "Let him have it."'

'I think I'd rather talk about Maria Callas's top notes. Let's just enjoy our few days, darling. No law, nothing nasty.' She bent her head to concentrate on her lobster salad and it was some time before either looked up. The waiter refilled Ferelith's glass and as she looked at her husband over the top of it, she groaned. 'Oh no, it's impossible. You'll never guess who has just walked in – but it can't be him. He's in jail.'

'I can't turn around in a restaurant and stare.'

'A man has just come in with several friends and he looks just like . . .'

'Rogers,' interrupted Angus. 'He won his appeal, darling. I'm sorry. I didn't want to spoil our weekend by telling you.'

'Has he deliberately followed us to London?'

'That's paranoia, Ferelith. Come on. We'll go back to the hotel and have coffee and brandy in our suite and you can try convincing me about tenors.'

But the lovely weekend was ruined and the Websters left early next morning for Edinburgh and their never-ending workload.

1952 had also brought Ferelith an ever-growing list of juvenile crime.

'Would you wallop a child if you had one, Simon?' she asked one day. It was the kind of leading question she felt that she could not ask Angus.

'Depends, and depends what you mean by wallop. I don't think a good smack ever hurt anyone. Gets the message across, short and sharp. Why?'

'I'm getting so many of these vandalism things and I'm finding the attitude of the parents in some cases almost extraordinary. Do you know I have never represented a child who causes any trouble at all at home. Good as gold, helps Mum with the dishes and then goes out and breaks every window in every car in the street. Old Oliver thinks just bringing the little darlings into Court is enough punishment but I think all a court appearance does is fill them with curiosity. There's certainly no fear there.'

'You hankering back to the good old forties and the birch?'

'I see the same little blighters time after time now, Simon. A few years ago, one crime one punishment, and we rarely saw the same faces in the juvenile court. Look at this now. Four boys, all, according to their mums, "good as gold at home, he is", all nine or ten and all deliberately breaking car windows. What do you think would happen if the punishment was that Mum and Dad had to make good the damage?'

'Most of them couldn't afford it, so we're back at square one.'

'Well, something had better be done or we're heading for a great deal of trouble. Tell these mums, politely of course, that I wouldn't touch their boys' defence but this one now . . .' She handed Simon a brief.

'You're out of your tree. They're as guilty as this little lot.'

Ferelith paraphrased for him. 'Robin Hood and his merry men, robbing the rich, in this case the local poultry farm, but who are the poor in this case, Simon? Little Robin Hood, aged all of twelve says he stole the chickens. Why? How many chickens did he and his merry men rustle . . . ? Seven. Whose mum is going to cook seven hens? No, these were stolen to order and what we need to get is not these little villains but the person who is buying their chickens. I'll have a word with the Advocate Depute: we'll see if we can get them off with a caution and then we'll watch them like hawks.'

The Lord Advocate's wife did have power. The boys, obviously guilty, were cautioned and released and over the next few months leading up to Christmas it was found that they were spending quite a bit of time talking to a butcher in one of the better areas of the city.

A few days before Christmas they were followed as they made their laborious way to the butcher's shop. It is, after all, very difficult to carry four geese, five ducks, and two hens – the hens' keeper had already lost most of his flock in a previous raid – when you and your companions are only twelve years old.

Police Constable Christie arrested Mr Andrews, the butcher, when he saw him passing coin of the realm to the boys in exchange for the stolen poultry. Mr Andrews was further said to have been heard to declare the scheme 'a nice little earner' which is obviously what Robin Hood and his now not so merry men had also thought.

Lord Whitfield sentenced the boys to three months each in a Remand Home and Mr Andrews received six months at Her Majesty's pleasure for receiving stolen goods.

'I'd like to have been able to prove he actively encouraged them to steal, Angus,' she told her husband over dinner that same night. 'But it was his word against our little folk heroes'.'

'Perhaps he was telling the truth,' said Angus. 'After all, young Robin could easily have suggested the whole thing.'

Ferelith looked at him demurely over the rim of her coffee cup. 'Oh, no, darling, his mum said he was as good as gold in the house.'

A NEW ELIZABETHAN age was ushered in with incredible pomp and circumstance on the 2nd of June 1953, a day that Ferelith spent trying to save a woman caught shoplifting from going to prison. She did not succeeed. Her client had failed to mention to Simon, the instructing solicitor, that she had a suspended sentence already for failure to pay fines. Ferelith knew that her client had previously passed through the usual sequence – conditional discharges, probation orders but no one had told her of the suspended sentence and the Judge felt that he had no alternative but to impose a custodial sentence.

'Poverty is such a bloody trap, Simon,' she despaired.

'Lots of poor women don't steal, sweetness.'

'Oh, don't be so bloody patronizing.'

'Ferelith Gallagher, I never cease to be amazed at the language of so-called good Catholics when they are not getting their own way. She should have told us and we could have worked something out.'

'But why didn't she tell us? She couldn't make herself believe that she might go to prison. She stole because she's poor and she couldn't pay the fine because she's poor and now she's in jail because she's poor. I really loathe my job sometimes. What happens to the children?'

'There is a decent granny in this instance, who'll keep them for her.'

'And how old is granny?'

Simon looked around to see what there was to hand that his favourite advocate might throw at him. 'Granny is forty.' He did not need to remind Lady Webster of her own age.

She was only too aware of the fact that in a few short months she would be forty years old, the same age as the granny who was now bravely looking after her oldest daughter's children while that daughter was in prison.

'You'll be a Q.C. before you're forty, darling,' said Angus one night at dinner. 'You can pick up the baton of Dame Margaret Kydd and you can carry it farther, into even higher office.'

Ferelith had raised her wine glass and toasted him. 'And you'll be Lord Chancellor before then. Remember how we once talked of my taking silk before you became Lord Advocate and I haven't even got that far yet. But I would love to see you become Lord Chancellor: there's no one more able for the job.'

He had got up from the table and walked round to refill her glass. 'I'm not sure that I want that,' he said, putting his left hand with its broad, gold wedding band on her bare shoulder. 'It's important to me that you become a Q.C. but I really am quite happy with my career. There's nothing else in life that I want, except perhaps that you should be free of these whispers of nepotism.'

She put up her left hand to touch his hand that still rested very gently on her skin. The emeralds in her engagement ring caught fire from the candles and she watched them sparkle. 'We'll get them anyway, my angel.'

The pressure on her shoulder grew heavier for a moment and then he walked away from her to his own place. 'I want to protect you from everything, Ferelith, and I can't and that knowledge almost destroys me.'

'I was a law student when we met, and a lawyer when we married, Angus. I had already received everything nasty that life had to throw. Nothing that happens outside these four beautiful walls touches any essential part of me. All I want is for life to be as satisfying for you as it is for me.'

He said nothing but he smiled and toasted her again across the table, and Ferelith looked into his eyes and, not for the first time, wondered if she was being as truthful as she wanted to be. It was not satisfying for Angus. One thing was needed to make his life complete and he had never once asked for it.

His eyes were asking a question now and she answered by ringing the bell for Karen.

'I don't feel like coffee, darling.' She smiled at him. 'An early night?'

She rose and he got up and walked round the table to hold the door for her. Two minutes later Karen came up the stairs from the kitchen with the heavy silver tray she insisted on using to carry away dirty plates.

'I've got some lovely cheese,' she began before she realized that the room was empty. She lifted her head and looked at the ceiling above her head but she could hear nothing.

'I bet he was like Rhett Butler and just whisked her up the stairs. It was that dress, all that bare shoulder, just inflamed his passions,' she said, and then, since not even her fertile imagination could picture dull, quiet Angus Webster overcome by passion, she laughed and cleared the table.

Ferelith lay awake for hours after Angus's very

real and very satisfactory passion had died down
and he had fallen asleep. His head still rested against
her and she held him protectively as he slept. He was
in his late fifties. If it did not happen now, it should
never happen. But what would it do to her career?
The only person to be pleased immediately by her
decision, if indeed she made it, would be Father
Munro, the priest of the little parish church she
attended when they stayed with Blair and Emma.
Deliberate contraception was, according to Father
Munro, against the law of God.

The next morning, while she was still under the
softening influences of the previous night's thoughts
and desires and doubts, she made an appointment
with her gynaecologist.

After he had listened to her he examined her
thoroughly and pronounced her healthy. 'And as
for having a baby, some would say that you have
left it a bit late but if it doesn't happen now, Ferelith,
it shouldn't happen.'

'It's in God's hands,' she said mockingly.

'And Angus's. All I will say is that if the two
of you have a fairly regular sex life, save up for
a day or two to give his sperm a chance to build
up.'

'I'm going through to Ayr for a week.'

'Perfect. If there is anyone who will live like a
monk for seven days it will be Angus Webster.'

'This is a highly embarrassing conversation, Jim.'

'Good heavens. You're an advocate. Don't tell me
you haven't had fruity conversations about sex with
hundreds of clients.'

'The sex life being discussed wasn't my own.'

'Men in their eighties have fathered children,
Ferelith, and so it's unlikely that there will be a
problem. If you don't want to tell Angus, and that's

your decision, just be aware of your best chance for success.'

'I've left it so late that I might not conceive, Jim. If I tell Angus that I'm trying to get pregnant he'll be overjoyed and his distress if I don't will be just as powerful.'

She walked to her office feeling vulnerable for the first time since the early days after her first aborted marriage when she had half-prayed that she was pregnant and at the same time had prayed feverishly that she wasn't. She turned as if to go back to the doctor's office to ask him to put a coil back in.

I'm mad, she thought. I'm mad. I don't want a child. I'm almost forty. I'm too old. Angus is too old for disturbed nights and colic and teething and, oh God, toilet training. I went through all these arguments before and always decided that it was wrong to have a baby. I know Angus would love a child. I would love Angus's baby, my baby, wouldn't I, even when it got in the way of my career. Career? What a selfish woman I am. No, I'm not, I'm not. I told Angus I didn't want children. He agreed. And he's too old now.

Then she admitted to herself that, in all probability, Angus would adjust happily and that she was the one who would find the adjustment hard.

Too hard. It wouldn't be fair to a baby to have me for a mother. I want to be Lord Advocate. I do not want to be a mother and I can't be both. I can't be Lord Advocate either. The world isn't ready yet but a baby isn't my second prize. I don't want motherhood as a compensation. What have I done? It's not too late. I can have another coil fitted. Maybe I'm too old anyway. Maybe Angus is too old.

She blushed then in the street as she remembered how easily Angus had proved last night that he was not an old man but a man in his prime, a gentle man, a caring and considerate man who had never ever asked her for the one thing she withheld from him.

As usual she loved her time in circuit. Several times a year she travelled to conduct defences in various cities in Scotland. It was perfect when Angus too was in the same town but his position kept him more often in Edinburgh or London these days and she missed him dreadfully. In Ayr she stayed with her old friend from university days, Elspeth Baxter, who, with her husband, was a GP in the seaside community. They worked too hard all day, ate and drank too much each evening, and talked and talked and talked.

She said nothing when Elspeth told her that she and Michael had decided to have one more child, 'and even if it's another boy, we won't change our minds in a few years. Four is enough.'

'You said that about two and you said it ad nauseam about three.'

'Three is such an unsatisfactory number, don't you think?'

'Of children?' Ferelith asked drily.

'No. The numeral itself. It's so full of myth and legend. Three's a disappointment. The three witches in *Macbeth*.'

'You do realize that if it is a girl, you'll be all hot and bothered, terrified that the poor wee thing will feel all alone with all those big brothers and you'll decide she needs a sister, and you'll go on producing, trying to get your family all nicely symmetrical.'

'She can't produce without my help and four is *it*,' said Michael as he rose to offer them brandy.

'Thank God for that,' laughed Ferelith. 'No, not

for the brandy, for putting your foot down. We can't afford all these godchildren.'

'Just as well you two decided not to have any. Children are unbelievably expensive . . .'

Elspeth, her hands clasped protectively over her stomach, which was as flat as Ferelith had ever seen it, went on bemoaning the problems of parenthood. Ferelith switched off and sat comfortably on the couch, her bare feet comfortably tucked up under her and felt a ghostly fluttering in her womb.

I won't think about it, she thought. I won't think of the joy in Angus's eyes if I tell him one day that he is to be a father. And I won't pretend I'm tired when he wants to make love on Friday night when I get home because, whatever Jim says, I'm not going to cold-bloodedly save his seed for a big chance. '*Who is the patron saint of motherhood*? It has to be Mary, the Virgin Mary.'

'It's St Gerald, or is it St Jerome? I'm sure it's a man and a G or a J,' said Elspeth, and Ferelith laughed because she had asked her question out loud. It never occurred to Elspeth that Ferelith was asking the question for herself.

Despite her best intentions, she was as nervous as a new bride when she got home on Friday afternoon.

'You're jumpy, darling,' said Angus with concern. 'Too much chatting with Elspeth, I should think.'

'No, it was wonderful to be with them.'

'She's not a restful woman. I've never been sure what a dry old stick like Michael sees in her. Gosh, perhaps I'm the dry old stick. I'm ten years older than Michael.'

'Neither you nor Michael is dry or old. Michael is perhaps a little serious for his . . . gosh, he is a dry old stick, isn't he . . . but he's just right for Elspeth as you, Angus Webster, are right for me.'

He smiled. 'Shall we dine at La Dolce Vita tonight?'

La Dolce Vita had become his favourite restaurant because he said it reminded him of their honeymoon in Venice.

Ferelith thought quickly. She was tired. If they dined out, especially at the madly popular Italian restaurant, they would meet too many of their friends, eat too much food, drink too much wine.

'Hasn't Karen been looking after you?'

He looked a little guilty. 'Yes, and in fact I've already been to La Dolce this week. I took young Fiona' – a young solicitor in Simon's firm – 'on Wednesday night. We were both abandoned and she couldn't afford it on her own.'

Yes, he needed a child; it would save him collecting waifs and strays. 'We could stay at home then, darling. I'm sure I can find something, even spaghetti with a pesto sauce if you must have Italian.'

'Sounds great,' he said with alacrity. 'I'll open some chianti and I'll do some antipasto while you're making the pesto.'

Ferelith sighed and then smiled at his retreating back. She had meant to open a jar of pesto sauce. Now she was committed to measuring basil and pine nuts, garlic and oil, and grating parmesan. But it was worth it, and soon the heavenly smell of a really good Genoese pesto mixed with the aroma of prosciutto crudo, salami, and marinated artichoke hearts that Angus was arranging on a plate.

'We must go back to Venice, Ferelith,' he said as they sat at the table with the debris of the meal. 'Do

you remember that little place down the alley near
. . . oh, what was it near?'

'Santa Zaccharia.'

'You're wonderful,' he said and raised his wine
glass. 'Next summer?'

She did not immediately agree and he asked
again. 'Next year, darling, shall we try to go back? Of
course you know Italy so well and the world is full
of wonderful places and since the war, it's possible
to go anywhere. Goodness, how many times have
we said we must go to Paris. Unfinished business
in Paris, wasn't there, darling?'

'Yes, the Opera House. I couldn't afford it when
I was there.' Ferelith stood up. 'Let's clear away
for Karen, Angus. And yes, darling, I can think of
nothing I'd like better than to go back to Italy with
you. You still have to take me out in a gondola.'

She did not say next summer, she did not say, unless
I'm very busy, unless we are very busy, but he seemed
to be happy with her answer. Together they cleared
the table, rinsed the dishes and stacked them neatly
in the sink and then, their arms around one another,
they climbed the stairs to their bedroom.

By Christmas she had almost convinced herself that
she was no longer thinking about motherhood. She
was too busy: Angus was too busy. They were apart
a great deal and even though, when they were
together, everything was wonderful and very very
satisfactory, there was still no sign of a pregnancy.

'That's that,' she would say when she allowed the
thoughts to surface. 'Obviously I have left it too late
and really it's so much more sensible this way. How
could I possibly cope?' Quite happily, or at least with
resignation, she went back to the ever-increasing pile
of briefs.

In early December she had taken two days off to do some Christmas shopping in London while Angus was also there. She loved London for shopping and sightseeing, music and restaurants but did not look forward to moving there if Angus ever became Lord Chancellor. She kept those thoughts to herself.

The phone was ringing as she let herself into their Edinburgh house on Wednesday night.

'There's that bluidy phone again,' said Karen unnecessarily. 'It'll be Mr Osborne. He's been phoning every two minutes since yesterday.'

'Thank you, Karen.' She handed the housekeeper her briefcase and picked up the receiver trying to shrug herself out of her coat at the same time.

'Did it get into the London news?' It was Simon's voice. 'The Fiscal killed it up here, of course, but when he was found . . .'

'Simon, what are you talking about?'

'Maggie Sturrock. She knifed Bert.'

Ferelith stepped out of her shoes and sat down heavily in the chair by the telephone. Maggie. How long had she known Maggie Sturrock? Almost all her life, it seemed. 'Go on,' was all she said.

'The usual story of course. He beat her up yet again: all the neighbours testify that he was in grand form. Wee Charlie tried to hold him off, deflect his arm or something and he went for him. The boy said his dad was throttling him – his throat is heavily bruised – and Maggie went berserk, ran into the kitchen, picked up a knife and stabbed him . . . about thirty times.'

Ferelith felt sick and, for a moment, could say nothing.

'Are you all right, Ferelith?'

'Poor Maggie.'

'She wants us, you really. I'll find out when we can see her.'

'Fine.'

His voice was concerned: there was none of his affected femininity. 'Are you all right, sweetness? Is Angus at home?'

'Yes, I'm fine, just desperately sorry for the Maggie Sturrocks of this world, and no, Angus has one more day in London.'

'Rather him than me. Have a good stiff drink and I'll see you tomorrow.'

He rang off and Ferelith went into the kitchen where Karen was getting ready to prepare a meal.

'Don't worry about me, Karen. I had dinner with Lord Webster before I left. I'll have some cocoa and go to bed.'

She sat at the table and sipped the hot sweet drink from a cheery pottery mug she had bought in Italy. Had Angus been at home he would have realized, by her use of this old favourite, just how desperately upset she was.

Simon and Ferelith had been dealing with the tribulations of Maggie Sturrock almost since before they had qualified. Maggie had attended Dominic's cooking class at the University Settlement and Ferelith had first met her there. She had always been impressed by her courage and her willingness to try to better her lot in life. Unfortunately for Maggie, Ferelith thought, she had married Bert Sturrock because she was expecting his child and had lived with his violent abuse of her body, her mind, and her soul, ever since.

And God dammit, she thinks she deserves his abuse. Why? Because he had no respect for her because she had given in to his demands for sex 'to prove that you love me'. Dear God, do the Bert

Sturrocks of this world understand anything at all about love?

A more important question was whether or not the Prosecuting Advocate and the Judge and Jury really understood anything about domestic violence. Too often the police failed to act in cases that were labelled 'domestic'. There were firmly entrenched attitudes in society about the roles of men and women. Ferelith knew that if she were to ask ten advocates if they agreed that men had the right to beat up their wives and children most would say 'no'. But in Court it would soon be obvious that too many men felt that what happened within the four walls of a home was a matter for the people living there. Too many platitudes about such things as the 'sanctity of marriage' were mouthed daily. Men were often released with no more than a severe dressing-down from the duty sergeant. This had been the case quite often in the battles between Maggie and her violent husband.

'She asked for it,' was a perfectly adequate defence and several times Maggie had been told not to nag Bert about his drinking.

'If I leave him, Miss Gallagher, what aboot my weans? I cannae take them because there is naewhere fer me to go. Where could I get a job? I havenae even got a decent frock to wear. Who'd hire me and whit could I dae? All I've ever done is have bairns and wash dishes. I'd be worrit sick aboot Mary, my wee lassie. Whit if he turned tae her? He needs . . . it . . . regular,' she added with a blush as if ashamed to say something about sex in front of someone who, in her eyes, had obviously never been touched by it.

Ferelith had an unwritten but remembered catalogue of the ills suffered by Maggie Sturrock.

Bert was a waster. The only time in his life that

he had been employed had been for four and a half months in 1941 when His Majesty had finally asked Bert to do his duty. Bert's commanding officer had very soon discovered that he had enough problems with the opposite side without adding Bert to his list and had thrown him out. Whereupon Bert had returned to Edinburgh to limp around pretending that he had been invalided out, to making life a misery for Maggie and his children. Seven times he had been thrown in jail for wife beating and every single time Maggie had taken him back.

'Jist where am I supposed to go wi' five bairns?' she had asked Ferelith again and again, not angrily, merely with acceptance of the status quo. 'God alone kens where he gets money but he aye seems tae be able tae get us a loaf and there's aye tatties in oor bit gairden and sometimes a cabbage or a Brussels sprout. Wouldn't it be nice no tae ever hae tae eat another Brussels sprout?'

Ferelith, who had spent seventeen years in an orphanage where an unbelievable number of Brussels sprouts had been consumed year after year could only agree with her.

But now Maggie had had enough. Constant beatings of her own person she could, as she had said often enough, 'thole', but abuse of her children? No. Maggie the lion had roared and she had killed in defence of her young, but what would the Law say?

'I kent fine whit I wis daein', Miss Gallagher. I was that calm, I couldnae believe it. The bluid wis rinnin' doon ma face but a' I could think on wis my wee Charlie standin' up fer us and gettin' leathered. He wid hae kilt him: the bairn wis blue. I hit Bert wi' the knife the once but he didnae stop chokin' Charlie an' I don't ken whit happened but I could see masel lifting the knife and stickin' it in him and liftin' the knife and stickin' it in him and there must hae been noise but I couldnae hear nothin' and then wee Charlie wis hingin' on my skirt and greetin', Mammy, Mammy, and I wis fell tired and sat doon. You'll no let Bert's family get my weans: they're a bad lot. I'd raither they wis pit in a hame.'

Not calm, Maggie. Catatonic, decided Ferelith. She did not know what she was doing. She could hear and see and feel nothing. The action of her arm had been an automatic response to the throttling of the boy.

But Maggie Sturrock had accepted that she had murdered her husband and for that *crime* she expected to die.

'Not if I can help it,' decided Ferelith Gallagher Webster and brought the whole might of her intellect and training to work.

18

THE FACT THAT Maggie Sturrock had struck out in defence, not of herself, but of her son, weighed heavily in her favour. Against this was the knowledge of the surely unnecessary violence with which she had killed her husband.

'The first knife wound,' said a forensic scientist, 'would have been quite enough.'

There were over thirty wounds in Bert's body. According to her own traumatized son, Maggie had calmly, without screaming or yelling in any way, thrust the knife into his father again and again.

'I couldnae get her tae stop,' young Charlie, his throat still swollen from the brutal strength of his father's hands, cried to Ferelith. 'Mammy didnae seem to even ken I wis there. She looked at me that funny when she finally stopped and I think she jist stopped hittin' him because she wis exhausted.'

Added to the evidence of the thirty knife wounds was the unpalatable fact that Maggie had, according to many eminent and knowledgeable people, deliberately courted Bert's violence.

'Why did she take him back again and again?' asked the public, both male and female.

Maggie's doctor gave eloquent testimony to the misery of her existence with her husband but her very dignity and composure in the face of cross-examination acted against her. She was too calm, too unemotional.

'You knew what you were doing, Mrs Sturrock, when you wielded that knife and stuck it over thirty

times into the body of your husband, and I say too
that you enjoyed it,' said the Advocate Depute.

'I needed tae make him stop hitting the wean,'
said Maggie calmly. 'There wis nae other way
tae de it.'

'And you enjoyed it, Mrs Sturrock?'

Maggie looked at him out of thousand-year-old
eyes. 'I didnae feel onything. I jist has tae stop
him.'

Maggie Sturrock was not helping her defence at
all. Ferelith, who had seen too many clients talk
themselves into long prison sentences, decided to
try a new tack. 'We'll have to try to persuade the
Jury that in the face of severe provocation and real
fear for her son, Maggie was temporarily insane,
Simon.'

'According to most judges and juries, temporarily
insane people do not deliberately go into the kitchen
to get a bread knife.'

'But they do.'

Ferelith ran her hands through her hair. She was
tired. This case was taking more out of her than
any other. Her whole being wanted to get Maggie
off and every day she could see a death sentence
getting nearer and nearer to her client.

'God, I wish I wasn't so tired, Simon,' she said
and he noted the dark shadows under her eyes and
the loss of weight.

'You're taking too much out of yourself, Ferelith.
When did you and Angus last go out somewhere
nice for a quiet dinner?'

'I dine quietly with Angus every night that we're
at home together,' said Ferelith which was not really
an answer to the question. Sometimes she felt that
she and Angus were doomed to spend the rest of
their lives passing one another in doorways as one

came in and the other went out. 'You know he'd be the last person in the world to try to stop me doing my best for Maggie. If only I get get the Jury to see that she is traumatized by the fact that she murdered her husband —'

Simon interrupted. 'Can't you get her to break down, relive some of the beatings? If she comes across scared and desperate, she'll get the Jury on her side. Right now she's not making a very good impression.'

'Why, in the name of all that's wonderful, should she have to . . . why should she have to sell herself? Can't you see that she's pulling resources out of some inner place she didn't even know she had to help her deal with this. She's distancing herself from the murder, from the years and years of brutality and fear, in order to be able to stand up there in the witness box just to hear herself being described as "unnaturally calm and composed". Did you hear Fenton suggest . . . ?' Ferelith stopped to compose herself and took a sip of water.

'Ferelith, why are you letting this case get to you so much? You're making yourself ill.' Simon was on his feet, his usual indolent pose gone.

'I'm not ill, Simon,' said Ferelith putting the glass back on the table. 'I'm fighting mad. He suggested that she liked being beaten up. He told her that if she hadn't enjoyed it, she would have left Sturrock. What banana boat did that Neanderthal man come up the Clyde on? She stayed for her children. Can't you stone-age men get that through your thick heads? There was nowhere for her to go and she stayed to protect them: she took years and years of rape and beatings for her children.' Ferelith broke down and started to cry, great sobs that tore at her. Simon took one look and went to the telephone to

ring Angus's office. Then he put his arms around
Ferelith and held her until the paroxysm of crying
had stopped.

'I'm holding you to stop you throwing something
heavy at me, sweetness. Angus is on his way
here to take you home. No, don't argue and don't
struggle. I'm stronger than I look and it would be
so dreadfully embarrassing if anyone came in and
found us rolling on the floor in a parody of immortal
passion. You need a good night's rest. Angus agrees.
I'll talk to Maggie's doctors and see if we can get
some sympathy for the abuse.'

'"I'll talk to Mrs Sturrock's doctors", Simon, not
Maggie's. She is entitled to some dignity. Women
don't like strange men calling them by their Chris-
tian names and they certainly hate the old school
"Sturrock" or "Gallagher".'

She looked at him, her friend, her dear friend.
'Why do I attack you when I'm angry, Simon? My
best of friends. Anyway, not even her doctor, and
he's sympathetic, knows the extent of the abuse,
Simon. Women who are being beaten up hide the
evidence. They pretend they've fallen downstairs.
They don't go to the hospital unless they're so badly
beaten that something is broken or they're bleeding
so badly that they're frightened of dying and leaving
their kids. She never told her doctor about the times
Sturrock raped her.'

'Ferelith, he was her husband. A husband can't
rape his wife. I mean . . . marriage, he's entitled
. . .' Simon flustered in the face of Ferelith's obvious
contempt for his opinion. 'Aren't wives supposed
to submit to their husbands? Doesn't it say that in
the Bible?'

She stood up calmly and looked at him. 'Dear
God in Heaven, Simon, if a decent man like you

thinks a husband can do anything he likes to his wife . . .'

'I didn't say that.'

'You said a husband cannot rape his wife. Rape is violence, Simon. It means to take by force what has been withheld. Most men will say, "Maybe tomorrow?" if a wife says, "I'm too tired", or "I don't feel well" or "you're drunk", but not the Bert Sturrocks of this world. He took what he wanted whenever he wanted. He raped her in front of their own children, Simon. And then they wonder that violence and degradation are self-perpetuating. God, if only there was one decent relative to keep the children. That will be held against the poor woman too.'

The door opened before Simon could ask her what would be held against her client and the Lord Advocate came in. Ferelith's defences crumpled again and she went into the haven of her husband's arms.

'I think she's fighting the flu, Angus,' said Simon. 'Take her home and feed her hot lemon and honey with a shot of whisky. She did that to me once when I had plumbed the depths. Works a treat.'

'Sounds wonderful,' said Angus. 'I'll have some too. Come on, darling, you're letting this case get to you and that is no good for you or for your client.'

'Do you know what one of the newspapers printed this morning, Angus? "Is Maggie Sturrock a good mother? If she is, then we don't want her to hang because she should be there to look after her children. If she is a bad mother, then it doesn't really matter." We're talking about someone's life and we're saying "it doesn't really matter". Excuse me, I have to go to the Ladies before we go home.' She pulled herself from her husband's arms and hurried out and the two men were left looking at one another.

'This case is really getting to her, Simon.'

'I've known her over twenty years, Angus, and I've never seen her as emotional as this. What is it about Maggie Sturrock that has got to her like this?'

'She feels helpless. There are no tricks she can pull, no playing to the gallery, and Mrs Sturrock's attitude isn't helping. Maggie killed him: she admits it and she is showing no remorse. If she could just be made to work on the susceptibilities of the Jury. I know there are too many men but men have sympathetic natures too. If only she'd say something like, "I never meant to kill him."'

'But did she murder him and does she deserve to die?'

'An eye for an eye?'

'The fact that the children are in care and have been in care so often is a strike against Maggie. Her children have been in care, ergo, their mother is a bad mother and they are better off without her. I wish we could make more of psychiatric evidence: if we could prove that she was criminally insane or had some other mental disorder.'

'I'm sure the day is not far off when the psychological state of the accused will be important but right now it's a kind of mumbo-jumbo world that no one understands. To me it's obvious that Maggie was operating in a state of diminished responsibility. Nothing has come up to show her as a violent person: she never even spanked her children. Bert did too much of that. But Ferelith is having a hard job convincing those eleven men and four women that Maggie did not know what she was doing when she ran into the kitchen for a knife. Why not the rolling pin or a broom? Why did she deliberately open a drawer and take out a knife? And why did she go on and on knifing her husband? Because she was not in her right mind.'

'What would you do? How would you handle the defence?'

'Ferelith has the instinctive feel of a good jury advocate. She'll get them on her side and she'll get them on Maggie's if she can persuade Maggie to emote more. There are, as you know, Simon, so many unspoken prejudices in a case like this. Ferelith naturally empathizes with Maggie. She understands what motivates her. If anyone can get her off, Ferelith can.'

'Well, thank you, M'Lord.' They had not heard Ferelith return. She looked a little better with slight colour in her usually pale cheeks. 'Let's go home and have some scrambled eggs and then I'll spend some time working out how to explain Maggie's detachment to the Jury. It is so frightening how little time there is to deal with life and death.'

'You are going home to bed, Mrs Webster,' said Angus severely. 'Please, darling, you will be unable to help Maggie if you tire yourself out. You have spent more hours than necessary on this case as it is.'

Ferelith pulled away from his arm. 'How can you say that? Simon thinks men are entitled to do what they bloody well like with their wives and you think your wife shouldn't get too tired defending Maggie Sturrock. Dear God, what chance does she have of justice? I'll go home, Angus Webster, because I want to go home, not because the two big strong men in my life are telling me to go home, and after I have made some scrambled eggs, I will work on my client's defence and I will take as many hours as it takes.'

'Sitting up in bed comfortably,' suggested Simon. She ignored him and stalked out.

'You're a braver man than I am, Simon,' said Lord Webster as he hurried out after his wife.

A light supper and an early night seemed to do wonders for Ferelith's health.

The *Mens Rea*, the advocate's term for the state of mind of the accused at the time of the incident, had to be explained to the Court. That is, Ferelith had to make the Court understand Maggie's intention. To succeed as a defence to murder, she had to be able to prove that Maggie acted in self-defence and in defence of her son. The Jury might be prepared to accept force, even leading to death, if they could be made to believe that stabbing Bert was the only way Maggie and Charlie could escape death themselves. The insurmountable stumbling blocks were the number of blows struck and Maggie's detachment. Ferelith strove to show that years and years of brutal conditioning had made Maggie Sturrock accept her husband's brutality. She did not seek it, she did not enjoy it, but she saw no way out of the vicious cycle. Eloquently and movingly she painted a vivid picture of a woman who, as a young and idealistic girl, had acted wrongly.

'She loved Bert Sturrock: she, like many other innocent and loving young women, gave in to the pleas of her young man for sex to prove, in his words, that she loved him. Some of you might say that was wrong: you might think it immoral. Was it not immoral for that young man to ask such a pledge? Should he not have said, "I will prove my love for you by staying chaste with you until we are married." Maggie gave in and she paid the price and she went on paying it for year after year of degradation and brutality where she herself came to believe that she was no good, that she did deserve Bert's violence. And then, on that fateful night, when most happy and loving families, no matter how poor their circumstances, were looking forward to the joyous and loving season of Christmas, Bert Sturrock subjected his wife to a vicious beating, a beating so severe that a young boy dared his father's anger and brutality to try to save his mother. And what happened to that brave boy? His father, his father, ladies and gentlemen, tried to strangle him to death. And Mrs Sturrock saw her son turning blue and something inside snapped, not because of the beating she had received, but because of this innocent and brave boy. In her own words you heard her say that she saw nothing, heard nothing, was aware of nothing but her child struggling for his very life in the hands of the man who had given him that life, and in that state of consciousness she went to the kitchen and she took a knife and she stabbed and stabbed her husband until she heard her boy cry, "I'm safe." Who among us would have acted differently in the defence of the baby we had nurtured in the womb? Maggie Sturrock killed her husband, ladies and gentlemen, but she did not murder him.'

She sat down wearily in her chair and Simon looked at her anxiously as, with trembling hands, she sipped water from a glass. He watched as a very subdued jury left the room to begin their deliberations. What were they thinking? What would they decide?

It was Maggie Sturrock who consoled Ferelith. 'You're no looking weel, Miss Gallagher, and I want tae say now, afore they come back, that naebody could hae done better fer me. I killed him, lassie.

I'm no proud that I've taen a life but it's all over fer me now. You ken, Mr Osborne, this time in the jail has been the longest time in thirty-five years that naebody's belted me one. It's my bairns. They'll be fine in care, won't they? Naebody'll be on at them for whit I did, will they?'

Ferelith looked at her. The weeks in jail had actually been physically beneficial to Maggie. She had lost some weight, probably because her diet was slightly better than that which she was used to.

I wonder if she ever made any of the casseroles Dominic taught the girls to make, Ferelith thought, or did she lose heart for sensible cooking too?

The neat blue dress that Ferelith herself had bought for her client sat well on her frame and the colour suited her blue eyes. A shadow of the pretty young girl whom Ferelith had first seen all those years ago was visible now in the ravaged face.

She's even standing taller these days and has that been bad or good? Bad probably. The Jury would have preferred her to look more cowed, to be unable to meet the advocates' eyes.

'Jury's back, Miss Gallagher.' So soon. So soon. The Court Officer was already at the door.

Ferelith felt her stomach flip over with dread. She wanted to retch, to be violently sick. She breathed deeply and looked at Simon.

'My God, Simon, they've been gone twenty minutes. How can they decide in twenty minutes? I take longer than that to decide what to wear in the morning.'

They walked back from their waiting room and as always, Ferelith was conscious of the many people, innocent and guilty, who had walked these corridors in fear and trepidation, throughout the years.

They were back in the courtroom. Ferelith and Maggie took their places, Simon just behind for support. The Judge came in with the Court Official and the mace and then for a few minutes Ferelith experienced what she felt Maggie must have experienced when she had killed Bert. There was a swimming, humming noise in her ears. She knew she was doing what her long training had taught her to do but she was acting like an automaton: she saw the hazy figures of the Jury and the Judge and the Advocate Depute and all the court officials. She was aware of the mace, that great symbol of regal authority hanging on the wall behind the Judge, but she could hear nothing.

And then Simon was helping her into her seat and Maggie was standing there with her children around her and they were laughing and crying and flashbulbs were popping and then Ferelith knew.

'Not guilty?' she asked in amazement and still with that far away voice as if this was all happening to someone else, 'but they couldn't possibly find her not guilty.' She grabbed Simon's gown. 'They found her not guilty?'

'Not proven,' he said and in front of any interested spectator, he kissed her. 'You won, Ferelith, you won.'

ON THE 10TH of January 1955 the contralto, Marian Anderson, became the first black singer ever to sing at the Metropolitan Opera House in New York. Angus, who had been on a courtesy visit to the Supreme Court of the United States, was so entranced by her voice, her age, and her achievement, that he had to telephone Ferelith from New York to share his experience with her immediately rather than to wait for his return. He telephoned every day when he was away from home anyway and this time he was anxious to contact her because he had been worried about her health over Christmas and the New Year and had been on the point of cancelling his trip when the Not Proven verdict had come in.

'I'll rest at home for a few days, darling,' Ferelith had persuaded him. 'Go to New York. I'd adore to come with you, I'm madly jealous, but maybe next time.'

'When I get back we'll talk about that holiday we were going to have. Somewhere for some sunshine or Paris or anywhere else you want to go?'

Now he tried to convey to her the excitement generated by the national acceptance of the great contralto.

'It was the *Masked Ball*, darling, Verdi. She sang Ulrica and it was electrifying. Toscanini says hers is a voice that comes along once every hundred years and I feel privileged to have heard it and in the

States in the Met. Let's not go to Italy after all for our holiday. Let's try to find out where she's singing in the summer. She tends to do concerts . . .'

Ferelith listened to the bubbling excitement of his voice and her heart lurched with love and happiness. 'Why are you so excited by one singer and a contralto at that?'

'Because the United States grew up a bit last night: that's exciting. She's black, sweetheart, and there she was accepted as a singer and a great one in a country where blacks and whites can't sit on the same bus. Where children of different colours can't sit in the same classroom. Her glorious voice was like a breath of clean fresh air. You remember how we heard Toscanini yelling *vergogna* at the orchestra when we were at Pietro's ordination? Well, no one was shouting "shame" at anyone last night. The place went wild.'

'And Angus Webster went wilder than anyone.'

'I behaved,' he said mock sternly, 'with my usual magisterial decorum but I did send flowers. Have you any idea of her age? She's sixty this year. It's taken her all this time to be acknowledged, to succeed. I thought you would be delighted for her. And since you, at forty, are a mere child, I thought, when I get home tomorrow, we could talk about your application for silk.'

'That'll be nice, dear.' Ferelith smiled and he could not see the smile but he sensed it.

'You have wanted to take silk for years, Ferelith, and especially after the Sturrock case, you are bound to be accepted, not as my wife, but on your own.'

'Yes, Angus. We'll talk about it tomorrow.'

Lord Webster was not at all happy with his telephone call. Lady Webster, on the other hand, was delighted with her half of it.

But we won't be chasing Marian Anderson this summer, Angus Webster, no matter how wonderful she is.

Angus's flight reached Edinburgh in mid-morning and Ferelith was there to meet him.

'You're glowing, darling,' he said as he kissed her. 'Either it is this cold frosty air or the rest since the end of the case has been just what you needed. I was so proud of you and I want you to be the first female Q.C. and, why not Ferelith, the first female Lord Advocate?'

'That's nice, dear,' she said again and he looked at her strangely but said nothing. 'Nice that I'm glowing,' she said, a hint of laughter in her grey-green eyes.

What colour were they? It seemed to depend on her mood and the weather.

'You seem to have put back a little of the weight you lost, darling. I'll tell you now that I was really worried when you were defending Mrs Sturrock.'

'Oh, it was nothing. Fatigue, worry. Everything is fine now. I shall amaze you with how healthy I am.' She turned and led the way to where she had parked the car.

'Do you want to go into the office?' she asked when Angus had stowed his suitcase and his duty-frees and the countless magazines he always seemed to accumulate on journeys. 'I thought you might like a nap first and then we could have a lovely lunch at La Bella Napoli.'

'Only if a nap is a euphemism for what I hope it is.'

She smiled that tantalizing smile again and turned the car into the road leading out of the airport.

'You are behaving very oddly, Mrs Webster,' he said finally. 'I was actually surprised to see you this morning: I thought you might already be up to your ears in a new case.'

Ferelith slowed down at the approach to a roundabout and appeared to give her full attention to the difficulties involved in steering her course safely.

'I'm glad you have lost your fear of this car,' Angus went on as Ferelith had not answered him.

She had learned to drive in Angus's powerful Jaguar but she drove as seldom as possible. Usually Angus drove, as he actually enjoyed it, but Ferelith preferred that he not drive after a long flight.

'It's a nice car,' she said. 'Had you thought of changing it?'

'Why on earth should I change it? The mileage is remarkable for its age: it's not as if we go any great distance in it. Don't tell me you've seen something you'd prefer? I always thought a car for you was merely something that took you conveniently from A to B.'

'And so it is. We'll talk about it after your nap.'

'Our nap?'

'Wicked old thing, you. You'll have to think of a good excuse for Karen.'

'Give her some shopping to do – as far away from the New Town as possible.'

'I'm only teasing you. I've given her a day off to hit the after-Christmas sales. I'm going to ring Simon after lunch too, darling, to ask him to dinner. He had to have Traviata put down and he's really desolate.'

For Edinburgh the road from the airport was fairly quiet and they were soon at home.

'Apart from your opera programme, did you bring me anything?' Ferelith teased when he abandoned his attempts to unpack his suitcase.

'I didn't bring you my programme. I'm keeping that for myself. That's an "I was there" programme. I brought you some nylons from Saks on Fifth Avenue.'

'Is New York as exciting as everyone says it is?'

'Nowhere is exciting when you aren't there, my darling,' said Angus and proceeded to prove to their mutual satisfaction just how very exciting windy Edinburgh could be.

Later they drove down to Tollcross to the restaurant and Ferelith surprised her husband by asking for champagne.

'To Marian Anderson,' she said when the waiter had poured the first glasses and left them alone.

'Miss Anderson,' agreed Angus.

They drank.

'And to Baby Webster,' said Ferelith looking over her glass at her husband.

'To Baby Web . . .' he began and then he put his glass down so abruptly that the champagne spilled over on to the immaculate white cloth. He looked at his wife.

Her lovely eyes sparkled at him assuring him that he had heard what he had hoped he had heard. He leaned across the table and grabbed her hand making the stones in her engagement ring bite into her flesh. She did not feel the pain.

'Ferelith, but you can't . . . we agreed. We've taken steps.'

'I un-took them, Angus, months ago.'

He lifted both of her hands and kissed them very gently.

'You're going to have a baby?'

'We're going to have a baby and, oh Angus, I'm thrilled and terrified but mainly thrilled, in fact ecstatically happy.'

'Oh my darling girl, so am I.' They sat holding hands and just looking at one another. A baby. Neither could quite believe that this miracle was going to happen. Angus looked at his wife and saw her as he had seen her only an hour or two earlier. He would be much gentler from now on: he would take great care of her.

'You wonderful, wonderful girl,' he said.

'Woman, Angus. I'll go along with wonderful woman.'

'Should you be drinking alcohol? And you need food. Shall we order?'

'Yes, I should be drinking my celebratory glass of champagne and yes, I need food.'

Angus summoned their waiter and soon Ferelith's favourite antipasto was on the table between them.

'The car?' he said.

'Not a family car.'

'You are right. Let's get one of those marvellous estate wagons.'

She laughed and speared a marinated artichoke. 'It's only one baby, not a rugby team.'

At that glorious thought he leaned back in his chair and put his fork down. 'We have to go home. I keep wanting to do crazy things like kiss your feet and that is definitely not acceptable for a Lord Advocate.'

'It is in the privacy of his own home, but I'm starving. I've worked very hard this morning,' she said archly, 'and I have to go home and prepare a nice dinner for Simon.'

'No, you mustn't strain in any way, darling. We'll eat out or I'll ring Simon and tell him to come back in . . . how long?'

'In six months. So no holiday in Venice, and now you know why I couldn't get excited at the thought of a second honeymoon. I couldn't tell you until I was quite sure. Venice will wait. We can even take the baby. But we can't cancel poor Simon. He's awfully upset about Traviata and I cancelled our meeting this morning to fetch you from the airport. I'll have some work to do after dinner and you can catch up on your sleep.'

Angus signalled to the waiter to remove the antipasto. 'Just salad for Lady Webster and *linguini con funghi* for me and a tossed salad. And water.

'Ferelith Webster, you are avoiding my eyes. You are going to tell Simon that you are resigning?'

'No.'

'No. You mean not yet, not for a few weeks yet. When did you find out? Who told you? I mean, how does one . . . this is silly but I've never been . . . intimate with a pregnant woman before?'

'I should hope not,' she teased and then took pity on him. 'I went to see Jim a few days ago and I guessed for myself on the last day of the trial. All the fatigue, the nausea, I put it down to overwork, to stress. And then I came in after the Jury came back and there were such strange things going on in me and around me and I felt the baby move. Jim says he's too small but Jim isn't pregnant and he's never been pregnant. I am and the baby, our baby, introduced himself. He said, Mummy, I'm so sorry you've been feeling awful but I'm here now and we'll be fine. And he was right. I started feeling better and I want to share my joy, our joy with everyone. We'll ring your sister, then Blair and Emma, and Jane and Jamie, and all the di Rollos and Elspeth. Some doctor, Elspeth. She thought I was talking about her,' she said cryptically, but he was not sufficiently interested in Elspeth to ask for an explanation. 'Then we'll tell Simon and maybe old Oliver but then we'll keep it a secret until I've finished the work that I have on hand.'

'Ferelith, a pregnant woman can't practise at the Bar.'

'Why not?'

'It's not done.'

'Why not? Finish your linguini and we'll go home. I'm perfectly healthy, Angus. I'm a teeny-weeny bit old to have a baby and I will take no more instructions until after he's born but —'

'After he's born?' Angus interrupted. 'Ferelith, my wife is not going back to work. It's unbelievably unsuitable.'

Ferelith touched his hand gently. 'Finish your linguini, dear, and we'll discuss this at home.'

Angus called for his bill and for the waiter to remove his unfinished meal. He did not speak until they were in the car and heading home. 'I will not allow my wife to work in her condition and that is final, and I will not allow my daughter's mother to go out to work either. It is totally unsuitable.'

'How do you feel about your son's mother taking silk?'

Angus was so angry that he stalled the car at the west end of Princes Street; and because he was angry he flooded the engine and took so long to restart the car that there was a huge tailback of honking cars. It did not help that the policeman on duty at the corner recognized him and tried to ease the situation.

'Sometimes I can almost understand what drives men to violence,' he said through clenched teeth as they reached their home.

'What a dreadful thing to say. Scratch a liberal and he's every bit as outdated and prejudiced as anybody else.'

'You're being childish.'

'And you're being medieval, prehistoric. "My woman doesn't go out to work."' Ferelith hurried up the steps and threw open the door and almost slammed it closed again in her husband's face. 'I'm furiously angry,' she said unnecessarily.

She could see Angus withdraw. She had seen him do it over the years in Court but he had never yet done it to her. They had never had a flaming row. Neither of them was prone to shouting and raging. Now her anger frightened her.

'I suggest that you lie down and rest,' he said quietly and she could see how hard he was trying to control himself and she almost capitulated. 'Your condition . . .' he began and she exploded.

'My condition? How dare you, Angus Webster. You are like every other arrogant male. You don't like what I am saying and so you take refuge in stupid stereotypes. We should have moved on from the Ancient Greeks who gave us the word hysterical and stuck it as a label on every mother who did or said something her lord and master didn't like. My womb is not governing my actions: I am not affected by the cycles of the moon.'

She stood at the foot of the stairs trembling with anger and misery and looked at him. He did not look any happier than she. Poor Angus, she thought. He has wanted a baby so much and now I tell him there is to be a baby and I spoil it by fighting with him and he's afraid to say anything to me because he has always felt there was something holy and mystical about pregnancy and there is, dear God, there is, but he has to realize it's a perfectly natural state.

'You do know that Simon's Traviata was a Fidelio until she had kittens and he saw that he was a she. She had them perfectly happily and easily.'

'Don't be childish, Ferelith: you are not a cat. You are my wife and I don't want you exhibiting yourself and your condition in court.'

'Exhibiting myself?' She almost choked. 'That antediluvian gown that advocates wear would hide anything. No one will even know I'm pregnant. I don't intend to go into labour in court number eleven but I will finish the work I have agreed to do and if you don't like the idea, you can . . . you can . . .'

She could feel the words 'Get out' forming themselves on the end of her tongue and she swallowed them and ran up the stairs to the sanctuary of her bedroom. She sat down on the bed and looked at herself in the wardrobe mirror. At the enormity of what she had almost said she started to cry and she did not hear Angus open the door and cross the room to her. He held her, sobbing, in his arms until she was quiet.

'I think my perfect mix of cerebral and emotional has gone somewhat skewwhiff. This was supposed to be the loveliest day in our marriage.'

'And it is.'

'If I give in.' Ferelith looked at him and took a deep breath. He was not going to like what she had to say but she could not be dishonest. 'Angus, I still intend to apply for silk. Don't you see, advocacy is the perfect job for a mother?'

'Why do you want to work at all? You don't need to work.'

'Oh darling, I do. While I'm useful, I want to work. The baby will change things. I'm not the same woman now that I was three months ago. In six months' time I will be a mother and I'll be changed again. Maybe my aspirations will change but I want to leave the options open. Sweetheart, I'm like your

wonderful Marian Anderson. I've changed things
for the better, and she's not finished and neither
am I. Can't you understand?'

'No, but I'll try.'

'That's all I ask.'

Angus was unhappy about Ferelith's decision to
continue working but in the days and weeks that followed he was amazed by her energy. He delighted
in her slowly changing shape and made countless
plans for their unborn child.

Ferelith did not announce her pregnancy to her
colleagues but she did announce her intention to
apply for silk. This was a courtesy not always
given by all advocates. After all if one was rejected
and had not made a general announcement it was
sometimes possible to lick the painful wound of
failure in private. If one did announce, one knew
that one's hopes and aspirations, one's talent or lack
of it, one's education, experience, in fact everything,
would be a hot subject of discussion for weeks if not
months.

Ferelith decided to make her application public.

'A woman?'

'Well, there is Margaret Kydd.'

'Then that's enough surely.'

'Is there no end to her ambition? Old Webster had
better look to his laurels: she'll be after his job next.'

'I hear Ferelith Gallagher has applied for silk.
She'll get it, of course. I mean if one only had the
Lord Advocate to put in a good word . . .'

'Nonsense, she's a damned good advocate and
she's done her time. Brilliant in Court.'

'Brilliant? She's an assertive, aggressive, unfeminine woman and Webster should be ashamed of
himself to allow it.'

And steadier heads tried to discuss why it was perfectly noble for a man to be assertive and even aggressive in the defence of his client but not permissible for a female.

Aware of all the arguments Ferelith sailed through her pregnancy on a cloud of euphoria.

It became generally known that the Lord Advocate and his wife were to have a child and Ferelith experienced another change of attitude in Court on the few times she appeared before her voluntary withdrawal from public life.

'I was so frustrated, Angus, I could have wept,' she said one night at dinner. 'Old Ironsides has been particularly hostile to me since I first appeared before him and today he behaved like my uncle. He almost said, "There, there, lovey, sit down and put your feet up and I won't argue with you." And his Lordship stopped proceedings when I took a sip of water to ask me if I was tired. He actually said, "We must all remember your condition." My client didn't know my "condition" as he called it until he said that and now she thinks I'm a fallen woman. "You really understand where I'm coming from," says she.'

Angus, who had met no prejudice of any kind in court or out of it, tried to sympathise.

'You are absolutely delighted that I'm the little pregnant wife at home now, aren't you? Admit it.'

'I'm absolutely delighted that my wife is *enceinte*.' began Angus.

'You Victorian, you. You can't even say pregnant.'

'Of course I can. I merely wanted to point out that his father has a smattering of learning. Actually, Ferelith, I want to rent a bus and watch it drive around Edinburgh with a banner up that says, "Ferelith Webster is pregnant and I did it."'

She got up and went to him. 'Darling Angus, you are pleased and proud and you won't mind if it's a boy or a girl.'

'I would have difficulty if it were anything else,' he teased her. 'Ferelith Webster, you continue to make me the happiest and proudest man in the world.'

'Oh, it's nothing,' she said. 'Now put your hand there and feel him kick. Definitely a rugby player.'

They sat for some time communicating with one another and their unborn child and then Ferelith jumped up. 'I forgot to ring Pietro. Everyone in Edinburgh knows I'm a fallen woman but not the man who is going to baptize the little treasure.'

James Gallagher Webster was born very easily on the 21st of June 1955 and it was a few weeks before his mother had time to read the papers. She scoured the newspapers that referred to the date of her precious child's birth and found that after a two-day trial, a jury of ten good men and two good women, had taken twenty-five minutes to find one Ruth Ellis guilty of murder in the first degree. Mrs Ellis was hanged at Holloway on the 13th of July, just a few days before Jamie was baptized.

July 13th was also the day on which Lady Webster was told that she had been awarded silk and would now be a Queen's Counsel.

'Well Jamie?' asked Ferelith and at her voice the baby opened his eyes and looked up at her face. He continued to suck and she watched him tenderly. 'This is the most beautiful time, Jamie my love,' she told him. 'So much tenderness flows from me that I feel the world should be able to see it. I love you so much – and your daddy. Daddy is the nicest man in the world, Jamie, and I hope you will grow up to be just like him.'

James Gallagher Webster burped loudly and regurgitated some milk and his mother laughed.

'Not an accepted way to conclude an argument, young man, but effective, I must admit.'

'Am I disturbing you two?' Angus stood in the doorway of the baby's room.

Ferelith smiled at him. 'Come and join us. We're having a mother to son talk and he told me what he thinks by spitting at me. I told him I wanted him to be just like you and he thought I meant I wanted him to be a lawyer: he hates the idea.'

Angus took the baby and expertly began to burp him. 'What does he think of having a working mother?'

'I haven't asked him that yet. Where did you learn to get rid of wind?'

'Not in the Court of Session, although perhaps thumping one or two people on the back might be rather a good idea,' said Angus, giving the baby back to his mother. 'I'm a quick study. I'm going to try a nappy as soon as he's finished.'

Ferelith smiled at her husband who was looking absurdly young in his pyjamas and not at all like a Lord Advocate. 'Nappies are serious business.'

'So is being a father. When you go back to work . . .'

'I haven't decided yet,' said Ferelith quickly.

'Oh, I think you have, darling. I saw your face when you read about the Ruth Ellis case. I saw your face when I called you Ferelith Gallagher Q.C.'

'I want to be Jamie's mother.'

'I gave the matter a great deal of thought. Advocacy is actually quite a good job for a woman. If he's sick you can stay at home with him and remember, I want to be an involved father too. Sometimes I'll be free to look after him.'

Ferelith bent her head over the baby to hide the ready tears. 'Oh Angus, I still want it all, not today, not until Jamie is weaned, but I do want to continue.'

'That's what I want too. You're a brilliant advocate and there are people out there who need you.'

'More than this precious mite?'

'Differently. And he has a father who is now going to send his mummy off to bed while he struggles with his first nappy pins. Go on, I won't stick the pins in him. We're going to have the first of many man to man chats.'

Ferelith kissed the drowsy baby and handed him to his father. 'Did I ever tell you that I love you very much, Angus Webster?'

'Not nearly enough. We'll get back to that later. Goodnight, Ferelith Gallagher Q.C.'

'Ferelith Webster Q.C.'

He looked up from his struggles with the pins and looked solemnly into her smiling eyes.

'Yes, we like that, don't we, Jamie? Ferelith Webster. Q.C.'

Harvest of Courage

For my sisters,
Anne, Nancy and Kathryn

Thank you to my nephew Eli Colner and his friend David Schertzer who rescued this story from the depths of Eli's father's computer – and never once laughed.

Chapter One

In the spring of 1900 Mairi McGloughlin discovered that she loved the land. She was just nine years old: in fact she had just passed – not celebrated – her ninth birthday. With her best friend, Violet Anderson, she was walking home from the village school. They skipped and walked down Pansy Lane and then Mairi saw the first of the year's snowdrops, virginal white, the lovely heads standing straight and tall on delicate stems, their dark green leaves cradling them protectively.

'Look, Violet,' she said, her voice full of awe, 'snowdrops.'

Violet skipped on the spot, not losing the beat. 'Seventy-eight, seventy-nine – they're jist flooers, Mairi – eighty-four, eighty-five.'

Mairi knelt down in the damp soil beside the flowers and she spoke for herself. 'No, they're not, Violet, they're more, they're harbingers of spring.'

She was top of the class and had seen that posh word in one of the Dominie's reserved books.

'Harbingers of spring,' she said again, liking the sound of the phrase. 'Look at them, Violet. They've come up out of the ground and they're pure white; the muck hasnae stuck to them.'

'Ach, you're daft, so you are, Mairi McGloughlin. Of course dirt doesnae stick to them.'

'Well, why not, since you're so smart, Violet Anderson? Why doesn't muck stick to them?'

For a moment Violet was perplexed. She had not expected to be questioned on something unquestionable, on an irrefutable fact. 'It just disnae because . . . because God made them.'

'Aye, and he made Billy Soutar tae and all the mud in Angus is stuck tae him.'

At the thought of Billy Soutar, the little girls dissolved into laughter and ran giggling down the path, all thoughts of flowers and muck and their place in the great scheme of things gone from their minds.

They parted at the end of the lane. Mairi had to continue another mile to the farmhouse but Violet's father's tied cottage sat four-square to the road almost beside the path. Her mother was in the garden throwing potato peelings to the hens that bustled frenetically around her feet as if terrified that there would not be enough for all.

'There's scones jist oot the oven, lassies,' she called as she went on feeding the hens, 'and a nice jug of fresh milk in the larder, oor Violet.'

Mairi sighed. Pheemie Anderson was a fine baker. 'I cannae the day, Mrs Anderson. I've a pot of soup tae put on for the week.' The pot of soup would have been ready if her brother, Ian, had not let the fire go out. Ian's head was usually busy with anything but what he was supposed to be doing and yesterday he had got so involved watching a blackbird building a nest that he had forgotten not only to keep the range stoked but also to bring in the cows. Mairi had gone for the cows but too late to save her brother from their father's righteous anger. This morning Ian had been too sore to go to the school and Mairi had lied and told the Dominie that he had a cold. Mr Morrison had said nothing but at hometime he had given Mairi a lovely bound Shakespeare.

'If Ian is still unwell tomorrow, tell him to read *Richard II* and I want him to go on with his history book and the composition he was going to write for me.'

2

Glowing, Mairi had put the precious book carefully in her bag. She and Ian and the teacher's horrible son, Robin, were the only children who were allowed to read the reserved books. Ian and Robin had fought for the position of top of the class for seven years since the day they had entered the little school together. Sometimes Robin was top, sometimes Ian. Robin always beat Ian in the arithmetic examinations and Ian beat Robin at compositions. Aggregate scores were what counted for top place and Mairi was hoping that Ian would be Dux. Then maybe, just maybe, Father would allow him to stay on at the school beyond the date when most farm boys left.

'He'll need tae count well enough tae buy in seed, no be diddled, and tae pay his men whit they're worth. He doesnae need tae speak poems.' That was Father, who would never understand his son, mainly because he would not try.

Mairi carried on up the road until she reached the farm-house. The dogs, Dog and Ben, rushed out to meet her and she hugged them both, careless of the fact that they were working dogs and not, according to Father, to be petted like lap dogs. Dogs were the most satisfactory of all animals. They loved totally and without question; everything these strange human creatures did was perfect and Mairi, with her cuddles and scratching of just the right spot under the ears, was the most perfect of all. They even tolerated Ian's forgetfulness and waited patiently when he forgot to feed them. Their master did not have their forgiving nature.

'Oh, you beautiful babies,' crooned Mairi. 'Have you missed me then?'

Their tails wagging vigorously, to show her how much she had been missed, they followed her into the house.

'You'd best lie down in the kitchen while I see where Ian is.'

If they could have, they would have told her that Ian was ploughing with his father. Mr McGloughlin had promised his wife that the children would attend school but here was

3

Ian, perfectly well and doing nothing. He did not have to sit down to help with the plough.

When Mairi realized that the house was empty, she cut herself a slice from a loaf of bread that she had baked herself. She spread it liberally with their own butter and sat down at the scrubbed kitchen table to eat it. Then she changed from her school frock into a working day dress and began to prepare vegetables for the soup: carrots, turnips, leeks and a cabbage all grown either in the garden or on the farm. She washed some of their own barley and left it sitting in a bowl of water while the stock simmered on the range. The stock she had made from the bone of the mutton joint that had been their Sunday and Monday dinner. The soup started, she peeled potatoes and then went out into the garden to gather some of the last of the Brussels sprouts. How good it would be when the spring vegetables began to appear; Brussels sprouts were, unfortunately, such a serviceable vegetable. Mairi could not think of one good thing to say about them and, in fact, sometimes wondered why farmers bothered to grow them. She was only nine years old, not a great age, but, in all that time of living and experiencing, she had never met anyone who admitted to liking them.

'When I'm choosing the garden vegetables,' Mairi informed a particularly tough plant, 'there will be no sprouts.' She sat back on her heels beside the plants. There would be flowers. That's what there would be and something called asparagus that she'd seen in one of the Dominie's books, and strawberries, of course, which grew beautifully in Angus soil under Angus skies, and potatoes, even though Father grew them on the farm. The Dominie had a book about growing vegetables and it said that potatoes cleaned the ground and left it nice and ready for the next crop. Yes, asparagus. Mairi had never eaten, never even seen asparagus, but the gentry liked it and so it must be good. The Laird had a glass house called a succession house and he grew peaches in it. *Peaches*. Mairi had seen them when the Laird had given a

4

picnic for his tenants. Oh, earth, soil, good clean dirt was a marvellous thing; it grew potatoes and peaches both. Even the word peach was good. *Peach*. When she was a farmer she would have a succession house and she would have a peach tree in it. The Laird would help her. He was a nice old man. He did not chuck her under the chin and expect her to like it as so many elderly and not so elderly men did. He had spoken to her, one gardener to another. Yes, she would not be afraid to ask the Laird. No doubt he had asparagus. She would go to see it at the next picnic.

Mairi jumped up. She had better get the sprouts and the tatties on. If Ian had done nothing to annoy Father they would have a nice time sitting around the table together, even though the soup would not be at its best until tomorrow. But if she made a nice Shepherd's pie and that and the sprouts were ready to be served just as Father walked in from the fields, maybe he would speak to Ian with the soft voice he always used for Mairi and that her brother very rarely heard addressed to himself. She stopped at the back door, her eye caught by a glimpse of white against the garden wall – more snowdrops.

'When I'm the farmer,' began Mairi, and then she stopped, for she would never be the farmer. She was a girl. She would grow up and keep house for her father until Ian married and then, unless she herself married, she would share the chores with her sister-in-law, for it was Ian who would be the farmer, Ian, who was only completely happy when he was reading a story or scribbling away in his secret notebook.

'It's daft,' said nine-year-old Mairi McGloughlin, 'but it's the way it is and there's nout I can do about it.' She thought for a moment and smiled a slow sweet smile that was older than time. 'I'll marry Jack Black and bully him.'

Her future decided, Miss McGloughlin hurried into the kitchen and finished preparing the evening meal. Then there were a few precious minutes to do her homework. She was clever like Ian and the horrible Robin – what a

5

sissy name for a laddie – and so the sums took her no time at all. The parsing and analysis of the three sentences took her a little longer because she was happier just reading and understanding lovely words than cluttering up her mind with parts of speech and suchlike nonsense. Ian now, and that spoiled brat who lived in the Schoolhouse, could happily parse and analyze all the day long. She was about to say that such a failing showed just how horrid was Robin Morrison when she realized that the same label would have to attach itself to her beloved Ian. She vented her spleen on Robin by viciously slicing two sprouts into slivers and tossing them into the soup pot. Father would have been sure to ask her what on earth she was trying to do to his laboriously grown vegetables. Sprouts were cooked whole. Everybody knew that.

Colin McGloughlin and his son, Ian, were welcomed home by the smell of good food beautifully cooked. Ian had managed to keep his mind on his work all afternoon long and so his father was as pleased with him as he ever got. A good hammering had done the boy the world of good, which proved that Ian did not need 'patient understanding' as the Dominie was always saying, but discipline. There was a time for books and a time for remembering to mend the fire and, of the two, the fire was the more important. Without a fire, wee Mairi could not cook and he had never yet seen Ian ready to eat his books instead of a succulent Shepherd's pie. For a moment Colin toyed with the idea of approaching the School Board to allow Mairi to stay at home. There was necessity; he was a widower with two children. Ach no, he had promised Ellen and forbye, the lassie was only nine. She could finish the primary school and then she could stay at home where she belonged and take care of the house. She would not do hard farm work, not his wee lassie. Too much work had killed her mother, a shop girl from the town who should never have married herself on a farmer. But Mairi should be spared the hard work that was the lot of every daughter of the farm and if she did marry, and she had to he supposed, she should marry onto a farm that was owner occupied where there was a bit of extra money for a kitchen maid as well as a dairy maid. But not yet, not for a long time yet.

The little family ate their meal and washed it down with mugs of hot sweet tea. Then Colin went to the fire and sat down, the dogs at his feet. He would sit for an hour or two and then, once he had seen the children to bed, he would take himself off to his lonely room.

Ian too left the table and after assuring himself that his father was safely ensconced in the inglenook, he took the book that Mairi had brought him from the Dominie and carried it with pride and care to a seat on the other side of the roaring fire. He was soon deeply involved in the fourteenth century and totally removed from the world around him. Mairi accepted that she would clear the table and wash the dishes; that she would put the oats to soak for the morning's porridge and that she would fill the stone pigs that warmed the beds. That was woman's work. She could barely keep her eyes open by the time her jobs were finished.

'I'm away tae my bed,' she announced to her father and to her brother but neither heard her. She was not hurt. She did not expect a loving and protracted goodnight ritual. She smiled fondly at her menfolk as if they were her children and took herself off up the oak staircase to her little room under the eaves. She liked her room with its view over the fields towards the Firth of Tay. It was dark and she was tired and cold, but once she was stripped to her vest and knickers she pulled the handmade patchwork quilt from her bed, wrapped it around her shoulders, and sat on the window seat looking out at the night. There were one or two fishing boats on the water. In the moonlight, against the dark sky, they looked like etchings. Mairi waited and waited and there, at last, was the train. It ran like a wheeled jewel box between the fields and the sea. It was

7

going to Dundee, to Edinburgh, to York, maybe even to London itself.

'I'll be on you one day, Train,' she told it. 'Maybe all the way to London, but at least as far as Dundee. You wait and see and I'll have a red coat and a red hat and black leather gloves.'

Satisfied that the nightly ritual had been concluded successfully, she went to bed.

She was able to sleep late for in those days of late February it was still dark at six o'clock. No need to wash in cold water. Was there not always – well, nearly always – a kettle murmuring away beside the soup at the back of the black iron range? She made tea – Father liked a really good strong cup of tea first thing in the morning – before she carried a ewer of hot water back up to the basin that sat on her dresser. She pulled on her petticoats and her hand-knit stockings. It was far too cold to stand there in her knickers just to make sure that her neck was clean.

Ian was coming in from the byre when she went downstairs again to stir the porridge.

'Did you do your composition last night?' she asked him as he slumped tiredly at the table.

His face lit up and he sat up straight, his early morning labours already forgotten. 'Aye, and it's grand. I'll easy beat Robin. I've used near every big word I know.'

'Mr Morrison says whiles a wee word is better nor a big one.'

Ian looked up at her from the superiority of his eleven years. 'You don't know what you're talking about, Mairi McGloughlin. Big words, correctly used, show an educated mind.'

'But you and ratty Robin only look up big words in the Dominie's dictionary. I cannae see much education in that. I think one of thon parrots could do the same.'

Ian refused to answer which was usually a sign that he knew he was beaten but refused to accept it. 'Hurry up

8

with the porridge, Mairi. You still have all the pieces to make.'

'Your wee sister has only the two hands, lad. Get aff your backside and pour the tea.'

The children had not heard their father come in but when they did, they sprang, Ian to do as he was told, Mairi to her brother's defence.

'Ian's jist in from the byre, Dad. We'll have calves and lambs soon. Lambs first, do you think? I hope I can raise one this year. Wouldn't that be nice?'

'No, it wouldn't, lass, because it would mean that I had lost a ewe, most like.'

'Well, if it was like Snowdrop refusing one of her twins again, I could raise that.'

'If she does and if we find it before it starves to death or the crows get it.' Colin turned to his son. 'There's a good job for you on Saturday, Ian. Take the shotgun and get some crows.'

'Teach me to shoot, Dad,' begged Mairi. 'I bet I'd be better than anyone.'

'Shooting's not for girls, lambkin.'

'There were women shooting at the Laird's Ne'erday party.'

'Gentry's different.'

'Women shot in the Wild West, Dad,' put in Ian.

For a moment Colin looked angry and then he started to laugh. 'I'm picturing my wee Mairi like one of they women on the Wild West Show. Who are you going to shoot, Mairi Kathryn McGloughlin, gin your daddy teaches you to shoot?'

Mairi smiled. She had won, as usual. 'Stinky Robin Morrison and even stinkier Billy Soutar.'

'I don't know what you have against Robin. He's really very nice.'

'He's a pain. He thinks he's special jist because his father is the Dominie.'

9

Ian jumped to the defence of his friend. 'That's not true, Mairi. Robin is great.'

'Robin's great. Robin's great,' Mairi sneered. 'Well, think what you like, Ian McGloughlin, but *I* don't like him.'

'If the two of you don't get your porridge eaten,' said their father mildly, 'it'll be Robin's father you have to worry about.'

Mairi looked at her father quickly and then at the wag-at-the-wall clock. 'What a fleg you gave me,' she laughed. 'We've hours yet.' She ladled out the porridge and the children sat down and began to eat. Their father took his bowl and ate from it as he walked to the door.

'Straight home the pair of you,' he said, 'and I'll be ready for my tea as soon as the sun goes down. Mind you feed the stirks, our Ian, just as soon as you change out of your school clothes.'

He was gone and Ian breathed a little easier. He was rarely relaxed around his father, unaware that his nervousness communicated itself to the man and made the situation worse. Mairi felt no lightening of the atmosphere. She was a sunny child; she adored her brother and she worshipped her father. She missed her mother who had died three years earlier but time made the pain bearable and because she had been so young when her mother had died, she did not know that she missed certain attentions. If the deficits in her upbringing had been pointed out to her she would have denied their existence vociferously. She had everything she wanted and needed. There were twice-yearly visits from interfering, although well-meaning, relatives but there was, more importantly, Ian and the dogs and occasionally a lamb, and she had, as she knew fine well, big Colin McGloughlin to fight all her battles for her.

Mairi cleared the table, washed the dishes, made up pieces for herself, her brother, and an extra one for daft Billy Soutar who, as usual, would have none, and only then did she pick up her books and leave the house. She did not lock the door. No one apart from their father would enter the house until she and Ian came back from school.

'Robin Morrison, get your head out of that book and fetch some coal. Jack the Carter shovelled it into the shed for me. Your father isn't up to it.'

Lizzie Morrison looked at her son, saw his too-long, too-thin arms sticking out from the ends of his jacket.

'Neither are you, laddie,' she thought, but she said nothing. If she did, he would go out and shovel coal until he was exhausted. 'Just fill the coal scuttle, Robin, and then clear this table so that I can set the tea.'

Robin looked up vaguely at his mother; it took him time to get from 1485 to 1900.

'Coal,' she said again firmly. 'Fill the scuttle and clear the table.'

Robin began to pile the books.

'Coal,' she said again. '*Now*. If I don't get coal, you don't get your tea.'

The boy stopped. 'Sorry, Mother, I wasn't really paying attention. Well, I mean, I wasn't *not* paying attention but my mind . . .' He looked at the set of his mother's jaw. 'I'll get the coal.'

He looked regretfully at the book. A few more minutes; if she had only given him a few more minutes. He went outside and the beauty of the night stopped him. He reached up his hands towards the stars. He could touch them if he stretched.

'Maybe that one's dead, laddie.'

His father was standing near the gate that separated school and Schoolhouse.

'Dead? How can it be dead and it shining and twinkling so brightly?'

Robin knew the answer, but he loved allowing his father to show his erudition.

Euan Morrison pointed to a star above the Schoolhouse. 'Perhaps that star has burned itself out but, because it takes the light so long to reach the earth, the only way you can tell if it's dead is to stand right here and watch till the light goes out.'

The door opened and light spilled out from a fire that was still very much alive. So was the voice that floated along on the light and, like the fire, it was warm and welcoming. 'If you two don't stop your star gazing, there'll be no tea for either one of you. Euan, it's near the boy's bedtime and you've been sitting in that cold classroom since four o'clock.'

'Don't fuss, Lizzie. The fire's embers are still sending out warmth. Robin has the coal situation in hand, haven't you, lad, and I'll help with the table. Is that mince and onions I smell?' Deftly he steered his wife away from the steps to give his son time to do his chore.

Robin, the heavy scuttle held before him in both hands, walked stiff-legged into the kitchen a few minutes later. He had overfilled the container so that its weight bent him almost double, and it was impossible for him to bend his knees.

'Laddie, you've too much in there.'

Robin lowered the scuttle to the hearth and stretched thankfully. 'Saves going out again, Dad.' He laughed suddenly. 'We should be like the Romans and put in central heating systems.'

Euan was about to discuss the feasibility of the plan together with the probable objections of the Educational Authorities when his wife interrupted.

'Robin Morrison, there is far too much nonsense in your head. Wash your hands and finish that table. That's not a fitting job for your father.'

Euan winked at his son and went on placing forks and spoons. 'Wee Mairi McGloughlin beat everyone in the big class at spelling today, Lizzie. She's bright.'

'She's a pert wee madam. Her father ruins her.'

'Och, he's doing a grand job raising those bairns since his wife passed away.'

'He's too hard on Ian.'

'No harder than I am on Robin. He just has a wee difficulty coping with a better mind than his own. I wish I'd made more of an effort to get to know the mother, a quiet, shy lassie, never very robust. Perhaps the children, Ian in brains at least, favour her. Colin McGloughlin is an intelligent man but he seems to think intelligence is a weakness in a labourer, as if brains and brawn don't go naturally together.'

'Ian doesn't want to be a farmer, Mother. He wants to travel, see the world, write about it. We're going to go together, to Greece, to Italy . . .'

Euan frowned. 'Fine dreams, Robin, but where would the likes of us find the money for such travel? You might have a chance if you get a place at the university' – he looked at his wife and smiled – 'and not get yourself tied up with a wife and a family before you graduate, but Ian. He has no chance of breaking out of his life pattern. In a way he's lucky. His father has a lease on a good farm. The McGloughlins have been tenants on Windydykes farm for three generations. Ian will take over from his father, the fourth generation. Hard work, but he'll have a job for life and a house, a warmer more convenient house than this one.'

'Mairi hates me.'

'No, Robin. She's just protective of her brother. If you were not here, he would be the undisputed top of the class.'

'He's cleverer than I am.'

'You are both intelligent boys. Each of you could go to university but Ian won't need a university education, even if his father could afford it. Now, Mairi's brain is wasted on a girl.' Too late he saw his wife's quick frown of displeasure.

13

'You have to agree, Lizzie. What use on a farm is a girl who can recite Shakespeare and Milton?'

Lizzie Morrison stood up and the anger emanating from her was almost palpable. It was a sore point with her that almost every female member of the farming community, including nine-year-old Mairi McGloughlin, was a better cook than she was. She had married and set her not inconsiderable intelligence to trying to master all the domestic chores she had never learned as a child, but she was still not satisfied with her achievements. 'So it doesn't take intelligence to run a house on a pittance, Euan Morrison. Well, we all know how intelligent you and Robin are. Fine, there's bread dough proving for tomorrow. It should yield – no, why should I tell you, anyone should be able to work that out. And Colin McGloughlin brought another rabbit. You can work out how to skin it, clean it, and cook it for tomorrow's dinner, and I'll be locking the bedroom door, so work out how the two of you can get yourselves and your amazing intellects into the same wee bed.'

She left the room, slamming the door behind her and Robin looked nervously at his father. Euan smiled.

'Quite a woman, your mother. I could have told her that the Bible says that a woman should do as her husband bids her but I can hear her explaining that since she never had the opportunity to finish at the university she is therefore too stupid to read the good book. If you have finished your meal, away to your bed. I'll crawl in beside you later, when I've figured out how to deal with a dead rabbit.'

Robin said nothing. He would have liked more food but the tension in the air was too threatening. He whispered, 'Goodnight,' and ran up the stairs. When he was washed and in his night shirt he got into his narrow bed and squeezed himself as close to the wall as possible so as to leave room for his father.

14

But when he woke in the night he was alone in the bed and there was muffled laughter from the bedroom on the other side of the wall. Robin smiled and went back to sleep.

Chapter Two

Jack Black reined in his horse and took in the beauty of the picture in front of him. Sixteen-year-old Mairi McGloughlin was standing on a barrel, her arms stretched above her head towards the kitten that stayed tantalizingly just out of her reach and, every now and again, batted at the outstretched fingers with a soft paw.

Jack stayed looking and appreciating the slim waist, the rounded hips, the swelling breasts against the stuff of her dress. He edged his horse close to the barrel and, reaching up, scooped the kitten from the roof and placed it in her arms. She had been so involved in her battle with her pet that she had not heard him approach and she looked first startled and then pleased.

'Thank you, Jack. Hello, Bluebell.' With her free hand Mairi patted the white nose of the old Bay.

'Let me help you down.'

'I can manage.'

He moved the horse away so that she had room to jump and she landed on the ground beside him in a flurry of brown skirts and white petticoats.

Colin McGloughlin watched the encounter from the kitchen window and he put down his pipe, stuck his hat on his head and went out. 'Hello, Jack. You'll have a message from your father?'

'No, Colin, for Mairi, and Ian, of course. There's going to be a dance in the Kirk Hall next Friday. I thought we could make up a table.'

16

'If you can get Ian to go then Mairi can go, but he's not a lad for the dancing. Prefers to sit under a tree with a book in his hand.'

'I'll make him come, Jack,' said Mairi. 'Is it just for the young farmers?'

'Aye. Will you help with the supper? We thought stovies. Edith is in charge but Robin Morrison will be back from the university and so maybe her head won't be working as well as it normally does.'

Mairi frowned. 'Is his lordship coming then? You'll get Ian. He'll not turn up to dance with your sister but he'll come to swop poetry with his friend.'

'Best not tell Edith that. She's happier thinking the two of them are after her.'

Colin looked at the strong, handsome, young man. 'That's no a respectful way to talk about your sister, Jack.'

'Oh, all the lassies like tae think they're driving us wild, Colin. Do you no mind yourself at our age?'

'I mind myself fine,' said Colin coldly. 'Mairi, it's time there was a meal on the table. Will you join us, Jack?'

'My mother's expecting me, and I still have to go to Peesie Acres.' Jack smiled down at the girl, sure of his looks, his charm, his position as the son of the biggest farmer in the district. 'You'll help in the kitchen then, Mairi, and you'll save the last dance for me.'

'Oh, I don't know, Jack Black. I might be up to my elbows in soap suds like I was at the Ne'erday dance . . .'

'Ach, you were only a wee lassie at the New Year . . .'

'Or I might dance with my brother. Who knows?'

He laughed and turned his horse away. 'Edith'll come by to make lists; she's a grand one for list making. I'll see the two of you next Friday.'

Father and daughter watched him ride away.

'He really fancies himself,' said Mairi and Colin's heart lightened. She would not be the only girl in the district to find Jack Black attractive and, although he knew he would

17

have to give her up some day, he was not yet ready. She was too young. He remembered the picture of blossoming womanhood he had seen on the barrel.

'Don't let me catch you climbing on barrels again. It's not ladylike and, forbye, it's dangerous.'

'I couldn't get the kitten down.'

'I'm over forty years on a farm, lass. I've never yet seen a cat that couldn't get out of the situation it was in, gin it wanted to.'

She tucked her hand into his arm. 'But I wanted him then, Dad,' she told him simply. 'Come on. I've got lettuce soup, a trout Ian caught this morning, new potatoes, and fresh peas just out of their pods. I hear Mrs Morrison is under the weather. She's not over the cold she caught in February. That Schoolhouse needs money spent on it. It's damp. Robin's nose used to run as often as Billy Soutar's.'

'Robin Morrison's nose never ran in its life.'

'You have an awful respect for education, Dad, if you think that a man is above such things just because he can do the twelve times table faster than anybody else – and besides, he couldn't do it faster than me, if I'd put my mind to it.'

She served the soup and looked at the tureen measuringly. 'I've made an awful lot of this soup. It'll go off since there's cream in it. I know,' she said brightly as if she had just that moment thought of it, 'I'll take what Ian won't eat to Mrs Morrison. That's the first thing that goes when a woman's not feeling her best, her wish to cook. They're probably eating bread and cheese. Who is going to shake off a winter cold eating shop-bought bread?'

If her father thought it strange that she had not expressed concern for their neighbour until she had heard that Mrs Morrison's son was to be at home, he said nothing.

'We're not waiting on your brother then?'

'He's shearing. He has some bread and mutton and can get some water from the burn.'

'Charlie's with him?'

18

'No, he's taken the extra ewes to the market in Forfar.'

Colin handed her his empty plate for a refill. 'God help my sheep.'

She looked at him, delicate eyebrows raised. 'They're hardly your problem once they're sold, Dad.'

'The ones getting clippit by your forgetful brother, I meant.'

Father and daughter laughed for a moment at their memories of some of Ian's disasters.

'Dad. You're not fair to Ian. He'll do a grand job.'

'Aye, if he keeps his mind on the cutting and doesnae wander away thinking on how beautifully the wool grows from the skin or some daftlike nonsense. I dinnae want them with funny haircuts.'

Mairi laughed. 'He didn't write a poem about sheep sheering, did he?'

Colin watched her deftly bone the trout. 'Sometimes I think it's a wee bit of a shame that you're not a boy, Mairi. I could hae let the laddie go to the university. It would hae been a big sacrifice but we could hae managed and you could hae worked the farm.'

'I can still work the farm, Dad. Charlie promised to teach me to plough since you won't, and I bet I could clip sheep. I've watched you and Charlie often enough.'

'You're a wee bit lassie. You're no built for hauling sheep around or harnessing yourself tae a horse and following a plough. I catch you yoked tae a horse and Charlie'll be at the next hiring fair.'

'Isn't this a grand fish,' she said ignoring his anger. 'Ian should hae been born tae the Schoolhouse and Robin Morrison tae the farm. He's better at tattie howking than Ian, and really enjoys getting his hands mucky.'

'Aye, because he does it once a year tae earn a few bob for his schooling. Day and night, summer and winter, mud and snow, is a different thing. You'll make some farmer a good wife one day.'

'Jack Black for instance?'

'You could dae worse. His father owns his land and it's right beside us. You'd be near me and when I'm . . . when Ian is farmer here, you and Jack could keep an eye on him.'

'What eye I had left from watching Jack,' said Mairi drily.

Her father looked at her. Jack, like Ian, was the only son of a farmer and so he had been bred up from the time he could walk to work the land. She could not question his ability. What else did she mean? That rumour that had gone around before the New Year that his mother's kitchen maid had left in tears and disgrace . . . ! How would his sheltered Mairi hear such tales? Ian, even if he was aware of them, would say nothing and Edith would not spread distasteful rumours about her own brother.

'I was talking about the future, lassie. I'm in no hurry to give you up. Ian would need tae marry first.'

'Is that a fact?' asked Mairi laughing. 'Let me tell you, Father dear, I will marry when I choose and so far I haven't seen anyone worth the marrying. I'll away and make you some tea and then I'll take this soup to poor Mrs Morrison.'

'What your mother would say if she could hear the cheeky way you have of talking to your father. Whit a hoyden you would be with a university education.'

'Mrs Morrison has been to the university.'

'Aye, and whit a waste of good money that was. She didn't finish and she never worked a day in her life.'

Mairi sighed. 'That's the kind of marriage I want, Dad. When you see this man and you know he's the one for you and nothing else matters. Forbye, though, she's helped the Dominie times he's been ill and no single woman teacher available. That's been using her education.'

'Education. The woman can talk to you in Latin and Greek and there's the Dominie and Robin thin as two rakes because she can't cook. Do you know what she said to your mother once? "There are more important things in life, Mrs McGloughlin, than recipes for fish."'

'I'll take some of my scones as well,' said Mairi.

'Will I come to meet you, lass?'

'With it as light as day until two o'clock in the morning? I won't be long.'

He said nothing when he noticed that she had changed her dress, but instead took the mug she handed him and went to the fireplace and sat down. He did not pick up a book although there were books in plenty in the house. Reading was something Ian did, and, more often than Colin knew, Mairi. He sat and relaxed into his chair. He scarcely looked up when Ian entered.

'Mairi's left you some tea, lad. Soup's in a tin plate keeping warm in the scullery. Clipping done?'

'Aye. What was Jack Black wanting?'

'You didnae see him?'

'No, but that old horse of his left us a present.'

Colin stood up. 'I didnae notice. I'll away and put it on your sister's flooers. Jack was asking the two of you to a dance at the Kirk Hall.'

'I'm no going to any dance.'

'Aye, you are, for your sister wants tae go and forbye, Robin's going.'

'Robin?' Ian looked around the room as if his sister might be hiding under a cushion. 'Where's Mairi?'

'Away tae the Schoolhouse with some soup for Mistress Morrison.'

'Away tae plague Robin more like. I'll away ben and get my tea.'

Mairi was unsure of her motive in taking soup and scones to the school teacher's wife. Since she had left the small country school she had had little contact with the Morrisons. Ian and Robin had remained friends when they had gone

21

on to secondary school in Arbroath and, even after Robin had won a scholarship to a boarding school, the boys had continued to see one another, at least when Robin was at home. But Mairi resented Robin who was having the chance that she knew her brother deserved. Sometimes she felt that, had the Dominie tried harder, her father might have relented and allowed Ian to continue his formal education. But Mr Morrison had accepted the status quo and Ian had left school on his fourteenth birthday. His sole contact with books and learning seemed to be Robin's periodic visits but Mairi suspected that the Dominie loaned her brother books and discussed them with him whenever there was an opportunity. For most of the year there was no time for long chats but in the winter when there was little light for working, as long as the inbye animals were fed and watered and their bedding changed regularly, Colin had no objection to his son's visits to the Schoolhouse. But Mairi had no reason to visit her former teacher and, until tonight, no intention of doing so.

She walked carefully up the farm road, taking time to admire the beauty of the briar roses and the honeysuckle twining in the hedges. She was conscious of the indescribable and ethereally beautiful Scottish summer evening light when a lilac blueness seems to hang over everything and, if she had not been carrying a pail of soup in her hands, she would have raised them in supplication to the self same sky to show her awareness of her oneness with the world around her.

'How can he say he wants to leave this? How could anyone ever want to live anywhere else?'

Mairi was well aware of the struggle for survival that her father and brother fought almost every day of their lives. She had seen them return from the fields too tired from hours of back-breaking labour even to eat. She knew too that Colin had never considered living in any other way. Ian loved the land; he saw beauty in an unfolding leaf, the innocence in the play of a young animal. Had he not written poem after

22

poem to those same delights and yet, when he spoke at all about himself, it was always to say how much he wanted to get away, away from the things he loved.

How strange. Mairi loved the land and her love made her want to cleave even closer to it. How was it possible to love something and to want desperately to go away from it?

The Dominie was in his garden and, as he stood up from his hoeing, his face expressed his delight and surprise at seeing her.

'Soup, Mairi, how very thoughtful of you. Mrs Morrison enjoys lettuce soup but just hasn't had the energy for cooking this summer.'

'Goodness, Dominie, it cooks itself. I'll take it into the back kitchen.'

He put down his hoe, obviously glad of an opportunity to rest. 'No, no, lass. Let me take you in the front door, Mrs Morrison will be overjoyed to have a visitor and, as for me, a wee crack with a former star pupil is always a delight. You're enjoying being the mistress of the farm? Your brother tells me you rule with a rod of iron.'

Mairi blushed to the roots of her hair and vowed silently to make Ian regret his flippancy. She made her menfolk do only what was good for them. 'Ian's a blether. Hello, Mrs Morrison. I hope you don't mind, but I made too much soup for the three of us.'

Lizzie Morrison rose with a smile of welcome and Mairi had to stifle a gasp at the difference a few months had made. The Dominie's wife had always been slim, but now she was almost emaciated. Her face was thin and pale and her great eyes looked too big for their sockets. Her hair, which had always curled around her head in soft feathery curls, was dry and lifeless. Her voice, too, was lifeless but she did try to make it bright and there was no doubt about the warmth of her welcome.

'Oh, Mairi, how very kind of you. We have missed seeing Ian this past summer. The Dominie misses Robin so much

23

and Ian is almost as dear to him. But come, my dear, sit down and tell me what you are doing.'

Mr Morrison, with a murmured, 'I'll move the kettle onto the fire,' took the pail and the plate of scones and went off to the scullery and Mairi was forced to sit down. She felt stupid and awkward. What had she been doing? Nothing. Nothing but washing, ironing, cooking, cleaning. What was there of interest in that?

'I grew roses this summer,' she said, 'Bourbons and gallicas . . .'

Mrs Morrison sniffed, her eyes closed. What a strange way for a grown woman to behave.

'Oh, I can almost smell them, Mairi,' she said, 'and what else did you grow?'

'Canterbury Bells and Hollyhocks.'

'I should like to see your garden, Mairi. I suppose you have no need to grow vegetables?'

'But I do, to get them young and sweet. Even potatoes.'

'Your father keeps us in potatoes and cabbages, carrots and turnips in season. He's a fine man and Ian is very like him.'

'Ian? But Ian is nothing like our father, Mrs Morrison. Why, Ian is a . . . a poet.'

'And your father isn't? I think all men who work with the land are poets, Mairi, especially the big, gentle ones like your father.' For a moment she looked embarrassed but was saved by her husband's entrance.

'Have you made us tea, Euan? And here's a poet can make a cup of tea, Mairi.'

'But not scones, my dear. The scones are Mairi's.'

Mairi looked up and her eye was caught by a sepia portrait of Robin, so starched, so formal. He did not look like the boy who had plagued her in the playground. Or had he ever plagued her? Was it not Ian who had said, 'Go away, Mairi. This is a boys' game.'

'How is Robin?' she asked politely. 'I hear he is enjoying the university.'

'He is a very new student, my dear,' said the Dominie, 'and like many new students has made his share of mistakes but he ended his first year well and, having managed to just scrape through his examinations, is vowing to do better next year.'

'And what will he do with this fine education?' asked Mairi and surprised herself by the bitterness in her voice.

If the Morrisons noticed, and probably they were too innocent and gentle to believe they had heard it, they said nothing except, 'Well, here is his mother who would like to see her son a doctor or a lawyer, but would you believe, Mairi, our Robin wants to teach.'

'To teach?' Mairi almost screeched. 'Not here surely?'

'He has fallen in love with our magnificent capital city. Perhaps his future lies there, but he will start in Angus, probably in Arbroath since that is where the nearest secondary school is. Robin will teach Latin and Greek. There is little need for Latin and Greek here.'

'Latin and Greek. I would have liked fine to learn those languages, Dominie. One day, I'm thinking, farm girls will learn them.'

The Morrisons laughed politely and Mairi, a picture in her head of herself reciting Homer to a milk cow, laughed with them.

'Pigs might fly, as Bridie O'Sullivan is always saying,' she said, and stood up to go.

'Wait, child. I'll put the soup into a pot and give you back your pail.'

'No matter, Mrs Morrison, I'll drop in when I'm passing.'

'Or Robin could bring it over some evening when Ian is at home,' suggested Mrs Morrison.

'Aye, he could do that. Ian's in most nights and if he's out, he's lying by the burn with a book, probably one of yours, Dominie.'

They saw her to the gate and Mairi turned when she reached the entrance to Pansy Lane. They were standing watching her, the Dominie's arm around his wife.

'Aye,' thought Mairi again. 'That's the kind of marriage I want,' and she raised her arm in salute before picking up her skirts and running like a child down the path to the farm.

Chapter Three

The band was ready: Edith on the piano, George Trace on the fiddle and Maggie McLeod on the accordion. Maggie looked a bit awkward, she so wee and the accordion so big, but nobody laughed because everyone in the Kirk Hall had seen her throw bags of tatties on to her father's cart. A feisty wee soul was Maggie and it was a brave man who would meddle with her.

Mairi McGloughlin found her toes tapping in anticipation and she had no idea how her vitality and eagerness transmitted themselves to the watching farm boys. She had made her dress and she was pleased with the soft frill around her throat, at the end of each narrow wrist-length sleeve, and around the whirling hem. Green was a colour that suited her burnished auburn curls and large green eyes, and well she knew it.

'You'll save a dance for me, Mairi,' and there was Robin.

If only he had asked properly and humbly like the rest of the boys – except Ian – in the hall.

'I don't know that I have a space left, Robin Morrison.'

He laughed. 'Duty done, Mairi,' he teased and sauntered off over to where Ian stood awkwardly, obviously wishing he were anywhere else.

Mairi tossed her curls with vexation. Robin was not quite so good-looking as Jack but he was a better, more courteous dancer, and what was more, he seemed unaware of his attractiveness. All the girls in the room wanted to dance with him.

'Only because he's a good dancer,' said Mairi angrily to herself, 'and a girl who hasn't had too much practice looks better when she's dancing with someone who knows what he's doing.'

'Don't tell me I heard you turn down Robin Morrison, Mairi?' Edith, released from the piano for a moment, was at her elbow. 'You must be daft. He is the best dancer in the hall, apart from our Jack and I can't imagine why anyone would want to dance with him.'

Mairi looked over to where Robin and Ian were standing, their faces animated with their interest in each other and in their discussion. She tried to see them objectively. Robin was too tall, too thin, and his too-long dark hair hung dejectedly around his ears. Ian was his father's son, with the strong legs and broad shoulders of a working farmer. His skin was weatherbeaten and his eyes shone out a brilliant blue against the tanned skin. They were fine-looking men, Robin perhaps a slightly poetic, Byronic figure, although she would die a thousand deaths before she would let him know she thought so. Ian looked . . . trustworthy, capable, kind: fine-looking young men, both of them. A girl could count herself lucky to attract either one of them.

'And doesn't Robin know it?'

She turned and looked across the hall to where Jack was sitting, one girl, who should have known better, on his lap and another sitting in a chair gazing at him as if every word that fell from his lips was gold.

'We don't see our brothers the way other girls see them, Edith. Your Jack is very handsome.'

'Oh, he's not on a par with your Ian, or Robin. Robin's beautiful, don't you think?'

'I think he looks as if he could use a few plates of stovies,' said Mairi disparagingly. Ian was a big man and every inch on him solid muscle. No one would ever say Mairi McGloughlin didn't know how to feed her men.

Edith looked hopefully at the clock on the wall and

sighed. 'It's too early for supper. You'd better get a dance or two first.'

'Unfortunately girls have to be asked.'

'Goodness, Mairi, you're not one of those awful modern women who think they should do the asking?'

'I don't care who does the asking; it's having to smile sweetly and say yes to every corrie-footed farmer who asks that bothers me.'

Edith looked at her and laughed slyly. 'I didn't notice you smiling sweetly at Robin.'

'Och, he's not a man . . . well, I mean it's different with Robin and I didn't exactly say no, I just said maybe.'

He would not ask again, she knew that. She knew too that even if he did ask, something in her would make her say no.

Mairi McGloughlin was beginning to wish that she had stayed at home.

'I'd better get back to the piano. Pity you can't play, Mairi. Boys love it and besides, I'm dying to dance.'

For years, sitting in the schoolroom, Mairi had envied Edith with a longing that was almost palpable. Imagine being able to sit in front of a piano, look at a page of funny little black squiggles, and begin to make music, music that could make you dream, music that could make you cry, music that could make you dance. But, yes, if you were sitting up there at the piano, you could hardly be whirling and twirling around on the floor. She smiled and the smile caught at Jack Black's notoriously unselective heart. He dumped the girl from his knee, crossed the floor and presented himself to Mairi.

'I'm sure you said yes to Broon's Reel, Mairi. Let's get ourselves into a decent set.'

Mairi went, conscious that most girls were looking at her with envy and completely unconcerned about the young man whose name was already on her card. To give her her due, she had not looked at her card and had forgotten completely about him.

Sinclair, the Minister's son, saw Mairi's rejection as just one more cross on his troubled way and would have accepted it. Not so Violet, Mairi's one-time best friend.

'Sinclair, did you not say you had this dance with Mairi McGloughlin?'

Her young clear voice carried across the hall. Mairi stopped in mid-step and blushed to the roots of her hair but Jack laughed and, grabbing her arm, whirled her around in a proprietary way that annoyed Ian. Everything about Jack Black annoyed Ian.

He walked across the hall to Sinclair. 'Did she promise this dance, Sinclair?'

Sinclair blushed like Mairi. 'It's not worth making anything of it, Ian. She forgot, that's all. Can't expect a beautiful girl like Mairi to—'

'My father would expect his daughter to dance with Billy Soutar if she's given her word. I'll stop the dance.'

Robin, who had followed his friend across the floor, put a restraining hand on Ian's arm. 'Don't make a scene, Ian. She's thoughtless; that's hardly a crime.'

'My father spoils her but he'd not allow her to be rude.'

'Would he prefer his son embarrass her in front of a roomful of people? Sweet little Violet has already done that.'

'Embarrass her? Our Mairi?'

'She's desperately sorry.'

'That's why she's dancing like one of them dervishes with her skirts flying higher than any decent girl's should?'

'Exactly and forbye, she's only a lassie. Leave her alone and she'll apologize to Sinclair. If you do the big brother routine she'll stick her heels in like Carrie Kennedy's old goat and not be moved for love nor money.'

Ian looked at his friend and then back at Sinclair. 'Is that enough, Sinclair? Will I leave her to say she's sorry?'

'I'm so surprised she agreed to dance with me anyway. I can understand her preferring Jack.'

'For God's sake, man, stand up for yourself.'

Sinclair winced at his language. 'I'll stand up for what I feel is important, Ian, like taking the Lord's name in vain.'

Ian looked down and had the feeling that subtly Sinclair had changed and then, before he could analyze the change, the feeling was gone and once more timid, harmless Sinclair was there.

He turned away. 'Let me know if she doesn't apologize.'

Followed by Robin he walked back to their chairs against the wall. 'Look at her,' he fumed as he watched his sister sail, like a beautiful yacht, down the length of the hall, her energetic steps allowing her to keep pace easily with Jack's longer strides.

Robin was looking and what he saw was confusing him. 'She's grown up, Ian. When did your wee Mairi grow up?'

Ian looked at his friend in disgust. 'For Heaven's sake, Robin, it's just Mairi. Anyone would think you were St Paul on the road to Damascus with your tongue hanging out like an old dog needing a drink. Come on outside for a while.'

'I want to ask Mairi to dance.'

'You did.'

'I know but I didn't really mean it and now I do.'

'And you think she'll say yes? You'll never learn about women, Robin. Mairi can't abide you. And even if she did, she'd die rather than dance with you now.'

Robin looked at his friend in stunned silence. Mairi disliked him? He had known that she resented the times when he had beaten her beloved brother, but that she disliked him . . . No, surely not. Well, she would never know how much her dislike hurt him.

'You know Edith will be taking a break in a while and she's got awfully pretty, don't you think?'

'Well, she's certainly prettier than Maggie McLeod.'

'You are turning into an old grouch, Ian. Why on earth did you come to the dance if you're not going to enjoy yourself?'

31

'I came to see you,' said Ian angrily, and then added the second truth. 'My faither made me come to look after our Mairi. I doubt he could, the mood she's in.'

'Well, there's the end of the dance. I'm away to talk to Edith.'

Ian stood angrily and watched his friend cross the hall. He saw the way everyone, boys and girls alike, smiled and nodded as the Dominie's son passed them. He had always been popular, his position as the teacher's son and brightest pupil rarely held against him. In fact, everyone in the world, with the exception of Mairi McGloughlin, recognized the worth that was Robin.

'I'll thank you not to make a talking point of my sister.' The words were out before Ian thought. His fist connected with Jack's jaw before the other boy had even had a chance to protect himself. In amazement, horror, and some pride, Ian looked down at the sprawled figure of his sister's dancing partner. But not for long. With an oath that easily drowned out the squeals of excitement from various young ladies and words of encouragement from several farm boys, Jack had jumped again to his feet and thrown himself at Ian.

They went at one another with strength but without skill. The other boys formed a circle around them and the girls stood squacking outside that.

Robin jumped down from the platform where he had begun to ask Edith for a dance and pushed his way through the excited young people.

'Stop it,' he yelled but neither of the opponents heard him.

'Come on, Ian, it's the Kirk Hall.'

It's doubtful that they would have paid attention had he told them they were in the Kirk itself. Robin grabbed Jack and pulled him back just as Ian swung a blow at Jack's jaw. It connected, of course, with Robin and sent him to the floor in a crowd of multicoloured stars.

The shrieking stopped, the shouts of enthusiastic encouragement died away as the young people looked down at Robin.

'Now look at what you made me do.' Poor Robin heard Ian's voice yelling at Mairi and he smiled as he pulled himself to his feet. Edith was there to help him stand up.

'Oh, Robin, you poor lamb. I'll make you a nice cup of tea. And you'd best away home, our Jack, afore I tell Faither.'

'You too, Mairi,' Robin heard Ian say and he looked back to see Mairi, her face white with fear and embarrassment, burst into tears and run from the room followed by her brother. He would have gone after them but it was remarkably comfortable being propped up by Edith. Was she aware of how close her well-formed bosom was to his swollen jaw? He hoped not for he would have hated for her to move away.

She did though while she made him tea, having first given him a wet cloth to hold to his face.

'You're going to have a magnificent black eye,' she said. 'You were so brave, Robin, to get between Ian and Jack like that.'

'Stupid, more like,' groaned Robin who was beginning to wonder how he would explain his bruises to his parents.

He was not, of course, the only young man with explanations to manufacture. Colin McGloughlin was not at all pleased to have his daughter return home in tears and when he heard the story, told reluctantly by his son and somewhat hysterically by his daughter, was unsure as to which of his offspring he should berate first. As usual he chose Ian, only to have Mairi – as usual – jump to her brother's defence.

'Don't yell at Ian. It was my fault. I did promise Sinclair but I had forgotten until Violet reminded me.'

Colin looked at his dishevelled offspring. 'Oh, go to bed, the pair of you,' he said and went back to his account books.

*   *   *

33

It was several days before Robin showed his face outside the Schoolhouse. He had been concussed when his head hit the floor – not, he assured his father, when Ian's fist hit his jaw – and he suffered from headaches for a few days. When his rather splendid black and purple bruising had changed to an unfortunate bilious yellow he made his way to the farmhouse with the pot in which Mairi had carried the soup. Ian and Colin were not yet home from the fields and Mairi was in the kitchen preparing their evening meal. She flushed when she saw Robin standing there.

He had known that she would be alone and he had known that she would be embarrassed and possibly annoyed to see him and yet he had been unable to prevent himself from coming. Why did she dislike him? What had he ever done to deserve her animosity? The questions rankled.

'Ian's still in the fields,' she said angrily. 'A farmer uses all the hours God gives him in the summer. Even a brilliant Greek and Latin scholar should know that.'

'Take your pot, Mairi McGloughlin, before I put your head in it.' Robin was well and truly fed up. He had had a painful and ignominious few days; his mother had been distressed and all for the sake of this Madam. He thrust the pot at her. 'It's a pity your father never gave you a few of the skelps he was so keen to give Ian; it would have been the making of you.'

For the second time in less than a week Robin found himself on the receiving end of a McGloughlin fist but this time he saw it coming. He grabbed her hand and pulled her forward, fully intending to slap her with his other hand and found to his surprise that he had pulled her into his arms. Her beautiful green eyes sparkled up at him like those of a furious wildcat and he bent his head and kissed her full on her soft yielding lips. Stunned, she stayed quiet for a second and then Robin felt her respond.

He was eighteen years old and had never kissed anyone except his mother and he had not done that for several years.

34

This was very different. It was wonderful until Mairi came to her senses. She kicked him hard in the shins and when he released her with a yelp of pain she pushed him as hard as she could. He stumbled backwards and fell over the theekit pump that stood just outside the scullery door.

It was painful and it was humiliating. He looked up at her. One minute she had been kissing him so that every nerve-ending in his body tingled with the hints of unknown delights and the next she was kicking and slapping him.

'That's it,' he yelled. 'Edith's right, Mairi McGloughlin. You'll end up an old maid and serve you right.'

She stood above him, her face red with fury, her eyes full of unshed tears, and then as suddenly as she had become a fury she deflated.

'I hate you, Robin Morrison, and I'd choose to be an old maid rather than have anything to do with the likes of a Mammy's boy like you.'

Then she burst into tears and fled back into the farmhouse, slamming the door so hard behind her that the old stone house seemed to rock on its foundations.

Chapter Four

Robin Morrison, after promising faithfully to write to Edith Black, returned to the University of Edinburgh and decided to get a very good degree.

'And that'll show her,' he announced to his suitcase as he tightened the extra leather strap he had fastened around it, the catch not being reliable. He had little desire to 'show' Edith anything. Edith was a clinger and there were times when a chap wanted to cling and times when he wanted to be clung to, but pleasant as a little dalliance was, there were other things in life.

After his first year, Robin did not usually return home for the university holidays since jobs were more readily available in the city, but he did return in the summer of 1910. Robin Morrison was going abroad, to Florence, to study for a year in the places he had read and dreamed about since he first learned to read.

Ian had the news first.

He was sitting at the fireside waiting for Mairi to bring the soup to the table. He and his father and their hired men had been ploughing all day and they were dirty and exhausted. Ian had been slumped in his chair almost too tired to eat and forgetting completely that it was four weeks since he had heard from Robin who was normally a faithful correspondent. Mairi had put the letter up on the fireplace propped against the Wallie dug, that bone china ornament no self-respecting Edwardian household would have been without and, softened by her brother's obvious exhaustion, she brought it to him.

'This came today, Ian; it's from Robin.'

Immediately Ian brightened. These letters were his passport to a world in which he should belong but from which he was barred by poverty. Robin told him everything: classes, professors, university social events, opinions, political, religious, whatever . . . Robin shared with his friend. Ian never once complained of how much he missed their meetings and had taken to going to the Schoolhouse once a week, where he discussed the world past, present and future with the Dominie, and which he used as a library.

Now he carefully opened the letter and read the closely written thin sheets again and again and just this once allowed his heart to fill with grief that he too should not see Rome and Florence or one day, maybe next summer, ancient Greece.

'Dad, Mairi,' he called. 'Come and hear this. Is it not wonderful? Robin's won a scholarship to the University of Florence. A whole year, Mairi! He's going to Italy for a whole year. He's studying his daft old Romans, of course, but he plans to go on walking tours, to Venice, Mairi, and to Rome and, would you believe, Dad, Greece. He hopes, if he can save enough on his food, to get to Greece before he comes home for his last year in Edinburgh. What I would do to go with him!'

He handed Mairi the letter to read and sat back down in his seat. 'He'll send me postcards and he'll sketch.'

Colin looked at his son and not for the first time wondered if he had done the wrong thing by forcing the boy on to the land. No, no, no. The land was constant. People needed food. Therefore, although he would have to work all the hours God gave him, Ian had a job, a life. How many young people in this glorious new century could say the same with any security? Weren't machines taking jobs every day, even on farms? Hadn't he seen a bit in the paper about a machine cried a tractor? Couldn't it plough an entire farm in a meenit with just the one driver?

'All well and good, lad,' said Colin as he moved to his

37

place at the head of the scrubbed table, 'and I'll like fine tae see his postcards, but whit kind of a job is he going tae have at the end of all this?'

'Teaching, Dad, but that's not important. He'll have seen things, maybe even put his hand on stones touched by Cicero and Plato and . . .'

'If you want ancient stones, laddie, there's plenty here on the farm. The Picts is as ancient as your Romans and Greeks and forbye they spoke decent Scots.'

Ian stood up angrily. 'We don't know what they spoke, because we're none of us clever enough to read their stones.'

'Soup,' Mairi almost yelled. Ian must be distressed. He rarely argued with his father and certainly not over education and learning. She pushed him gently towards his seat. 'I'm glad Robin's coming home afore he goes gallivanting. I doubt his mother'll live through many more winters in that draughty old house. The doctor's bike's fair worn a new path to the Schoolhouse.'

'Aye, I think from the tone of Robin's letters that his father isn't telling him the whole truth; he knows his mother's poorly but I doubt he knows how often she's really ill.'

'Why has he no been home lately, lad?'

'Work, Dad. He's worked as a postie and he's worked . . . he's worked in a bar. Not everyone who goes in a bar gets drunk, you know,' he added defensively, 'and he needs money since his father makes next to nothing as a Dominie.'

'Then why in the name of heaven is the laddie set to be a teacher? Forbye there's only about two bairns at the most that wants tae learn Latin and Greek.'

'Robin sees teaching as a calling, like to the Church. Teachers want to make the world a better place.'

'So do farmers, but we want a decent wage for it.'

'You'll be glad to see Robin, Ian,' broke in Mairi. 'Goodness, have you spoken to him since that awful dance?'

38

'The dance wasn't awful, Mairi McGloughlin, you were,' said Ian with his rare smile.

'Stop it, you two. Sometimes I think you're getting younger instead of older. This is grand soup, lass. I'll have another bowl.'

Mairi picked up her father's plate and went through to the scullery. Rome, Florence, maybe even Athens. Robin would see all of them and she would stay at home content to see Dundee. No, she would not. She could live nowhere else but, oh, to see somewhere else, Edinburgh even, or London. It would be grand to look at famous buildings that sometimes seemed to exist only in books. Robin would see the wonders of the ancient world; he would speak in a language that she could not understand.

'What are you thinking about, Mairi? Here's Faither wondering if you've burned the soup.'

Ian was behind her, his bowl in his hand, Oliver Twist begging.

'Aren't you jealous, Ian? Robin away to Italy and you, that's just as clever, stuck behind a plough.'

'Jealous, no. Unhappy, yes. But I'll go abroad one day, Mairi, and I'll relish every minute the more for having been denied. And in the meantime Robin will share.'

'Oh, aye, Lord Bountiful. He'll send you a postcard and not feel guilty.'

'Good Heavens, lassie, why should Robin feel guilty? It's no his fault I couldnae stay on at the school, that I wasnae born rich. One day people will want to read the words I write and they'll pay to read them and I'll go to France and see castles and vineyards. Will I take you with me, my wee sister?'

Mairi did not doubt him. 'Will you come back? I'll go with you but I'd need to come back.'

'Of course I'll come back, especially if I'm not forced to stay, but first we'd better get the dinner on the table or neither one of us will be going anywhere.'

*   *   *

Robin came home but he was rarely at the farm. Ian was too busy and besides Robin wanted to spend time with his parents.

'Robin'll be away abroad afore I've had a chance to talk to him,' Ian complained to his sister, when he finally came in, exhausted. It was very late but still daylight and Mairi had been ironing while she waited for her menfolk to come home from harvesting.

'You'll be through by Sunday if this fine spell holds,' Mairi heard herself saying. 'Invite them back after Church for their dinner.'

Ian hugged her in one of his rare gestures of affection. 'You're sweet, Mairi McGloughlin, and I'll run away down to the Schoolhouse afore I eat and ask them.'

Then he spoiled it. 'You'll be nice, won't you, to Robin?'

Mairi stamped the hot iron down on his shirt as if she wished her brother were still inside it. 'I hope I know how to behave in my father's house, polite and . . . and ladylike.'

'Och, Mairi, can you no just be yourself?' He stared at her aghast but she smiled.

'Away afore you hang yourself,' she said and, with a sigh of relief, Ian stuck his cap on his head and went back out.

It was nearly an hour later when he returned and his father had already eaten.

'I'm sorry I took so long,' Ian apologized. 'Robin and I got talking about the Romantics and the Realists. I fair enjoy a chat like that, Mairi, and Mrs Morrison offered to make me a piece . . .' He looked up at his frowning sister. 'But, of course, I couldn't stay and miss this.'

Mairi still held on to the plate of delicious-smelling rabbit pie. Harvest was a good time to make easy catches. She struggled with inclination and desire and then capitulated and sat down, after giving her starving brother his plate.

'Come on, tell me, what's Romantics and Realists?'

Ian's eyes twinkled at her over the top of a full fork and when he had finished chewing and savouring he told her.

'Realists is people like Hardy and Wells, and a French fellow, Emile Zola, and they write about life as it really is. You know, you see the dirt swept under the carpet, and then the Romantics are writers like Lord Tennyson and Rudyard Kipling, softer stuff, poems and such like, "Come into the garden, Maud."'

'Surely poets are Realists?'

'Yes and no. They paint the world as they see it and that might not be the way you see it. And it's the subject as well. You wouldn't write a poem about anything nasty, like wringing a hen's neck, or a scuffle in Arbroath on a Saturday night.'

'Your friend Tennyson wrote about war. I cannae think of a less romantic subject.'

'That was then. We're civilized. War's a thing of the past.'

'If women were runnng the world it would be,' snapped Mairi and went off to put the oats on to soak for the morning.

Robin Morrison went to Italy and Mairi found herself, like Ian, looking for his letters. Not that she cared a fig for Robin but a first-hand account of foreign travel was interesting and educational. But there was more to life than watching for the postman's bike. The farming year turned unrelentingly on its axis from one harvest and immediate ploughing and planting to the next. By October the harvest was over and the fields were being readied for the next year's crops. Turnips were piled for winter feed and the constant repairing of binders and tack and the thousand other things that were indispensable occupied Colin and Ian indoors during the long winter nights.

They had a break at New Year and Colin kept an open door for any of the neighbours who wanted to come in for

41

a dram and a bit of Mairi's Black Bun or the more delicate shortbread she baked. It was the only day of the year that the McGloughlins saw their father the worse for wear. He drank dram for dram with his neighbours and grew maudlin and sentimental until he fell asleep in his chair by the fire and was carried up to bed by his son, no longer Colin's laddie but a man, suddenly grown bigger and stronger than his father. In the morning Colin was up as usual and if his mouth was dry and his skull a throbbing mass he said nothing and no one, not even Mairi, dared ask him how he fared.

Soon after Ne'erday came the seedtime, the sowing of oats and spring barley. Then, without drawing a breath, it was time to prepare the ground for the root crops, especially the potatoes. The farmers painted a living picture on the soil with little awareness of the beauty they were creating but still with an appreciation of the world around them and even big men like Colin McGloughlin would stop and admire the delicacy of the primroses that peeped out from every turn. He would tell his horses to stop while he pulled a bunch, roots and all, for his daughter's garden.

Then the weather turned warm enough for Colin to roll up his sleeves and unbutton his shirt, not to the waist, merely a decorous button or two – had his daughter not been nearby he would have liked fine often to remove shirt and singlet both – and get on with thinning out the turnips. And always, always the farmer watched the progress of the grain. The seeds were sown and the fields were watched for the magical overnight when thousands of little green soldiers suddenly appeared above the ground. They did not spring into action like those of the Greek hero . . . but bided their time growing taller until the summer sun turned their heads gold. Then Colin and other farmers like him all over Angus and further afield would lean over a fence and look and swither about whether or not to cut now – could they not hear the grains rustling and whispering in their silken beds, and surely this fine spell could not last? – or should they pray for good weather and wait another five or maybe six days?

And then the word miraculously went round that the harvest was ready and McGloughlin was hiring. Men and women, but not his wee lassie, could work ten or even twelve hours a day, stopping at noon for a piece and a cup of tea. Colin did not give ale, not until the day's work was done, and then he and Ian would dish it out from a pail to men and women both, and Mairi would watch from her bedroom window and wish that she could run like the children among their elders and listen to the stories, often bawdy, always funny.

Robin had seen a different harvest in Italy, the grape, but the camaraderie had been the same, and oh, how Mairi Kathryn McGloughlin would have liked to kirtle her skirts above her knees and stamp those grapes, but wild horses could not have pulled that admission from her.

When the haystacks were standing in the fields it was time to dig the potatoes and to find time to laugh at the fat bellies of the golden turnips that vigorously pushed themselves from their earthy bed; they could wait there until the frost and no harm done. And the work filled days, and nights marched on and at the end of the harvest when September was telling the trees that it was time to wind down in preparation for winter, Robin Morrison returned home from Italy and he brought Mairi a small glass fish from a fabled city where there were no streets and the buildings floated in water like the lilies on the duckpond.

Mairi was amazed. No one outside her immediate family had ever given her a gift before. In fact she could count on the fingers of one hand the presents she had had in her entire life: a cloth doll, a book, ribbons when the tinkers came with their wares, a peach from the Laird at the picnic, wonderful but not much, oh, and primroses still wet with dew.

She looked at the little fish with its golden tail defiantly flipping and its little pink body shimmering in the afternoon sunlight and she knew that it was the most beautiful thing that anyone would ever give her and, while her heart melted inside her, she frowned.

'Why, Robin?'

He did not misunderstand. 'Because it reminded me of you.'

She blushed. It was so achingly delicate and lovely. 'Of me?'

'Yes. Look at it. It's saying, "Here I am, ready to take on the world." I saw it and I thought of you.'

Her fingers clenched themselves around the tiny work of art and she seemed to feel the little heart beat and she could not hurl it at him because it would break.

'I hate you, Robin Morrison,' she said and once again slammed the door in his face.

Chapter Five

There was a harvest dance in the village hall. The hairst was over and the fruit of several months of back-breaking labour – with some help from the variable Scottish climate – was gathered in. It had been a good harvest and grain and seed potatoes had been sent south on the train, that same train which Mairi watched from her bedroom window.

Colin added his figures and then added them again. Yes, it had been a good harvest.

'Here, Mairi,' he said as he turned from his chair at the table to where his children stood watching and waiting breathlessly for the smile or the frown that would tell all. 'Buy a new frock for the harvest dance. You could do with a new shirt, our Ian, but I'm sure you'll find a book.'

Buy? A dress from a shop? Wordlessly Mairi clutched the coins to her and thought delightedly of which shop should be honoured by her patronage. She would put on her Sunday coat and hat and – she would take the train to Dundee! One of the big shops would be sure to have the dress that would make Robin Morrison regret that he saw her as a feisty termagant.

'Dundee?' bawled Colin. 'On the train on your lane? You shall not and I can't go with you because of the cattle sales. Ian, you'll take your sister into Dundee on Saturday and make sure she sticks to the High Street . . . maybe Reform Street, at a pinch.'

Ian groaned and Mairi grinned. She could handle Ian.

She turned from her brother with a swish of skirts. 'You

45

can away and find yourself a bookshop. With a big publisher in Dundee, there's bound to be a bookshop for brainy folk, or were you planning on buying that new shirt you need?' she teased as she slipped into the kitchen. If she was going into a shop she would need to make sure she had on the cleanest underwear that the sales lady had ever seen. She would wash her gloves too and maybe her Sunday frock. If the weather held she could get it out and dried and ironed tomorrow.

'Don't let her out of your sight, lad,' warned Colin on the Saturday morning. 'Didn't I see the smile of pure mischief she gave when she heard me say I was busy. If there's enough money left after the train fares, take her to Lamb's restaurant at the top of Reform Street for her dinner, or Draffen's if she gets stuck there in the dress department.'

'Don't you want to take her, Dad?'

Colin turned from the pegs at the door with his cap in his hand. His face and voice were serious. 'More than anything, laddie, but you've not experience enough for the sales and besides, I ken fine you're dying to buy yourself your own book.'

Ian flushed and Colin laughed but it was a gentle, understanding laugh. 'You've my frame, Ian, but your mother's brain and I'm pleased that you're clever. Write your poems if you like. I've nae objections whiles if the work's done properly.'

He had said more than he meant to say and he was embarrassed. Daft saft gowk that he was. He took refuge in simulated annoyance. 'Are you going then or do you plan tae walk sixteen miles?'

Mairi squeaked with nervousness. She had rushed downstairs in a flurry of skirts and a too-generous application of bottled toilet water. Now she looked at the clock and at her father. 'You have the worst sense of humour in the whole of Angus,' she told him.

'Jist as well I've the worst nose as well,' he said drily. 'You've as much scent on as would dae five lassies.'

He wished he had said nothing – it would have blown out the train windows on the way to Dundee – for here was Mairi squeaking again and rushing back upstairs to scrub her neck and behind her ears.

'I'll need tae take the pair of you in to Arbroath,' he told Ian who had resettled himself with the paper. 'Serves me right for getting between a woman and the impression she wants to make.'

Ian looked up. 'A woman? It's only Mairi.'

'Exactly,' said Colin and went out to hitch up his horse.

When his sister, now smelling slightly of carbolic soap, joined him on the cart Ian took a good look at her. Goodness, she was even sitting differently, her back straight, her knees together, her cotton-gloved hands demurely in her lap. Ian watched the hands. They did not look as if they could deal the unwary a sharp blow but he knew to his cost that they could.

Her eyes were shining with excitement and it was obvious that she wanted to forget that she was this mysterious creature called *woman* and jump up and down with joy on the bench the way she would have done – yesterday. He was more full of trepidation himself but he was looking forward to being on the train and to taking Mairi for a meal at a real restaurant. He lifted his own chin a little.

Colin left them at the station. He did not promise to meet them on their return; a new dress and a book would hardly weigh his children down on the four-mile walk home. Mairi and Ian, in their turn, could barely wait for him to go. This was their adventure and they met it unflinchingly in their different ways.

Ian bought the tickets, trying to sound as if he bought tickets for train journeys every other day. Mairi sat on the very edge of the wooden seat and then almost jumped up and began to pace the platform and then, at last, at last, the train came steaming and snorting and roaring around the corner and by some miracle hissed itself to a halt right in front of the platform. For a moment Ian panicked. How did the doors open? – but the guard was there and when he and Mairi were seated on a hard bench across from two elderly ladies who smiled at Mairi's dancing eyes, the guard waved his little green flag and the train wound itself up and belched out of the station.

And there was the sea, and, oh look, our farm and our house and there's my window and today the train can see *me* and I can't see it because I am inside it and I am going to Dundee where I will buy a ready-made dress for a dance.

Carnoustie came rushing to meet them with its magnificent golf course and beautiful hotel.

'Look, Ian, look. I'm sure you have to be a millionaire to stay there.'

And there was Monifieth and Broughty Ferry with houses like palaces – and then Dundee. The noise, the smell, was overwhelming.

'What do I smell, Ian?'

'Fish and, I don't know, beer, I think.'

'Can I smell jute?'

Ian frowned and tried the air like a dog on the scent. 'I don't know what jute smells like. Now come on, Mairi, take my hand crossing the road. I've never seen so many carts and, look at the carriages! They cannae be going to the Kirk on a Saturday.'

'It's ladies going shopping – like me,' laughed Mairi and, ignoring his hand, she danced away from him. He cursed under his breath and followed her.

How did she know so unerringly where she was going? They were on the High Street where the smell of fish from open shop fronts was more pervasive.

'Now Draffen's is just down there, Ian. You go and find a bookshop and then come back for me and we'll go for our tea like jute barons.'

He did as he was bid. He wanted to go but it would have been useless to argue anyway and so Mairi Kathryn McGloughlin found herself in the middle of Dundee on a Saturday afternoon with nearly three pounds in her purse. She would not go into the shop, not just yet. She would walk and she would look and she would remember.

The first thing Mairi noticed was that most of the women who were shopping were extremely well dressed. She would see a carriage draw up at the front of a shop; the door would open and first a highly polished boot of the finest soft leather would emerge, to be followed by yards of the best material excellently tailored. On top of all would be a hat – and such a hat! Perhaps there was a large brim – Mairi favoured them – and piled around the crown and trailing over the brim would be yards of fine tulle or silk or feathers. Superb. One hat made her laugh. For all the world, the elderly lady who was wearing it looked as if she had balanced on her head one of Father's finest cabbages.

'And she had to pay a lot more than Dad gets for his cabbages,' Mairi said to herself as she stored the memory to share later with her brother.

A sudden gust of wind reminded her that it was almost October, by blowing some leaves along the gutter, and Mairi, in her best coat, shivered. And that was when she noticed the children. Children of all ages and sizes, all of them dirty and all of them without shoes. They did not seem to care as they ran in and out among the shoppers, getting in the way, their shabby clothes doing little to protect them from the elements.

'Noo watch oot for some of that lot, hen,' advised a portly middle-aged woman who had come out of one of the fish shops. 'They're nae better than they should be and they'll hae your purse if you're no careful. Just come in from the country, have you? They'll have you marked.'

She bustled off and Mairi tightly clutched her purse with its precious coins and sighed at the knowledge that she did not look nearly so sophisticated as she had hoped. Then she brightened. She was going to buy a shop-made dress. No one would mistake her for a country girl then. She turned and hurried off to Draffen's.

And there at the door was one of the children, a girl with uncombed, tangled hair and the loveliest blue eyes peeping out from a grimy tear-streaked face.

'Got a ha'penny, Miss?' she whined, rubbing one bare foot against the other leg as if to warm it.

Mairi had the woman's words of warning in her head and so she did not reach for her purse immediately.

'And if I have and I give it to you, what will you do with it?'

'Gie it tae meh mam for some bread,' came the answer. The girl looked up at Mairi and opened those incredible blue eyes even wider.

Mairi loosened the string on her purse. 'And where's your mother?'

The girl lowered her head. Mairi saw the thin shoulders shake and she heard a sniff. 'In her bed, Miss, coughing and sneezing and that weak she cannae lift her heid.'

'Tuberculosis?'

'We cannae afford the doctor, Miss, but if you gie me a penny I can get her some food.'

Mairi knew that tuberculosis was one of the diseases that was prevalent in Dundee. The conditions in which many of the poorest people lived, herded into tenements that were damp and vermin-infested, encouraged such illnesses.

She looked at the girl who was once more staring at her with those eyes that said, never in my life have I told an untruth.

'If I give you some money will you buy your mother some nourishing broth?'

The tangled mop of hair nodded vigorously.

Mairi took out a shilling. She could still afford a store-bought dress. She looked down into the child's eager, hungry

50

eyes. Perhaps she was lying but her body could not lie. It told a tale of hunger and perhaps abuse. She thrust the purse at the girl.

'Here, take it, get your mother a doctor and buy yourself some hot food.'

The girl grabbed the purse and stood for a moment poised like a little bird for flight. 'You mean it? You'll no yell that I robbed you?'

'No.'

The girl began to back slowly away from Mairi as if she did not quite believe her and then when she was some few feet away she turned and disappeared into the Saturday shoppers and Mairi was left alone on the pavement. She shrugged her shoulders. Maybe the girl was lying but she, Mairi McGloughlin, had three frocks in her cupboard and good food on the table every day of her life.

'I can look at the dresses in Draffen's and make something over,' she told herself and feeling thoroughly depressed – is virtue really its own reward? – she went into the hallowed sanctuary that until today she had only read about.

The shop smelled of perfume, expensive perfume, quite a difference from the street outside, and Mairi's heart lifted. There were more important things in life than new dresses and many of them were free. She pretended that she was the daughter of one of the jute barons and that a little maid walked behind her ready to carry any parcels lest *Madame* exhaust herself. This was such a strange picture even to Madame that she laughed out loud and was frowned upon by several of the extremely superior-looking sales assistants.

Mairi walked up several flights of stairs and lost herself in china and hats and materials and lingerie. She stood close to an elderly lady who was buying a dinner service for her daughter. Several attendants scurried around with different patterns and at last *the* pattern was selected.

'Everything,' ordered the customer.

'For eight, Madam?' asked the senior sales assistant solicitously.

'Good gracious, no. For twelve,' said the dowager and Mairi noticed that apart from her signature in a little book she was required to give no further information.

'They must know her,' thought Mairi. 'I bet she owns the shop but if I did I'd be nicer to the hired help.'

She stayed in the china department long enough to choose her own pattern, lots and lots of delicate flowers on white china so fragile that Mairi feared her work-worn hands might break it.

She found a sales assistant in hats who knew perfectly well that her young customer could not afford her models but who was obviously tired of putting hats on imperfect heads. Mairi found herself glad that she had given away her money, for a totally impractical summer model – greatly reduced to three shillings and ninepence, *'and maybe they'd take the ninepence off too'* – was perfect on Miss McGloughlin's auburn curls.

'Those yellow roses do suit you,' said the assistant and Mairi, looking at the wide-brimmed hat with its huge cabbage roses, was forced to agree.

'Such a shame I didn't see it a few months ago,' said Miss McGloughlin shamelessly and the girls parted company, both delighted with the past half hour.

She did not venture into gowns but went instead to look at materials while she congratulated herself that really to make one's own clothes was so much more sensible and original. She finished with a visit to the overly modest lingerie department where she asked to see a satin chemise and smiled at the sales girl who could not make up her mind whether the girl on the other side of the counter could or could not afford any of her delicate frivolities.

'Too chilly in the country,' Mairi dismissed the expensive nothings and went to meet her brother.

At first he did not notice her empty hands, being too

busy with his own brand-new book on whose fly leaf he had already written *Ian Colin McGloughlin*.

'Look, Mairi, Palgrave's *Golden Treasury*, first published in 1871 and this edition with additional poems reprinted every year since 1907. Come on, we'll go to Lamb's because I didn't spend all the money Dad gave me and I'll let you read a few of the poems.'

They were in the restaurant and seated at a table before Ian noticed that there was no precious parcel.

'Och, Mairi, you couldn't make up your mind. Do you want to get a later train?'

'I gave the money away.'

At the sound of the words, Mairi's heart began to thud rapidly. She had given away all of Dad's hard-earned money, Ian's too, of course.

'Dad'll kill me,' she whispered.

Ian looked at her. She had done some pretty appalling things for which Colin had scolded her severely but nothing so stupid as this.

'No, he won't. Come on,' he said, standing up, 'we'll use the tea money for a frock.'

Mairi looked at him and smiled. He was the world's very nicest young man, easily. 'No, we won't,' she said. 'It was to a poor wee girl whose mother's got a terrible disease.'

'Och, Mairi, a terrible drink problem, more like,' said Ian when she had finished telling him the tale. 'You found yourself another Billy Soutar. You shouldnae be let out without a keeper.'

'Would you care to order?' asked a refined voice above them.

'Yes,' said Ian, 'please. Two haddock and chips with bread and butter and tea, and two cakes please, a yellow one and a pink one.'

At the thought of a pink cake Mairi sat back and looked ten years old again. Ian stared at her, wondering at the strange ways of women, and knew that if Colin was angry, his anger would be directed against his son.

But apart from vowing that if his children were ever let loose in a city again, he and his hired man would both be with them, Colin said nothing.

Chapter Six

The weather broke on the day of the harvest dance and rain clouds scudded down from the North and vented their anger on Forfarshire.

Colin looked out of the window at an already darkened afternoon and watched the great beeches bending and bowing before the fury of the wind. 'You'd be better tae stay by the fire the night, lassie. It's no weather tae let a dog out in.'

'I am not a dog,' smiled his daughter as she pirouetted before him in the dress she had just turned up. 'And I am going to dance every dance tonight. I'll wear my coat, Dad, and my boots – till I get there.'

Colin smiled at the picture of his daughter dancing with her great, heavy, but very necessary, boots.

'I'll take you in the trap and come back for the pair of you. I'm no leaving one of my horses oot in weather like this.'

Mairi chose not to argue. She would not win and so the effort would have been wasted. She just prayed that no one else would be arriving at the same time to see her being brought to the party like a little girl.

Five of her friends and acquaintances turned up at the same moment, the Blacks driven by Jack himself, and Robin, who had been given a lift by a young married couple from a farm nearer to the village and the Schoolhouse. This was no night to stand around greeting one another and Mairi was delighted since she had no wish to even speak to Robin Morrison. She had, however, a lowering suspicion that he felt exactly the same way about her and she determined to show him that she cared nothing for him or his opinions.

She filled her card with initials, mostly J.B., and knew without a doubt that she was the most popular and therefore envied young girl at the dance. She danced too with Sinclair who was also enjoying his last few days at home before the university term began. When Robin and his partner were near her in the course of a dance she could hear her own laughter, louder and sillier than anyone else's, and she hated herself.

'You sound like auld Agnes Dalrymple when she gets a dram at Ne'erday,' remonstrated Ian. 'What's bothering you?'

'Nothing,' said Mairi and danced past him laughing louder than ever.

At the second interval several of the young men went outside 'to see if it's still raining'.

'They're away for a smoke,' complained Edith. 'I've tried it, have you, Mairi? I've stopped though because Robin says it's a terrible unfeminine smell. I wouldn't like to be thought unfeminine. Would you?'

'I don't care what Mister Morrison thinks about me.'

'That's obvious, if you don't mind my saying so, or the other boys either. One or two of them were giving you . . . knowing looks.'

Mairi gasped. She would die of embarrassment; she prayed for the ground to open and swallow her up, or for the roof to be blown off, anything that might make this dreadful evening end.

'You have a foul mouth, Edith Black, and just mind that no one washes it out with carbolic soap.'

Trembling, Mairi turned away and hurried outside. Edith must not see how much she had hurt her. The men were huddled under a tree and so Mairi slipped out and ran around the corner to the back of the hall to the ruins of the old church. She leaned against a broken stone pillar and began

56

to cry, until eventually the peace of the building stole over her and she relaxed, stopped sobbing, and wiped her nose.

'Oh, I hate you, Robin Morrison,' she breathed into the silence.

'I know.' The voice was sad. 'You've been telling me for years and I keep asking myself why?'

Robin emerged from behind another pile of stone. He looked wary. 'Don't yell at me, Mairi. I only followed you because one or two of the lads have had a dram or two – they brought flasks – and a man with a drink can be awful silly.'

'Not half so silly as some women without drink,' sniffed Mairi.

He came closer and she saw that he had her coat. 'You'll catch your death,' he said as he slipped it around her shoulders.

She could not thank him. Instead she asked him how his mother was keeping.

'I see an awful difference in her since I went away,' he said sadly. 'Her letters were always so brave, so full of me and what I was doing, and when I asked her how she was, she ignored that bit and I let myself think that was because it was so inconsequential, her health, I mean.'

What could she say? They stood silently together listening to rainwater running off the broken roof and dropping from sightless windows.

'Could I ask you to keep an eye on her for me, Mairi? Ian doesn't notice; he's not really too interested in people he doesn't love. He notices your dad and you – his letters are full of you – and he sees me but . . .'

'Everyone else he cares about is a dead poet,' Mairi finished for him and they both laughed.

'I don't think that's strictly true but it's near enough.' He straightened up off the pillar against which he had been leaning. 'We'd better go in or we'll be talked about.'

She walked ahead of him back around the hall and at the

door she stopped. 'If I think there's a change I'll make sure Ian tells you.'

The door opened and there stood Jack. 'Well, where have you been, Mairi? The dance has started and since my partner was missing, I couldn't get into a set.'

'I don't think I have to tell you anything about my activities, Jack, but I'm sorry if I've missed the dance. I was talking to . . . an old friend.' She could almost feel Robin relax behind her as she took Jack's arm and went into the hall with him.

For the rest of the evening she was a model of propriety, dancing with all the young men to whom she had promised a dance, saying little and laughing less. Sometimes she saw Robin across the hall but he avoided her eyes and she turned away from him too. He was her old enemy; she had disliked him all her life and nothing had changed. But it had. He had cared enough for her – or for Ian – to watch over her and he had shared his worry about his mother's health. Little things? Major things? She did not know. She welcomed her father so heartily that he worried and could hardly wait to get her off to bed so that he could quiz his son.

'Mairi? She had a great time. Danced every dance. She was pleased tae see you because she was ready for her bed and maybe she was pleased to have half the men in the area miserable because she left early. Don't ask me about women. I just let her get on with it and stay out of her way.'

Colin stood up and Ian remembered how his father had towered above him when he was a child, terrifying him into stupidity.

'You didn't let anybody bother her?'

'Dad, she had every able-bodied man in the area wanting tae dance with her. She was even outside with Robin for a few minutes.'

Colin relaxed. Robin? She would be all right with Robin. 'I don't want her outside with Jack Black.'

'I think she'll make her own mind up about Jack, Dad.

58

You're the one reminded me she's no a wee lassie. She's near twenty. She'll be worrying soon that she's an auld maid.'

'An auld maid, my Mairi, never! Mind you, I'm in no hurry tae let some man have her and you watch her with Jack Black.'

He stomped off up the stairs leaving Ian to lock the doors and mend the fires. Ian looked around the comfortable homely room when he had finished, picked up his precious book, and followed his father upstairs.

Suddenly his father had faith in him? Misguided or was it just that the older man had no real notion of what a single-minded young woman could do? In his own room he looked at his strong farmer's hands.

'I couldnae begin to keep an eye on our wee Mairi but I can make sure Jack Black knows I'll break every bone in his body if any harm comes near her.'

Jack Black, of course, had no intention of harming Miss McGloughlin in any way. He had become quite used to being the most sought-after young man in the area and he did not much like it when the Dominie's son came home for holidays. This had been a very pleasant year with him off stravaiging all over Europe. But he had come back and he and Mairi had been outside together during the dance. If a girl was not loose, and Mairi was certainly not that, she went outside only with someone very special, someone with whom she was walking out. Jack had got used to thinking of Mairi as Ian's wee sister who would be there whenever he sought her out and here she was outside with Robin Morrison. He thought long and hard about his plan of campaign.

He had been told often enough by the females of his acquaintance that a well-set-up man on a horse was a splendid and even exciting sight.

On the day after the dance, after the church service and

the ritual of Sunday dinner was over and all the elders were snoring gently by the fire, hands resting on well-fed stomachs, he saddled Bluebell, still handsome in spite of his advanced age, and rode slowly over to the McGloughlins' farm. He carried with him the first of the autumn's brambles, picked by Edith and ready for a pie.

In answer to his prayers, Mairi was outside surveying the damage done to her flowers by the storm.

'Can I help you tie them up, Mairi?' he asked in a sympathetic voice. 'I just rode over with these brambles I picked before church but I'll be happy to help you repair the damage.'

Mairi had looked up at the sound of his voice and now she smiled as she took Edith's hard-won brambles. 'How lovely, Jack, we'll have these with cream tonight. None of ours are ripe enough yet. Where did these come from? That sheltered spot by the burn, I suppose.'

Jack had absolutely no idea and so he mumbled and stayed on his horse.

'I'll take these inside,' Mairi said. 'Come in and have a cup of tea with us, Jack.'

Jack was aware of exactly where he stood with Mairi's father and he knew why. He hesitated. 'If you bring the twine . . .' he began.

'Not on a Sunday, Jack. It's only necessary work that gets done here on the Sabbath. Look, Dad,' she said as Colin appeared in the doorway, 'look at these lovely berries Jack picked. I've asked him in for a cup of tea with us.'

Colin looked from the berries to their donor. 'You have early brambles, Jack. Kind of you to share. I take it your mother has as many as she needs.'

'Oh, aye, and it's Edith makes the jellies in our house. A grand hand with jam and jelly is our Edith.'

Colin grunted. 'Well, tie up Bluebell, and come in for a cuppa. Ian's away tae the Schoolhouse if you wanted a crack with him.'

'Who would want to talk to Ian when Mairi was in the same room, Colin,' said Jack and Mairi blushed while Colin watched her with trepidation clutching his insides.

'Talking's fine,' he said and led the way into the farmhouse.

Jack sat down at the fireside across from Colin while Mairi made some tea and buttered scones. She had been happy all day notwithstanding the devastation wrought in her flower garden by the wind, and the men could hear her singing.

'Pretty sound,' said Jack gingerly.

Colin was none too fond of Jack. He had watched him grow, a wild, spoiled young lad, and he knew the truth in some of the rumours that sometimes swept the area, but he found himself smiling at the young man who relaxed perceptibly. 'Aye, she has a sweet voice. A woman singing at her work is a comfortable sound.'

'You wouldn't say that if you could hear our Edith,' said Jack. 'If she would just stick to the piano playing we'd be happier.'

They laughed together companionably and Mairi saw them and the dull day brightened further.

'It was good of the wind to stay away till the hairst was over,' she said as she encouraged the men to eat. 'The shepherds say we're in for a bad winter.'

'Ach, if there's anyone with more gloom and doom in him than an Angus farmer,' laughed Jack, 'it's an Angus shepherd.'

'I wouldn't like to be marooned up past Hunter's Path with snow up to the window sills,' said Mairi as she poured Jack a second cup of tea, giving him, at the same time, her most devastating smile.

There was more than one handsome young shepherd up in the hills. Jack suddenly realized that he would have to be more careful with Miss McGloughlin.

'No reason for you ever tae be that far up the Glen, is

61

there, Mairi?' he asked anxiously. She had danced with two of the boys from the Glen, now that he minded.

'A bad snow comes,' said Colin, 'she'll be snug and safe by my fireside.'

Jack heard the unspoken warning and applied himself to his scones. They were delicious, as was the home-made jam. The room was clean and tidy, not nearly so luxurious as his father's own much grander farmhouse, but it was rather pleasant to sit across the table from a very pretty girl even with her father glowering at him from beneath shaggy eyebrows.

He did not outstay his welcome. He complimented his host on the warmth of his fire and his hostess on the lightness of her scones and then he left. Mairi saw him to the door.

'I could come by and tie up those flowers for you tomorrow, Mairi,' he offered as they stood together beside the placid Bluebell.

'Ian or my dad'll do it, Jack. They have me fair spoiled between them.'

'Will you walk home from church with me next Sunday – if the weather's fine?'

He had not meant to say it. He had no real idea of why he had come; he knew only that it was suddenly very important that he did come and that Mairi begin to walk out with him.

Mairi looked up at him and wondered if he would bring her a coat on a cold night.

Jack turned from her and easily climbed into his saddle.

A good-looking man on a fine-looking horse is . . . pleasant to look at, thought Miss McGloughlin, and agreed to walk with him – depending on the state of the weather.

'Walking home with Jack Black, lass? Ian'll walk too,' decided Colin. He did not want his daughter's name linked with that of the handsome young farmer.

Mairi looked at her father in exasperation. 'Ian will not

either, Dad. This isn't a declaration. It's just a walk; two people walking home from church together.'

'Your brother likes a walk.'

'Then he can walk in the other direction. Dad, Jack and I will walk home from church. Half of Angus is on that road on a Sunday morning. What in the name of Heaven do you think we're going to do?'

Embarrassed, Colin blustered, 'What a way to talk to your father? What do you think we're going to do, indeed. Jack Black has not the best reputation, Mairi, and I don't want my daughter's name mixed with his.'

'That old story about his mother's kitchen lassie having a baby? Honestly, Dad. If you could see the way the girls hang on poor Jack. He just attracts gossip.'

'I don't want mud attaching itself tae my lassie. Jack's dad owns his farm. He's a good-looking laddie and knows it. He's spoiled, Mairi, used tae getting what he wants.'

'Me too, Dad,' laughed Mairi and almost danced past him into the kitchen where she began to wash dishes. Once again she was singing.

Colin sat down by the fire with his paper but no matter how he tried he could not follow the news. Instead he saw all the advantages to be gained from having Jack Black as a son-in-law. If anyone could tame him, Mairi could.

'But not yet,' said Colin fiercely to the column that reported the disgraceful price of potatoes by the ton. 'No, my wee lassie.'

His wee lassie went for her walk watched over by all her elders and betters and it was seen that Jack never so much as laid a hand on Colin's lassie but instead watched her solicitously as she walked demurely beside him – but not too close.

And the young couple walked home every Sunday after that when the weather was fine. And then one day Jack asked Colin if he might drop by the farm and sit with Mairi in the

63

front room and Colin agreed. Next they went by train to Dundee where they watched a theatrical performance. Jack was bored to tears but Mairi was enchanted by the whole thing and he found himself thinking that he could watch her face, as she watched the actors, for the rest of his life. He planned to kiss her when he walked her home from the station; he could feel excitement building up inside him and he was terrified that it would show, but Mairi noticed nothing and when she saw her father with his trap at the station she ran to him in excitement and not in disappointment.

'There's snow threatening, Jack, and she has on her light shoes,' explained Colin as he avoided the young man's eyes.

'Oh, Dad, it was wonderful,' sang Mairi, completely unaware of the undercurrent. 'I think I will leave home and become an actress. Don't you think that must be the most wonderful . . . well, you can hardly call it a job, can you?'

'You'll dae fine looking after the house and the family, Mairi,' said Colin gruffly but Jack calculated that if he took Mairi's side – and he was sure she had no real desire to leave home – he would rise in her estimation.

'I think she'd make a wonderful actress, Colin, in fact I bet you could do anything you wanted to do, Mairi.'

'Until tonight all I've ever wanted to do is be a farmer.'

Both men hooted with laughter, drawn together by their patient tolerance of the silly twittering of their women. 'A farmer? Surely you mean a farmer's wife?'

'No, I don't,' said Mairi angrily as they trotted along. 'I've far more interest in the farm than Ian and maybe even you, Jack, and I wouldn't be the first woman to run a farm.'

'Ach, women forced by circumstance, lassie, and that end up mare man than woman. I'll no have my wee lassie knocked aboot by life, no while I can help it.'

Jack took his courage in both hands and pressed Mairi's hands into her lap. 'I'll make sure life delivers no blows either,' the pressure and his smile said and Mairi found

64

herself getting warmer and wishing, for the first time, that Colin had not met them at the station.

'The fire'll need a shovel of coal,' said Colin as he jumped down from the trap at the door of the farmhouse. 'I'll away and tend tae it and then I'll put the horse away.'

Suddenly shy, they watched him walk into the house.

'It was a lovely . . .' they began together.

'I really enjoyed the play, Jack,' said Mairi. 'It was kind of you to buy the tickets.'

'You don't really want to be an actress, do you, Mairi?'

'It must be a lovely glamorous life. Staying in hotels, having all your meals cooked, and people bringing you flowers.'

'I'll bring you flowers,' he offered, and pressed his lips to hers.

Miss McGloughlin was surprised but not frightened; she had expected to be kissed at least twice before. Since she did not struggle and, in fact, returned some of the pressure, Jack became a little more demanding. He had kissed girls before. Mairi sensed that he was no amateur and the effect he was having on her was not unpleasant, so she cooperated.

'I'll away and untack the horse,' they heard Colin bellow from the house in warning. Mairi laughed. There was no one in the house – Ian was at the Schoolhouse for his weekly meeting with the Dominie – but Jack drew away from her just as she was prepared to become even more enthusiastic. Regrettable but there would be another time.

For the first time she sensed her power. Oh, yes, there would be another time.

By the end of the year everyone knew that Mairi McGloughlin and Jack Black were walking out. He had even been seen buying a bouquet in the town's flower shop.

'Perfect for Mairi,' said the neighbours. 'Jack'll heir that farm and Mairi'll be near her faither. Who could ask for anything more?'

Mairi herself asked that question more than once. When

Jack was with her she was excited and happy. His kisses set her body in a whirl of sensations and it was he and not she who put limits on their experimentation. But when she was alone in the house, doing her chores, preparing vegetables, washing clothes, completing one of the thousand tasks that had to be done every day, she would sometimes find herself full of a longing for something she could not understand.

'I want . . . more,' sighed Mairi, but more of what she did not know.

Chapter Seven

Snow fell. Mairi stood in the silence and let the weightless flakes melt on her hands. Such incredible beauty, but what chaos it caused. The school was closed. No children could walk through that relentless accumulation. Colin and Ian worked for hours clearing paths to the animals and as soon as they had cleared a way another fall mocked their attempts to master the elements.

'Where's it coming from?' an exhausted Colin asked no one in particular, but his son said *Russia* and was told to keep his smart remarks to himself.

Unlike many of their neighbours, the little family were snug and warm in their kitchen. Ian had cut logs in every spare minute for months past and there was a huge pile keeping dry under an old canvas just at the back door. The cellar still had some good lumps of coal and plenty of dross that could go on the back of the fire to keep it in during the longest and coldest nights.

'They'll be struggling at the Schoolhouse,' said Ian. 'I cut logs for them and I know they had half a cart of coal the last time the boat came in but the place is that draughty.'

'How is Mrs Morrison?' Mairi asked, suddenly mindful of her promise to Robin.

'She never complains and she wouldn't let me tell Robin. Nothing is to disturb his chance of a good degree.'

'Gin his mother dies this winter, whit are his chances of finishing?' asked Colin and Mairi, stricken, looked from one to the other.

'She's not dying, is she?' she asked. 'I promised Robin I'd make sure you told him, Ian.'

'I wish you'd spoken to me, Mairi. I wrote to him just before Ne'erday with her usual story that she was fine.'

Guiltily, Mairi remembered how absorbed she had been and still was in her meetings with Jack. 'I've been . . . busy,' she said. She got up and went to the window and looked out at the snow-covered fields. So beautiful. So dangerous.

'I think I'll walk over to the Schoolhouse and see how she is. I promised Robin and I haven't kept my promise.'

'You're going nowhere in weather like this, Mairi,' said Colin from the fireside. 'Some drifts could swallow up a wee thing like you.'

'I'll go with her, Dad, and see to the cattle when we get back.'

Colin looked at them steadily for a moment and then turned back to the fire. 'See if they're needing ocht we can help them with, and dinnae let your wee sister fall in the burn.'

'He always has to have the last word,' said Mairi to her brother as, well wrapped up against the cold, they set off for the Schoolhouse.

Ian glanced at her but said nothing. If he said what he was thinking she would only yell at him, little shrew that she was. He pushed her gently as if to knock her off balance and she picked up some snow and threw it at him and together they began to run or wade as quickly as they could through the drifts towards the school road. Mairi's face was soon rosy with cold and effort and she felt so hot that she unwound the thick scarf she had wrapped around her neck.

Ian examined her critically when she was so involved with keeping her feet that she had no time to wonder what her brother was thinking.

'Why, our Mairi is pretty,' Ian thought to himself. 'Her eyes are sparkling like the frost on the burn and the sun is

68

turning her hair to copper.' Then he spoiled it by deciding that his sister looked about ten years old.

'You're seeing an awful lot of Jack these days, Mairi, what with the dancing and the theatre.'

'So?'

'Nothing. Just that it's hard to think of you being married to someone and not being at home with Dad and me.'

'Married? Who said anything about being married?'

'It's what usually happens around here when people walk out together.'

'Does it happen because it's expected by the neighbours? I certainly won't do anything just because that's the way it's done. Jack and I are . . . friends.'

'Is that all? I mean, do you let him kiss you?' asked Ian bravely. 'I hear he's kissed every girl in Angus.'

'Is that so?'

Colin recognized danger but had no idea how to extricate himself from it. 'There's been talk,' he began and he would have done better to keep quiet.

'He's told me all about it, Mr Perfect. Just because a man is handsome and his father owns his own land . . . girls chase him, Ian, and it's not fair. That girl was no better than she should be and was walking out with two of their men. No doubt one of them is the father.'

Ian blushed. 'You shouldn't speak of such things.'

'Oh, what hypocrites men are. Jack told me before he asked me to walk out with him. He said it was only fair and it's only fair that he should be judged innocent until someone finds him guilty and, as far as I know, he's never even been accused . . . out loud that is, by the girl herself, or her family.'

Since it was rumoured in the countryside that Jack's father had withdrawn a great deal of money – over a hundred pounds – on the day the servant girl left his wife's employ, Ian said nothing. Arguing against his sister's involvement with the young farmer seemed only to make her more anxious to defend him and, to be fair, Jack had been a model of decorum since he started courting Mairi McGloughlin. He was pleased that the difficulty of walking made it easy to remain quiet, involved in the business of putting one foot in front of the other and pulling it out again. Several times Mairi stumbled and would have fallen but for his strong arms and although she pushed him away and told him roundly what she thought of men who considered women weak, helpless creatures to be cosseted, she was smiling.

'Women,' he thought. 'Just when you think you've got their measure they change completely.'

They had reached the Schoolhouse where a slender column of grey smoke showed that someone was trying to keep a fire alight.

'They're a handless pair,' said Ian. 'They fall apart when Robin's not here. I think they're only beginning to realize just how much of the practical work he did around the house.'

'It's a son's place,' said Mairi. She would find no praise for Robin Morrison.

The Dominie greeted them at the door with his usual charm and with obvious delight at seeing them.

'Come in, come in,' he said. 'What a great pleasure. Mrs Morrison will be delighted. She's not too well, you know, but you two are the tonic she needs.'

They followed his gaunt figure into the front room where Mrs Morrison was sitting in a chair by the fire whose feeble flame tried to do battle with the cold and damp of the old house.

'It's not drawing very well, Dominie,' said Ian. 'When was the chimney swept last?'

'The School Board takes care of things like that, Ian. They're very good, you know.'

'Well, let me see if I can get a better blaze for you.'

'And you sit by me, Mairi, while Euan makes us a nice cup of tea. You bring the sun into a room with you, child. Is it just that burnished head or is it personality too?'

70

Embarrassed, Mairi took refuge in laughter. She well knew that she had never been a great favourite of Robin's mother. She must indeed be sick to find Mairi McGloughlin a welcome tonic.

'I'm glad we've had such a fall, Mairi. Euan needs a rest. The school takes all his energy and then he has to come home to a useless wife. We have enjoyed today, sitting together and talking. He's been reading to me.' Her eyes fell on the book turned upside down on a chair. Euclid.

'She actually likes Euclid,' thought Mairi and wondered a little about the life of these two people in this cold inhospitable house, so much grander than the farmhouse but so much colder. But there was a warmth, an atmosphere, and when Mairi saw the sick woman smile at her husband as he came in with a tray of ill-assorted cups and saucers, weak tea, and stale biscuits, she realized that the warmth was love.

'They don't notice the cold and the damp, not when they're together. They probably sit here, read Euclid to one another, and talk about Robin,' she thought.

'Have you heard from Robin recently?'

'Oh yes,' the Dominie answered. 'He writes every week. Can you believe, Mairi, that he is in his final year? In June he graduates with a Masters degree.'

'That's what I'm waiting for,' smiled Mrs Morrison. 'June, when all the roses are out, we will take the train to Edinburgh to see our boy become a Master of Arts, just like his dear father.'

'That will be a lovely day,' said Mairi but she saw the look that passed between husband and wife and knew that though they hoped for a fine June day, they were almost sure that only one of them would see it.

She was quiet as they walked home, retracing their own footsteps in the bright moonlight. When they reached the farm, Ian turned to go off to feed the cattle.

'You'll write to Robin tonight, Ian.'

'She looked better as we were leaving.'

'She knows she's dying and she wants her son. She'll not see the spring flowers, never mind the roses.'

'I'll write.'

She heard a sob as he turned and stumbled to the byre and, for the first time, Mairi wondered if her brother remembered their own mother.

'He must remember; he had been old enough. Poor Ian and now poor Robin.'

Ian wrote the letter and, next morning, he walked through the snow to Arbroath to post it.

Robin and another, even fiercer, snowstorm arrived together.

The McGloughlins were in their front room; the fire blazed brightly, sending odd shadows dancing and gyrating on the walls.

'Remember when we were wee,' Mairi spoke into the silence. 'You used to make up stories about the shadow men, scary ones.'

Her brother did not answer and she looked at him. He sat in his chair with his head cocked like a pointer dog.

'Can you hear something?'

'If Robin came in on the train he'll get lost on the way from Arbroath.'

'He'll hardly have got your letter yet.'

'He wouldn't wait for the weekend, Mairi. He would come as soon as he read the letter. I have an awful feeling.' He jumped up. 'I'm going to walk to Arbroath to meet the train.'

'You're out of your mind, lad. This is no a night for a dog tae be out.' Colin stood up as if he would physically prevent his son from going out into the snow.

'I'll take a lantern, Dad. Robin has no sense of direction, never has had. If he steps into a ditch he'll lose his way.'

'You're an idiot, laddie. You're going out to walk five

72

miles to meet someone who is probably sitting on his backside by his fire in Edinburgh reading one of they great books.'

'If he's out there, he'll die.'

Colin reached for his coat. 'Hap up the fire, lass, and keep it going all night if you have to. I'll need to go with him. He'll start thinking how beautiful the moonlight is on the snow and freeze tae death in a ditch while he's thinking on a poem.'

Mairi said nothing. She looked from one to the other as they wrapped themselves up. She believed that Ian's instincts were right. Robin Morrison was out there in the storm. Whether Colin believed or not, she could not tell, but something was telling the older man to go.

'We'll take the dog,' said Colin, 'and the crook tae fish your daft brother out of the drifts and then I'll belt him with it when we get hame. Cat got your tongue, lassie? It's got my brains, both of them.'

The door closed behind them and Mairi ran to the window and pushed aside the curtain. She could see two large huddled shapes and a small bobbing light and she watched them until they disappeared into the swirling snow.

'I'll make soup. I can't sit by the fire and imagine them out there. Oh, Robin Morrison, if anything happens to them because of you . . .'

She forced herself to concentrate on cutting woody carrots and turnips meant for the cattle into perfect shapes. She would not think, she would not.

And outside in the storm Ian and Colin struggled together unerringly towards Arbroath. The dog followed in their footsteps. He did not question, merely accepted, as always, the strange conduct of these Gods who ruled his life. If he was called upon to die for them he would do so without thinking. They were the reason for his existence and although he would have been more comfortable by the fire, he was happier here.

73

'I couldn't manage without you, Dad,' said Ian as his father's strong arms pulled him for more than the first time from a drift. Colin had walked this way for over forty years in every weather. He knew where they were by the feel of the stone of a wall, by the texture of the gnarled trunk of a tree. He thought his son was a fool and he looked forward, with pleasure, to telling him so when they got home. Imagining the words he would use almost made him smile as he wiped the freezing snow from his eyes. But there was no time to smile, time only to struggle on, to keep the boy on the path, to pray that the snow would stop.

'Where is it coming from?' he asked as they helped one another up after losing their balance once more in a drift that looked a few inches deep and turned out to be at least three feet.

Exhausted they clung together, too tired even to push themselves apart.

'Canada?' croaked Ian and was delighted to hear his father's laugh.

What if Robin wasn't out here? What would his father say if Robin was snug and warm in his Edinburgh boarding house?

'He'll kill me,' he said as he had said a thousand times through his childhood and then he realized that his father would say nothing. He wished he could say, *I love you, Dad*, but he never had said it before and during a snow storm when they had to fight for their lives was hardly the time to start.

They reached what passed for a main road and the way was clearer because there was some shelter from an avenue of trees. Colin stood for a moment to get his bearings and then, unhesitatingly, pressed on and Ian and the dog went with him. Because the going was easier they both became aware of how wet and cold they now were. More than once each had stepped up to his waist in a drift and the snow now made itself felt as it invaded

74

every inch of the material that covered the lower half of their bodies.

'We'll have to go all the way into town,' thought Ian. 'Otherwise we'll never know if we've missed him.' For a moment he lifted his head to look before him into the swirling snow instead of at the road just ahead of his feet. 'I have no idea where I am. It must be worse for Robin. Is he out here somewhere?'

At that moment Colin plunged up to his neck in a drift and Ian turned swiftly to pull the older man up.

'I'm sorry, Dad, I'm sorry; this is madness.'

'Aye, but the right kind, laddie,' gasped Colin and shaking off his son's hand he went on. He was happy, unbelievably happy. He had worked with his son in all weathers and they had shared a kind of companionship but this, this struggle with the elements, was different. He had the greater guile; the lad had the greater strength. 'Comes tae us all, tae tak a back seat to our own lads.' He wished he could tell the boy, say, *We're a great pair*, but he didn't know how.

They found Robin less than a mile from the town. He had fallen into a ditch and lost, not only his balance, but also his sense of direction and had, in fact, just realized that he was struggling back into the town. The snow had taken pity on him and had, for a moment, abated to show the lights of Arbroath.

They helped him take off his rubber boots and empty out the snow and freezing water.

'Good job nane of yer professors can see you now, Robin. You look like a drowned rat.'

'Thanks a lot.' Robin tried to smile between teeth that were chattering together with cold.

'We'll need tae mak you run, Robin laddie, or you'll tak your death,' said Colin. 'Ian'll tak the one arm and I'll tak the other. You wouldnae think on coming back tae the farm afore you go home? Mairi aye has water on and she'll be making soup tae keep her mind busy.'

75

Robin shook his head and tried to get going under his own steam. He would love to go to the cosy little farmhouse, where a pretty girl would be waiting with hot food and maybe a warm welcome. Knowing Mairi though, he assumed she would be furious with him because her father and brother were in danger, but at least she would feed him and dry him off. He well knew that had the McGloughlins been a few minutes later he would have died out here so close to the town and yet so far away from safety. What friends they were. He did not ask them what had brought them out. It would be days before his mind would work on that. He accepted their presence, their strength, and thanked God for them. One day, when his body and mind were once more functioning properly, he would thank them too.

They said no more as they struggled the rest of the way. The snowfall had stopped and it was fatigue that was their enemy now, but doggedly the farmers plodded on, holding the slighter man between them and, at last, when all three were deciding that they could take not one more step, they saw the Schoolhouse with one little lamp shining from an upstairs window.

Ian was the one with enough strength left to raise the knocker and they waited for several minutes until at last the door was opened. Mr Morrison stood in the doorway, a candle in his hand. He saw his son and, with a cry of joy, clasped the soaked young man to his heart.

'She knew you'd come. "I'm waiting for my Robin," she said. Take off your coat and go straight upstairs. Come in, Mr McGloughlin, and you too, Ian.'

'I've left my lassie, Dominie,' began Colin.

'Mairi will understand. She's going, you see, and I don't know what to do.'

Colin had lived through this night years before.

'Go to your sister, Ian. I'll stay here and see to what needs to be done.'

He put his arm around the man he had always respected

and of whom he had often been in awe. Tonight it was the man of learning who was so sadly in need of the man of the soil.

'We'll be fine the night, laddie,' he said to Ian who had reached the gate. 'Come back the morn and you'll know what to bring.'

Ian nodded. 'Mairi,' he said to himself. 'I'll bring Mairi.'

Chapter Eight

Farmers from all over the area came to dig out the road for Mrs Morrison's hearse. Robin, looking out of the Schoolhouse window at the dawn spreading over a frozen landscape, was startled to see small moving black dots and, as he watched, the dots became larger and he saw that they were men, men and boys and even women, each with a shovel.

Nature had not helped. It was as frozen as Robin's heart and the roads were impassable. At first he did not realize why so many people were struggling through the deep frozen drifts and then when he saw the shovels he knew. Somehow the word had spread through the farms that the Dominie's wife was dead and that the Schoolhouse was cut off from the roads.

'We'll dig her oot,' someone had said.

The local carpenter-cum-undertaker had dug his dignified way in and made the simple coffin in the front room. It was cold in there; even the usual feeble fire had been allowed to go out for the body was there and, had the weather been kind, would have been buried days ago. But the other downstairs rooms were warm and cosy. Had they ever been so cosy? Robin thought as he watched a silent Mairi McGloughlin cut large slices of bread to make sandwiches for the people who were digging the path from house to gate and the road from the Schoolhouse to the Kirk yard. The doctor had managed to get through almost twenty-four hours after his mother had died peacefully in her husband's arms and the Minister, too old and frail to be safe far from his own fireside, had arrived on the back of Charlie Thomson's biggest Clydesdale. The horse had managed only part of the way. Even with his great feet wrapped in sacks, not to pay silent homage to the dead but to prevent him slipping, the animal was unsafe on the road.

'Do ye ken, I walked clear across the dyke,' Robin heard one farm lad say to another. 'The drifts are that high the dyke's buried and I knew I'd lost my way when I ended up to my neck in snaw. Luckily oor Bob was with me and pulled me oot, and him laughing like a loon. When this is feenished I'll see how he likes freezin snaw doon the back of his neck.'

'My mother is dead,' thought Robin, 'and they can dig through appalling conditions and still have fun.' He had been to school with the lads and knew that they could find joy in almost anything. But they had not found joy in school and none at all in his mother who had had few of the skills of which their mothers were justifiably proud. 'I'd dig for them,' he thought, 'but would they ask me or would I even find out that they needed help?'

He looked across at Mairi who smiled at him. 'They're good people,' she said. 'They mean no disrespect by laughing.'

'Mum would like to hear them laugh. She always regretted that she couldn't communicate well.'

Mairi turned away, embarrassed. Some of the children had thought that the Dominie's wife believed herself a cut above them because of her education. Many had revered her just because of it. Probably she would have preferred something in between.

'How is your father this morning?'

'She had prepared him,' said Robin bitterly. 'I should have been here.'

'She was so proud of you, Robin. She wanted nothing

79

to get in the way of your education, your degree. She'll be there with you, when the roses bloom, always.'

She had no idea why she had said that but she knew it was true. When Robin Morrison stood up at the grand university of Edinburgh in his cap and gown, when the roses bloomed in voluptuous abandon all over the country, his mother would be there.

'Robin, Robin, laddie.' It was the Dominie. 'Have you seen them? Boys – and girls – I taught, now grown men and women, are here with us, caring, helping.'

Robin suddenly pulled himself out of his daze. 'And I'm in here, warm. I'll away out to help, and I'll send your dad in, Mairi. He's worked like three men, the past few days.'

Mairi smiled. 'That's the way he always works,' she said and went back to her sandwiches.

Edith came later, and Mrs Black, and they made soup and Edith's famous stovies, and the men and women of the farms sat quietly, ill at ease in the Schoolhouse, and ate their dinner, and then went back to work again. The older men struggled back to their own yards to feed animals but at last the work was done.

'It'll be the morn's morn, Dominie,' said Charlie Thomson. 'There's more snow coming and we'd best get her buried.'

'Thank you, Mr Thomson. I appreciate all your efforts. And you, Robin, my boy, I want you on the first train to Edinburgh after we've said goodbye to her.'

'I can't leave you, Dad, not yet, not alone.'

'I'm not alone, laddie, and the children will be back as soon as the roads are passable.' He put his hand gently on his son's shoulder. 'Who can give up with a school full of children to teach? You're going back to work for your degree; that's the only thing in the world she wanted.'

Robin did return to Edinburgh on the first train to get through and in June he graduated with First Class honours.

Mairi and Ian read about it in the local paper under the heading: LOCAL BOY'S SUCCESS.

Mairi looked out on her patch of garden where the roses danced in all their splendour. 'What now?' she asked her brother.

'Oxford. Can you imagine, Mairi? Robin's going to Oxford, and then probably a fine job in a great school somewhere in the city. The Dominie's so proud. He wanted me to go with him, you know, to the graduation, and if I could have got to Edinburgh and back all in the one day . . .'

'With two rivers to cross? There's a dream to write a poem about, Ian. Eighty miles and two rivers and back in your own bed on the same day. Pigs might fly.'

They laughed at the old childhood joke.

'I'll go to Oxford,' said Ian. 'I'll stand there and I'll touch the stones and I'll breathe in the poetry. You can come too, Mairi. I bet Robin would like that.'

Mairi turned away. Robin had said nothing to her since he had stood watching her cut the sandwiches. She had known that he was too distressed, too incapable of thinking, and he had walked away from the Kirk yard without turning back.

'Jack's asked me to marry him,' she said. 'I doubt he'd be keen on his wife going off to some English city to see another man.' She turned on Ian angrily as he looked as if he was about to question her further. 'Away out from under my feet, you and your local boy's success story.'

When he was gone she picked up the paper and read the item through again. There was even a picture of Robin, even more formal and somehow remote than the one she had seen in the front room of the Schoolhouse. 'I'd like fine to go to Oxford, Robin, but would it be to see you or to see the city?'

She put the paper away and hurried on with her tasks, for Jack was coming and they were going to a tennis party, and she knew that he would find a way to get her on her own to ask her again, and she would go because being with Jack was exciting.

He arrived just as she was finishing washing up the dishes from their evening meal and was forced to sit in the front room with Colin while she hurried upstairs to put on her tennis dress of heavy white cotton. She had altered an old one the better to resemble the lovely dress worn by the celebrated Mrs Mavrogordato during her mixed doubles match on the hallowed greens of the All England Tennis Club.

'It's a wonder she could play, let alone win,' mused Mairi as she buttoned hundreds of little white buttons, down the front and on the cuffs of her dress. 'At least I look nice and it's not so hot in the evenings.' She blew her damp hair up from her forehead, wished desperately that she had some lip rouge and then descended the staircase. Well she knew the effect she was creating, but if she had expected to captivate her father as well as Jack, he gave her no satisfaction, telling her only that it would be impossible to get the dress clean if the courts were dusty.

'No one will be able to play for looking at you, Mairi,' breathed Jack, getting as close to her as he dared. 'You're beautiful.'

'She's well enough,' said Colin, 'And she's to be back by eleven at the latest. It's early up these mornings.'

'I may not bring her back at all,' said Jack daringly.

Colin looked at him for a long cold moment that made Jack sweat in his long-sleeved white flannel shirt.

'Then it's me will be after you with a shotgun, not that I'll need it.'

'Och, Dad, Jack's only joking. We'll see you later,' said Mairi crossly and almost pulled Jack out of the door.

'I don't know that I am, joking I mean,' said Jack and he in turn pulled Mairi into his arms and kissed her firmly, his tongue trying gently to force open her lips.

She pulled away. 'Don't be silly, Jack, not here, at the very window.'

'I'll wait until after the tea,' promised Jack, 'and then I want an answer, Mairi McGloughlin.'

She looked at him provocatively and took to her heels like a hoyden as he came after her and it was two rather breathless tennis players who arrived at the little local club.

'You didn't get chased by Tyler's bull, did you?' asked Sinclair, who was chairman. 'You'd best sit down and draw your breath and hope you're not on first.'

They played singles and doubles and enjoyed themselves heartily until ten o'clock. The long evening still stretched clear before them but most of the young men were ruled by the soil and their animals and knew that they would have to be up early next morning.

'We'll have our tea now,' decided the chairman and Mairi was delegated to pouring, not tea, but the cool and refreshing barley water made by the minister's wife.

'I told Robin all about you and Jack,' smiled Edith. 'I thought it only right to wish him well at Oxford and to bring him up to date with local gossip.'

'That was kind.' Mairi forced a smile. 'But you can't have given him gossip about me, Edith, because there is no gossip to tell.'

Edith laughed archly. 'I know my brother. He always gets what he wants and . . . so do I.' She danced off to press sandwiches on the other players leaving Mairi to fume with rage.

'What have you been saying to Edith about me?' she asked Jack furiously when he came to sit beside her. She flushed as she thought of things that Jack might have said, private things between two people who cared for one another.

'Just that I'm mad about you,' said Jack. 'What else is there to tell?'

'Nothing, and that's how it will stay.' Mairi got up and went to do her share of the dish washing. She wanted to go home and she wanted to go alone.

Jack followed her. 'Mairi, wait. What's Edith been saying to upset you?'

What had Edith said? Nothing really. Except that she had been writing to Robin Morrison.

'I don't like being gossiped about.'

'Gossip? My dad says if I don't stop talking about you he'll move into the barn for some peace. Is that gossip? Edith's jealous because I'm always talking about your hair or your scones, or your light hand with a sponge. Come on, let me walk you home.'

Mairi hesitated. She liked Jack. She liked walking home with him and stopping in the shade of some great tree where they could sit for a few minutes until Jack's lips and hands became too demanding. It was exciting, a little naughty, but nothing wrong. 'I don't know, Jack. I did want to, very much, but now I don't want you to ask me to marry you again. I'm not ready.'

'Oh, you're ready all right,' laughed Jack and it was not a pleasant sound. 'Let me show you just how ready you are.'

She pushed him away and he made to catch her, then he thought of her father's eyes when he had said, *I won't need a gun*, and he let her go.

'Don't think I'll hang around waiting. There's a wheen of girls ready and willing to take your place.'

'Then let them,' said Mairi coldly.

She hurried home up the lovely country lane, taking no pleasure in the briar roses intertwined among the hedges. She went over and over the evening in her mind.

'Robin Morrison,' she said out loud. 'The evening went wrong when Edith talked about horrible, nasty Robin Morrison.'

She managed to let herself into the farmhouse and

up to her room without disturbing her father or her brother.

As usual she stood at the window to watch the train.

She played her game. 'I'll be on you one day. I'll go to Edinburgh, to London, maybe even to Oxford. And what will I do in Oxford? I'll walk in the sunshine and I'll pretend I don't see the imploring eyes of Robin Morrison.'

But why that thought should make her cry, she did not know.

Chapter Nine

'It's not right,' said Ian quietly. The words fell into the hot air that had been flying around the room and hung there like grubby washing on a line. No one wanted to look at them.

'War's not right either,' said his father quietly, 'but there is a war and we're in it whether we like it or not.'

'Kier Hardie says we should be for peace not for war.'

'Aye, and he chose to make his peace speech from the plinth of Nelson's column. That's whit clever fellows like you and Robin would cry. Irony, is it no, him being such a great fighting sailor?'

'Why can't you ever say, "Clever fellows like me", Dad. Everyone else, according to you, is clever but you're the one that's saying it. There's nout wrong with your brain.'

'There something up with yours if you think that helping the oppressed is wrong.'

Ian stood up, his huge frame sending the room scurrying into its own shadows. 'That's not what I said and tell me, Mister Clever, who's the faither that skelped me for fighting with Robin at the primary school? Violence doesn't solve anything, Dad.'

'I walloped you because you were bigger and stronger than Robin and wrong into the bargain. Belgium's wee. Germany's big and needs skelping.'

'Your argument is too simple, Dad,' Ian started again but Mairi interrupted. She was tired of this war that had been raging since some prince or other had been assassinated in a place called Sarajevo and by a boy scarce nineteen years old.

86

'It really doesn't matter,' she said, 'since neither of you will be involved; you're needed here on the land.'

That was true but many, many young men from the area had already enlisted, anxious to be part of what they saw as an exciting moment in history. By September of 1914 the Scottish Division of Lord Kitchener's First 100,000 or K1 as they were called, had begun to assemble. They were sent away from the hills and glens of Scotland to Bordon, near Aldershot in the south of England. They had thought to win the war quickly, whip the Germans, and return home, with medals for bravery, to their sweethearts, their mothers, their wives. But too many were already dead in places called Ypres, the Marne . . . One farm boy had been on a ship, a submarine, that had dived under five rows of mines, torpedoed a Turkish battleship, *Messudiyeh*, and got back safely. The news that he had been killed not by the enemy but in a freak accident had reached his elderly parents on the same day that a letter had informed them that he had won this brand new medal, the Distinguished Service Medal, that the King himself had established.

'Where in the name o' God is the Dardanelles and whit guid is a medal gan tae dae his mam at her age?' had been the feeling of many of his friends who had stayed at home on the land.

The Earl of Dalhousie, whose family had owned or still owned the land that most of them farmed, was injured by a bursting shell while he saw action with the Scots Guards.

'Aye, his legs and arms baith hit by shrapnel,' was the chatter in the bothies. 'He's a guid man and oor ain. We wish him well.'

Every Friday the muster roll of those who had answered the call grew longer and longer in the pages of the *Herald*, among them the names of the one or two who thought that a certain young lady's eyes might light up with pleasure at the sight of a young man who sported a shiny new medal. For different reasons they went. But not Ian McGloughlin.

And night after night Ian lay awake and worried, for he knew that farming would not keep him safe much longer. He had never believed that the war would be over quickly. In fact he could not see how it would ever end. What would he say when the letter came, this year, next year, for the huge open maw of the great war machine would never close and would devour more and more of Scotland's finest and, one day, one day very soon, there would be Conscription?

'I cannot agree that the way to solve our problems is to take up arms against some other farmer's son.'

Wars should be fought around a table, with these great powerful men sitting there and arguing until they agreed on what was right for all. What good did blowing a country to bits, destroying cities, farms, rivers do? He could not believe that French farmers wanted to fight. He shuddered at the thought of the devastation of the land. How long would it take the fields, that were today running with blood, to recover? Where would next year's wheat grow? What about the Germans? Did they like fighting? He had never met a German but in the paper they looked much like him. The Dominie had told him of great poets who spoke German, of great musicians who spoke German. There had to be farmers among these Germans too.

'Fightin's no the way to handle this,' he said again into the silence.

'You'd better no let anybody in the village hear you talk like that, Ian. They'll be crying you a coward.'

Ian looked at his father in surprise. He had never considered that. A coward? Was he a coward?

He felt an icy hand clutch his heart. 'You don't think I'm feart?'

Colin looked up at him. 'No, laddie,' he said and his voice was sincere, 'but then, I'm your daddy.'

Mairi threw her mending down on the rag rug before the fire. 'Enough,' she said. 'It's Christmas, the birthday of the Prince of Peace. There's hypocrisy for you. Now, we'll have no more talk of war, or cowards or anything else in this house. The war is nothing to do with us.'

Ian smiled sadly at her. 'Not talking about it won't make it go away, Mairi. Sinclair's joined up; his mother's devastated. And we'll have Robin in afore too long.'

Robin. Mairi deliberately kept her face turned to the fire. Robin. How little they had seen of him since his mother's death. He had gained a second degree at Oxford University and was now teaching in Rome. The Dominie had gone with him for a holiday and had returned, refreshed but alone, to the Schoolhouse. Robin's letters to Ian arrived religiously and so she supposed that his father must hear often too. And Edith, did she receive letters from Italy? Now that she was no longer walking out with Jack, Mairi's path seldom crossed Edith's. Both young women were polite to one another but at a distance.

'I don't care if he's writing to her,' Mairi thought while she made herself pretend an interest in the Minister's son. 'Sinclair Sutherland in the Army? But Sinclair wouldn't hurt a fly.'

'It'll be mair nor flies he'll be hurtin,' said Colin but Ian said nothing at all.

He did not know that, that very year, a No-Conscription fellowship had been formed and that there were already 16,000 members. He did not hear that the Anabaptists and the Quakers had adopted a completely Pacifist Doctrine. Had Robin been at home, no doubt he would have told him and they would have discussed and argued as they had done all their lives, but Robin was not at home.

When he did come home, the young men did not debate pacifism.

The first they knew that Robin was back was when Colin went to answer a knocking at the door and found the young schoolmaster on his step. He had not seen Robin for some time and was surprised at how the boy had grown, filled out, matured. He was as handsome as ever, his dark hair falling untidily about his lean scholarly face.

'Can't I come in, Mr McGloughlin?' said Robin at last into the silence.

Colin grabbed him. 'Laddie, laddie, I near didn't recognize you. Come away in. Goodness, you're near as big as my Ian.'

Robin laughed. 'It's the sun. It pulled me up.'

'Aye,' said Colin seriously. 'I'll bet it pulls the crops and all. Will you have had time to look at the fields?'

'Rome's not the best place to study agriculture, Mr McGloughlin, although I've seen oranges and lemons growing on trees, would you believe.'

Robin had taken off his coat and was seated at the fire when Mairi came in from the kitchen. She had been baking and her hair was escaping from its pins, her face was red from the heat of the ovens, and her hands were covered in flour. But this handsome man of the world was only Robin, the bane of her childhood. Impulsively she hurried forward and then when she went to touch him, she saw her flour-covered hands and drew back.

'Robin,' she said and was aware of her flying hair and her apron over her oldest, dullest dress.

'Mairi, how good to see you. I hope you don't mind my dropping in.'

'No, no. You'll stay to supper? You just missed Ian, but he'll be back soon.' She was sounding like all the dizzy girls she disliked; all of a flutter because a handsome man had come in – and Robin was handsome. He looked nothing at all like the boy she had quarrelled with all her life, but then he smiled at her, his shy sweet smile, and he was Robin, and she wondered why she had ever believed that she disliked him.

'Gosh, it's wonderful to see you, Mairi,' he said. 'You're like a breath of fresh air.'

A breath of fresh air? Not very romantic but why on earth

90

was she coupling Robin Morrison and romance? One had nothing to do with the other.

'You're home, Robin? We didn't expect you until the summer. Do they take days off at Christmas in Italy?'

'I've resigned. I came home to tell my father and then, of course, my oldest friend. I'm enlisting at the start of the year.'

'Well done, lad,' said Colin and he shook Robin's hand.

Mairi stared at them aghast. They were grinning, well pleased with one another. 'I'll go and finish my pie,' she said and doubted that they had even noticed that she had left the room.

In the kitchen she put another plate to warm, and then finished her pastry. Her hands continued to perform their tasks automatically although her mind was busy with Robin and with what she had just learned as she had stood in that comfortable, friendly little room. No, not that Robin was going off to war. That was vitally important and would certainly affect her later. No, no. This was knowledge that was much more important in the great scheme of things, if indeed, there was a Divine plan, and how could there be if selfish men were allowed to maim and mutilate all in the name of achieving a lasting peace?

'I love him,' said Mairi McGloughlin to the pie crust that hid the mortal remains of an old hen. 'I have loved him all my life, and I have fought with him and driven him away and now he is going to war and it's all such a stupid waste.'

She did not know that she was crying until she heard Ian's gentle voice from the door. 'Mairi, love, that's not onions. What is it?'

She gulped and wiped her nose with her oven cloth. 'Nothing,' she said, opening the clothes boiler and throwing in the cloth. 'Nothing except that stupid friend of yours coming just at dinner time.'

His eyes lit up. 'Robin, you can't mean Robin.' He was already pulling off his wet clothes. 'Don't worry, Mairi, he can have half mine,' he said and he was gone into the front room.

'Stupid man,' seethed Mairi. 'Even the best of them, thick as a barn door. As if I couldn't add a tattie or two, and look at me in my old frock and Robin's been in Rome, Rome, the Eternal City, whatever that means, but Italian women are beautiful.'

Robin explained why Rome had been called the Eternal City as he devoured a plate of her chicken pie. 'Boy, that was good,' he said as he handed her his empty plate for a small second helping, the portion he did have to share with Ian. 'I really liked Italian food but home food is better.'

'Your father?' asked Mairi, suddenly feeling guilty. 'You should have brought him, Robin.'

'He's never been fussy about food. My mum wasn't the best cook in the world and his mind is too full at the moment to be good company, but I'd appreciate it if you'd go to see him now and again while I'm away. You're too necessary on the land, I suppose, Ian. Bad luck.'

'Ian, don't,' said Mairi but Ian was too honest ever to dissemble.

'I don't believe this is the right way to go about it, Robin. I wouldn't go to war even if I could.'

Both young men had gone white and they avoided looking at one another.

'He'll see sense in a month or two,' said Colin jovially, 'if it's not all over by then.'

'I won't see sense then, Dad, because I see it perfectly clearly now. You're a scholar, Robin. You should be in your classroom teaching the bairns about the stupidity of war.'

'There won't be bairns anywhere in Europe for me to teach if I don't go now. It won't be over in a few months, Mr McGloughlin. It'll take years, so the sooner I go and do my bit the better for everyone.' He stood up. 'Thank you for the pie, Mairi. It was delicious. Mr McGloughlin.'

He said nothing to Ian; he did not even look at him. He

walked to the door, took his coat and hat from the peg and walked out into the night. When the door closed behind him the family sat still in their chairs at the table. At last Ian spoke. 'He thinks I'm a shirker. He knows me better than anyone else in the entire world and he thinks I'm a shirker.' He pushed back his chair so that its legs protested, shrieking along the floor, and then stumbled from the room.

'Robin couldn't think Ian's scared, Dad. He couldn't.'

'"There won't be bairns anywhere in Europe to teach." Did you hear him, lassie? Here was me thinking jist of us, but there's bairns all over Europe affected by this. If I wasn't an auld man, I'd away and fight with Robin. Ian's no feart. It's all that poetry the Dominie stuffed in his heid when he should have been working on the farm with me. What bluidy good did education do my boy?'

Mairi found herself alone with the remains of the meal. She sat for a while looking at the gravy congealing on the plates and then she stood up stiffly, like an aged crone, and began to clear up.

'Dear God, where is it written that women are doomed to do nothing but clean up the messes men leave behind them? It's women who will clean up the mess from this war.'

She ran to the door, picked up her heavy old tweed coat and let herself out into the night after Robin. All evening she had been doing things automatically. Now, in the dark and the rain that lashed at her remorselessly, she found her way automatically to the Schoolhouse.

Robin was sitting hunched over an excuse for a fire when he heard her knocking and he opened the door just as she realized what she was doing and was turning to run back to the farm.

'Mairi, what on earth are you doing? You look like a drowned rat. Come on in,' he finished, dragging her inside and closing the door behind her. 'Damn it, you shouldn't be here. My father has gone to bed. What will people think?'

'I don't care what people think. I care what you think about Ian.'

He took her wet coat and hung it up on a peg by the door. 'Come and sit by the fire. Does your father know you're here . . . no, he can't know. This was silly, Mairi. What if anyone saw you? There are people in the village with nothing better to do than peep out from behind their curtains.'

She ignored that. It was unimportant. 'Ian's not a coward,' she burst out.

He laughed. 'God, will you ever grow up or are you going to spend your entire life fighting your brother's battles, real and imaginary.'

She slapped him hard and they were children again. He grabbed her arms and shook her and looked down into her angry face. 'I had almost forgotten how pretty you are,' he said and kissed her.

For a lovely moment Mairi felt herself relax and the pressure on her lips became harder and then she remembered what he had just said and she pulled herself free and swung her arm back. He caught it easily before she could hit him.

'Ian and I were always sure we would never make a lady out of you,' he said and then was sorry when he saw the tears spring into her lovely eyes.

She turned and stumbled to the door, grabbed her wet coat and ran out. He followed her but slipped on wet moss that had been allowed to grow on the top step and hurtled ignominiously to the ground. Mairi heard him cry out and stopped for a moment in her pell-mell flight but when she turned round he was pulling himself to his feet and so she turned again and ran into the darkness.

Robin stood tentatively for a moment looking after her. He had to have broken something with a fall like that but although his right ankle hurt badly when he put his weight on his foot, he was able to walk. He stopped at the top of the short flight of stairs to ease the pain and suddenly he remembered standing there with his father half a lifetime ago, watching the stars.

How simple life had been then: lessons, exploring the natural world with Ian, the unwanted Mairi constantly tagging along behind, reading poetry, trying to write some and discovering with excitement and pleasure that this was where Ian definitely had the greater gift. Mother had been here then with her inability to bake a cake and her ability to help with Latin homework when Dad wasn't looking. Now she was gone, Dad was becoming more and more of a recluse. Mairi was a woman and one who disturbed him – he remembered the warm softness of her lips – and Ian. What was Ian?

'He's my friend,' decided Robin as he hobbled into the house, 'and that is all that matters.'

Chapter Ten

Early in January Robin went off to Dundee to join the army. He was, his father told Colin and Ian with a mixture of pride and sadness, *officer material*.

'But that's good, Dominie.' Colin, with his own son safe beside him, tried to cheer him up. 'They'll get the best of everything, the officers.'

'Certainly,' agreed the Dominie. 'Including the best chance of being shot.'

What could one say to a response like that? Colin, out of his depth, muttered something innocuous, and hurried off to look after his cattle.

'He'll be well trained, Dominie,' said Ian.

'Oh, aye, laddie, but read your history books; you always liked history, Ian. You'll find it's the boy officers who are first in the firing line. I shall trust in God, lad.' He looked at Ian shrewdly. 'He told me of your decision. He respects it, you know. Doesn't understand it but he respects it. He'll need letters from friends more than ever. Don't let his initial reaction spoil a lifetime of friendship.'

Ian smiled. His heart felt lighter. It would have been unbearable to have Robin hate him. 'Thanks, Dominie. I've promised my dad that I'll keep my mouth shut for now, but, gin anyone asks me, I'll have to say what I think.'

'Don't court disaster, lad. I'm glad you've never been one for the pub on a Saturday night; drink's a sure fly way of loosening the tongue. Keep your own counsel and pray for a just ending to this war, for all our sakes.'

He turned and Ian watched him walk off to a house that would be cold and damp and empty. He could not remember that his home had been damp and cold and cheerless after the death of his mother but then his father was practical and there had been family and neighbours. Had the Dominie no one now that his wife was dead and his son had gone to war? The Minister, surely? They would be the same class. But Robin, his friend, the one person in the world who believed that Ian McGloughlin could become a writer, had gone off to war and wanted letters from his friends.

'He doesn't hate me; he respects my decision. I'll write and tell him what that means to me.'

Then there was the Dominie. Robin would be concerned for his father's well-being.

'I'll maybe ask Mairi to make him scones now and again and maybe some soup.'

Mairi had no objections to helping the schoolmaster. 'But he doesn't need charity, Ian. He won't want me going in there with food and surely he can afford to get someone in from one of the cottages.'

'He'd maybe never think on it.'

'Well, if I talk to anyone who might do for him I'll let you know,' said Mairi and put the Dominie out of her head. Robin refused to leave her thoughts though. She was glad that his fall had not injured him but she regretted slapping him. Too often her mind seemed to dwell on that kiss. It had not been the same as a kiss from Jack which had excited and terrified at one and the same time. This had been gentle.

'Oh, I will waste no more of my time on Robin Morrison. Goodness, I doubt we'll see him here for a year or two and then it will be off again to Rome or Athens. He'll have no time for a tiny village school in Scotland. And besides, I have more than enough to worry about here.'

As the spring slowly pushed the winter away, the routine of the farmhouse followed what it had been for years and years, as long as anyone could remember. Up at first light,

97

a full day of endless back-breaking chores, home with the setting sun for a meal and a wash, and then, if there was any energy left, reading and his almost secret writing for Ian, clerical chores for Colin, and the occasional visit to friends. For Mairi there was constant work to keep the family fed and clean. There was her garden to tend, and her chickens, and with the spring, a lamb, sometimes two, to bottle feed. She loved this time-consuming chore and enjoyed leaning back in an old chair while the small white bundle at her feet sucked vigorously from an old baby bottle.

'If you'd stop wiggling that ridiculous tail,' she would tell the lamb, 'you would have more energy for eating,' but it paid no attention and went on sucking and wiggling in a twinned ecstasy.

The Dominie reported, through Ian, that Robin was training near Dundee. He was learning to march, and to salute.

'The Dominie's no sure how much his learning will help him fight the Hun,' reported Ian, 'but he's learning to dig trenches or to order other folk to dig them while he learns all about sending messages. Have you thought of that, Dad? If you're a General sitting in one hole, how do you tell the General in a hole five miles away that you're running out of ammunition?'

'It'll be a boy on a bike,' suggested Colin. 'It's aye a boy on a bike.'

'I hope they're teaching him to shoot,' said Mairi quietly.

'I wish them luck,' laughed Colin. 'Goodness knows I tried and that boy couldnae hit the barn door. You should be there looking out for him . . .' he began and then, appalled at what he was saying, he turned away in embarrassment.

'We cannae hide from this, Dad, at least not here by ourselves. I'd look out for Robin; I always have. But where do I stop?'

'Whit aboot Mairi? How far would you go for Mairi?'

'Ach, Dad, that's different.'

98

'Stop it, both of you. I can take care of myself, thank you, and both of you into the bargain, great lumps that you are. Now go, get to bed for you have to be up at the crack tomorrow.'

They went sheepishly, almost happy to be bullied, and Mairi watched them and then sank into her chair by the fire. She sat for a while just watching the sparks jump from one piece of wood to another and then she slipped out of the chair and knelt down beside it.

'Don't let him be killed,' she prayed, but to whom was she praying and who was the subject of her prayer?

Wearily she picked herself up and climbed the stairs after her father and brother.

'I'll look in on the Dominie,' she promised herself. 'There'll be someone in the farms happy to make a little extra money by doing for him. One fewer thing for Robin . . . or anyone else to worry over.'

The whole town of Dundee turned out to watch their men march away, and countless people from the farms and glens too. Impossible to tell a farmer from a fisherman in a kilt. They were all the same and the women of the town gave their kisses and hugs freely to all unless, of course, they had a man of their own to cling to, a husband, a son, a brother. Mairi stood on the street outside the West Station and remembered the first time she had seen the place when she had come to buy a dress with Ian and had given her money away to a little beggar girl. She looked around. Maybe that girl, grown older, was somewhere in this hysterical crowd. She could hear the pipes as the Battalion marched out of Dudhope Castle, that ancient fortress that had once been the home of John Graham, Bonnie Dundee, the best of all the bonnie fechters. The bands were playing 'Bonnie Dundee'. She recognized the tune as did the huge throng, the cheery cheeky notes brightening the heart and lifting the spirits. Were there braver, finer soldiers anywhere than these lads?

'Goodness, they must fairly be skipping if they have to march to that,' thought Mairi and in a wee while noticed that the tune had changed, to give the pipers, or the soldiers, a slight rest. It was 'Scotland the Brave' that rang out and then again the music changed to a pibroch, a series of musical variations that Mairi did not know.

A bent, gnarled old man beside her enlightened her. 'Isn't it the Pibroch of Donnil Dhu.' He smiled up at her through blackened teeth as he began to caper around in the cold. 'Does it not ever make you want to dance, lassie?' and Mairi watched him jigging away among the crowds. She laughed, for a second forgetting why she was here and then she remembered that Robin was going away to war and she had to see him, had to.

But she could not. She was too small and the crowds were too dense. She pushed and shoved and managed to force herself through the mass to see the men march into the station. He was tall, not so tall as Ian but taller than average. She should spot him easily but there were so many tall strapping men among those men of the Fourth Battalion, the Black Watch. She waited until the troop train had pulled out of the station and then she felt such a sense of loss, of desolation, that she put her head down and began to cry.

'Your sweetheart gone, my child?' asked a gentle voice and she looked up through tear-filled eyes to see a clergyman peering solicitously down at her.

Sweetheart? What could she say?

She shook her head. 'It was Robin,' she said, 'just Robin, and I couldn't see him.'

'No doubt he saw you, my dear, and that surely is the more important thing. He knew you were here?'

'No.'

'If you were anywhere near the front of the crowd he saw you. Think of that and go home and write the first of many letters.'

Mairi smiled a wavery smile as she decided to walk into

the town to look at the shops. Her train would not be leaving for another hour and by the time she got home, Colin and Ian would be in from the fields reading a note that said: *Soup keeping hot on the grate.*

She had better have some purchases to explain her trip to Dundee. But they saw her face and asked no questions.

By mid-September 1915, the Fourth Battalion, the Black Watch, were down to some four hundred men and twenty-one officers. Second lieutenant Robin Morrison was still alive, at least his body moved and did as it was asked to do, but he himself was gone. He had come under fire first at a place called Neuve-Chapelle, and then there had been Ypres where the Germans had used poison gas as a weapon.

April, and instead of a sky full of larks there had been a sky full of choking, burning yellow smoke. He had remembered Ian's frst letter in which he had tried to explain his position and he had scoffed. But now, after six months that had changed him from a loving, cheerful boy to an automaton, he did not scoff. He could not think; he could not pray. He had even stopped worrying that he might disgrace himself by showing fear. For the first few months that real terror had marched or crawled through the trenches beside him. He did not want to die but he was not afraid of death and he did not fear pain. He had met pain before and conquered it but he was afraid and he did not know what he feared.

Perhaps it was the noise. Noise was constant, whining, shrieking, thudding, swishing, screaming, sobbing. But worse than the noise was that endless fraction of a second of utter stillness between the dull thud that said a shell had landed and the appalling roar it made when it exploded. Robin had prayed once that a shell might put an end to this misery but instead he endured the silent eternity, then the roar, then he felt his head almost jerked from his shoulders and he picked himself up out of the muddy blood bath or the bloody mud bath, face scorched, hair singed and he screamed *why* but no sound came from his mouth.

Would it never end? They were all dead. He looked around and the carnage made him vomit and that dry retching only made him feel worse. Surely, surely he was not alone; far better to be honourably dead than to be here in Hell alone.

'Whit did you cry this place?' a cheery voice asked behind him, adding *Sir*, as an evident afterthought.

Robin looked through the blood that was pouring down his face into the dirty but unmarked face of his corporal, a regular soldier who had run away from the jute mills twelve years before because soldiering was at least a regular job.

Robin found a fairly clean handkerchief in his pocket and wiped the blood from his eyes, anything to stop him throwing his arms around the older man for comfort. 'Loos,' he said at last. 'As in "All Hell's let, et cetera, et cetera,"' and they laughed together for a moment as only soldiers can.

'You're no hurt, sir?' asked Corporal Wallace. 'Bad, I mean, for I think it's jist the two of us in here.'

Tentatively Robin felt his head, his ears. No holes that he could find. 'No,' he said. 'Surface stuff, I think. The head always bleeds like mad.'

He was himself again and he was responsible for this man and this trench, or what was left of it. He would not lose his nerve again.

Of the twenty-one officers of the Fourth Battalion, the Black Watch, twenty were killed or wounded at Loos together with two hundred and thirty-five of the enlisted men. It was the end of the Battalion which was forced to amalgamate with the Fifth Battalion. For Dundee and parts of Angus and Fife it was also an end, for almost every home, from closes in the city itself to stately homes in the countryside around, was affected. Death had no favourites. His selection was catholic, indiscriminate. He did not ask, *Is there anyone at home to feed the children left behind?* He

102

spared no thought for the old mother left alone with no child to succour her last years. He did not care how many prayed to join their loved ones soon.

But on a wee farm near Dundee in the lovely fertile Angus countryside the Dominie proudly told Mairi that Robin was now a Captain.

'He says because no one else was left alive, Mairi. What sights my boy has seen. You will write to him, Mairi, keep him normal. He must know there is some point to this.'

'But there isn't,' said Ian and turned away from his sister and his former schoolmaster, the father of his friend, who sadly watched him go.

Chapter Eleven

Hard work, good weather, and better luck brought in a good harvest in 1915. While Robin was suffering in France, Ian suffered, in a different way, in Scotland. He knew that 1916 would not bring the end of the war. He read every paper he could get his hands on, talked with the Dominie, and could see no end at all. He kept away from the village as much as possible but Colin insisted on Sunday morning appearances at the wee Kirk in the village and that was where everyone met in the pleasant sunshine to talk about, not the harvest, but the war.

And the talk was always the same.

'Did you hear that Jimmy Simpson frae the Knock, him that's married on Bert Thomson's eldest lassie, has joined the Navy?'

'And Angus Watson's twa eldest boys have gone tae try fer the Airforce. Seems auld Angus can manage fine with his youngest and the wife.'

And the lads from . . . here, there, and everywhere in between. War was exciting, better than following the back end of a horse up and down the fields in the same old monotonous way. Soldiers, sailors, and these brand-new exciting airmen got regular wages which were sent back to mothers and wives at home.

And at last the question that had worried some for a time was uttered aloud. 'You'll be going now, Ian. Yer dad and auld Charlie and Mairi can manage. You'll be wanting the Black Watch like the Dominie's Robin. You were aye as thick as thieves.'

'I won't be joining the Black Watch,' answered Ian quietly and felt his father tense beside him.

'Don't say you fancy flying through the air in a wee bit machine? Raither you than me, laddie.'

'I won't be joining anything.'

'Ach away. Your auld man's no needing you and your country is.'

Colin tried but to no avail. Ian had wanted to utter the words for months, had longed to hear them said aloud so that he and everyone else could adjust.

'I don't believe in war as an answer to international problems,' he said quietly and then he looked squarely at his interrogator. 'I won't go, even when they tell me to go.'

No one knew what to say. They stood edging from foot to foot, coughing discreetly, and then found an excuse to hurry away. And then one turned, spat in the road, and uttered one word.

'Scrimshanker.'

'What the Hell does that mean?' asked Colin furiously. He did not know the word but he certainly recognized the tone in which it was said.

'Let's get home, Dad, Mairi,' said Ian. 'It's just ignorance. I'm not a coward and some people are saying that people like me are cowards, shirkers, scrimshankers.'

Mairi had been avoiding Edith since she had stopped walking out with Jack but now she saw the look of disdain that passed between Edith and her mother and it made her very angry. She hurried after her brother and slipped her hand into his. He smiled down at her.

'Brave wee Mairi,' he said. 'I'm not a coward. I thought all this out independently of anyone and now I have to act fearlessly on my own moral convictions. It is wrong to kill another human being. Men are making money out of death. There's men all over Europe retiring as millionaires on the money they're making out of misery. That's wrong, that profiteers, safe and warm far from the battlefields, should make money while men die in horror.'

He stopped talking, the longest speech he had ever made in his entire life, and Mairi could only squeeze his arm in comfort and support.

Colin caught up with them. 'Can you thole it, laddie?'

'Aye, Dad. The question is, can you?'

'No more, no more,' begged Mairi. 'Listen, Dad. Did you hear Willie Webster's Clydesdale made eighty pounds at the sale yesterday?'

Colin was so shocked that he stopped walking. 'Away! It never did. That's twice the annual wage of the man that looks efter it.'

'A good Clydesdale is irreplaceable, Dad. Men are expendable.'

Was there nothing they could talk about that would keep this hideous war away?

'Mr Morrison missed the Kirk this morning,' said Mairi after a while.

'I meant to tell you,' said Ian. 'An old friend of his has come out of retirement to teach in Dundee. The Dominie's away through for the weekend. That's a nice wee break for him.'

'More than profiteers doing well out of the war then,' said Mairi. 'If more men join up they'll be desperate enough to have married women teaching in the schools.'

'Ach, it'll never get that bad, lassie,' laughed Colin and lightened the atmosphere. 'Noo, let's have oor dinner and then I have a wheen paper work to do. You should maybe have a look at it with me, Ian, and you too, lassie. I'm bringing my rotation records up to date because we're due for a new seven-year lease and I want the Factor tae see that everything's been done right. The war's good for farmers, Ian. I can sell as much food as I can grow. We'll maybe look into getting a bit more land. My best field has tae lie fallow this next season.'

'Maybe the government will lighten the rules, Dad. Isn't producing food more important just now than letting the land rest?'

'Short-sighted, lass. You have tae look ahead on a farm, no just what's growing this year but what the land will bear in ten years.'

When they reached the farmhouse, Mairi hurried upstairs to change out of her best Sunday dress and then came downstairs to dish up the scalding hot soup made from the carcass of the old hen that would provide the second course. Sunday dinner was always the same: soup, then a roast of some kind with homegrown vegetables, followed by heavy pudding in the cold months and lighter milk puddings in the summer.

'Isn't it a shame the strawberrries and rasps are over?' said Mairi to her father who was sitting at the fireside, his fingers scratching the ears of the dog who lay devotedly at his feet. 'There was that much fruit I've way too many jars of jam in the store cupboard.'

'Aye, but you're right, lassie, soft fruits are better the way God made them. There's nothing better than fresh fruit.'

'I had raspberries in white wine at the Big House last year at the picnic,' Ian announced as he came in from the steading.

His father and sister looked at him, one in awe, the other in amazement.

'What did they taste like?' asked Mairi.

'How did they get you to drink sich a daft thing as wine, and white at that?'

Ian laughed. 'There's some as doesn't see a great country yokel when they look at me.'

Colin looked at his son and saw a tall, well-formed and yes, a good-looking young man, with wide clear eyes, and a firm well-shaped mouth.

'The Laird's niece? It was her, wasn't it? Oh, you sly old thing, Ian McGloughlin.'

107

'They asked for you, Mairi. The Laird had peaches in his wine; he said you would have liked that, rather than the strawberries. He gave me a peach for you but I put it down somewhere and forgot it.'

Over a year it had taken him to tell her. Typical. Mairi smiled as she turned away to attend to her sauce. This strong brave Ian was still her brother who could forget everything if his mind was stirred by something beautiful. Miss Arabella Huntingdon was beautiful. Ian and a lassie? No. He had never been interested in the lasses.

'Come on, let's have dinner and this year I'll go and get my own peach.'

'The picnic is usually in August and here we are at the beginning of October. Maybe there won't be one this year, not with the war.'

But there was and neither Mairi nor Ian realized that it was because Miss Huntingdon had persuaded her uncle, much against his better judgement.

It was to be different. In former years everything had been provided free for the tenants but in 1915 the Laird charged a shilling for each family and a halfpenny entrance to all the games. All monies collected were to go to war charities.

'You go, Mairi, and pay our shilling. I don't think it's a good idea for Ian and me to go and there's too much work here.'

'I'm going, Dad,' said Ian. 'I'll do all my chores before I go but I'm not ashamed of my stance and people can say what they like.'

Colin looked out of his windows, windows that Mairi kept clear and shining, no matter how dusty or dirty the steading became. 'I don't want to provoke anything, not in the Laird's grounds. Some of the ither tenants have already lost kin.'

'I won't provoke anything, Dad, and I'm happy to explain my point of view to anyone that wants to talk to me.'

'We must go, Dad, and you have to enter the shooting

and throwing the hay bale and you too, Ian. It's for the war effort. We can't have our neighbours saying we're not doing our part. The Blacks will be there and the Sutherlands and the Dominie. It'd be a good time to talk to him about taking a lassie into service if he's needing help.'

'Won't the lasses all be working on the land, Mairi?'

'There's still plenty in the tied cottages with more mouths to feed than money coming in, Dad.'

'Well, we can hope for a bad day and a cancellation,' sighed Colin and his children looked at him, Ian with a heart full of guilt.

It is difficult to be noble if your nobility causes distress to the people you love. Ian decided to be very circumspect. He would be a good and dutiful son. He would take part in all the competitions, even the shooting, and if he shot well and Miss Huntingdon saw his success, no doubt Colin would be pleased.

Ian was not the only one who was making resolutions about the Tenants' picnic. Because it was to be held in October which can be a lovely month in Angus or a wild one, depending on its mood, Mairi decided to buy a light-weight woollen suit that she had seen advertised in the *Courier* for three guineas. D. M. Brown's was offering the suit in blue, green, or a light grey and so Miss McGloughlin took the train into Dundee with not three but four guineas in her purse. The suit, which she wanted in green, had a very masculine line and needed, she decided, a soft feminine blouse to make it just perfect. This time she allowed nothing to dissuade her from her self-appointed task and a very happy young lady swept, with head held high, from the Dundee shop a mere two hours after entering it. Buying the suit, although she had tried on one in each of the colours, had taken only thirty minutes but oh, the difficulty of buying a blouse.

She sat on the train and looked, not at the countryside, but at the two brown paper parcels on her tweed-covered lap. She could hardly wait to show off her purchases. The

109

McGloughlins would present a united, and even elegant, front to their neighbours.

And so they did, for Colin and his son were both well-set-up men who wore their Sunday suits with easy assurance, and Mairi looked lovely both because she was pretty and perhaps more importantly because she felt good.

Her pleasure in her suit was diminished a little when she saw the ravishing outfits worn by the Laird's wife and niece. A three-guinea off-the-peg suit is no match for haute couture when it is worn by elegant women and Arabella Huntingdon and her aunt were both tall and slender. They greeted their guests politely although Mairi felt sure that Miss Huntingdon's eyes grew warmer when she addressed Ian.

'They would make a lovely couple,' thought Mairi but sensibly kept her opinions to herself.

Even if Ian had wished, they could not linger and the family went off to enter the competitions and to wander around the gardens, no longer in full flower, but tidied and prepared for winter.

'Sir Humphrey is such a good gardener,' sighed Mairi as she bent down to smell some of the bushes that had replaced the summer flowers. 'The last time I was here, this garden was an orgy of colour. Now look, it's all green, or bits of yellow, but it's still lovely and some of these leaves have a pleasant smell. I bet they would be especially nice after rain.'

She looked up and saw Edith, Jack, and their parents walking towards them.

The families saw one another at the same time but it was too late to pretend that they had not. The two farmers, of course, felt no qualms about greeting one another. The fact that their children were no longer friends meant nothing.

'Nice to see you, Mairi,' said Jack. 'I like your new costume, you look very . . .'

'Nice,' said Edith, waspishly.

'I was going to say, sophisticated,' said Jack and then

110

turned to Ian. 'Haven't seen you in ages, Ian. Come on and I'll take you on at the shooting.'

'It's only men I have a problem shooting, Jack, if you were looking for an easy prize. I hae nae qualms about targets.'

Jack blushed to the roots of his hair. 'I wasn't thinking about your politics, more whit you were like when we left the school.'

'I've improved,' said Ian simply. 'Come on then. Sorry I was so touchy. Are you going to watch us, girls?'

'Rupert Grey-Watson is home on leave,' said Edith. 'Mother and I were on our way to pay our respects.'

'Away you go then, Edith,' said her loving brother. 'But he'll not look at a bean pole like you when the juicy Arabella is around,' he added unkindly.

'Are you coming, Mairi, or do you want to swoon over the delicate Rupert?'

'She'd much rather swoon over his father,' teased Ian. 'Isn't that right, Mairi. Unless of course, young Rupert can grow peaches.'

Mairi fell into step beside them. 'I don't know why you men have to pretend to be so tough all the time. And Rupert isn't delicate,' she added as she caught a glimpse of the young cavalry officer who was walking with his mother and cousin on the other side of the garden. Edith and her mother were hurrying towards them and, for a moment, Mairi thought that Rupert might pull his mother and cousin into a path that would take them away from the advancing women but, if he had considered it, he changed his mind and bravely stood his ground and waited.

'Captain Grey-Watson, we are so proud of you.' She could hear Mrs Black's voice. So too could Jack who was looking extremely uncomfortable.

'Our Edith's given up hope of catching Robin Morrison; he hasn't written to her in months. Now she's after bigger game.'

Ian stopped and turned Jack around to face him. 'Jack, if you can't stop being nasty, find yourself someone else to play with,' he said and stalked off in the direction of the shooting range.

'Touchy, touchy,' said Jack. 'Come on, Mairi. I'll take you for tea and scones.'

'Thanks, Jack, but I'm having tea with my dad.'

She went to walk off after her brother but Jack looked so lost and he had once, after all, been quite dear to her. She took pity on him. 'How have you been though? I haven't seen you for ages.'

'Fine, but I'm thinking of joining up. It'd be great to see a foreign country and hae a crack at Jerry. I'm nearly twenty-five, Mairi, and I'm still living with my parents, being told what to do.'

'You're a partner now?'

'Name only. My dad is so used to being the boss, it never occurs to him to ask anyone else for advice. Truth is, he's usually right.'

Mairi thought of her father and brother who worked harmoniously together season after season. Any blemishes in their relationship had been smoothed out long since and even Ian's pacifism would not change their respect for one another.

'It would be worse to be the younger Harper though, Jack, wouldn't it? It must be awful to have your brother tell you what to do all day.'

Jack looked round and saw an ironwork garden seat. 'Come and sit down for a bit,' and when Mairi did so he added, 'you haven't heard then?'

'Heard what?'

'Tam's gone for a soldier. Left Jim as tenant. Wanted to get away from his wife, I think.'

Mairi ignored that reflection on domestic harmony. Every farm was changing. Who would have thought that Tam Harper, thirty if he was a day, would have enlisted?

112

'It'll just be the Blacks and the McGloughlins without serving soldiers,' she said.

'Not if I go and, besides, two of our lads have gone since the news of Loos came through. They were so angry at our losses they just disappeared overnight. My dad'll keep their jobs for them. He'll be decent that way. Mairi, if I go, will you write to me? Everyone else I know is keeping company or married.'

Mairi laughed. 'That's hardly a compliment, Jack.'

'Ach, you know fine what I mean and we always got on.'

'If you go, Jack, I'll think about it.' She got up from the seat. 'Come on. Ian will be waiting to take your money.'

'All prizes to our brave lads in uniform,' smiled Jack and he took her arm.

They walked off between the beech hedges and came face to face with Rupert and Arabella. Rupert smiled and stepped back to let them walk before him and Arabella said, 'Are you enjoying the picnic, Miss McGloughlin?'

Mairi blushed. It had not occurred to her that the young aristocrat would remember her among so many tenants, but before she could answer Arabella showed who was really remembered by adding, 'My cousin here tells me that Mr McGloughlin is the finest shot in the area. We hoped to see him compete, perhaps against Rupert.'

'My father and brother are both excellent shots, Miss Huntingdon, and so too is Mr Black.'

'Then we'll have a wager, Bella,' said Rupert. 'Five guineas tells me that I can beat either Mr McGloughlin.'

'Done,' said Arabella, clapping her gloved hands together. 'Either way the Charity will profit. Come along, Miss McGloughlin; let us find your brother and, of course, your father.'

Chapter Twelve

Afterwards Mairi could never remember how a day that had started so agreeably could have ended in such an unpleasant way. She went with Arabella past the front of the great house and into the side gardens, followed by Rupert Grey-Watson who was making heavy weather of light chit-chat with the nervous Jack, until they came to the area that had been set as a shooting range.

Two of the Laird's grooms were in charge of the guns, the shot, and the targets which were old chipped plates and saucers that had been collected for weeks by the children of the local primary school. The younger undergardeners took turns throwing a target into the air; it was all very light-hearted because, while most of the boys had no skill in throwing, one of them was the leading light of the local cricket team. His plates went higher and wider than those thrown by the others and were usually harder to hit because he threw as he bowled, a different route every time.

First Ian shot against Jack. They appeared to be evenly matched and Mairi stood beside Miss Arabella and watched her as she, with shining eyes, watched Ian.

'This,' Mairi decided, 'is a very unexpected and exciting new development.'

'Mr McGloughlin is very good, isn't he?' breathed Arabella.

'He gets lots of practice shooting crows.'

'No doubt harder to hit than pheasant, Bella,' said Rupert. 'I think I may lose my bet.'

Ian won the first match and then Rupert shot against Jack, who was so nervous at having been singled out for attention by the local aristocracy that all his shots went wide.

'Bad luck,' said Rupert generously. 'It's that gun, you know. I meant to tell my father to have it looked at. We'll have another go after your friend has trounced me.'

Rupert looked around at the crowd who were gathering to watch the excitement. 'Where's the senior Mr McGloughlin?' he asked. 'I'd like to shoot against him.'

But Colin had wanted no part of a sideshow in which he was a component of the entertainment and had gone off to throw horseshoes with several other farmers.

'Bad show,' smiled Rupert. 'One hears what a first-rate shot he is; it would have been jolly good fun to shoot against him.'

'I'm sure Mr Ian McGloughlin is just as good,' said Arabella, looking at Mairi for confirmation.

'I don't know,' said Mairi simply. 'Shooting crows is just part of his job.'

'Like being a soldier,' said an unknown voice from the crowd.

Rupert laughed. 'I do hope there's more to soldiering than shooting. Will you shoot against me, McGloughlin?'

'Aye, sir, for the Charity.'

'Splendid. We'll have ten plates each, and we'll have Gus throw for us.'

Mairi could tell nothing of what Ian was thinking from his face, which was set and almost cold.

The first plate was thrown – and was immediately shot out of the sky. The second, the third. On and on it went and the crowd grew louder and louder as they cheered, but it soon became obvious that they were shouting only for Rupert Grey-Watson.

Mairi, who had been standing quietly beside Miss Huntingdon, her fingernails digging into the palms of her hands, began to shout encouragement to her brother, and then Arabella, too, dropped all pretence of being neutral and joined her. The girls forgot for a moment that they were aristocrat and peasant and they yelled naturally for the young man in whom each had an interest. They looked at one another and laughed.

The first match was a draw.

'Shall we try again, McGloughlin?'

'There's many here could give you a good match, sir,' said Ian, who hated being in the limelight, today more than ever.

Rupert looked at the young farmer shrewdly. 'There's more going on here than a shooting match. Why is no one, apart from my cousin and your charming sister, cheering you on?

'Never mind,' he added quickly as Ian struggled for a truthful answer. 'I need to beat you.' He turned to one of the undergardeners. 'Run up to the house and ask Mrs Potter for some kitchen cups; the plates are too easy.'

The cups were brought by Rupert's parents and the crowd moved back respectfully. Sir Humphrey was a popular landlord.

'I'm putting a wager on McGloughlin,' he told his son, 'and Mama is backing you. We have twenty-four cups; Mrs Potter won't let you have any more but I have brought these in case we have a second draw.' He took two tiny bone-china egg cups out of his jacket pocket. 'Think you can hit that, young Ian?'

'He can hit onything bar a Hun,' came that voice from the crowd and Mairi gasped.

Ian stood stock-still and looked into his landlord's eyes.

'That the way the wind blows, is it?' asked Sir Humphrey. 'Well, I'm sure you have your reasons. Let the match begin.'

Rupert had lowered his gun and was looking at it as it pointed to the ground as if it was the most important thing he had ever examined.

'Rupert,' said his father.

Rupert looked from his father to his mother who was pointedly looking into the distance, then back to his cousin who was white and shaking, and then to Ian.

'C.O.?' he asked.

'I believe this war to be wrong, sir.'

'And what will you say when we come for you, because we will, you know?'

'I will say what I have just said.'

'That'll take guts, McGloughlin. You shoot first.'

He stepped back and Ian moved forward to the firing line and then, with a soft rustle of silk petticoats, Miss Arabella Huntingdon ran forward and spoke softly to Ian. He smiled at her but said nothing and she stepped back beside Mairi.

Ian missed the first cup and the crowd went wild with enthusiasm. Rupert fired and scored. Ian then hit three in a row and Rupert hit two and missed his fourth. Three all.

Five all. Seven six to Ian. Nine seven to Rupert. Nine eight. Nine all. Ten all. Eleven ten. Twelve eleven to Ian and Rupert still to fire.

'Save the last shell for the coward,' yelled that horrid hidden voice.

Ian turned white, but not with fear, and Rupert stepped forward.

'I see no cowards on this side of the line,' he said. 'I do not agree with Mr McGloughlin's views but I am prepared to fight for his right to express them, not only with the enemy but with anyone here who dares to show his face and make his challenge.'

There was muttering from the crowd but for once it was not against Ian.

'Throw your egg cups, Father,' said Rupert, and, as Sir Humphrey did so, both young men fired and the shattered china fell to the ground.

They stood looking at one another. Ian held out his hand. Rupert looked at it until Ian flushed and withdrew it.

117

'I have lost too many friends,' said Rupert. 'We should have met in happier times,' and he turned and walked away.

Arabella stood looking after him. Her aunt and uncle still stood, obviously disagreeing, and then Lady Grey-Watson called, 'Arabella,' and, without waiting, began to walk after her son.

Mairi was with Ian who was now white with distress.

'Well done, lad,' said Sir Humphrey. 'Forgive my son.'

'Forgive him, sir, for what?'

'You have chosen a hard path, young man. There will be Conscription within the next few months. If you need help, at any time, don't hesitate to use my name.'

'I'll plough my own furrow, Sir Humphrey, but thank you, sir.'

This time it was Sir Humphrey who extended his hand and Ian took it and found his fingers grasped in a hand that reminded him uncomfortably of his father's.

'Bella,' said Sir Humphrey as he turned away.

She stood for a moment and then she turned again to Ian. 'I do think you're perfectly splendid. I should like to give you my scarf but . . . I suppose that's quite silly.'

'Not silly,' said Ian. 'I am going into battle, Miss Huntingdon.'

Her scarf was of the finest silk and must have cost more than Mairi's entire outfit but Bella slipped it from her neck and held it out to Ian, and Mairi saw her shy, gawky brother take the scarf, kiss it gently, and slip it inside his shirt.

'Well, we'd better go and find Dad afore he hears all about this little fracas from someone else,' said Ian, as if the most momentous event in his life had not just occurred.

Mairi went with him and they followed in the wake of the crowd. She was frightened and exhilarated. Ian had won, or at least, since Rupert had not tried to hit his last cup, he had equalled the shooting of the young army officer; that

118

was gratifying. Then there were Arabella's muttered words – how she would love to know what they were, but knew that she could not ask – and the giving of the favour. But there had been Rupert's reaction to the news that Ian was a conscientious objector, and more horrifying, for Rupert had behaved with gentlemanly self-control throughout, the shouted words from the heckler.

'*Save the last shot for the coward.*' Surely no one would want to kill Ian for his stance? Rupert was prepared to fight for Ian's beliefs, which was amusing in a twisted kind of way since Ian, who was the stronger of the two, would not fight for himself. But the man in the crowd had to be someone known to them, someone who had perhaps shared their table or their fireside at some time over the years.

'I won't think about it. The war will be over, it will, and Arabella Huntingdon has given Ian her scarf.'

Arabella. What a beautiful name, so much more glamorous and sophisticated than Mairi. Could she mention the scarf to Ian? The days when she could tease him and worry him like an annoying fly that buzzed constantly just out of reach were over.

'Here's Dad. And by the look on his face, he knows.'

'I hear you won the shooting. Good lad. It's a lot of money for the Charity and here's the Laird told me that if you weren't to tenant one of the best farms he'd have you for gamekeeper.'

So he would, when the time came, be given the tenancy. Even conscientious objectors could be good farmers. But what if Rupert was the Laird by that time? Colin was younger than Sir Humphrey.

'He's a good man, the Laird,' said Ian.

'There's at least three people told me about Sam Jarvie heckling you—' began Colin when Mairi interrupted.

'Sam Jarvie? Him that has taken his dinner with us near once a week for years?'

'He's not been himself since he lost his boy, Mairi.'

'You're always too ready to make excuses, Dad. It was horrible the way they muttered at Ian, like dogs when the biggest one's got a bone they want, all ready to nip in at the right minute.'

'Let's go home, Dad. We did what we came to do. I'm sorry you didn't get your tea, Mairi.'

'Tea? There's nobody bakes better than me anyway,' said Miss McGloughlin saucily and they walked home together, with Ian and Colin teasing her by going through a long litany of local bakers – 'except for Pheemie Anderson, except for Betty Starkie . . .'

Ian was quieter than usual that evening and went upstairs early.

'He'll be away to write a poem, or maybe a letter to Robin,' said Colin, and Mairi, who felt sure that her brother was sitting at his window looking towards the big house and holding a delicate silk scarf between hard, work-worn fingers, smiled and said nothing.

They were both right and both wrong. Ian did spend a lot of time holding the scarf, sniffing its faint perfume, holding its softness against his weather-beaten face. He tried to write a poem but all he could write was one word: Arabella. He tore the poem out of his notebook and folded it with the scarf which he replaced inside his shirt. Then he wrote to Robin.

I want to do it now, to get it over, but that would hurt my father and Mairi, but as soon as Conscription is announced, and that must be soon, I will do it.

We did not speak to your father, and Mairi wanted to see if he needed somebody to help in the house, not her, but some other woman in the farm toon. I'm sure she'll see to it soon, if you want her to do so.

The news from the War Front is more horrific than ever, and we pray for you. The Minister leads prayers

120

for servicemen each Sunday. He must think, especially, of Sinclair; Sinclair who, at school, was terrified of both you and me and, even more, of Mairi, and who has now been decorated for 'conspicuous gallantry in the face of the enemy'.

He did not write of his embarrassment when Rupert Grey-Watson had refused to shake hands with him, and he did not write of the scarf.

Chapter Thirteen

The war was no closer to ending. It was escalating. By the end of 1915, Britain, France, and Italy had declared war on Bulgaria and by the end of March 1916, when Colin was looking forward to the springtime lambing, Albania and Romania had opened up hostilities against Austria, Germany was at war with Poland, and Great Britain had instituted a conscription policy.

'I can't keep who's fighting with who straight in my mind,' said Colin. 'Have you ever heard of half these wee places, Ian?'

Ian was staring into the fire and seemed not to hear and with an exasperated shrug Colin went back to his newspaper.

Ian stared on as if the answers to the questions that plagued him and would not let him sleep were to be found in the flames. Then abruptly he stood up and looked down at his father.

Colin lowered the paper. 'Well, laddie? Something on your mind?'

Still Ian stood and Colin looked at his tall young son with all the marks of manhood on him and he smiled up at the boy. 'Cat got your tongue, laddie?'

Ian returned the smile but did not answer. 'Goodnight, Dad,' he said and Colin heard him walk to the door, open it, and then climb the stairs to his room.

'Damn and blast the bluidy Kaiser,' Colin said and returned to his paper where he saw that the Canadian

Pacific Railway was advertising for farm hands and domestic servants to travel from Liverpool to Canada in search of a better life, and that it was expected that trade sheep would fetch at least forty shillings per live hundredweight in the Forfar Sales.

'We'll hope there's still some farmhands around in April tae sell the beasts,' mused Colin and set his mind to pondering if there was anything left in the house fit to donate to the Queen Mary's Needlework Guild's appeal for donations.

Upstairs Mairi slept and Ian sat at his table in his nightshirt and set about writing a difficult letter. He had tried, several times, to find both the time and the words to tell his father everything that was in his heart but the words would not come. Now he sat with his pen in his hand and watched the ink drip from the nib back into the old inkwell. He took a deep breath and began to write and this time the words flowed from his brain, from his heart, on to the paper.

It's a matter of a few weeks, a few months before they find they need agricultural labourers too, Dad. I'm a strong, healthy man and they will come soon and tell me, 'Your country needs you.' And I will tell them that I will not fight, I will not take the life of another man. They will say, 'Would you protect your wee sister, by force, if she were attacked?' and I will have to say, 'Yes, I would do everything in my power to keep her from harm,' and so they will tell me that I have no right to object to war, for surely it is only a matter of degree.

But what I say is, 'If someone asked me to murder a child, what would God and my fellow man expect me to do or say? No, and again No. But asking me to join the army and to kill children legally is barbaric. In war it is always the innocent who suffer. War brings starvation, poverty, illness, deformities, disease, and it brutalizes. Decent human beings become brutalized by the very brutality they practise and I know they cannot change back.'

I have gone into Dundee to tell the recruiting sergeant that I will not fight but I will cook food, or cut down trees, or drive wagons, or whatever kind of job they can find for me. I will let you know what happens as soon as I can. Don't worry about me. I have to do what my conscience tells me is right. Ask Mairi to tell her I have taken her favour into battle.

Your loving son,
Ian

The recruiting sergeant had no idea what to do with Ian McGloughlin.

'Laddie, there's Boards being set up all over the place tae hear them as has been called and disnae want tae go. Whit the Hell am I supposed tae dae with you?'

'I thought you would know,' said Ian.

'Why don't you away hame tae your ferm and maybe this bluidy war'll be over afore we get to the M's.'

'I can't do that. It's now a point of honour.'

The sergeant looked at him. 'Honour's got precious little tae dae with onything, laddie. Away hame.'

'I've come to join up. There must be somewhere for me to go.'

The sergeant was saved from the effort of answering by the entrance of an officer. 'New recruit? Well-set-up lad. Just what we need.'

'He's C.O., sir.'

'Not on my patch he isn't. Got your papers?'

'I haven't been conscripted,' said Ian and deliberately left out the sir. 'I'm here to enlist.'

'In what, the ruddy ballet corps?' If you haven't been conscripted and you're a shrinking violet, get the hell out of this office.'

He turned away but Ian stood stock-still and waited. His stomach was churning, just as it had countless times in his childhood when he knew that his father had gone for the shaving strap that hung by the fire. But he had gone too far to back down now.

'Surely I'm not the only man who's come in here and said he was a conscientious objector. There must be somewhere for me to go.'

'Man?' The officer turned and looked vaguely around the room. 'Man? Do you see a man, besides ourselves, in here, Sergeant?'

Ian would not be cowed and he would not be angered. 'I am fit and healthy and have worked on a farm since I was a wee boy. There must be something I can do.'

'You can go to jail for the night at least, you useless scrimshanker. Put him in a cell, Sergeant, and I'll see what Major Graham has to say in the morning.'

Whatever Ian had expected, it was not to find himself in a narrow prison cell. There was a rather dubious-looking mattress on the floor, a threadbare blanket and a hard pillow. Ian poked the mattress gingerly with his foot and then decided to remain standing for what was left of the day.

It was the longest day he had ever lived through. He could hear vague noises from the office but no one came near him for hours. At a few minutes past seven in the evening the sergeant came in with a cheese sandwich and a mug of hot, sweet tea.

'The Major's a decent man and he'll ken how tae handle this,' he said. 'I'll bring you a po for your convenience and you can empty it the morn's morn when I come back. Ye fancy a jam butty for your breakfast – ma missus'll mak ye one.'

He was gone and Ian, for the first time in his entire life, was completely alone and in complete darkness. He crouched down against a corner of his cell, wrapped the blanket around his shoulders, and waited for the morning.

It was a long time coming. Every hour or so Ian stood up and slapped his arms against his body in a futile attempt to keep the circulation going. He was stiff and cold and hungry and he thought he could almost smell Mairi's soup simmering away on the back of the fire. It would be warm there in the kitchen with the firelight throwing shadows on the walls. Mairi might be singing or humming as she went about her countless jobs; his father's long legs would be stretched out to the warmth of the fire and he would sigh now and again as he thought of his son.

'I'll be able to tell you the morn, Dad,' he said into the darkness, and his voice startled him as it exploded the silence. He crouched down again against the wall and tried to recall the words of Arnold's 'The Scholar Gypsy' that he and Robin had tried to learn one summer so long ago as they sat under a tree by the stream. He recalled the first ten lines and then another ten and then the lines began to run together in his head and he fell asleep, only to wake later colder and stiffer than before. He was on his feet walking around the perimeter of the cell when he heard the door open.

It was the sergeant. 'We're out of jam, lad, but there's some dripping in the bap. I'll make you a cup of tea. Looks like you could do with being warmed up.'

Gratefully Ian took the soft roll and ate it quickly. He would have liked to wash too and to shave but there was no water and his bag with his razor and his change of clothes was still in the office.

'Why didn't you just wait for call-up, lad?' asked the sergeant when he came back. 'You'd have saved the both of us a lot of trouble and Captain McNeil's a right bugger when he's crossed.'

'Surely not all jobs in the Army are done by fighting men? There must be non-combatant groups.'

'Aye, there are, but they had the decency to wait till they were called up. Why couldn't you wait and go before the

126

Board according to regulations. Regulations make life easier for everybody.'

Ian had never expected to feel sorry for the military. 'I'm sorry, but I couldn't live any longer with the threat of Conscription hanging over my head. It's just a matter of time.'

'Hell of a lot can happen in a few weeks, laddie, even in a few hours. I got hit two days after I reached Belgium; was hardly worth being that bluidy sea sick. And now you're upsetting this nice little job.'

They heard the office door open and the sergeant turned to leave. 'That'll be his nibs. We'll see what he's come up with during the night.'

But the immaculately dressed officer who came into the little cell was not Captain McNeil but Major Graham. And the Major was very angry.

'What is this man's crime, Sergeant?'

'He's a C.O., sir.'

'I wasn't aware that that was a crime. Why are you here, boy?' he asked, turning to Ian.

'I came to enlist in some kind of non-combative corps, sir.'

'Been conscripted?'

'No, sir, not yet. I'm a farmer. Well, I'm working with my father.'

'And why do you want to enlist?'

'I can't not do something, sir.'

'Get this man some shaving water.'

Everything Major Graham did was done quickly. By ten o'clock, Ian found himself on a train bound for Berwick-on-Tweed and two days later he was learning to drive an ambulance. Three weeks later he was remembering the sergeant as he hung on to the sides of a ship as it heaved and tossed across the Channel. If his night in a prison cell had seemed endless, this journey across a stormy sea was eternity.

'Nothing can be worse than this,' was his only coherent thought throughout the entire voyage.

Mairi and Colin heard from him two weeks after the awful morning when Mairi had found his room empty and the letter on his table.

'He says he's learning tae drive. What aboot that, Mairi? Oor Ian, driving like one of the toffs.'

'Thank God he's safe,' said Mairi and burst into tears.

Colin had no idea how safe driving an ambulance in a war zone might be but he said nothing. He was so relieved to know, at last, where his son was. When Mairi had brought him the letter his first impulse had been to go into Dundee and demand that Ian return to the farm. He was needed. The war was good for farmers. They could sell as much as they could grow or raise and that was necessary war work. But he had read the letter again and again and the words had affected him.

'I'll never understand him, my own flesh and blood. Where did he get these daft ideas from? War's not legal murder . . . it's, it's . . . war and that's not murder.'

Now he looked helplessly at Mairi and had no idea how to calm her tears. 'Ach, lassie, he aye wanted to go abroad,' he said but that only made Mairi cry more than ever.

'Oh, I hate Robin Morrison,' she said and ran into the kitchen. Colin stayed in the front room and heard what sounded like his daughter throwing pots around.

'Women,' he sighed in exasperation. Why she had chosen to mention the Dominie's son, he could not imagine. He did not understand that Mairi was comparing her brother's first overseas trip with that of Robin. He did not know that she had kissed Robin and slapped him on the same night. He could not know that she prayed daily for a message from him. He did not realize that her love for Robin and her fear for his safety were now bound up again with her love and fear for Ian. He decided, wisely, to stay out of the kitchen.

Mairi stopped banging the pots around and began to peel potatoes, a mindless task that allowed her to think. She would write to Ian. She would write as often as she could and she would tell him everything that happened. She would describe every leaf unfurling on every tree; she would note where the swallows built their nests and she would tell him of the antics of the babies as they leaned precariously out of the nests. She would tell him when a salmon was caught in the burn and she would describe the antics of lambs and calves as they played by their mothers in the flower-strewn fields. She would start immediately after supper.

First she told him of her unimaginable pride in her big brother.

Dad's not saying much except a man's got to do what he believes to be right, but he's very proud of you. He spent the whole of teatime telling me about every test you had ever taken at school.

'The Dominie always said our Ian was a brain.' If he said that once he said it a thousand times, and then he talked about the picnic and how you won the shooting and Sir Humphrey's respect. Sir Humphrey rode over a few days ago and Dad told him you'd joined the Army.

'I thought the lad would see sense,' said Sir Humphrey.

'He's aye seen sense, Sir Humphrey,' said Dad. 'It's me that couldnae see.'

I sent Miss Huntingdon a note and told her what you said. Dad doesn't want to know about that. 'He's got mair than enough problems,' was all he said.

Miss Huntingdon answered Mairi's note in person. One afternoon when Mairi was wringing blankets before hanging them out to dry, Arabella, accompanied by a groom, rode into the steading. Mairi looked at the beautifully attired girl on her superb blood-horse and glanced down at her own dress, soaked in spite of her huge apron, and she could have wept. Instead she wiped her soapy hands on a dry corner of the apron and went forward to meet her visitor.

'Miss Huntingdon,' she said.

Arabella turned to the groom. 'Walk the horses, Ewan,' and when he had complied she turned back to Mairi. 'I'm sorry to disturb you at a busy time . . .'

'It's always a busy time on a working farm.' Mairi was angry and she did not know why. Somehow she felt that Arabella had to see what Ian's life was like. He was a farmer, not a poetic dreamer.

'Ian,' said Arabella. 'Mr McGloughlin . . . he has gone into battle, your note said. He has joined the Army then?'

'No,' said Mairi. 'He has been sent to a non-combatant corps. He's going to France to drive ambulances.'

Arabella's face grew pink with excitement and she clasped her gloved hands together. 'Oh, how wonderful, true to himself. You must be so proud of him.'

'He didn't need to go; he wasn't conscripted,' said Mairi mulishly.

'I know, I mean I know that farmers are still exempt. Please, Miss McGloughlin, will you tell him that . . .'

She stopped as if she was unable to continue and looked at Mairi.

Mairi smiled. 'Why don't you tell him yourself, Miss Huntingdon?'

Arabella seemed to be considering many questions. 'Yes,' she said after a while. 'We must all help our brave . . . men. It would be a kindness to send a letter, a simple message of encouragement, wouldn't it?'

'I have the address in the house.' Again Mairi compared her plain homespun dress with the tailored clothes of the other girl. She might as well see everything, she thought.

'Would you like to step inside out of the wind, Miss Huntingdon, and I'll write the address for you.'

Arabella followed her into the house, stepping straight

130

from the farm yard into the front room. Mairi looked at her home for a moment through the other girl's eyes and she was ashamed and then she was even more ashamed when Arabella said delightedly, 'Why, how comfortable this room is, and how your furniture shines.'

'I use vinegar and water; my mother put store by the old ways.'

'And no wonder.' Arabella looked up at the ceiling which was astonishingly close even to her own head. 'Mr McGloughlin must find some difficulty in standing erect.'

'No, oh, you mean Ian. Yes, he stoops. I don't suppose he even thinks of it any more.'

'And how useful to be able to change a gas mantle without standing on a stool as the people at home do,' said Arabella and blushed furiously. 'If I may trouble you . . .'

Mairi hurried to the desk where Colin kept his accounts and copied the address that Ian had given them on to a piece of notepaper. Arabella took it, folded it neatly and tucked it into a pocket of her dashing little jacket. 'Thank you,' she said. 'And do forgive me for disturbing you.'

She hurried over to her groom who was waiting by the horses, stepped into his hands and was pushed up into her saddle. She did not look round as they trotted away.

Mairi went back to her mangle and finished wringing out the blankets which she then pegged out on the drying green. She stood watching the wind whipping them up into a wild dance but she was seeing the delicate and lovely figure of Arabella Huntingdon standing in the front room of the house.

'She's seen where you live, Ian, and she's seen *how* we live. Maybe she'll be too fine a lady to write to one of her uncle's tenants. And if she is, Ian, then she's not worth your interest in her.'

131

Chapter Fourteen

It wasn't mud; it was slurpy, sucking clay. It reminded him of the sound the pigs made as they sucked up their scraps: slurp, slurp, slurp.

He stood in it, some places three to five feet deep, and listened to the high explosives dropping all around him.

There were about twenty of them in the dug-out, packed tight like fish in a tin. The water came up to his knees. He looked at it lapping there like the sea on the beach at Carnoustie. Oh, just to slip down under the water. There would be cold, wet sand and shells; there would be shells and it would be salty and the seaweed would drift in front of his tired eyes until he closed them and then he would sleep, sleep, sleep, away from this madness.

His ambulance was a pile of charred metal somewhere near a place called Arras. The wounded who had been in it were charred embers too. He had to get back to them, he had to. Maybe someone had survived. Please, even just one. The soldier who had pulled him out of the blazing van, and had held him in an iron grip while the ambulance became a funeral pyre, had insisted that no one could possibly have survived the direct hit, let alone the fire. But he had to see for himself. He would wait for nightfall and then he would climb out and go back. He was an ambulance driver. He had to stay with his ambulance.

No one saw him go. He crept out of the dug-out like some primeval creature emerging out of the mud and onto dry land and he slithered back in the direction from which he thought

132

the men had brought him. Eventually, when he was too tired to crawl any farther and too distraught to care whether or not he would be shot, he stood up and began haltingly to limp along the road.

By morning he was miles from the battlefield and he lay down in the shelter of a hedge and fell asleep.

He woke, cold, stiff, and hungry, but he was used to these sensations. He could hardly remember when he had not been cold or stiff or hungry. He stood up, slapped his arms, jumped feebly up and down and began to walk.

The joy to be away from the mud! But these were fields where men like his father had toiled for hundreds of years, coaxing a living from the reluctant soil. Now there was nothing. Not a blade of grass, not an insect. He walked on. Once or twice that first day a shadow passed overhead. It was a hawk floating, floating on the wind as he hunted carrion. There were bodies. Dear God: he would not let those birds have the bodies, dead boys who sat there for days, for weeks, with their dead eyes staring out to see if someone would come to bury them, to give them some dignity. He straightened the bodies as best he could, so that there was only the obscenity of death, no lewd gestures, no naked limbs grotesquely offered.

The sun came out and the smell rising from the fields made him sick. He fell asleep in his own vomit, not a decent healthy sleep but the exhausted state of a mind and body that is at the end of its tether. When he started awake he heard himself mumbling, 'As before,' and knew that was his prayer for the dead, and for the living dead in this war, for he had no words of prayer left. Now he expected God, if there was still a God, to know that he meant those same prayers that he had said a lifetime ago when he was young and sensitive, when he had been able to think and to feel.

He had absolutely no idea where he was but he did know that he was dying of hunger. When had he last eaten? Yesterday or was it the day before that? He passed

133

a burned-out farmhouse and searched desperately for something, anything, that he could eat, but there was nothing.

He was unconscious when the patrol found him and he did not wake when they laid him in the back of a wagon and carried him back to their post.

He was aware of sounds, of voices that he could not understand. The smell of mown hay drifted in through the open windows on the wings of heat. Hay? Heat? How could it be? It was April, no it was May or perhaps June. Yes, he must have been in France a month or two. He had had a letter, two letters from Mairi and . . . he groped wildly at his chest . . . one from Bella.

'Bella,' he cried and woke up.

'*Bien,*' said a voice and then he felt a cool cloth on his forehead and strong arms lifting him up. A cup of water was held to his mouth and he gulped it feverishly.

'Thank you,' he said and he looked around.

He was in a hospital ward and a nurse was standing beside him. He heard her speak to someone he could not see and then she lowered him against the pillows.

The doctor came then and examined him and he spoke but Ian did not understand.

'British?' asked the doctor when he had finished poking and prying and Ian gasped, 'Yes.'

'*Bien,*' said the doctor and left him.

Later a man came who told him that to be a deserter was 'ver' bad theeng, not nice', and Ian wondered what on earth he was talking about.

But he forgot it when an orderly brought him a meal, soup, hot and thick, not like the watery rubbish he had been eating with his unit. He did not recognize the flavour but he believed that it was the most wonderful taste he had ever experienced.

The man who spoke some English came back and asked him questions but his English was so poor and Ian was so weak that he did not think he was making a good

134

job of his answers. The man seemed to think he was a deserter.

'I was looking for my ambulance,' he said over and over again.

'Regiment?' the man asked.

'Non-combatant corps,' Ian said but the face peering into his looked blank.

'Conscientious objector,' he tried. 'Pacifist.'

That was understood. The man stood up abruptly. 'We shoot *canaille* in France,' he said and stalked away.

Ian never saw him again but two days later the first nurse helped him to dress in trousers and a shirt that did not belong to him and leaning on her arm he went out and was assisted into a car. There were three French soldiers in the car and they said nothing to Ian, possibly because they spoke no English and he spoke no French, and he was driven off.

They drove for hours and, to Ian's surprise, it was autumn. They had passed one or two fields where crops had been allowed to grow or, more likely, had narrowly missed being laid waste, as had much of France. He put his hand in his pocket and the nervous soldier beside him pushed a rifle butt into his stomach. Ian removed his hand and with it the personal effects the nurse had given him, the letters from Mairi and Arabella.

'Ah,' laughed the soldier, '*votr' amante*,' and he laughed knowingly and Ian, who had no idea what he had said, smiled since that seemed the best thing to do in the circumstances.

At last they came to a small town that showed few signs of having been devastated by approaching or retreating armies. They stopped at a large building in the centre and Ian was hustled inside. He was, once more, in prison.

Again he found himself in a narrow cell with a board to lie on, a piece of wood that was supposed to act as a pillow and a thin blanket which he did not think he would need, the day had been so hot and dry.

It was two days before he was allowed out of the cell and

135

that was the day he was brought before an officer who spoke good English.

He answered the questions which were hurled at his head by a dry voice.

'Ian McGloughlin, Non-Combatant Corps, Ambulance Driver.'

'You were without uniform, identification, had been wounded, and were certainly without ambulance.'

He did wait while Ian tried to explain.

'I am an ambulance driver. My vehicle was hit by enemy fire. I was pulled out by some men of the Gordon Highlanders. The vehicle was burned with my patients inside. The Highlanders took me with them, patched me up, but I worried about my ambulance. Maybe it didn't burn completely; I had to get back to see. I just left the unit and started walking back, I think in the right direction. The last name I remember is Ypres.'

The officer looked at him from under thick black eyebrows. His eyes too were dark in his suntanned face. 'You walked a long way, *mon brave*, and you say to find a burned-out ambulance?'

'I had to see for myself. I was responsible for those men. They were all hit, every one.'

'You know what happens to deserters?'

'I did not desert.'

The officer shrugged. 'You have heard that conscientious objectors have been executed here in France? British C.O.s. You are, how they say, in between the devil and a very hard rock. The world wishes to shoot you.'

Ian said nothing.

'I believe your crazy story, *Monsieur* Ambulance Driver. We will keep you here, maybe a little more comfortable, until we can get some of your own people to take you off my hand. There are enough already here to feed.'

He stood up and walked out and Ian was left standing by the table. He remained there for some time and after a while was conscious that his legs were having some difficulty in supporting him. Should he sit in the officer's chair or wait to fall down? He compromised by leaning against the wooden table. And that was where he was when the orderly came back to take him to his cell.

The next few days were not too unpleasant. At six in the morning he was roused and given coffee. He had never had coffee before and he thought he would be unlikely to want to drink it again but at least it was hot and wet. From seven until nine thirty he went into the yard to exercise with the other prisoners and at ten he was given some soup. *Champignon*, the mushroom, became his first French word. He smiled to think how surprised Mairi would be to hear that the most delicious and nourishing soup could be made from something that grew wild all over the farm. From ten thirty to almost four o'clock he was back in the yard and once one of the guards allowed the prisoners to play football. Language barriers dissolved as they ran madly about the dusty square. Ian limped or hobbled as best he could up and down; sometime in the past few months, possibly when the ambulance was hit, he had injured his leg but he was unable to remember much about the time he had been in France. Some memories were very clear and other things were a haze.

Still, he would remember these dusty, sunny days, especially the football day when everyone seemed to forget that they were prisoners, and gave themselves up to keeping a deflated ball from anyone else.

The game ended, and the exercise period, and they went in, as usual, for more soup, this time thicker and with more vegetables, mainly potatoes. After this meal they went out into the yard again and this time Ian was able to read as he walked up and down or sat in the shade. There were few books in the prison and only one in English, a tattered copy of *Pilgrim's Progress*, and since no one else wanted it, he was able to have it every day. At seven o'clock he was locked once more in his cell where there was nothing to do but stare at the walls until the light went out at nine. He would spend the time reading and re-reading Arabella's stilted, formal little note that wished him well and he would compose answers in his head. He refined them and refined them and laughed to realize that, even without paper or pencil, he was once more writing poetry.

'Well, it's certain naebody'll ever see these poems, since they cannae get written.'

His French hiatus came to a rude end one morning when he was taken out of his cell, not to the exercise yard, but to the interrogating office and saw, to his horror, that the British officer they had found to interview him was his old adversary, Captain McNeil.

'Should I save the Government the cost of a Court Martial and shoot you here and now, McGloughlin, you lily-livered bag of scum?' he said, pointing a service revolver at Ian's chest.

'I have done nothing wrong, sir,' said Ian stoically, although his heart was beating uncomfortably hard in his chest.

'First you're too scared to fight, to do your duty to your King and country, and then you desert your post. You'll be shot, McGloughlin, and I hope I'm there to see justice carried out.'

Chapter Fifteen

They had lived through this scenario before. Jack was on his horse beside the theekit pump in the yard and she was on the barrel, but it was a different horse and she was not looking for a kitten, she was cleaning out a rone. She had to work all day, every day, anything to keep her mind from worrying, worrying.

'You shouldn't be doing jobs like that, Mairi. What's yer dad thinking on?'

'He's thinking on the fact that his son is missing in action, if you must know, Jack, and he has no idea that I am cleaning the rones.'

Jack dismounted and held up his hands to her. 'Come down, Mairi, and let me do that for you; it's no a lassie's job.'

Mairi looked down at him and saw how he had changed in the past two years. The eyes no longer danced with devilment. Jack Black had grown up. She allowed him to help her down from the barrel.

'Any job that needs doing is a lassie's job these days, Jack. There's a war on, in case you haven't noticed.'

He turned white beneath his ruddy complexion and she could have bitten her tongue. She had meant to be flippant, not to hurt.

'I went up against the Board, Mairi. All legal. I'm needed on the farm.'

'Oh, Jack, I'm sorry. I didn't mean anything. I wouldn't wish going to war on my worst enemy and you were never that.'

To her surprise he seized her hands. 'Then you'll start walking out with me again, Mairi?'

She pulled her hands away and started to walk towards the house. 'We've been through this . . .'

He interrupted her. 'Who are you waiting for, lass? Some daft prince tae come riding by on a white stallion? Could you no accept a man on an auld bay?'

Who was she waiting for? A picture of Robin Morrison came, unbidden, into her head. He must get leave soon. He had returned once to Britain but only to a hospital in England to recover from dysentery. His father had said that Robin was ashamed that, while his friends were dying around him, he had succumbed to a disease of the bowels. He had left the hospital as soon as he was able to stand upright and was once more 'somewhere over there'. Robin, Robin's father, Ian, so many people to worry about and now Jack standing here gripping her hands again and looking at her with sad cowlike eyes. It was easier to give in than to fight.

'We can go to the pictures now and again if you like, Jack, but only as friends.'

'Och, Mairi, that'll be great. In the paper it says that we get plays and even opera in the toon these days. Whatever you'd like. I'll get the best tickets.'

'Opera? Italians screaming at one another in Italian? I wouldn't understand a word of anything like that, Jack. A good murder story or a tragedy – no, maybe not. There's enough tragedy to go around just now, isn't there?'

Immediately he was calm, concerned. 'No further word then?'

'He's disappeared into thin air. His ambulance was hit and all the wounded in it were burned to death. They say he was pulled out, but by whom?'

'Maybe the Gerries got him and he's in a camp somewhere.'

She looked at him and he saw brave far-seeing eyes. 'He's not dead, Jack. I would know. He's been the closest person

140

to me in the world since I was six years old. I would know,' she stated again.

'It's a mess over there,' he said. 'Letters take months to get out and he was maybe hurt a wee bit when his ambulance got hit.' He thought of his old school mate actually driving an ambulance. 'I wish I could drive a car. A doctor in Dundee's got one. Everybody'll have one in a year or two.'

Mairi dismissed such nonsense. 'Aye, and in two shakes of a ram's tail, we'll all be using these tractors they had at the Highland Show. Farming without horses, I ask you.'

'I'm surprised at you, Mairi. If there was ever a woman that was running helter skelter into the twentieth century it was you. I thought you'd welcome change.'

Mairi sat down on the old iron set at the farmhouse door and Jack sat beside her, his bonnet in his hands.

'Things have changed too much in the last few years, Jack. I can't keep up. So many gone, too many dead, too many missing like Ian and Sinclair, lads who should be marrying and settling down here. I want the old days back.' She stopped and let her mind remember the old days, school days when every new day was a miracle, the only concern being whether or not Robin Morrison would beat Ian to the Dux's medal, and he had, he had. And now Ian was missing somewhere in France and Robin was so far away, not only in distance but in experience. She could never meet either of them on the same terms again. She heard Robin's voice – *when are you going to stop fighting your brother's battles?* – and she began to cry.

Jack jumped up from the seat. 'Crivvens, Mairi, don't greet. Here's your father coming. He'll think I've said something.'

But Colin was too excited to notice his daughter's quickly dried tears. He was walking, almost running up the path, dogs gambolling like puppies at his heels, so infected were they by their master's good spirits.

141

'I met the Postie and saved his auld legs a walk,' he shouted. 'A letter, Mairi, a letter from Ian. He's alive.' For the first time he noticed Jack. 'Hello, lad. Your father sent you for something? Come on in and Mairi'll make us some tea while I read this again. I didnae take it all in the first time.'

He hurried into the house but Mairi still sat. Ian alive? Her knees felt very weak as if they could not possibly support her if she were to stand up now. They had had one telegram from the War Office to tell them that Ian was missing and that had arrived weeks after their last letter from Ian himself. What if this letter had been written before the telegram was sent? What if Colin's joy were to be dashed to pieces again? She could not bear that.

'Mairi. Are you all right?' It was Jack. Jack being gentle and sympathetic; goodness, how much more was to change? That at least was a change for the better and Mairi looked up at him and smiled. He was all right, Jack, not nearly so bad as most people said; a little spoiled, nothing more.

'Thanks, Jack, it was just a shock, that's all. Thinking about Ian and talking about him and there was Dad with a letter. Didn't seem real for a moment. Let's go in and see what Ian has to say.'

Colin was sitting at the table and the light had indeed gone out of his eyes again. Even his shoulders sagged as if his great back could no longer hold up their weight.

'They're saying he's a deserter, Mairi. They're going to shoot my boy.' He held up Ian's letter and Mairi took it in trembling fingers and began to read.

Try not to worry because I know it will be all right. The truth will come out; it always does. Isn't that what you always said, Dad? The French Colonel believes me and he is speaking for me.

142

In the meantime, I'm in jail, but it's not too bad. Some of the jailors are decent men and some are right buggers, but isn't that what life is like everywhere. If the worst happens, believe that I was only trying to find my way back to my unit, which seems to have been wiped out in the raid that hit my ambulance. I had to see them for myself, my patients. You do understand that. I was responsible for them, and the Colonel thinks that I was probably concussed; it wasn't treated because it was a bit difficult there for a while, and so, when I left the boys who picked me up, I didn't really know what I was doing. They're letting another officer come in to question me. It will probably depend on whether or not he believes me. Mairi, if anyone asks about me, tell them I carry the letter everywhere.

Your loving son and brother,
Ian C. McGloughlin

'What's he talking about, Mairi, if anyone asks for him?'

'Later, Dad.' She could not tell him about Arabella Huntingdon while Jack was in the room.

'This sounds a bit scary, Colin,' said Jack. 'Him being in a French jail. They shoot . . .' Too late he realized what he was saying.

'My son never ran away from anything in his life, Jack Black. He volunteered for this bluidy war he docsnac believe in and he wantit tae do his job properly. Gin he was injured when his ambulance got hit, he should hae had medical attention.'

'But who will speak for him, Dad? Who will tell this officer that he's a good brave man?'

Colin leaned forward at the table and put his head in his hands. He was scared stiff. His laddie was in a French prison and they wanted to shoot him. For the first time in his life he had absolutely no idea what to do.

Mairi put her hand on his broad shoulders and picked

143

up the letter. 'This French Colonel is going to speak for him.'

'Whit good's a Frenchman tae my boy?' Colin would not be consoled.

'I'd better away home,' said Jack. 'It's not a good time to stop.'

Colin did not even acknowledge him as Mairi walked with Jack to the door.

'I'm sorry, Mairi. If there's anything I can do . . . ?'

Mairi smiled bravely up at him. 'Thanks, Jack, but I've had an idea.'

'And you'll not change your mind about going to the pictures with me?'

'Maybe you'll change your mind about wanting to be seen with the sister of a deserter?'

'Oh, I'd never do that, Mairi,' said Jack as he turned his horse round and prepared to mount.

'Wrong answer,' said Mairi as she watched him ride away. 'You should have said: *Ian's no deserter.*'

She returned to the farmhouse where Colin was still sitting, head in hands. 'Dad, it's a bit early for your tea. I'd like to go out for a bit. I won't be long.'

He said nothing and Mairi looked at him sadly, her big strong father who had handled everything always, and hurried upstairs where she washed her face quickly, brushed her hair into some order and put on her Sunday dress. She was going to the Big House.

'Sir Humphrey,' said the very superior person who answered the clanging bell on the front door, 'is not at home,' and he went to shut the door in her face.

'Please,' begged Mairi, 'I suppose I should have gone to the servants' entrance; I wasn't thinking. I *have* to see the Laird. It's really important.'

Inexorably the door was closing on her. 'Please,' begged Mairi.

'Good heavens, Beaton. There's no need to manhandle

callers.' Rupert Grey-Watson in a dinner jacket and bow tie had come into the hall.

Mairi had never seen a man in evening dress before. He looked, he looked . . . so . . . so right. She smiled at the young man and he smiled back.

'You should really have gone to the other door. The housekeeper would have answered that one, but come along in and Beaton will show you down to her room.'

Mairi stepped into the hall but refused to go with the butler. 'I came hoping to see the Laird,' she said and was grateful that her voice did not squeak nearly so much as she had thought it would. 'He did say if he could do anything . . .'

'I thought you were looking for employment, Miss, Miss . . .' He abandoned the effort to remember the insignificant daughter of one of his father's poorer tenants. 'M'father's in Town, I'm afraid . . .'

He broke off as they heard a door farther down the great hall open, and he turned. Arabella Huntingdon in a lovely dark blue satin dinner gown stood in the doorway.

'It's nothing, Bella, just one of the tenants with a problem. I suppose it is a problem?'

He looked down at Mairi again. 'I say, you're the sister of, what was his name, terrific shot?'

'Ian McGloughlin.'

'Miss McGloughlin.' Arabella had hurried forward. She had a lace handkerchief in her hands and she lifted it in a graceful gesture to her lips. 'Miss McGloughlin,' she said again. 'Is anything wrong?'

'Come into the library,' said Rupert. 'The entire household is going to hear your business if we stand out here wittering at one another.'

He propelled Mairi into the room that Arabella had just left and even in her distress, Mairi could see how beautiful it was, with its high ornate ceilings, its huge windows draped with dark blue velvet curtains that were held back by gold

145

cords, its dark shiny bookcases with shelf after shelf of dark leather-bound books.

'I'm sorry to disturb you,' Mairi said. Somehow the room calmed her. She was no longer afraid. 'We have had a distressing letter from my brother and I hoped to ask Sir Humphrey to . . . intervene, use his influence, I don't know.'

'Sit down, Miss McGloughlin,' said Arabella gently. 'Rupert, be an angel and pour us some wine.'

As he turned to do her bidding she whispered agitatedly to Mairi, 'Don't mention my letter, please. Ah, Rupert, how nice. Here, Miss McGloughlin, sip this slowly. It's one of my uncle's best clarets.'

'Claret doesn't travel,' said Rupert. 'Just as well, or he'd have taken it with him. Now, let's have the problem, Miss McGloughlin.'

Mairi put the glass down carefully on a little table by her seat and clenched her hands on her lap. She had to say the right thing, she had to. Arabella was on her side, she knew, but she could tell nothing from Rupert's demeanour. And he was the one who could help, if he chose.

'Ian volunteered in the spring. He became an ambulance driver and he was sent to France. So many battles, he said, and no rest between. They have to try to get the wounded out. He wrote about how content he was. He hates the war but he felt he was doing something useful, something that wasn't against his principles. Then he disappeared and we heard that his entire unit was hit by aircraft fire; Ian was missing, presumed dead. But now he's sent a letter. He's in prison and they say he's a deserter.'

Arabella gasped and again the useless little scrap of lace went to her lips. Rupert gave her a strange look but turned to Mairi.

'Explain, Miss McGloughlin.'

'He was pulled out of his burning ambulance by some men of the Gordon Highlanders but they wouldn't let him

146

go back; he wanted to check his passengers. He *needed* to check them. They were his responsibility. He thinks he was injured because he's lost a few months, can't understand where July and August went, but he tried to go back, in case, just . . . I know it sounds strange but he needed to see for himself. A French patrol found him and he's in jail. The French Colonel knows he's not a deserter but it depends on . . .' She could say no more.

Rupert's face was cold. 'And what do you expect my father to do, Miss McGloughlin?'

'He said, if there was ever anything he could do.'

'He has no military rank, no influence.'

Arabella almost sprang up from her chair. 'But you do, Rupert. You're a lawyer and a soldier. You know Ian would never desert. I think he's so wonderful to try to find his men.'

'Your feelings are embarrassingly obvious, Bella, and would do nothing in a court of law. Evidence is what's needed, not hysterical outpourings from silly little girls.'

White-faced, Mairi stood up. She had failed. She would leave before she humiliated herself further. 'Thank you for your patience,' she said quietly. 'I'm sorry to have disturbed you.'

'Do sit down, Miss McGloughlin,' said Rupert. 'My father would at least expect to find out as much as I can about your brother. He had him in mind as gamekeeper here one day and, Lord knows but good servants are getting harder and harder to find.'

Chapter Sixteen

In March 1917 the German Army retreated to the Hindenburg Line and on 6 April the United States of America entered the conflict by declaring war on Germany. In May American destroyers arrived in Britain, which had been suffering from the unrestricted German submarine warfare.

Mairi helped her furious father deliver two sets of twin calves, male and female. Colin was angry because he knew that for some reason the males would be useless. Male twins always were. Thank God most of the sheep were dropping twins or even triplets in some cases; no problems with male lambs. Another good year. The war was good for farmers, good enough that Colin could send a donation to the Scottish Rural Workers' Friendly Society which had told members that there were now fifteen thousand members on active service and so even more money was needed to help the Society make small sickness and disability payments. Everyone was looking for money. Churches wanted funds to help with Sunday morning refreshments to soldiers. A Parcel Fund for Prisoners of War had started.

Colin worked as he had never worked before and he had always been tireless. Only by exhausting his mind and his body could he hope to fall asleep when he reached the haven of the old double bed he had slept in alone for over twenty years.

'When's somebody going to ask for a donation for people like me, Mairi?' he asked in despair as he watched his daughter work beside him. He had never wanted her to soil her hands with farm work. Useless for her to tell him that she was happy. How could she be happy?

But Mairi was happy, as happy as she could be. She loved tying herself into a pair of Ian's old trousers and working outside, day in, day out. She loved watching the sky in all its moods; she enjoyed seeing lambs making up games to play with one another. If only, if only . . . but she would not think, she would not allow herself to think.

'Mairi.'

The voice from behind her was a voice she dreamed about but had not heard for too long. She forgot that she was wearing her brother's clothes; she forgot that her nails were broken and her hands were dirty. She turned round and joy shone out of her eyes.

'Robin,' she said and threw herself into his arms and then, rigid with embarrassment, she pulled herself back. 'Sorry,' she stumbled. 'It's just so lovely to have someone come back alive.'

She sensed him pull away too. She looked up at him. There were grey wings of hair above his ears. Robin? Grey? He was only twenty-eight. I'm twenty-six. We forgot to celebrate my birthday. She laughed ruefully and Robin smiled, relaxed again.

'Do I look so funny?'

'No, you look . . . distinguished. As you should, a decorated soldier.'

'I've only just heard about Ian. Can you tell me what happened? I didn't write because I didn't know, Mairi, not because I didn't care.'

'It's so wrong, so very wrong.' She looked up at him again and this time she saw the lines of pain etched into his face. 'Come in and sit down, Robin. I have some soup on.'

He went with her and she saw that his left leg was stiff. 'You didn't get that skiting down the Schoolhouse steps, did you?' she said, and was delighted to hear his shout of joyous boyish laughter.

149

'I could have wrung your neck, Mairi McGloughlin. That hurt like Hell. Small consolation to note that you did look back to make sure I hadn't broken my neck.'

He went to the table and she noted that he was glad to sit. He saw her looking at him and sat up straight. 'I'm almost fit,' he said. 'One more check up by the medics and it's back to work.'

'Work? Is that what you call it?'

'Calling it work keeps me sane, Mairi. *Back to killing Germans* doesn't fill me with enthusiasm.' He grabbed her hand and looked at the dirt engrained in her fingers. 'Who first said war is Hell?'

'Probably one of your silly old Romans,' she said but she did not pull her hand away. 'I'll get the soup, Robin,' she said gently, 'and then we'll talk.'

He released her and she went into the kitchen and tried to scrub her hands clean and then she filled two bowls with her vegetable soup and carried them back into the front room.

'I've coddled a couple of eggs in the soup, Robin. We're allowed to keep any that are cracked and one of our hens has an awful habit of pushing one or two eggs out of the nest every now and again.'

'Long may she continue to be so clumsy,' he said as he almost inhaled the soup. 'We're having an awful lot of oatmeal brose at home just now.'

'Isn't Jessie Turnbull doing for your father? I thought she was a good housekeeper.'

'Oh, the place is immaculate and Dad says she kept good fires going last winter. She's doing the best with what she can get.'

'No flair,' Mairi pronounced complacently. 'I'll give you some of my oatmeal cakes to take home with you. Oatmeal, potatoes, a cracked egg . . .' She stopped talking. She was deliberately chattering to avoid talking about Ian.

'He did not desert his post,' she said.

'No one who knows Ian would ever think he did, Mairi.'

150

She smiled at him gratefully. 'I'll never be able to thank Captain Grey-Watson enough. I'm sure that his intervention prevented Ian from being shot. The officer who was sent in to question him was the one who had spoken to him when he went into Dundee to join up. He called him a Conchie, said he had never wanted to fight, but Rupert, Captain Grey-Watson, explained that Ian had enlisted before he was conscripted, and he was heading back for the battlefield when the French patrol found him. That was in his favour and the Highlanders sent a statement about kitting him out with bits and pieces because his uniform had to be destroyed. He had no identity tags or papers, nothing but a letter from me and . . . one from a friend.'

'Why is he in prison?'

'I don't know. It's not fair but Ian says nothing is fair and to remember that they could have shot him. He's in a prison camp, hard labour. They said it was a warning for others that they won't be treated so leniently. He had what was called a hearing, not a full court martial, and I think they didn't really know what to do with him.'

'Can I write to him?'

She looked at him steadily and saw Ian's best friend, Ian's oldest friend. They had gone travelling after all, but not together. For a moment she saw them, backs against an old tree, books of poetry in their hands. Where were those innocent boys now? Did they still live in the grown men?

'I'll get the address.' She went to the desk where Colin kept Ian's letters. 'There will always be this stigma, Robin,' she said, her back to him so that he could not see her face. 'He's in prison, doing hard labour, and so obviously he did something wrong; that's what people will think.'

He was behind her. She had heard him scrape the chair back from the table, listened to the uneven footsteps as he dragged his bad leg across the floor. He put his hands on her bowed shoulders and turned her round to face him. How easily she fitted into the circle of his arms.

'What people think doesn't matter, Mairi. It's what we *know* that matters.'

'Fine words, Robin.' She could not meet his eyes.

He lifted her chin with his right hand and bent slowly until his lips touched hers, gently, sweetly, the kiss of a child and then his arms went around her and he pulled her to him as if he could not get her close enough and his kiss became powerful, demanding, the kiss of a man. She could not move even had she wanted to move and she did not; she wanted to stay there for ever, with Robin's body blocking out the light, the pain, the worry.

He let her go. 'You'll notice I was careful to hold your hands down, Miss McGloughlin. My jaw has a long memory and I'm a wee bit frail at the moment.'

'I didn't hit you that hard,' she said and they were bickering again and then Robin stopped it by kissing her again and this time her hands were, of their own accord, around his neck and she was kissing him back as heartily as he was kissing her.

'And I look such a fright,' she said breathlessly as he released her rather abruptly.

He limped back to the table. 'I didn't notice,' he said and she wanted to hit him but she couldn't. She knew that she would never hit him again; she doubted that she would ever want to squabble with him again either. She wanted him to kiss her again. That had been very satisfactory. She had forgotten her old trousers, her broken finger nails, her untidy hair. She went to the table and sat down beside him and they looked at one another.

'What a lot of time I wasted thinking you were a wee nuisance.'

'I was.'

'I would like to kiss you again.'

'Me too.'

'I can't. You are having the most extraordinary effect on me.'

'I know. I used to have that effect on Jack too, but I liked it with you.'

He smiled. 'It won't be long now, Mairi. I think Russia and perhaps some of the smaller Eastern countries, places like Romania, will sue for peace soon. Everybody has had enough. Almost a whole generation has gone. Not just us but the French, the Germans, the Italians, the Russians. So much waste. You should have seen Italy before the war. Unbelievable beauty and history and art and music all tumbled together, and the smell of Italy, like nowhere else; lemons and garlic and olive oil and heat. Heat smells, Mairi, and it carries the smell of ripening fruit. I'm afraid to go again. La Belle France? Very little *belle* about it now.' He stood up. 'I have to go. When do you expect your father? I would like to have waited to see him but . . . oh Hell, Mairi, kiss me again and tell me that wasn't a dream.'

She was only too happy to comply and the next few minutes were among the loveliest the young couple had ever lived through. 'I must go,' he whispered against her mouth as he kissed her.

'I know,' she whispered back but she made no attempt to loosen herself from his strong arms. 'We have wasted so much time, Robin.'

'You never wrote to me once, not even when I was wounded.'

'I thought Edith . . .'

'Who's Edith?'

'Jack's sister.'

'Who's Jack?'

'I don't remember.'

This time Mairi broke free first. She had to while she could still think. 'He'll be in any minute, my father.'

'I won't wait,' said Robin from the door. 'My father will think I'm in a ditch somewhere.'

'Wait, wait, the oatmeal puddings.'

'Tomorrow, bring them tomorrow, in daylight when the

153

whole village can see you walking into our bachelor paradise and my father in school with his snotty-nosed bairns.'

Snotty-nosed. Billy Soutar. 'Oh, Robin, he's dead, Billy Soutar.'

'I know, but we're alive, Mairi, and from now on it's roses all the way.'

There were few roses growing for them. Robin went to see the medical board and was declared fit to return to his unit and soon she heard that he was somewhere in France and, as she read the papers, she prayed that he was nowhere near a place called Passchendaele or somewhere named Cambrai. She wrote to him every day and she wrote to Ian at his oddly named 'Home Office Work Centre' where he was building a road with several other ill-assorted prisoners.

Thank God they have sent a few skilled Irish navvies to show us what to do with the dynamite or we'd blow the whole place up and ourselves with it.

Ian did not mention Arabella and so Mairi felt that she could not mention the young aristocrat either. At least there seemed to be no ill treatment of prisoners in this work camp. Ian had been beaten up several times in his first prison and had spent a great deal of time in solitary confinement. Unlike too many others, he had not gone insane, possibly because he had continued to write his poetry in his head. Colin had been furiously angry when Ian had admitted to being bullied but the father's anger was directed, not against the bullies, but against his son.

'Why doesn't he lay a few of them out, Mairi? He's strong as an ox and a bully needs to be put in his place.'

'It's because he's stronger that he doesn't fight, Dad, and forbye, maybe there's one holding him while another one thumps him,' Mairi had said and had gone off to make Robin smile when he read her next letter by telling him all about the hopelessly inept Ian being let loose with dynamite.

It had been a great relief when Ian had been transferred to the work camp where some of the guards were soldiers too badly wounded to return to their units. If the powers that be had thought these men would make life miserable for the pacifists, they had miscalculated hopelessly. The war had taught the soldiers cruel lessons. They rejected the idea of war as wholeheartedly as did their prisoners.

Now Mairi sat at the table in the front room and watched rain streaming down the windows as she waited for Colin. She had not started their supper, for a tinker family camping in the nearby woods had brought her a trout and it would not be cooked until Colin was already seated at the table.

He was late. He had walked into Arbroath to pay some bills and to talk to the bank manager, but he should have been back by now. No doubt he had met another farmer at the bank and they were deep in the accounts of the prices of winter feed.

Mairi went back to her letter to Robin. She had just written: *and Jessie came over and I showed her how to make the puddings*, when the door opened and she looked up to see her father standing there staring at her. Something had happened; she just knew it but she would stay very calm.

'Ach, Dad, you're soaked. I'll fetch the bath and you can have a nice wash here in front of the fire while I cook the fish.' She was prattling. She did not want him to tell her.

He could feel her fear. He had to get it over with. 'I've joined up, lass,' he said wearily and stopped dejectedly in front of her, water soaking into the rag rug on which he stood.

They looked at one another steadily, giving and receiving messages in some wordless communication.

'Then you'll need your tea,' she said at last. 'I'll fill the bath and let you steep for a while.'

He waited until she had gone into the kitchen and then

155

he sat down on a wooden chair – he would not soak her cushions – and began to struggle with the knots on his boots. Mairi came in but she did not look at him as she put the tin bath in front of the hearth and began to fill it from the kettle bubbling away at the back of the fire. She took the empty kettle with her and he heard her going out to the yard to the theekit pump. He'd better lag it well in the morning. God knows when it would get done again.

She came back with some clean underclothes, his other shirt and trousers, a pail of hot water from her range and the cold water from the pump; this she put on the large hook that hung from the chimney. The hot water she emptied into the bath.

'I've another pail,' she said, 'and that should give you a nice hot bath. Don't take too long. Fish cooks before you have time to turn your back on it.'

'Mairi, please, lassie, I have to explain.'

'That you're so ashamed of your son that you'll go in his stead? Ian's not a coward, Dad; he's a braver man than you'll ever understand.'

'Ach, don't hate me, Mairi. It's just something I feel I have to do.'

'For the neighbours? And what about the farm, Dad?'

He looked stunned. 'I didnae even think on it,' he said after a pause. 'You'll manage, lassie. You've always been a better farmer than Ian.'

She did not smile. 'You'd best get your bath before the water gets cold.'

When he was undressed he lowered himself gingerly into the hot water, lay back enjoying the euphoric feeling that unaccustomed hot water always gave him, and then splashed loudly for fear that Mairi should come in and see him in his nakedness.

When he was finished he stepped out cautiously and pulled himself, half wet, into the dry clothes. Then he took the bath outside and emptied the dirty water into the drain. Mairi had his fish on the table when he returned.

'Sit down with me, lass. I'm leaving in the morning and there's a lot we have to talk about.'

She perched on the edge of her chair. She was not comfortable. She did not want to stay. He knew that if he said the wrong thing she would explode from the chair like a pheasant scared up by a dog.

'Can you understand that I'm scared and excited at the same time? I'm no an old man, Mairi, though I've behaved like one often enough since I lost your mam. My youth went with her and is buried in the Kirk yard but I've got a second chance now. This war is wrong but Ian sees the wrong wrongs. There are wrongs that decent men have to make better and the world is full of them the noo. Evil and wickedness is marching all over Europe and it has tae be stopped and I think I can help. I'm no an auld man, Mairi,' he said again, 'and too many laddies that don't ken what they're doing are being killt. Maybe if same mair aulder ones that ken the front end of a gun frae the back end were tae join me, we could lick the Hun in a month or two and be back tae help with the spring sowing and my boy would be out of that damned work camp and home where he should be.' He stopped talking and looked at her steadily. 'Will you care for our land here for me while I care for it over there?'

She nodded wordlessly.

'The Blacks'll help – gin ye need any help,' he added quickly, 'and just maybe they'll let Ian oot tae work the farm. I've heard of that being done. Even some fighting men have been released for a while tae help with the harvest.'

She looked up at him fearfully.

'No that that's why I did it but, you never ken, lass, it micht help my laddie, his auld man marching tae the front. I'm getting a kilt the morn. Your dad's in the Black Watch, Mairi McGloughlin, the finest regiment in the world, bar

157

none.' He stood up. 'Private Colin McGloughlin of the Fifth Battalion at your service, Madame.'

For the first time in over twenty years he enfolded his daughter in his arms and let her cry till she was exhausted. His face too was wet but men don't cry, do they?

Mairi went with him to the station the next morning. 'If you see Robin . . . ?'

'I'll no kiss him for you, lassie.' Colin hugged her. 'Noo that I'm in, it's just a matter of time, lass, and then I'll be back and I'll bring your Robin with me and we'll have a wedding Angus will talk about for years. You'll write tae me? Is there enough paper in Angus for all the letters you write?'

'More than enough,' Mairi said. She felt old this morning, old, old, old. Much older than her father who was babbling like a nervous schoolboy. 'I'll write as often as I can. The farm's lost its best worker . . .'

'Talk tae Jack. He's got broad shoulders. The neighbours will help if they can and maybe you'll get some of these land girls that wifie Macgregor is teaching. I have tae say the ones I've heard aboot are doing a grand job. Watch oot for the tinkers when they find oot I'm not in the house. You'll need to lock the door at night now and keep at least one dog in with you. Bluidy hell, the things I didn't think on when I was feeling that patriotic.'

'I'll be fine, Dad. I'll maybe get some woman in to live while you're away. I'll be fine.'

With that Colin had to be content and he stood at the window and watched his daughter until the train rounded a corner and she was gone.

Mairi squared her shoulders and went back to the farm. This was what she had always wanted, wasn't it, to run a farm? She would never ask Jack or his father for help and so she looked for help for herself and found it in the strangest place. There was a news item about a soldier's wife who was going to be put out of her council home because, out of the twenty-three shillings a week she had to live on, she could not afford rent. The woman had three children, two boys and a little girl. Mairi wrote to the paper offering them a home with part-time work for the mother and the two boys.

She wrote to her father.

The boys are a bit rough but the Dominie will soon straighten them out and they are both fascinated by the farm and are pleased to be away from the town. The wee girl's nice and I've given her all my old frocks. Do we ever throw anything away? Mrs Baxter, Milly, is clean and capable and she is going to take over the house while I work full time on the farm. She wants to try with the hens too and now that Angus and Bert have stopped chasing them, I'm sure everything will be fine. Can you imagine the bairns were scared witless by the dogs? The only ones they'd ever seen were fierce brutes. Imagine how awful to live all your life up a stair in a big tenement. They find it too quiet here but once they learn to listen they'll hear the night noises.

Milly and wee Jean are in your room and Milly is so grateful to have a home that I'm sure everything will work out well.

She did not tell him that Bert, the younger of the boys, had drawn pictures all over Ian's precious books, and she certainly did not tell either her father or her brother about the subject of his precocious artistic endeavours.

She told Colin instead how pretty the winter skyline was and he stood in a trench ankle-deep in water and tried desperately to picture his fields.

Later she told him that bread had gone up to an impossible 8½d for a small loaf and admitted that she had been allowed to send some to Ian in his prison camp where the food was barely enough for survival. Colin saw boys his son's age and younger die horribly every day, with nothing gained, and he began to think with his reason and not with his heart and he wondered how his boy was coping in a prison camp, he who had been happiest sitting under a tree. And he worried about the responsibility he had thrust on his daughter who had now accepted even more. How could she cope with the farm, and the house, and now a complete stranger and three children?

'It's 1917. It's got to end this year and I'll go home to my fields and Ian will come home, and Robin. He and Mairi will marry and this soldier will return and he'll take his wife and bairns back to their closie, and everything will be the way it was before this madness came over us all.'

Chapter Seventeen

Cleaning out the cattle shed was one of Mairi's least favourite jobs but it was one that had to be done. Colin had prided himself on the fact that his inbye cattle were always kept as fresh as possible and so Mairi was standing up to her knees in urine-soaked straw shovelling it into a pile as quickly as possible. Her back hurt and her arms hurt but at least she could no longer smell the warm sickly smell of the soiled straw. The human body, she often felt, was incredibly able to adapt itself. After a while the nose became so used to stink that it no longer noticed it.

She noticed the smell of the clean straw though. That first forkful conjured up visions of summer fields full of waving, dancing cereal crops and the feel of the warm sun as it turned the fields golden.

'Mairi, there's a mannie wants tae see you.' Jean Baxter, in one of Mairi's own outgrown frocks, was standing in the doorway. Jean should have been at school but, as a result of the recent bad weather, she had had a bad cold and her mother had kept her at home for a few days. Mairi had enjoyed helping the child with the work the Dominie had sent home but the experience had reminded her of how long it had been since she had picked up a book other than her father's account books. Now she smiled at Jean. Who could it be disturbing her in the middle of a busy day? Someone from the estate office? No, the lease was in order. 'Who is it, Jean? If it's a travelling salesman, tell him to talk to your mum.'

'It's yon mannie on the horse. Will you ask him to let me up while you two are talking?'

Jack? In the middle of a working day? Who was cleaning out his byres? She threw down her fork, pushed her hair back from her face with rather dirty hands and stomped in her wellington boots out into the steading. Jack was standing seemingly deep in contemplation of a large puddle which a kitten was patting tentatively. He smiled when he saw her.

'I know you said you didnae fancy this, Mairi, but it's never been sung in Arbroath afore and they say it's got some nice tunes in it.' He handed her an advertisement cut from the local paper and while she read it, he lifted Jean on to the old horse's back. 'Don't fret. He'll no move unless I tell him.'

Mari looked up from her reading. 'Friedrich Von Flotow? What kind of name is that? It's not Italian.'

'Well, the name of the man that wrote it isn't important. "Martha" is a good lassie's name and so it should be something to take our minds off the war for an hour or two. I cannae say I really fancy it myself, no having heard opera afore, but the main singer's Welsh, Mr Ewen Jones. The paper cries him, *the brilliant Welsh tenor*. If you don't fancy that they're doing one cried "Rigoletto" but that's bound to be Italians.'

Mairi looked at him. She did not want to get involved again but it would be nice to put on a dress and stockings and go out, leaving the house and the farm and all the problems that the last few years had brought, just for a few hours. 'Jack, you know I'm writing to Robin Morrison.'

He looked straight into her eyes. 'I heard. I'm asking you to go to the opera, not to get married, Mairi.'

'Well, thank you, Jack. This "Martha" would be nice.'

He grinned. 'Good. I'll get tickets.' He took her arm and led her away from the horse with its perfectly content passenger. 'How's your lodgers getting on? My mother met Mrs Baxter on the school road. She seems a nice enough body.'

162

'They're not lodgers, Jack, not strictly speaking. Milly is working for me and the boys work after school and on Saturday and they both worked full time during the tattie holidays. Anyone over twelve can work. Wee Jean there was furious that she's too young but I've said I'll find something for her to do to earn a few pennies.'

He looked at Jean who was leaning on the horse's neck whispering into his twitching ear. 'Seems a nice enough wee lassie. What are you going to do when your dad comes back?'

'Corporal Baxter will probably get back at the same time, so it will all work out.'

Jack shrugged. 'I hope so. You could end up with permanent lodgers.'

Mairi had worried about that self-same problem herself many many times. What if anything happened to Milly's husband? She could hardly throw the poor woman and her children out on the streets again when their presence became a nuisance.

'Jack, I'm in the middle of mucking out . . .' she began.

'I know,' he said with a smile. 'I could smell you from the gate.' He turned away. 'Tomorrow night then. It starts at quarter past eight so I'll fetch you about half past seven. Don't wear your wellies.'

She laughed and watched him as he walked back to the horse. He did not lift the girl down immediately but, instead, led the old horse around the steading a few times talking to Jean all the while. Where had Jack Black learned to get along so well with children? A new side. Mairi liked it and was smiling as she returned to her work.

She wrote to tell Robin that she was going to the opera. He had been several times when he lived in Rome and had enjoyed himself.

'Damn, should I wait to let Robin take me? Should this be something I experience first with him?'

Too late to think of that and Mairi allowed excitement to

build up as she prepared for her evening out. The boys were banished to the barn as she and Milly heated up kettles of water so that she could take a bath and wash her hair in front of the kitchen fire. Milly professed to be 'good with hair' and after Mairi had towel-dried her hair by the fire, Milly twisted the long auburn curls up into an elegant roll on top of her head.

'You're losing weight, lassie,' said Milly as she helped Mairi into her best costume, the one she had bought for the picnic, and had rarely worn since. 'You'll need tae dae something about that. A man likes a nice armful in his bed and your Robin with his Latin and Greek is nae different frae any other man.'

Bed? Mairi was shocked by the coarseness of Milly's speech but then she realized that Milly was, by her own lights, merely being practical.

'I'll put more butter on my bread in the morning,' she said lightly and Milly was scandalized.

'At three shillings and sixpence the pound when it should only be just over the two shillings? You will not! You'll jist have to stop running around madly daing the work of three men.'

'When the war's over, Milly.'

'Aye, we'll baith stay in bed all morning eating cakes.'

This picture was so funny that they both started to laugh.

'Goodness, is a belly laugh no fell good for you. There, lassie, you're a picture.'

Mairi had to agree. It was so long since she had made an effort that she was pleased with how she looked.

So was Jack. 'You look good enough to eat,' he said.

'Anything looks good after war rations, Jack,' said Mairi lightly. She did not like the sudden gleam in Jack's eyes.

'Can you no take a compliment, lassie? Oor Edith's like that an all. You say, *My that's a bonny blouse* and she says, *What are you after?*'

164

'Sorry, Jack. I'm out of practice.'

'And whose fault is that? Come on, we'll away and see what this Grand Opera is all about.'

They went to the Palace Theatre and found that they were not alone in seeking a respite from the cares of the day. Almost every seat was taken. Mairi sat beside Jack and enjoyed looking around at the rather care-worn opulence of the old theatre. Without exception, the audience had made an effort and she even saw a lady in a purple evening gown and a diamond necklace. At least she thought it was diamonds.

At last the gas lights were turned down and the music started. Oh, how different from dances at the Kirk Hall. This was Music with a capital M. Mairi sat and let it flow over her. At first she was distressed that she had no idea what the cast was singing about but she read the synopsis in the programme at the interval and then sat back just to enjoy the rest of the performance. John Ridding's English Opera and his Welsh tenor were an unqualified success.

'Pity they didn't say their words between their big songs,' was Jack's comment as they drank a cup of strong sweet tea before setting off on the dark road home.

'Oh, I loved it,' said Mairi thoughtlessly. 'I kept wondering whether Robin had heard this when he was in Italy . . .' Too late she realized what she was saying.

'That's nice,' said Jack. 'Thank you very much.'

'I didn't mean to hurt you, Jack. I told you about Robin.'

'You told me you were writing letters to him, not that you swoon about him every minute.'

'I don't and I'm sorry I hurt you. I'm very grateful that you took me to the opera, Jack.'

'All right.' He drained his cup and stood up. 'We'd best get on the road.'

Chastened, Mairi stood up. How stupid. She had never intended to hurt him and she was grateful that he had taken her out for the evening. She wanted to go home and write to Robin, telling him that she had loved the music and the singing and that she would love to go again. For two hours she had been lifted right out of herself, aware of nothing but the sound and the knowledge that even remotely she was in touch with the man she loved. One more thing, one more thing that they could share. She chattered inanely to Jack, trying to make amends, going over the costumes and the scenery and the cleverness of the lighting effects but he said nothing and eventually she gave up and they made the rest of their way in silence.

Mairi thought the journey would never end. She could hardly wait to see the lamplight shining out of the darkness. Milly would be there, and the children. Their homework would be done and the boys, no doubt, would be arguing about bedtime.

She was wrong. Angus and Bert had been so well behaved that, had their mother not had a great deal to think about, she might well have wondered why they had gone off so uncomplainingly after their sleepy sister.

Angus and Bert did not like Jack. They did not know why and would have argued fiercely if it had been pointed out to them that they were jealous. They knew only that Mairi belonged to them: her father, her brother, even her love were far away. She had given them a home and their mother dignity and they were her champions.

'He pits one finger on her and I'll hae his heid aff,' whispered Angus as they crept from the house.

'But what if she likes it,' argued Bert. He had seen a film and he knew that girls liked to be kissed.

'Likes it? Likes Jack Black when there's . . .' He realized in growing maturity that he had been about to say: 'there's me', and he shied away from such an admission '. . . when there's Robin Morrison.'

Bert said nothing but nodded his head in the dark. Yes, there was Robin Morrison. He crept along behind his big

166

brother until they were well clear of the steading and then he walked boldly beside him towards the town.

Unaware of his reception committee Jack stopped the buggy when they were almost within sight of the farmhouse.

'So you're grateful, Mairi. Show me how much,' he said and putting his arms around her pulled her to him and began to kiss her.

At first Mairi was too shocked to move and when he thought that she was acquiescing Jack began to kiss her more brutally and to her horror she felt his tongue thrusting into her mouth.

She gasped and pulled back, struggling, but he paid no attention. He held her with one hand as his free hand sought for the buttons on her coat and she began to struggle even more wildly.

'Oh, I like a bit of a fight, Mairi,' he said. 'Come on.' Now his hands were inside her coat and she could feel him fondling her breasts through the thin wool of her best dress.

He took his mouth off hers for a moment. 'Christ, Mairi, it's months since I've had a woman.'

He pushed her down on to the floor of the buggy and his hand was lifting her dress. She would die. She knew she would. She tried to cry out but his mouth, his horrible tongue choked her and then suddenly Jack stopped and she heard a voice.

'Get aff her right noo, you bluidy bastard or I'll blow your head off.'

The Baxter boys, such unprepossessing figures of legendary knights in shining armour, were standing beside the buggy and in the strong hands of thirteen-year-old Angus was Colin's favourite shotgun. It was pointing at Jack's stomach. No doubt Angus felt that 'blow your head off' sounded better than 'blow your stomach off'.

Mairi started to laugh hysterically and then to cry.

167

'Come on, Mairi,' said Bert. 'Gees your hand and come doon aff there. Mam's waiting up for you and we thought we'd come and meet you. She disnae ken that, mind, so dinnae tell her.'

Mairi found her hand held in the warm soft grasp of a twelve-year-old but there was strength there for he helped her down from the buggy and as she wavered his grip strengthened. Little boy Galahads. She loved them.

She stumbled away from Jack with the boys and then she was at the house and before the boys could hide the door was open and Milly was there.

'Mercy. What happened to you?' she asked, taking one look at Mairi's face and then another at those of her sons. She did not fail to notice the gun in her eldest child's young hands. 'You put that back right now afore I leather your backside. Just wait till your father gets home.'

'We saved Mairi, Mam,' explained Bert as Angus, too dignified to explain himself to his mother, stalked off to shut the shotgun in its cupboard. 'Thon mannie was trying you know what and we thought Mairi was liking it and then Angus saw she was trying to fight so he stuck the gun in his ribs. He got a real fleg, I'll tell you.'

'I'll bet he did,' said Milly and began to laugh and Mairi began to cry and found herself wrapped in a woman's arms and comforted.

'Away and tell your brother I think he's a wee treasure and I'll no tell your dad, and then put the kettle on and we'll all have some cocoa.'

'I was so lonely, Milly,' sobbed Mairi, 'and I wanted to put up my hair and go to the theatre and feel like a woman, not a farmer, and to forget Dad and Ian and even Robin just for a while.'

'I know, lassie, but listen tae me. If you was a millionaire what would you rather have, a bit steak or a quarter of mince?'

'Steak,' sniffed Mairi.

168

'Well then, men are like steak and mince, lass, and once you've found the one for you he's the steak and so you dinnae bother with mince. You wait fer yer steak, even if you have tae wait an affie time. Look at me. I met my Jim when I was in the Mills at fifteen and he joined up tae get a regular job. Twenty year we've been marrit and he's been away maist of that time but dae I go the dancin' with other soldiers' wives and maybe pick up a wee mannie for a night or two, I do not. I wait for Jim and it's mair than worth the days and nights of loneliness. He's my top steak.'

'And Robin's mine.'

'Then we'll wait thegither.'

'We will.'

'Good, now go and wash yer face and I'll make some cocoa and then we'll away tae bed for there's work waiting.'

Mairi thought of Jack and the unexpected or unwanted end to a pleasant evening for only a few minutes and then her healthy young body demanded sleep.

She woke early as always and washed and dressed in the dark before opening her curtains to look out at the farm and the sea way, way beyond. There were still some stars in the sky and a glimmer of moonlight stroked the water. As Mairi watched, the blue-grey of the sky became tinged with pink as the sun struggled to oust his sister moon from his place in the sky.

'Sun, moon, and stars in the sky together. Maybe I should wake the bairns to let them see.'

She decided to leave the young Baxters, deciding that the moon and the stars would have quite disappeared before the children's tousled heads could be forced from their pillows. It was pleasant to sit alone watching the play of light in the sky. The pink turned red, great huge burning banners stretching across the sky just where it met the grey-blue of the sea.

'Shepherd's warning? No, that's only when the red is

169

in the sky late in the morning, not now at the birth of the day.'

The remembrance that the world was at war cut across Mairi's day-dreaming. She thought of her father, her brother, and Robin. How beautiful was the sky under which they were waking to another day? She prayed that it was as lovely as this one. Colin and Ian were aware of the sky and the games the sun and the moon played at four-thirty on a winter morning. Was Robin? Had he ever seen the birth of a day? Or were all the soldiers from all the armies awake and alert as they waited for the sun to rise to show them how best to attack and kill their enemies?

'Oh, let them all see beauty,' Mairi thought sadly as she turned from the window and went downstairs and outside to the barns to the softly lowing cattle who pushed up their heads and blew softly at her as she walked across the steading.

Later that morning Mairi intercepted the postman on his bicycle. There were no letters for Mairi but two for Milly from friends in Dundee.

'She'll need them,' said the postie as he told Mairi grimly that among the list of names in the post office window was that of Corporal James Baxter – killed in action.

This time it was Mairi's arms that did the comforting.

Chapter Eighteen

Would the misery never end? Fourteen-year-old Angus Baxter ran away to join the Army. He was going to kill the German who had, according to the distraught boy, murdered his father.

It was the Dominie who went to Edinburgh to bring him home.

'He's a bright lad, Mairi,' he said when they had Angus upstairs and in bed, his mother sitting by his side. 'Another Ian. No poetic talent but a very good mathematical mind. I hoped to encourage Mrs Baxter to keep him at the school.' He looked at Mairi. 'Things are going to be very difficult now.'

Mairi sighed. 'They're all right here for now, Mr Morrison, and by the time the was is over we'll have thought of something.'

Things are going to be very difficult now. She supposed he meant that when Colin came home there would be no room for Milly and her children; one more problem. For herself Mairi could hardly see that things could get any worse than they were already. Both Colin and Robin had been wounded and were recuperating in the same hospital in France. Ian was somewhere in Italy – she could hardly bear it that war had taken him to the land he had dreamed of as a boy – and now, just as it seemed that Milly was able to walk around as if she no longer saw an unbridgeable chasm opening at her feet, Angus had frightened her like this. He was a big strapping lad and had fooled several people before one over-worked recruiting officer had taken a second look and sent him home to grow up.

'And I can't even write Robin a loving letter,' thought Mairi as she sat staring into the fire after the Dominie had left. How nice it would be to explain the difference between steak and mince but Robin had no real idea of how Mairi felt about him. His letters were the letters of a friend, as if he was somewhat embarrassed by his behaviour on his last leave. And she had taken her lead from him, as she had done all through their childhood. Robin and Ian led and Mairi followed along behind.

It would soon be the holidays. The school was closing for ten days, and, despite war shortages, there was going to be a party for the children in the Kirk Hall. Rumours abounded to the effect that Sir Humphrey was coming home for the holidays and that he intended to give every child in the school an orange. Mairi had been asked to help with the party; Edith Black, whose fiancé was a prisoner of war in Germany, was going to play the piano for games and even Violet, Mairi's first friend at school, was going to be there since she had four children who each spent some time at the school.

'Bert, you must try, for your mother's sake, to enjoy this party,' she told Milly's younger son, who was showing every sign of defying them both by not attending.

'It's a bairns' perty. I'm no gan near the place.'

'Yes, you are,' said Angus. 'Because I tellt the Dominie we'd baith come to keep the bairns in order.'

Mairi, who was sure she was going to hate the party as much as Bert did, watched anxiously to see how he would deal with being ordered around by his brother. Bert looked at Angus and saw how big and strong he was.

'You and me, the baith of us?'

'Oh, aye. The Dominie thocht you'd come for the orange but I said you couldnae be bought,' said Angus blandly as he tied his laces round and round his legs.

'Have I ever had an orange?'

'Aye, hundreds of them,' lied Angus, 'but no since this bluidy war stertit.'

Mairi was so glad that they were going to do what their poor mother wanted them to do that she turned a deaf ear to Angus's language. It would be good for Milly to get out of the house, which she had not left since the telegram had arrived. It was fitting that Christmas should be the time for her to start her painful journey back to a life without the hope of her husband returning.

'Get a lantern, Angus, and we'll be on our way,' she said and then turned as Milly came down the stairs with Jean.

Poor wee Jean. What agonies she must have endured to achieve those tortured plaits. She smiled tearfully at Mairi and got her coat from the pegs by the door.

Milly walked over to the fireplace and put the guard protectively in front of the damped-down coals. 'A wee poke when we get hame and we'll hae a nice wee blaze.'

'A Christmas party should be fun, Milly. Everybody will be there.'

'Everybody that's left, lassie.'

'Oh, Milly.' Mairi had thought that Milly's willingness to go to the party had signalled a new start. Perhaps it did.

'It'll get better.'

Milly looked at her and in her eyes Mairi saw the empty years stretching ahead. 'I'll endure it – for my bairns' sake. Och, dinnae fret, lassie. I'm tough, I'll survive, but it'll never get better. How can it?'

Mairi could say nothing. There were no words of comfort. She reached for her coat and followed the children out into the darkness.

They heard the sounds of revelry long before they reached the village. The piano, which even to Mairi's untrained ear sounded badly out of tune, was being played as if loudness might make up for accuracy but the children did not seem to mind. They were running from one side of the hall to the other, from the top to the bottom, bumping into one another, into angry and overworked mothers who thumped, without discrimination, whichever child they could reach, and they were having a wonderful time.

The hall had been decorated with holly but there were no candles. Some of the smallest children could have no memory of socials and parties when the hall had been ablaze with red candles. They did not mind. It was decorated. A piano was being played and they did not have to go to school for a whole week. Could life get better?

It could. For one magic night the war was forgotten, at least by the children, and at nine thirty, just as the Minister and the Dominie were beginning to whisper together about the lateness of the hour and the dangers involved in long walks home in the dark, someone heard the sound of a car and there was Sir Humphrey with his oranges – and his niece Arabella Huntingdon.

She was wearing silver grey furs and looked exotic and wonderful. Small children pressed close to her just to drink in her perfume or to touch the stuff of her coat. Jewels sparkled in her ears and on her soft white hands and Mairi, more than ever, was aware of her own reddened skin, her broken nails, her ugly, ugly, too large dress. And then Arabella smiled and Mairi, together with everyone else, was captivated again.

Bella left her uncle deep in conversation with the Minister and came over to Mairi who was watching the Dominie, flanked by his henchmen Angus and Bert, give out the precious oranges.

'Miss McGloughlin,' said Bella, 'how very lovely to see you again.'

Ian loves her and she is a fairytale creature who has forgotten him.

'It's nice to see you, Miss Huntingdon,' she said stiffly. She had to be polite, had to be. Arabella, after all, had

174

persuaded Rupert to exert his influence on Ian's behalf. 'You have been away a long time.'

'One has to do what one has to do,' said Arabella. 'My uncle and aunt want me to have the life they think a girl from my family ought to have. I have tried to play their game.' Suddenly she looked directly at Mairi and her face was no longer smiling. 'Have you heard from him lately? I'm so worried; there was such a ghastly battle at a place called Caporetto.'

'Caporetto?' Mairi's mind seemed sluggish.

'Italy. It went on for weeks and weeks and I tell myself that he was probably in quite a different part of Italy, probably sitting under an olive tree writing a poem . . . that's how I make myself see him, to keep myself sane.'

'You know where he is?' Mairi could hardly believe what she was hearing. Ian had never mentioned Bella and Mairi had hardly dared remind him of the Laird's niece.

Bella laughed. What a lovely musical sound. Several of the children who were stroking her coat looked up at her lovely face to hear the laughter better. 'He hasn't told you,' she said. 'What a wicked boy. Is he ashamed of me, do you think?'

'Perhaps you're the only lovely thing in his life, Miss Huntingdon, and he wants nothing to touch you.'

'Goodness, how lovely. You're a poet too. And do call me Bella. If we are to be sisters in the eyes of the law . . .'

'Goodness, Miss . . . Bella. No, I'm sorry, I can't. I can't take this in. I didn't think you and Ian . . .'

'I haven't seen him since the picnic. Those picnics were, well, you won't believe me if I say they were the highlights of my year. I saw Ian first when I was fourteen. He's so beautiful, isn't he?'

'Would you like a cup of tea, Miss . . . Bella? I need to sit down.'

'Me too. Let some of these little acolytes fetch tea for us. We can sit over here.'

She walked across the hall, children trailing in her wake like seagulls after a trawler, and sat down against the wall and Mairi had no choice but to follow her. Milly brought them tea and slices of the latest attempts at eggless cake. Arabella smiled up at her. 'You must be Mrs Baxter. We were so sorry to hear about your loss.'

Milly smiled but said nothing and Mairi drank some of her tea and wondered what on earth to say. Ian beautiful? Ian was a farmer's son who had almost been shot for desertion. What would Sir Humphrey have to say about that?

'It won't be easy, Mairi, but what is easy? My aunt will have a fit and Ian isn't terribly easy to convince either. He spouts all this stuff and nonsense about my being too good for him and miles above me and all that rot.'

'It isn't rot at all, Miss Huntingdon.'

Bella turned in her chair to look at Mairi. 'But I thought you would have been on my side.'

'I'm on my brother's side. Has he asked you to marry him?'

'Good gracious no. I have to do all the running. He has such fearfully outmoded ideas. I keep telling him that the war has changed everything. I was going to try with "love changes everything" but Ian would give me up out of love. Now I'm working on, "when you're acknowledged as an absolutely brilliant war poet, everyone will say you're marrying beneath you" but he hasn't replied to that one and so I'm frightened.'

Mairi was having trouble in taking in all that she was hearing. Ian and Sir Humphrey's niece, a debutante, a girl who had been presented to their Majesties at Court: they were writing to one another, had been for some time. 'I haven't heard in weeks,' she said at last. 'I've been so involved with poor Milly Baxter and her children, but quite often there's a huge gap and then three letters arrive at once . . .'

Arabella stood up. 'That's what I'm hoping. Uncle's

leaving. I must go. When you hear from Ian, you may tell him that I've told you of my feelings. Perhaps then he'll write to you about his. Funny, isn't it, but he's actually more of a snob than Rupert and that's saying something.'

She walked to the door chatting to all the little acolytes who followed her and when the door closed behind her the room seemed cold and empty and dark.

A few days later another visitor, Mr Sutherland the Minister, brought Mairi more bad news. Ian was missing, assumed captured by enemy soldiers.

She could not bear it; she could not. It was too much. Robin in hospital, Dad out but sent back to his unit, and now this.

'Do you know what day it is, Milly?' she asked as they sat side by side before the fire that Angus kept stoked for them. 'It's the first day of 1918. We should have the whisky out and black bun and a fiddler playing all the old tunes.'

'It'll get better, lassie.'

Who had said that last?

'He's been in prison, Milly. It nearly drove him insane. He'd rather be dead. Oh, God, I have to tell Bella.'

Milly lifted a spoon of the hot broth she was trying to make Mairi drink. 'Come on, lass.'

Mairi took the spoon from her and tried to smile. 'You think you're dealing with Jean, Milly.'

'Ach, we're all children when we're in pain. Who's Bella?'

And Mairi looked at her honest face and told her everything. 'But how can I tell her on New Year's Day? They're bound to be having a wonderful party.'

'It won't hurt to keep it till tomorrow. Let her have her fancy party.'

'He's a prisoner of war. He's alive and he'll come home. Right?'

'Right. And then your dad'll be back and your Robin

177

because this war has to end, Mairi. They won't go on until there's no one left to fire the guns.'

Mairi stood up. 'We'd best away to bed. There's more than enough work for the two of us tomorrow.'

'Give Angus some chores. He'll need to do some of your work or you'll no have time tae visit the lassie.'

'I wonder if I should just send her a note – I went to the front door there once – I'll not make that mistake again. I don't know what excuse I'd make for wanting to see her.'

'It's still better than letting her read it, lass.'

Milly was right, of course, but Mairi did not relish the embarrassment of being asked by a servant to state her business and she knew that would happen. She lay awake for most of the night worrying about Ian and trying to think of a reason for a farm girl to call on the daughter of the 'Big House' before eventually falling into an uneasy doze.

Milly was already awake and the porridge was plopping softly over the heat when she went downstairs the next morning.

'I'll do what has to be done here and then I'll walk over, Milly. Will you have a look at the logs, Angus? Maybe Bert could give you a wee hand and, Jean, you'll do the hens this morning for me, won't you?'

By one thirty she had no excuses left. She combed her hair, tied it back neatly, put on her coat and her boots and set off for Sir Humphrey's home. She rehearsed what she would say when a maid came to the back door to see who was knocking.

Arabella was walking in the garden, throwing sticks for her spaniel to retrieve. She saw Mairi on the driveway and, abandoning her puppy, hurried to meet her.

The cold air had made Arabella's cheeks pink and her eyes bright and she looked ethereally lovely. As usual she made Mairi feel plain and dowdy but she could not care about that today because she was going to extinguish the light in Bella's sparkling eyes.

178

'A prisoner? But he'll hate that.'

'He's alive . . . Bella.'

Arabella smiled. 'He hated prison. It wasn't so awful when they sent him up to the highlands to build roads but the prison cells were terrible, frightening. He couldn't write; they wouldn't give him paper and so he kept sane by memorizing his poetry. He's a genius, but you know that.'

Mairi hung her head. They had never taken Ian's poetry seriously. 'Men like Rupert wrote poetry.' She was startled to realize that she had spoken.

'Then what about Burns, Mairi? Men like Ian write poetry. You have no more news?'

'No, I'm sorry. The telegram came yesterday . . .'

'And while I was dancing in the ballroom, getting squiffy on champagne and toasting the end of the war that is bound to come, you were alone.'

Mairi felt exasperation rising. How melodramatic. Two poets together. Ian and Bella were perfect for one another. 'With Milly, Angus, Bert, and Jean, and a farm to run so that Ian will have a home to come back to. I'd best get back.'

'Yes, of course, and you'll let me know when you hear something. Oh, blast, I'm going to Town later this week. You must ring me on Auntie's new telephone; I'll give you her number.'

'I've never seen a telephone machine, Miss Huntingdon. There isn't one in the village.'

Bella looked at her and impulsively grasped Mairi's hand. 'You're angry, calling me Miss Huntingdon. I'm sorry. You will write to me though, just as soon as you hear something definite?'

'I'll write.'

Bella called the spaniel who was having a wonderful time rolling in the soft snow and Mairi stood and watched them make their way back to the luxury of the Big House. Ian would not be at ease there. There could be no future for him and Arabella Huntingdon, no matter how romantically they looked at their situation. And it was obvious that the young aristocrat was keeping her letter writing from her family or perhaps she tossed off her interest in Ian with a . . . *writing to one of the tenants, you know. One's got to do one's bit for our fighting men.*

Mairi remembered how Rupert had reminded Arabella pointedly that the young farmer was one of her uncle's tenants. And he was not even that. Colin was the tenant; Ian no more than a hired hand. A match between the two young people would never be allowed and, even if it were, how could Ian support a girl who wore furs and diamonds to a school party?

The only thing to do now was to write to Ian with love and support. And after that letter was written there was one to Colin who also needed support and then Robin . . . How wonderful to be able to pour her heart out to Robin but she would have to write him a friendly letter, telling him about the children's party and the oranges and Arabella Huntingdon's beautiful clothes, and then she would tell him that Ian was a prisoner of war and she would be so positive that everything was going to be well.

She did not have to write the letter, for when she got home Angus rushed out to tell her that the Dominie had walked to the farm to tell them that the war was over for Robin, who was being invalided out to recover at home.

Chapter Nineteen

'Hey, fermer, can ye no see ma sheets?'

The cheery cry rang out from the drying green and Mairi straightened up from the fire she was lighting to wave to her housekeeper.

'The wind will change, Milly, honestly.'

'I'll believe you,' shouted Milly, leaving the end of the quotation, *thousands wouldn't*, left unsaid.

Mairi laughed and went on with burning the stubble. She was months behind with the work on the farm; things just did not work so smoothly with Colin and Ian away. This had to be done and it was a shame that Milly had chosen to change the beds on the day she had elected to light fires so near the farmhouse. The wind would change – eventually.

Just as the war would end – eventually, and Ian and Colin would come home. And Robin? Mairi sighed. Robin would talk to her – eventually.

Oh, he did talk. He was painfully polite when a meeting could not be avoided but it was obvious that communicating with anyone at all was an almost unbearable burden.

'He's no the man he was, lassie,' said Milly. 'Your Robin is still there somewhere, but there's layers of experiences on that laddie and he has to learn to live with them afore he can think on living with anyone else.'

'But I don't want him to marry me – I mean, of course I do, but I know he's not ready. I'm terrified that he doesn't love me any more, that maybe he never loved me at all. He kissed me, Milly; he never said he loved me. Oh, damn, why is being an adult so difficult? Can't he see that I want to help him. If he'd talk to me, really talk, not just mutter things about it being a good spring for planting, I know I could help him.'

'Give him time. Give him space. My Jim used to jump up in the bed at night screaming bluidy murder; used to frighten the life out of me – and the bairns. It's whit they've seen, whit they've had to do.'

'I seem to have wasted so much time, Milly. I took years to realize how I felt about him and now, just when I thought that perhaps he cared for me too . . .' Suddenly Mairi looked up and saw Milly's kind, sympathetic face and she remembered that Milly had lost her husband and here was she, blubbering like a school girl.

'I'm sorry, Milly. I feel so ashamed.'

Milly wiped Mairi's face with her dishcloth, just as she did with Jean and occasionally Bert. 'Come on, let's have a cup of tea and a scone. There is nothing to be ashamed about, lass. Jim's dead, and I'll carry that grief for the rest of my life but surely that should make me better able to comfort. You helped me when Jim got killt, I help you when Robin gets hurt. Women always pick up the bits after their men, lass. The way of the world.'

Mairi looked at the older woman and again felt ashamed. Milly had loved her husband dearly, yet after allowing herself hardly any time to grieve, she was back at work, looking after the house, caring for her children and their grief, keeping a worried eye on her elder son who, of course, felt the loss of his father so much more than the younger children who had hardly known him, and being constantly, unfailingly cheerful.

'Milly, did you never think of joining any of the clubs . . . I don't know, knitting socks for servicemen or something like that?'

'My God, lassie, have you ever seen my knitting? Jim

182

didnae marry me for my knitting skills. I'm perfectly content here with you and the bairns.'

They both looked quickly out of the window as they heard a furious cry from Bert but it was no more than high spirits. It was good to see the three children running around happily, as if they had not a care in the world.

'This is a lovely place you've given us,' said Milly. 'Jim died knowing his family were safe. I'll never be able to thank you enough for that.'

Mairi followed her into the kitchen. One more worry that would not go away. What would become of Milly and the children when the war ended and the men came home?

Robin knew that he was hurting Mairi but he had no idea what to do about it. The wounds on his body were healing and the doctor at the hospital had assured him that the scars on his mind would heal too, given time.

But days passed and he felt worse, not better. He was home, alive. A girl was waiting for him to make some move; he just knew it. She was so tense when they met and he was taking every chance to ensure that they did not meet. He refused to accompany his father to church and he refused to stay in the room when the Minister came preaching forgiveness. He could never forgive. But the person he could not forgive was himself. He was alive and his friends were dead. But worse than that – other men were dead at his hand.

Every night he dreamed of the men he had killed. He saw their faces as they knelt before him, their hands together in supplication; he heard them begging him not to kill. He ignored their cries. Useless to tell himself that he had killed only once in arm-to-arm combat and his victim had been too busy trying to kill him to beg for anything. But still he saw them. He could smell them in the dream too. He smelled rotting putrefaction, the sickly sweet smell of warm blood. He gagged in his sleep.

Now he had begun to dream again about Mairi and they were not the dreams that had kept him sane – he laughed aloud at the thought of sanity – during those terrible days and months and years. In these dreams he was killing Mairi, not making love to her, and he woke trembling and sweating, resolved to stay away from her as much as possible. For maybe the killer in the dreams was the real Robin Morrison and if he found himself alone with her, maybe that horror would become a reality.

His father, so gentle so kind . . . could he tell him of the nightmares that plagued him? No, never. The Dominie was so happy to have his son home safe and well. Well. Robin sobbed again at the thought of being well. Dear God, how easy it was to fool everyone. Was there anyone in the world who knew him so well that he could confess his worries and feel relief and not guilt that he had added a burden to the loved one?

Ian. Ian, who had been his friend since their first day at school, he would listen and he would understand, even about Mairi he would understand.

Dear Ian,

I think I'm going mad. There, I've said it. I fooled the poor over-worked medic who wanted me to go to Craiglockhart. (There's someone there who specializes in people who've gone off their rocker a bit.) He said I would recover in time, but I'm getting worse, and what in the name of God will it do to my father if they lock me up in a loonie bin somewhere. Oh, Ian, why am I writing to you? You're a P.O.W. I should be writing letters to cheer you but, in spite of your poetry, you've always been the most stable person I know.

Does this letter sound fairly sane? See how clever I am but if I tell you about my dreams, night after night, that make me cry like a baby for my mother . . . I think I'm capable of killing someone I care for deeply . . .

there, there it's out, but I won't. I stay away from everyone. My father believes the Minister can help me but I can't bear to be in the same room with him. I think, if he spouts one more damn cliché about forgiveness and turning the other cheek, I'll strangle him with my bare hands. Father worries, I know he does, but he can't find answers to me in any of his books and so he's at a loss and the weight of guilt I feel is crushing me. He deserved a son who really was a hero, who deserved these bloody medals. Do you know, when I wore them, I felt them burning through my uniform into my flesh, but there are no marks. I can't see the marks . . .

He was crying. Bloody hell, he was crying and it would ruin his letter. He couldn't send it anyway, couldn't send such drivel to Ian in a prison camp, so it didn't matter about tear stains. He had to get out. Such a beautiful day. Was it a beautiful day in France too, in Germany, in Russia? No, Russia was too far away. There, he was thinking rationally. He was not mad. He would walk to the sea, away from Mairi; he could not meet Mairi because he might try to kiss her. Oh, sweet, sweet Mairi. How often had he dreamed of kissing her, of loving her, so strongly that he could feel her in his arms? Now, if he kissed her, maybe the dream would come back and he would find himself killing her. No, he would walk to the sea. He must stay as far away from her as possible.

His father saw his headlong flight down the road towards the coast as he stood at the window of the schoolroom listening to the primary four pupils reciting the six times table. As soon as he could he rang the bell for an afternoon break.

'You have all worked so hard on this fine afternoon,' he told the surprised children, 'that I have decided to award you a fifteen-minute playtime. Now, Maggie Stewart, you keep

185

an eye on the wee ones while I go into the house for a book I need.'

He hurried across the playground and into the house. It was empty and quiet. His heart was pounding. What had distressed Robin so much that he had been running, for it was not the run of an active young man out for exercise. It was terrified flight. He looked into all the rooms on the ground floor. Nothing. Everything was neat and tidy. Using the banister like an old man, he climbed the stairs and went into the room Robin had occupied since they had come to the village.

The letter was lying where Robin had left it and, at first, the Dominie ignored it. Letters were intensely private and not to be read by anyone but the intended recipient. The bed was neat, the window was open and the spring breeze was ruffling the letter so that it coquetted on the surface of the old school desk.

'His legs are too long for that desk,' thought the father practically.

The Dominie went to the window and looked out at the children running madly around the yard. What a pleasure an unexpected playtime was. Oh, to be so young and innocent and so easily made happy.

The letter. He looked at it. He had been writing a letter. Why would that upset him? Surely he might be upset by a letter he had received, not by one he was writing – unless, of course, he had to convey bad news.

He snatched up the paper and read the words and they struck at him so fiercely that he had to sit down on the edge of the iron bedstead. 'Oh, my baby, my boy,' his heart cried. 'What a burden of guilt and grief and fear. You couldn't hurt Mairi, my wee laddie, just as you can't disappoint me.'

The last words came back to haunt him. *When I wore them, I felt them burning into my flesh, but there are no marks.*

'Oh, Robin, my lamb, the marks are burned into your soul.'

He sat for some minutes. He had to get back to the children. He had made up his mind. He folded the letter, put it into an envelope and addressed it to Ian. Then he slipped it into the pocket of his gown and returned to the school.

None of the children dared to tell him that he had forgotten the book he had gone to the house to collect and the afternoon plodded on. He left as soon as he decently could that afternoon and walked into Arbroath where he posted the letter. He thought of Ian in prison receiving and reading such an outpouring of grief.

'Robin comes first. He's right. Ian has always been stable. If anyone can handle it, he can. Ian, Ian, help my lad,' he cried across the miles and then turned, dry eyed, and made the long walk back.

As he had hoped Robin had calmed down and had returned home before him.

'You're late, Father,' he said and his voice was normal although he was paler even than usual.

'I had to go to a meeting,' the Dominie lied. 'What did you do with yourself this afternoon?' He hoped he sounded casually interested.

'I went to the beach, had a grand walk. Clears the head no end.' He stopped and looked puzzled and somewhat unsure. He looked at his father. 'You know, sounds silly, but I thought I had been writing but there's no paper on my desk.'

'Gracious, Robin, you're beginning to sound just like me. I was quite sure I'd done the primary seven essays this morning and there they all were on my desk, untouched by human hand.'

Obligingly, Robin smiled. 'Some of that lot . . . perhaps yours was the first human hand that touched them.' He shook his head as if clearing away a fog. 'I was so sure . . .'

'Come and help me burn the Shepherd's pie we've been left for tea.' He walked quickly into the kitchen and was relieved to hear Robin following along behind him.

Chapter Twenty

Colin was delighted to read that his local football team was strenuously recruiting juvenile players. He was not so happy to read that it was because many of the adult players had enlisted and too many of them were never coming back.

'Here, Chay.' He handed the boy in the dug-out beside him the three-month-old copy of the *Herald* that Mairi had sent out. 'Were you no telling us you were a great goalie? Arbroath's looking for you, laddie. You're aboot the age they want, seventeen and never been kissed.'

The boy soldier laughed and took the paper and Colin watched him painstakingly spell out the words, his young soft mouth forming every consonant, every vowel, as he tried to decipher the article.

Eventually he finished the task. 'I'm free the morn, Sergeant. I'll drop in and let them hae a look at us.'

'Fine. I'll make sure naebody takes yer space.'

He sighed at his own pitiful attempt at humour. The boy beside him might well never have been kissed, but he had survived a bayonet wound, shrapnel in the shoulder, constant shelling, disease, hunger – and these all before his eighteenth birthday. Dear God in Heaven, this was all wrong. He remembered other articles in the papers his wee girl made such an effort to send to him. Pals' Battalions: boys who had grown up together, enlisted together and fought and died together. There were the Bantam Battalions, later known as the Demon Dwarves, who were first deemed too small to fight, and later were anxiously

189

conscripted into the Army where they fought and died like tigers.

He would have to write to Ian and tell him that he had been right all the time and that his father had been too thick-headed to see it. This wee laddie should be at hame trying out for his team, no dodging bullets, and my wee lassie should be married tae some nice lad, Robin Morrison maybe, and having healthy babies. Instead she's working like an Irish navvy. I promised her mam Mairi'd have it better than she did and what have I done to her? And her Ian, her son, her pride and joy – and mine too? Oor laddie with his scribble scribble aboot sunsets and sun on the water and the beauty of spider webs. Spider webs, for God's sake. I never took the time tae let him show me beauty in a spider's web. But I'll watch them with him yet. I'll listen tae him, and I'll try looking at things with his eyes. Dear God, does he even know I love him? Did I ever show him, tell him? I'll put it in the letter and he'll cringe with embarrassment, or maybe he'll no.

He sorted through his pockets but there was nothing and he called across to the boy who was still making heavy weather of the newspaper.

'Chay, you dinnae hae a bit paper?'

The boy looked through his pockets. 'No really, Sarge, but you can have my mam's envelope. I dinnae need that.'

He handed it over and Colin tore it open with his capable farmer's hands and smoothed it out gently. 'I need tae write tae my son,' he said as if an explanation was expected. 'There's such a lot I never told him.'

The boy looked at him. Sergeant McGloughlin with a son? He had thought that the man had been born an iron sergeant in the Fifth Battalion the Black Watch. Impossible to think of him out of uniform, out of mud and sweat, fathering a baby.

'Whit's his name, Sarge?' he dared.

'Ian. Grandest son any father could ask for.'

190

'Is he in the Regiment?'

Colin looked at the thin, undernourished, tired little face in front of him and saw instead Ian's handsome, sensitive face. 'No, he's a Conscientious Objector,' and he said it loudly and proudly. 'He fought two wars, Chay, the enemy and his own side and he won. He's in a prison camp in Germany now. I write tae him when I can but I just realized' – and here he was talking to himself and not to the young private – 'that I never write about anything important, like how much I love him, and admire him, about how proud I am that he can make beautiful images wi words, that, when this is all over, I'll be the first one tae tell him it was all wrong.'

He turned back to his envelope and did not see the boy soldier squirm with embarrassment at the use of a word like *love* and neither did he see the embarrassment replaced by a look of envy on the boy's face. He was trying to find the words. He knew that men on all sides were disillusioned with the war and were calling for peace talks. Colin no longer believed in what he was doing and he could see no way that the war could end in honour. For a while this year he had even believed that Britain would be defeated.

The Germans had mounted a terrible offensive in the west and had come close to Paris. They had lost 800,000 men but the Allies had lost more than a million troops.

'Sweet Jesus, a million men no returning to their mammies, their wives, their bairns. The world cannae recover. There cannae be many men left at all . . . if there are any. There's my Ian . . . in prison.'

He licked the tip of the pencil and bent again to his letter, but his ears, attuned to the soft bleating of a lost lamb, heard the whistle of the grenade as it flew over the rim of the trench. He saw it as if in slow motion. He felt himself unfold from the ground; he saw the startled look on young Chay's face as he became aware that death was seeking him.

'No,' screamed Colin. 'Not him, you bastard,' and he

threw his body over the boy and his back took the full impact of the explosion.

'Jesus Christ,' said Corporal Russell some time later as he helped the injured soldier out from under. 'What a mess.'

'The sergeant, Corporal, the sergeant,' screamed the boy. 'Where is he? I felt him pushing me out of the way.'

The corporal turned away for a second to school his heaving stomach. Then he turned back to Chay. 'You're wearing him, laddie,' was all he said.

Thirty-six hours later, on 11 November 1918, the last shot was fired in France.

Mairi received the notification of her father's death several days after what soon became known as Armistice Day; his name, with too many others, was posted up in the local post office and the Minister cycled out with the news. At first Mairi refused to accept it. Death was impossible. The war was over. They had seen it in the paper. They had participated in modest celebrations at the Kirk Hall. The war was over and prisoners of war would be released and soldiers would soon be returning to the bosom of their families.

'It's a mistake, Milly,' she said, pushing away the shot of Colin's whisky that Milly had unearthed from under the sink. 'The war's over. But you mustn't worry about you and the children; we'll work something out. That's what Dad will want. He was . . . he is so grateful that you're here. And Ian too. You'll like Ian. It will take a while for him to get home, I suppose. They'll have to go to Germany and find the prisoners, won't they? They'll hardly just open the doors and let them walk home. If they do,' and she started to laugh, 'we'll never find our Ian because he'll find a view somewhere and he'll sit down to write a poem. Did I tell you he was a poet?'

And Milly, with her age-old common sense, let her talk and talk. Eventually she slept and the young girl who had been Mairi McGloughlin died in that sleep, and the woman,

192

Mairi, was born. There had been too much sadness: Ian, Robin, and now Colin.

The Dominie had read the name Sergeant Colin McGloughlin and walked wearily home to tell his son. This would surely move him, show that somewhere under the remote stranger, Robin Morrison was still there.

But Robin looked horrified at the thought of offering Mairi his condolences – or anything else. 'You'll do the right thing, Dad. You'll tell her what we feel.' Robin, taller and thinner than ever, was hanging on to the mantelpiece for fear that his knees might buckle and he would fall forward into the flames. He swayed and his father made as if to support him.

'Don't touch me,' Robin snapped. 'I'm perfectly all right.'

Euan Morrison looked at his son. He was not all right. His body was healing but what about the wounds that he could not see?

'You'll come with me to pay our respects?'

Robin turned away almost violently. 'You go,' he said. 'I don't know what to say, how to say it.'

'Maybe it will be enough for you just to be there, Robin.'

'I can't.' He moved towards the door, to escape.

'Robin, I don't know what happened between you and Mairi but her father is dead and her brother is in a camp in Germany and God alone knows if he is still alive or when he'll come home if he is. She needs her friends.'

Defeated by a lifetime of habit Robin stopped but he did not turn to look at his father. 'You won't leave me . . .' He was the child Robin again, afraid in the dark.

'I won't leave you. Come on, get another woolly jumper and your coat; it's tipping it down out there.'

Robin did as he was told, climbed upstairs to his room where the bed for some years had been too short and he took a woollen pullover out of the chest of drawers, pulled it over his head and went back down to where his father was standing, Robin's coat in one hand and an old farm lantern in the other.

Robin allowed his father to help him on with his coat and then he took the lantern and walked first out of the Schoolhouse. He stood at the top of the steps waiting for the Dominie and remembered the time – a lifetime ago – when he had kissed Mairi, been slapped hard for his pains, and had then fallen ignominiously down the steps.

His father's hand was on his shoulder but instead of calming him, the touch seemed to fill him with panic.

'I can't,' he said. 'I can't,' and he sank down at his father's feet in the rain and began to sob.

The Dominie dropped to his knees and put his arms around his child. 'It's all right, Robin lad. It's all right.'

He helped the young man to his feet and into the house. Then he half carried him up the stairs, undressed him as if he was indeed just a little boy, and tucked him in.

'You have a rest, Robin. I'm going out for a wee while and when I come back I'll make some tea.'

Robin said nothing but his sobs had almost subsided and his father sat for a few minutes until all the shuddering had stopped and then he left.

But he did not turn right and head towards the McGloughlin farm. He turned left to the village and the doctor's house and was admitted to the front room where the doctor was sitting toasting his socks at a roaring fire.

'I hope you've come for a game of chess, Euan.'

'No.'

Dr Muirhead folded away his newspaper. 'Sit down, man, and have a dram.'

When he had poured the drinks he sat down in his chair facing his uninvited guest and said, 'Drink that first, and then tell me the problem. It's your laddie, I suppose.'

When Euan had finished telling him everything that Robin

had said or done since he had been invalided out, he sighed deeply and lay back in his chair, his hands round the crystal tumbler, and his eyes watching the fire.

'I can't help with mental problems, Euan. I'm way out of my depth here.'

Euan started up. 'I have to get back to him. I put him to bed. I never did that in my life before and here he is nearly thirty years of age.'

'Sit down and finish your dram. He'll sleep. I said I couldn't help but there are doctors who're specializing in psychiatry. There's a professor in Edinburgh, Rivers, an anthropologist, would you believe, but he's done wonders with some of our wounded lads. I could write to him for you.'

Euan sat up and his face was immediately happier and George Muirhead felt the weight of his calling heavier than he had ever felt it before. This trust: it frightened him sometimes. He couldn't possibly measure up all the time. He sighed. 'It'll take a few weeks, Euan. Finish up your dram and I'll come back with you and have a look at the boy.' He heard what he had just said. *The boy.* Robin Morrison had not been a boy for a long time.

'Damn, but I'm getting too old for this job,' he thought but he kept his thoughts to himself.

'Robin was an officer, wasn't he? That makes it easier. Rivers is in a hospital for officers in Edinburgh. Pity they released Robin from the hospital without letting a psychiatrist have a look at him. Still, doesn't sound as if he's a danger to himself or anyone else.'

Euan decided not to mention the contents of the letter.

Chapter Twenty-One

Thank God for the land. As the winter of 1918 passed, Mairi took refuge in making plans for the spring sowing. Sir Humphrey Grey-Watson's solicitor had assured her that Ian would have no trouble in taking over the tenancy.

Ian was coming home. She had had a letter dated November 1918.

Mairi wondered sadly if the letter might have been written on the very day that Colin had been killed but she tried to put that thought out of her head. What did it matter when it had been written? In late November, Ian was still alive, and so he would be coming home with all the thousands of other prisoners. It would take time. But Mairi and the land had time. Sometimes she felt that she had nothing else.

Ian's letter had hinted at changes in his life that he wanted to discuss with his father. She sighed and Milly who was sewing patches on her sons' trousers looked up.

'It was nice of the Laird to send that wee note, Mairi,' she said in hopes that remembering Sir Humphrey's kindness might cheer Mairi. 'And the Dominie, and the Blacks, and the Minister. Jings, everybody that's onybody has been in this house these past weeks.'

But not Robin, thought Mairi, not the only person who mattered. 'People are like that in the country,' was all she said.

'Och, had I been up a stair in Dundee when my man was killt, the neighbours would hae been at my door tae.'

Milly held the strong thread between her teeth and bit at

it until it broke and Mairi got up and went to her sewing box for her scissors.

'You'll break your teeth, Milly.'

'We had teeth afore we had scissors, lassie, but since you've got them, I'll use them.'

They heard the rattling of the old windows as the wind freshened and changed direction.

'Damn,' said Mairi as the room filled with smoke blown back down the old chimney piece. 'I forgot to get the sweep in.'

That had been one of the many jobs attended to by Colin.

The women coughed furiously for a few minutes and then Mairi went to the door and opened it a little. Smoke went out and snow blew in.

'The smell of wood smoke's braw though, Mairi,' laughed Milly as she joined her shivering landlady at the door. 'Better nor some of the stuff we used tae burn. Mind you, if the bairns are cauld you'll burn what you have.' She pulled her old cardigan round her shoulders. 'Come on, lassie. It's freezing with that door open.'

Obligingly Mairi closed the door. 'The world is so pretty with snow on it.'

'It's prettier and warmer without it,' said the practical Milly as she sat down again beside the fire.

She sewed steadily for a few minutes and then put down her mending. 'Mairi, can you sew?'

Startled, Mairi looked up. 'Sew? I'm sorry, Milly, do you need some help? Of course I can sew.'

'No, it's no that. I like my hands busy. I was jist thinking that your Ian'll have lost weight in a prison camp. Maybe we should be making him some new shirts, a wee welcome home present.'

'I haven't told him . . .' She still could not say the words *our father is dead*.

'Might as well keep the bad news till he gets home. It'd

be different if he was going to be years yet. One day soon he'll jist be here.' She looked at her employer. 'Are you hearing what I'm trying tae tell you, lassie? I've brought this up afore.'

Mairi looked up and there was such an expression of pain on her face that Milly's heart was touched. 'There won't be room for us, lass. He's the tenant. Even if he didn't want his dad's room, he'll need his own.'

Mairi saw the justice of this. In all probability Ian would prefer not to use the bigger room, unless he brought a bride to the farm. She saw the beautiful Arabella Huntingdon but could not picture the young aristocrat in this farmhouse. Poor Ian.

'You haven't started to look for somewhere, Milly? The children are happy here at the school, in the village. Ian won't want you to leave. We'll think of something. I can't bear for you to go. I would even miss Bert.'

They laughed. Bert was what was commonly known as a holy terror.

'He misses Jim but the Dominie's got the measure of him,' said Milly and then, more quietly, 'I'll have to go, Mairi. I can maybe get a job in the Mills.'

Mairi stood up. 'But not yet, not yet. Have the winter here at least.'

And so they left it although Mairi stayed awake for some time worrying. If she worried about Milly and her children it left less room to worry about Mairi McGloughlin. When she worried about herself and her future, her heart bled for Robin, Robin who had kissed her so sweetly and had talked of a future full of roses, but who had come back from the war and avoided her at every turn, who had not even come to say he was sorry that her father had been killed.

What had happened to him? What had happened to his love for her? For she knew that he did not love lightly. He had meant what he had said. What had she done to make him change his mind, because she must have done something.

A few days later Milly went to fetch the children from the school and Mairi found herself alone in the house. It was pleasant to sit and listen to the sounds that she had not heard since those three delightful but noisy children had come to stay: the tick-tock of the old clock on the mantel, the spitting of wet wood in the fire, the snores of the dogs as they lay at her feet.

'This is nice,' thought Mairi. 'I'd forgotten how comforting clocks and dogs are.'

She heard the sounds of someone approaching the door and looked up at the clock, surprised that Milly was home so quickly. She had thought she might walk in to the town, small as it was. Milly liked the country but she missed the bustle of Dundee.

Mairi got up and opened the door and Robin's father stood there. 'Twice I've tried to come and tell you, lass,' he said.

Her heart almost stopped beating. Tell her what? Robin. Something dreadful had happened to Robin. That was it; of course that was it. He had not come to see her because, because . . . No, no, hold on, Mairi, hold on. You would have known, had he been dead.

'Come in and sit down by the fire,' she said when she could speak. 'Tell me what, Dominie? Is something wrong with Robin?'

He looked at her and away again and it was shame and embarrassment that were in his face as well as grief. Then he faced her again.

'I won't dress the miserable truth in pretty clothes, Mairi. My boy is in a lunatic asylum. He's had another breakdown, a complete one this time. Thank God I spoke to Dr Muirhead.'

Mairi wasn't really taking in the words *lunatic* and *asylum*. She had expected to hear that final word, *dead*, and so her heart was slowing down and she was even conscious of relief.

'A lunatic asylum? Where?'

'He's been admitted to a hospital in Edinburgh.'

Edinburgh. It could have been a million miles away. How could she get to Edinburgh? No matter. She would get there. A lunatic asylum. What was that? A hiding place for the mad. Robin was mad. No, not Robin. But what was madness?

'Can I see him?' Desperately she prayed that she could deal with madness, with insanity. What was it? Perhaps if Robin had asked to see her . . . She remembered once falling in the mill pool. Her frock had bloomed like a giant flower up over her head and she had fought kicking to reach the surface, to breathe. She felt the same now. Then Ian and Robin, yes, Robin had pulled her from the pond, swept the weeds from her dress and begged her not to tell her father. Robin needed her.

'May I see him?' she asked again.

The Dominie looked surprised. 'You wouldn't want to see him where he is. I hated leaving him there.'

And Mairi began to hear what he was saying. 'Robin is mentally ill. That's what you're saying, Dominie.'

His face crumpled as if he was going to cry. 'Such a fine mind, a fine mind.'

Mairi McGloughlin had never been ill a day in her life. She had no experience of illness, having been so young when her mother had died and she knew nothing whatsoever about illnesses of the mind. But illness was illness. Some you could see and bandage up and some you could not. It was as simple as that and if it was not, then wishing and praying should make it so.

'He'll get better,' she said fiercely and the Dominie looked at her, startled by the note of determination in her voice. 'Of course, he'll get better. When may I see him?'

He sighed and handed his burden over to younger, stronger shoulders. 'Not yet, my dear. It's too early. He's . . .

well, they give him something to keep him quiet.' He leaned over and gripped her hand and it was the first time that he had ever touched her. 'I think he's afraid.'

The Dominie was an old man. Not in years; surely he could only be a few years older than Colin. But he looked old, old and frail.

Afraid? Robin afraid? Never, ever. Ian sometimes, but never Robin. His father was afraid too but this fear could be handled.

'Stay and have some soup with me, Mr Morrison, with me and Milly when she gets back. You remember Mrs Baxter?'

'Of course, my dear. I'll be glad to stay a while, Mairi.'

Mairi did not go to the kitchen to see to her soup. Instead she sat down beside Robin's father. This conversation was vitally important. She had to understand everything.

'Dominie, Robin's fear. Is he afraid of me? Afraid that I might hold him to promises? I won't. I thought I had made that clear when he first came home. I'm here to be his friend, if he wants that.'

The Dominie thought of the letter that he had sent, so rashly to Ian, and he thanked God that it had never arrived. Robin was afraid that he would kill someone very dear to him. He had been alone for months with his father and had shown no violence whatsoever, so the *someone dear* had to be someone else. He had always known that Mairi was very special to his son and he knew too that Robin had been desperately afraid ever to be alone with her.

'We don't know much about the way the mind works, Mairi, why one man's mind can take all the blows it's dealt and another man is destroyed by the same blows. I think every soldier has been changed by the war and even a few for the better but the change in Robin . . .' The father sat back and stared at the ceiling. 'He can't

201

cope. He tried to do it all on his own, refusing to believe he was ill, then he did ask for help but he never got it, and now, now he is in the only place where they have some idea of what to do to help him. I don't know if he will ever get better. He wouldn't expect you to wait, Mairi.'

Mince or steak? Steak or mince? There was no choice.

'If he loves me, Mr Morrison, it would never occur to me not to wait. I've waited so long already.'

'Do you understand what I am telling you? We know so little about mental illness.'

He slumped in the chair and she saw how hard that admission had been for him. Robin had been wounded twice in the war and his father had told of his injuries proudly. Honourable scars. But wounds to the mind, to the soul, wounds that could not be bandaged, were these not also honourable?

'He'll get better, Dominie,' she said again. 'You and I have to believe that and then Robin will believe too.'

'Mairi, you are still so young, so pretty . . .'

He was letting her go. He was casting her off. She could forget the gentle moments, the hope of a lifetime full of roses. Only one thing mattered. If Robin had asked him to set her free . . . She steeled herself to ask the question that would change the whole course of her life. 'Did Robin ask you to tell me that?'

He shook his head. 'He says nothing at all, nothing. He sits in a chair and looks at the wall or out of a window if the nurse has the chair turned that way.'

'He'll get better,' Mairi said again and she smiled at Robin's father. 'I'll fetch us some soup.'

Milly and the children came in from the village just as Mairi was ladling the soup into the bowls.

'Good,' Mairi called. 'You're just in time for supper. Wash your hands, Bert, and bring the scullery chairs to the table.'

'We cannae eat with the Dominie, Mairi,' hissed Milly. 'The bairns'll die of fright.'

'In here he's just a man with a son in hospital, Milly. The children will be good for him. You can talk to him about Angus staying on at the school.'

But instead Milly talked about returning to Dundee and Mr Morrison bravely set his own problem aside and applied himself to worrying about hers.

'I would suggest waiting until Ian comes home, Mrs Baxter. Come along, wee Jean, drink up your good soup while it's hot.' He waited to see that the girl was being obedient and turned back to her mother. 'You certainly don't want to start looking for a job and a home in the middle of winter. And have you thought of getting a cottage near here? Surely there are empty cottages on the Estate, Mairi?'

'It's the rent, Dominie. Mairi'll no need me when her brother comes home.'

Mairi took the big knife and started slicing some of her own bread. 'Ian said he has things to discuss with . . . Dad. Maybe he'll talk them over with me, but I don't think you should do anything, Milly, until we see what happens.'

'Are we going to stay here then?' asked Bert and Jean, and Mairi looked at Angus and saw that the answer meant a great deal to him.

'Yes,' said Mairi. 'We'll work something out.'

And only Mr Morrison knew that she was thinking about Robin.

She wrote to him that night when Mr Morrison had walked home and Milly and her children were all in bed. She did not refer to his illness, told him only about her work on the farm and then she added something about the antics of Bert. Robin, too, had been a schoolmaster. He would have met boys like Bert.

Mairi did not know that, in his camp in Germany, Ian

was writing to his friend. Mr Morrison's desperate appeal for help had just reached him and Ian had set aside the daily letter he was writing to Arabella to communicate with his old friend. He did not mention that Robin had been unable to finish the letter; he did not say that he assumed that it was Robin's desperate father who had sent it. He told him how his company of conscientious objectors had been captured by a German patrol. He did not tell Robin of the inhuman brutality meted out by men who should have known better but he did tell him of the humanity of others. And he told Robin what he had told no one else. He wrote of his love for Arabella.

Her love has kept me sane, Robin. No matter what happened, I would conjure up a picture of Bella, and I would challenge fate to throw at me whatever it would. I managed, somehow, to keep the scarf she gave me. It would have been so difficult to believe that she and her love were real had I had nothing. Letters go missing and sometimes they were so late that I would convince myself that she had stopped loving me. Why would a girl like that love a wreck like me? But she does, Robin, she does. Why, I don't know, but I will treasure her love and her faith in me every day of my life.

In battle, Robin, my dear friend, you did what you had to do and the girl you love – and I know it's my wee sister – will help you live with what you have had to do. You couldn't hurt her, Robin, not physically; it's not in you. And I think you're afraid that you are killing her love, not her, Robin, her love. But she's strong, Robin, and she's faithful, and she guards those she loves. Remember how we used to laugh at her, the cocky wee bantam, standing up for me that could lift her up with one hand. She'll lift you, Robin, as Bella lifts me. What did we do to deserve

204

such women? Don't question, old friend, accept, and be grateful. You, as you are, as you were, as you will be, are the man to whom she has given her heart. Take it and treat it gently.

Robin received that letter on a warm summer's day in 1919. His father, looking better than he had looked for some time, Robin noted, had brought him the letter with a pot of Mairi's strawberry jam.

The Dominie was nervous. He prayed the letter was not an answer to the one Robin had written, but Robin took the letter and the jam and he read the letter without speaking.

'Ian's got a girl,' he said, when he had finished reading. 'Someone called Bella. I don't remember a Bella anywhere in the village.'

'Perhaps it's someone he met in one of the camps, a nurse or such like.'

Robin looked at the pot of jam. 'Strawberries. I remember the smell of growing strawberries, Dad, and the warmth of the sun through my shirt as I picked them.'

'That'll be in the jam, laddie.'

Robin smiled. 'You're as much of a poet as Ian. This is Mairi's way of writing poetry. She and Ian are so alike; I never realized it before.' He was quiet for a moment. 'I wish I could see her smile.'

'She'll come to see you, Robin, if she thinks she's welcome. She would not want to intrude.'

Mairi intrude? Robin saw her small sturdy figure as it followed him and his friend all over the farm. She had intruded on him all her life. He tried to laugh and although it sounded more like a snort, his father took hope from it and courage.

'It's nice out here in the garden, lad. I could bring her some Sunday and you could walk around the garden. She always liked flowers.'

'I could show her the flowers I'm helping to grow. I've

205

tried to remember. Is it the spring flowers she likes, or is it the roses?'

'There were some white briars in a jam jar on the kitchen table.'

Robin smiled. 'White briar roses,' he said.

Chapter Twenty-Two

Ian arrived in England on 4 October 1919 and went first to Godalming in the pretty county of Surrey. When he had completed his business there he took the train to Scotland.

He walked from Arbroath and the weather matched his mood. It was a perfect autumn day. The sky was blue, the sun was shining, and the wind, a southwest wind, was not too strong but just strong enough to tumble the leaves that had already fallen along the grass verges. He whistled and he kicked them with the polished toe of his new shoes.

New shoes. Leather. For nearly two years he had worn strips of dirty cloth wrapped around his feet in a vain attempt to keep them warm. Arabella had wanted him to have shoes especially made by a London shoemaker but he had refused. What he could afford, he would have. He had allowed her to buy him one pair of cashmere socks, *but only this once, Bella, and just, if you must, as a welcome home gift.*

He thought of Bella now . . . no, when was she ever absent from his thoughts? He had been afraid that the girl of his dreams, the girl of the letters, would not be the girl who met him at Guildford. But she was and although they had met before only a few times, they knew as they walked towards one another down that station platform that they had been heading towards one another all their lives and that once they met and Ian held out his strong arms and enfolded the delicate girl to his heart, they would never again be apart. She was with him now, although she was still in her beautiful Surrey home. An elderly, and very disapproving, aunt had chaperoned the young couple because Lady Grey-Watson refused to have anything to do with either of them.

'I can't expect you to go through this for me, Bella,' he had cried, his lips against her golden hair.

And she had laughed and raised her face so that her lips met his. 'It's nothing to what you have gone through for me. And they'll come round because they love me and if they don't, I'll manage if you love me half as much as I love you.'

And he laughed now as, swinging his bag, he walked jauntily along, remembering the precious minutes they had spent trying to decide who loved the other more.

'Are you the daftie?' A broad Scottish voice broke through his romantic glow.

Ian looked down at the boy and an anger so fierce swept through him, that he, who had never raised his hand in anger during five years of Hell, felt that he might strike the child.

'The daftie?' he asked, although he already knew the answer.

'Aye, the daftie. The Dominie's son that was that clever, went tae Oxford and a'thing. Daft as a brush but he's coming home. You don't look daft. My mam says we'll no sleep safe in oor beds wi a daftie runnin loose.'

Ian looked in horror at the child for whom he and Robin had fought and nearly died.

What had Shakespeare said?

> I hate ingratitude more in a man
> Than lying, vainness, babbling, drunkenness,
> Or any taint of vice . . .

'Ask your mammie to pray that you'll ever be half the man he is,' he said and cursing himself for letting himself get angry, his mood soured, he walked the rest of the way home in silence.

He saw another boy, slightly older than the first ragamuffin, as he turned off the main road onto the one leading to the farm, and, at sight of him, the boy took to his heels and ran.

Ian laughed. 'That must be Mrs Baxter's Bert, the terror of the entire county, off to tell Mairi.'

Sure enough, when he breasted the brow of the hill and looked down towards the sea to where the farmhouse nestled comfortably among its fields, he saw his sister, it had to be his sister although this running creature was a woman, a woman with Mairi's wild red-gold hair. He too began to run and he caught her up in his arms and swung her around as he had done so often when they were children, before setting her on her feet. She looked up at him, her eyes shining with tears and her hair glinting gold where the sun hit it and, to his surprise, she burst into tears, and he held her like a baby and let her cry.

He was amazed. Mairi had never been the kind of little girl who took refuge in tears. She had been much tougher than he was and here she was, and he felt how slight she was, soaking his new, department shop shirt.

'It's all better now, Mairi,' he said softly. 'The war's over and I'm home and Robin will get better, I know he will . . .'

She sniffed loudly, made a tremendous effort and looked up at him through her tears. His appearance shocked her. He was so thin that he looked even taller than his six foot. He was a living walking scarecrow. Bella's hairdresser had tried to do something with the hair that had been kept tidy with the use of a kitchen knife but it would be some months before it grew properly and – it was not gold but silver. A boy had gone to war and an old man had come back. What had happened to his young strong manhood? She would not let him sense her horror. 'You know about Robin?'

As she spoke to her brother she thought of that first day when she had gone to the hospital in Edinburgh. She had been so nervous that she had been sick twice on the train. She had pictured the asylum, a huge grey sprawling building with iron bars on the windows. She had heard the screams of insane patients and she had smelled the nauseating carbolic smells of cleanliness and lack of hope. How could someone as fastidious and sensitive as the Dominie spend every free moment there? So simple, so simple. He loved his son.

And then she had arrived and she had walked up a tree-lined lane to a large sandstone building which stood benignly among its paved walks and abundant flower beds. A nurse in a starched white uniform had opened the door to her and she had smelled lavender and had seen the sun shining on old polished furniture and books. She had breathed a deep sigh of relief.

The nurse had obviously seen the reaction before. 'This is the twentieth century, my dear. There is illness here, and sadness, but there is hope and joy. Captain Morrison is in the garden with his father.'

Mairi looked up now at the gaunt face of her brother.

'He wrote to me,' he said simply and then he looked over her head towards the farmhouse. 'But Dad?' he asked. 'I thought he'd come out to welcome the prodigal . . .' He felt her tense in his arms and draw away from him. 'Mairi?'

There was no way to soften the blow, nothing that could be said that would make the pain go away. 'He's dead, Ian. He was killed almost a year ago, just a few hours before the Armistice.'

The pain hit him like a knife between the ribs: his father, the provider, the arbiter, the meter out of justice, the solid bulk of security, the teacher, and later the friend, dead. How had he not known that the world no longer contained Colin McGloughlin? He looked at the fields his father had loved, the dry-stone dykes he had helped him build or at least repair, the trees where they had sheltered with their pieces. They were the same. They had no right to be untouched.

'He was awarded the Victoria Cross, Ian. I wish you'd been there to receive it.'

He pushed down his pain to deal with later. Another blow that Mairi had coped with on her own. He looked down at her, saw that the round softness of the girl's face had been replaced by more mature womanly, but not matronly, lines. It was a too-thin face, but beautiful. Whoever would have thought Mairi McGloughlin would grow up beautiful?

'So much you've had to thole on your own, wee Mairi,' he said and wondered how he could do what he wanted if it meant leaving her alone again. Nothing was easy. She must go with him. Bella would insist.

She dimpled. 'Not on my own,' she said. 'I've had Milly and Angus who is wonderful and Jean who's a smaller Milly . . .'

'And don't forget Bert,' he said. 'It was Bert who told you.'

She laughed and they turned towards their home and began to walk to it.

'"There's a golden giant walking along the school road." That's how he announced you. "Has to be your brother and he's no getting my bed."'

He laughed. 'I'll sleep in the kitchen if it makes him feel better. It won't be for long.'

She took a quick look at his face but saw that he was not ready to talk. 'You'll be hungry,' she said.

'What would you do with yourself if you didn't have men to feed, Mairi? A good meal cures all the ills of a troubled world.' But he said that bitterly.

'It goes a good way,' she said simply. 'Bert and Angus will sleep at the Schoolhouse for a while. Mr Morrison is trying to cram Angus for his highers.'

'How is he?' And he knew that she knew he meant Mr Morrison and not Angus.

'Better now that Robin is improving. It was slow, slow progress, but definitely progress and then, after your letter

211

came, he seemed to accelerate. I visit him once a fortnight and now his father leaves us alone for a while. I think he expects, well, I'm not sure what he expects, but Robin is the same whether he's there or not.' She sighed and he looked down at her sadly.

'But he's not afraid to be alone with you?'

She looked at him in surprise. 'No. We walk in the gardens. Growing flowers is part of his therapy. He loves it and he's good at it. I don't know what we'll do in the winter. He seems nervous if I'm too close to him but at least we talk now, about books and music, the newspapers. We used to walk and stop to look at a flower and sometimes he'd pull one and thrust it at me. Now he tells me about them. Of course, it's Michaelmas daisies and chrysanthemums now.' She sighed and then looked up at Ian and smiled. 'He'll be glad that you're home.'

They were at the house and the next few minutes were taken up with introductions. Ian met Milly and recognized her, as he would have recognized her had he met her first in the street, from the descriptions in Mairi's letters, and then Angus, a quiet muscular boy who looked so much like an amalgam of the boys Robin and Ian that the adult Ian almost wept. Next he met Jean who was so tongue-tied that she could say not a word but constituted herself his slave and set herself to wait upon him, hand and foot, until he feared that he might step on her, and Bert, the pirate, whose wicked black eyes told him he would have to fight for his right to sleep in his own bed if he had not already abdicated that right.

'My father is dead and yours is too and I hope there was nothing left unsaid between you two,' he said, speaking to the boy who surprised his mother by dropping his pugnacious appearance and hanging on the back of Ian's chair in case he missed a word that the returning hero had to say.

He was disappointed. Ian had never been a loquacious

man and, especially when there was so much to be said, he found the process very difficult, if not impossible.

He answered the children's questions as truthfully as he could and Angus soon learned when he would not be drawn but young Bert worried at him like a dog at a bone until his mother, seeing Ian's exhaustion, sent him off, with his brother, to the Schoolhouse.

'I'm no sleepin there. Bad enough Mairi made us eat with the Dominie.'

Milly insisted and, after seeing Jean into bed, went off with her sons to ensure that Bert did not turn round and run back to the farm.

Mairi and Ian were alone.

'Funny not to see him sitting there with his paper and the dogs. He went to make up for me, didn't he?'

He was looking straight at her with those eyes that had always seen so much and she could not lie. 'Not exactly, Ian. He wanted it to be over and he was tired of boys being killed; he was always such a good shot. I think he thought if experienced men went it would help the laddies. He did help the laddies, Ian. Dad threw himself in the way of a grenade to save the life of a boy from Arbroath. He knew what he was doing. Such incredible bravery makes it bearable, I think.'

'Not for me. I never, all my life, did anything properly that he wanted me to do, and now, to know that he felt that he had to go and possibly die in my place . . .'

She threw herself down on the rag rug at his feet and held on to his hands as if he or she or both were drowning. 'It wasn't like that, Ian. It *wasn't*.'

'Oh, please, Mairi, spare me that. I have so much I need to talk over with you; plans that need to be made. First I have to know if you and Robin have come to some kind of arrangement.'

'It's not possible to "come to an arrangement", as you put it, with someone who is like a piece of glass, like the wee piece he brought me from Venice, so fragile that the least puff of wind will blow it over and smash it.'

He put his hand on her hair. 'You said he was improving.'

'He is. He is, but he's holding himself away from me. He's so polite to me. We were always so at ease with one another; he was just like you. I could scold him and argue with him and fight him. Now, I'm on my best behaviour. I don't want to scare him into thinking he has to marry me because he kissed me once or twice and said there'd be roses.' She shook her head and looked up at him and in the mischief in her eyes he saw his wee sister. 'Now, you, Ian McGloughlin, have you no news for me?'

He laughed. 'I've met a rare wee bully too. Just like you, doing what's good for me whether I like it or not.'

'And don't you like it?'

'I love it.'

They sat quietly for a moment, listening to the logs complaining in the flames.

'So all is well, Ian?'

'I sometimes can't believe it, Mairi, but Arabella Huntingdon loves your brother, and I love her. She wrote hundreds of letters to me. Sometimes I got none for weeks and then I'd get twenty on the one day and she'd numbered them so I know that some never turned up. She could have been dining and dancing with all her posh friends but she stayed at home writing to me.'

He went quiet and from the smile hovering around his lips Mairi knew that he was recalling some of Arabella's letters.

'And when are you going to see her? You *are* going to see her?'

He looked guilty and the first pangs of jealousy hit her and she tried to push them away. A sister was not nearly so important as a lover.

'I went there first, Mairi. I had to know . . . if she was

214

real, the girl who wrote the letters. We met in Edinburgh once, when I left the work camp, and she was so shy and so sweet and called me Mr McGloughlin and asked if she might write still when I was in France. I loved her then, I think. I hadn't before. What is love, Mairi, that chooses one against another and says, this is she? I'd been a wee bit embarrassed, you know, at the shooting, the Laird's niece, and then she smiled at me and gave me her scarf and I knew it was more than the scarf she was giving, but I was afraid that I didn't want her gift, that I couldn't appreciate it.' He looked up from the fire. 'You think I should have come to you first?'

She noticed that he did not say, *I should have come home first*, and so she lied. 'No, Ian, it was right for you to go there first.'

'I don't know what we're going to do. Her aunt and uncle are furious. Her parents are dead, poor wee lamb. Sitting here in the kitchen, I think I'm crazy to think I can marry her.'

'The tenancy, Ian?'

'I doubt they'd give it to me anyway and they won't give it to a woman, lass. If I leave here, you're homeless, and if I stay, who knows? Maybe Sir Humphrey will hound us out.'

'The agent says the lease is yours.'

'That's before Arabella told them. She kept it secret, Mairi, dated men in her own set, as they say.'

'Devious wee madam,' thought Mairi, and wondered when, if ever, he would realize that *she* had written her letters while working day and night to keep his home together, and apart from her one and only night at the opera with Jack, had dated no one *in her own set*.

'She won't want to live here.'

'Can you see her as a farmer's wife?' asked Ian and he laughed tenderly. 'But, Mairi, I have to tell you, I don't want to farm. I want to write. Thanks to Bella, I wrote all during the war, and . . .' He looked away from her as if embarrassed. 'I've sent some stuff to a journal. I won't let Bella help. I want to stay here and I'll work the farm, Mairi, I'll do the best job I can and when and if I start to make some money then I'll leave and marry Bella. She's rich, you see, in her own right, but I couldn't live on a woman.'

She had forgotten that Bella had known about his poetry. Bella had told her, her face alight with enthusiasm, that Ian was a genius, that he had memorized the poetry he was writing in his head because, in prison, he had had no paper.

She stood up. 'I'm tired, Ian, and I have to be up early.'

He stood up too and walked with her to the stair and at the bottom step she stopped and looked up at him. 'Please, Ian, you mustn't worry about me. I couldn't bear that. You stay here only as long as it takes to get yourself established. Bella thinks you're a genius.' She grinned up at him, the old, teasing Mairi. 'Mind you, women in love have nae judgement, or so I'm told, but I'd like to see your poems too, maybe, if you'd like me to see them.'

'I'd be honoured to have you read them, Miss McGloughlin. There's even one called "Mairi". It's about this horrible wee girl who plagued the life out of her long-suffering brother.' He stopped laughing and was suddenly serious. 'And there's one called "Friend". We'll take it with us when we go to see him.'

It was too much. She could bear no more. She moved quickly away up the stairs and when she had gone a few steps she turned and saw that he had not moved. He was so tall that she was eye to eye with him. 'I was so afraid there was no God, Ian, but there is. You brought Him back with you.' And she turned and ran lightly up the rest of the staircase.

Chapter Twenty-Three

The village postman cycled out to the farm more times in the last two months of 1919 than he had done in the whole of his career. Arabella wrote to Ian almost every day and Mairi soon learned to recognize her writing and her distinctive, expensive stationery. But other envelopes began to arrive too and Ian grinned or groaned each time he saw one, depending on its thickness.

These were letters from publishers interested in his poetry.

Just before Christmas Ian told Mairi that an extremely reputable publishing house had offered to bring out a limited edition of his poetry in the spring and, possibly more importantly to the lover, if not to the poet, Arabella was spending Christmas with her uncle at his Scottish estate.

'Now that I'm going to publish, Bella thinks Sir Humphrey will take me more seriously.'

Mairi looked up from the shirt she was sewing. 'And if he doesn't?'

'She's of age. I would prefer that she not be at outs with her family but . . . if it has to be . . .'

'You'll still marry her?'

'I don't expect you to understand, Mairi,' he said and she could hear the embarrassment in his voice, 'but I ache for her.'

Dear God in Heaven, how self-absorbed the nicest of men were. Women didn't ache, didn't lie awake night after night, longing, longing. Mairi sighed.

'Robin's father walked up with Bert this afternoon after school.'

Immediately Ian looked contrite. 'How is Robin? We'll visit again before the New Year if you like. Bella arrives on the twentieth. Perhaps just before that. What do you think?'

'He didn't come to talk about Robin, not mainly. It's Milly. He wants her to keep house for him. His daily is getting married at Ne'erday and since Milly will be looking for a job and a home' – she looked at him as if hoping that he would either confirm or deny this – 'and he already has the boys most of the time . . .'

'Sounds good, Mairi. An ideal solution.'

Mairi cut off the thread and folded up the shirt. It was a Christmas present for Ian but she assumed that he would not know that most of it had been sewn right under his very nose. 'An ideal solution to what, Ian?'

He had got up to put some coal on the fire but he recognized the iciness in her voice. 'Mairi, I'm sorry. Have I not been listening? My mind is so full of thoughts of seeing my work in print, in a book, Mairi, with covers and my name on the spine, and Bella, sitting where you're sitting, reading my new poems in her lovely voice. Ach, I'm selfish. I was thinking that if the Dominie needs Milly and has room for all of them in that cold barn they call a Schoolhouse, it would be an ideal solution.'

Arabella Huntingdon sitting in the front room reading poetry? He had left his brains as well as his naivety in that prison camp. 'Ian, we have to talk about the future. If you marry . . . when you marry Arabella, you don't expect her to live here?'

He laughed and it was his nice real Ian laugh. 'Can you see Bella living here?' He looked at his sister's white, set face. 'Gosh, Mairi, I didn't mean that it isn't a perfectly comfortable, probably the most comfortable of the small farms, but Arabella is a lady, oh, God, I didn't mean that either. What I mean is, she has her own home. I told you that. But I won't live with her there until I can support her.'

'And what about me?' She had not meant to say that; she had been absolutely determined that she would never say it but it was out now. Her fear was Ian's now.

'You can live with us,' he said easily, 'you know that. You're my wee sister. Bella wants to treat you like a sister.'

'But your Bella is a *lady*. I'm a farmer, Ian. That's all I've ever wanted to be, and if you leave I will have to leave too. They won't give a woman the lease, not a single woman my age.'

Obviously he had never thought the whole thing through. He was in love and his beloved loved him in return. Mundane, practical matters like leases had never crossed his mind.

'But you won't need it, Mairi. I've spoken to Bella. Where I go, you go.'

She was angry again. 'And if I don't want to go where you go? If I was old or married, then it would be different, I could run the farm with everyone's blessing, but since I'm still quite young and have no husband, they'll conveniently forget that I ran this farm for years with the help of a woman and two wee boys. The first man back from the war that has experience and wants a lease will get my home.'

'Robin?'

'Is going to Italy.'

There, she had said it and now the tears that she had kept dammed burst out of their prison. 'His father told me a week or so ago. Robin will leave the Sanitorium but he won't come home. He didn't want to be released back here, not yet, not until he's convinced himself that he's well.'

Ian remembered the urchin who had asked him if he was the daftie. Oh, yes, Robin would have to be quite sure of his mental health before he ran the gauntlet of the village.

'But then he'll come home and you'll marry?'

She managed to stop sobbing. Ian could not cope with tears and he had suffered so much; she did not want him to have to deal with them – not hers, Bella's maybe. If rich, beautiful women in love ever cried . . . ?

'We never once talked of marriage. We never said the words . . . marriage or love, never once.'

Ian wondered if he should tell her about the letter. *Robin is afraid that he might kill you.* No, he could not tell her. He took her in his arms, awkwardly. She was his sister. They were not used to embracing one another. 'Mairi, Robin loves you; I know he does. He's not a farmer. He's a teacher. And he won't teach here in the village. Where is the nearest town that needs a Classics master? Maybe Dundee, maybe Edinburgh. Who knows? When you marry Robin, you'll have to leave the farm. This way it's just a little earlier. I wish I could stay and be a farmer for you but I never wanted to farm. I will stay until I can afford to leave. If there hadn't been Bella, I would probably have stayed for ever and written my poems to keep me sane. But I love her and I need to be with her and I can't ask her to live here. You do see that?'

'Of course I do.' She blew her nose loudly and dried her eyes. 'I'm sorry and I never meant to cry and upset you. Goodness knows, if Robin asked me to go with him, I'd leave without even closing the door behind me, wouldn't I? And I don't expect you to stay here for me but, Ian, I couldn't live with you and Bella in a big mansion house. I'm a farmer. I don't know how to talk to her. I don't know how to dress. I'd embarrass you and I couldn't bear that.'

It was obvious that such a thought had never crossed his mind. 'Och, Mairi, you're havering. You and Bella always look so nice. But let's leave this for now, please. We'll talk to Bella and her aunt and uncle at Christmas.' He stood up because he was so excited that sitting down he could not contain his excitement. 'What a Ne'erday we'll have and then, because of Bella, we'll have to start celebrating Christmas in the English fashion. I've an idea, Mairi, for Bella and for Milly's bairns. We'll get a Christmas tree and put candles on it and presents under it for Bert and wee Jean, and maybe even Angus too, although he thinks he's grown up. What do you say?'

She could not bear to disappoint him and so she tried to sound enthusiastic. Was love enough to smooth all the bumpy paths that he was preparing to walk along? And what would Miss Arabella Huntingdon really think when she saw, daily, the conditions in which her love had grown up? There's nothing romantic about an outside privy, even in the height of summer.

Arabella came the first time when the house smelled of wood smoke and baking bread and Christmas cake. Mairi thought that she looked like a fairy lost from her Christmas tree in her silver white fur coat and tight little hat. She had gifts for under the tree and Milly and the children exclaimed over the beauty of the wrappings, paper and ribbons so expensive that Mairi blushed at the waste. She could not bring herself to thank Bella for the packages or exult at their beauty. All she could think of was that they made her home-made efforts look so provincial and she hated herself for her jealousy.

'Will you take some tea, Miss Huntingdon?' she asked stiffly and Bella looked at her in surprise.

She slipped off her fur coat and threw it over a chair and Jean and Bert, together, rushed to pick up the glorious creation. Jean fetched her mother's best padded coat hanger from the old wardrobe and they hung the coat up neatly on a nail at the door.

'Thank you, darlings,' said Bella but she was laughing and Mairi found herself hating her for her easy laughter.

'Mairi, please, we are to be sisters. You must call me Bella.'

'Bella' said Mairi and tried to say it naturally. 'You'll take some tea?'

And all the while Ian stood loving them both and wondering why on earth everything was going wrong. Bella tried

221

and Mairi tried but the visit was a trial for everyone and, too soon, before they had really talked, Bella stood up and Ian almost ran to get her lovely coat.

'I'll walk you back,' he whispered.

'Silly, I didn't walk all that way in these,' she said pointing to her soft leather boots. 'Uncle's motor is waiting. Let's take Bert and Jean. Come on, you two, if your mamma agrees you may have a ride in the motor.'

They ran in to the scullery shouting for Milly and Arabella looked at Mairi.

She seemed to sense that she should not offer such a treat to her and instead thanked her for the delicious baking. 'You must teach me, Mairi; if I am to be a farmer's wife, I must learn about the food that a farmer likes.'

'Ian's a poet, Bella, and has little idea about what he's eating. I'm sure your cook will manage.'

Oh, how she hated herself for that mean twisted voice that spat out these remarks. What was wrong? Was it that Arabella was so beautiful and elegant, and more importantly, nice, and did not deserve her animosity? Was it because she, Mairi, was jealous of the way that Bella and Ian looked at one another, at the way they let their hands touch over the homely tea table? How can I live in the same house and watch them love and know that Robin does not want me? Will I become the mean, twisted maiden aunt that their children will mock? She ran out after them into the beginnings of the first snow of the winter.

'Bella,' she called, 'Come back soon. This house is brighter with you in it.' And then she ran back inside because she was so embarrassed by her own spontaneity.

'Bonny lassie, that,' said Milly as she boiled the kettle for water for the dishes. 'She's no really seeing hersel as the wife of a working fermer, though, is she?'

'I don't think so, Milly. More like Marie Antoinette playing at being a shepherdess with her specially built perfect wee farm. Ian will give up the lease as soon as he's making a living from his writing and then they'll go to England and live in her big house.'

'I aye thought you had tae be dead tae make a living as a writer, if you ken what I mean.'

'The world wants to hear from the poets of the war; to make sure we don't get into such a mess again.'

'Well, amen to that, but what about you, lass? If I leave with the weans next week, you'll be on your own when Ian gets wed.'

'I'll manage, Milly. There'll be plenty of men needing work.' She would not worry Milly by telling her that it was highly unlikely that the Estate would give an unmarried woman a lease on the farm. If Ian and Bella were married before September, Mairi would be out of, not only her occupation, her life, but her home too.

Ian was not too sanguine about the prospects of an early wedding. 'I can hardly bear to be so close to her and know that we have to wait so long,' he told Mairi next morning as he poured fresh cream on his porridge. 'The Grey-Watsons won't even see me. Bella says she'll leave before Christmas if her uncle remains so obdurate . . .' He flushed as he saw her look of surprise at his vocabulary.

'Nothing else to do in prison but read what's there, Mairi. In Germany it was a German–English dictionary.'

Mairi smiled stiffly. He's beginning to sound like them, she thought. Even Robin, a Greek and Latin scholar, did not use such words around her.

'Obdurate? I suppose that means he's a thrawn old bugger.' She tried to smile.

He beamed warmly. 'Aye, but he'll come round. He loves Bella. He's been her guardian since she was three years old. He'll come round.'

Sir Humphrey agreed to meet Ian early on the morning of 24 December. It could only be a short meeting. There were so many social engagements that had to be fulfilled.

223

Ian, of course, had nothing to do but look after his stock; for working-class labouring farmers there were no social engagements.

Mairi pressed his suit and washed and ironed his best shirt. Then when he was dressing, she took her Christmas present from the little pile under the tree and took it up to him.

'Does it spoil Christmas if you open your present before Midnight?'

He took the parcel. 'Not if it's that lovely shirt a wee lassie has been working on for weeks.'

She smiled happily and went downstairs to wait. He had noticed. She would be more careful in . . . no, there was no future. His future was with Bella. He would never again sit by the fire in this farmhouse and pretend not to see his sister make his gift.

'But that's right,' Mairi told herself. 'That is the way it should be and it's what I want for him.'

When he had left for the Big House, she sat quietly reading by the fire. Since Ian had come back she had found renewed delight in the written word and in the few minutes each day when her hands were not busy she took one of Ian's books and made a new acquaintance or renewed an old one. She felt she might read a great deal more in the years ahead. It would be something to do, she thought, thoroughly sorry for herself.

Ian meanwhile had every right to feel sorry for himself. The interview with Sir Humphrey, his landlord, was not pleasant. He was shown into the magnificent panelled library where a fire was consuming, at one go, more wood than he would use all day, and where exotic hot-house flowers pretended that it was not mid-winter.

Sir Humphrey was seated behind his desk. He did not get up when Ian was announced and he did not ask him to sit. Ian stood in front of the desk and remembered how he had felt when the officers had tried to break his spirit. He had managed to resist then. He would not allow his spirit to be broken now.

'I have to say I'm surprised at your effrontery, McGloughlin. Can't say I expected it from your father's son.'

'I never expected to fall in love with your niece, Sir Humphrey, if that is the situation that insults you.'

'You're the uneducated son of a tenant farmer, man. You're not fit to clean her boots.'

If he had expected Ian to blush with shame at such an insult he was disappointed.

'I couldn't agree with you more, Sir Humphrey.' He would not say that it was Arabella who had done all the running. 'But I have fallen in love with her and, she with me.'

'She's a very wealthy young woman . . .' Ah, he had scored a hit. Ian pulled himself up and stood, if possible, taller and straighter, and a muscle worked in his jaw.

Sir Humphrey looked at him. 'Unworthy,' he said. 'I think I know that it's not her money, but, Ian,' and here he stood up, 'you must see that it wouldn't work. I know you are going to publish some poetry but, dear God in Heaven, do you seriously think being the author of some maudlin verses makes you the equal of a Huntingdon. You have nothing in common, lad. Bella thought it was romantic to champion you; you and she against the world. But when her world turns against her, and it will, then what? How long will the great Romance last?'

'If Bella's family and friends spurn her for marrying a decent hardworking man who will love and cherish her all her days, then she's maybe better off without them, Sir Humphrey.'

This time it was Ian who had scored the hit. Sir Humphrey went an alarming shade of red. 'How dare you! When did you leave school? When you were twelve, thirteen? How can you even converse with our kind of people?'

Ian laughed. 'Sir Humphrey, even for an aristocrat, Bella

225

is appallingly ignorant, but I'm remedying that. I came to ask, not for your permission, but for your blessing. If you can give us neither, then I will tell you that I will offer to let Bella go. I love her and would not harm her. But if she will not leave me, then as soon as I can afford it, I will marry Arabella Huntingdon.'

'We'll see about that. I own the house you live in, remember?'

Ian had not expected this. He would not get angry, he would not. He leaned forward and held on to the edge of the heavy oak desk. 'Then you would punish my sister too. I had not thought it of you, Sir Humphrey.'

The Laird slumped back down in his chair. 'If I throw you out to sleep under a hedge I play into your hands. Bella will merely insist that you move to Surrey with her. She is of age.' He picked up a pen, thrust it into a solid silver inkwell and then began to draw circles on the blotter in front of him. He looked up at Ian who still stood ramrod straight. 'Damn you, boy. Can't you see it's for you as well as Bella? She'll make you miserable in six months. She's used to balls and parties. Damn it all, she's welcome at Court.'

'And I'll take her away from all that? You do Bella an injustice, Sir Humphrey. She is a finer woman than you realize. If we think we can make a marriage work . . .'

Sir Humphrey stood up and went to the door and Ian had no choice but to follow him.

'Marriage between equals is difficult enough. You are just released from the prison camp, Ian. Is it love or pity? Give her a chance to really get to know you. Until October you'd met fewer than five times. Give yourself time.'

'I won't hurt her, Sir Humphrey. Try to convince her that she's making a mistake if you like. She must be sure in her own mind and heart.'

The sound Sir Humphrey made was almost a snort. 'Basic psychology. I tell her no. She'll dig her heels in. Damn it, I wash my hands of the pair of you. Invite her to your cottage.

226

Let the difference in your lifestyles speak for me. And you'd best emulate Kipling and win the Nobel prize with your writing. Even that might not be enough. I won't wish you the joys of the season. Good day to you.'

Ian walked out, head high, and managed to get to a bend in the driveway before being violently sick in the shrubbery. When he had recovered he turned and looked back at the great house. Was Sir Humphrey right? Was there too great a difference between them? Maybe Bella was living a fairy tale but this frog would never turn into a prince.

And then he saw her, running towards him down the driveway and he forgot all his good intentions and ran to meet her.

'My darling, my darling, we'll make it work. Ask Mairi if I may dine with you tomorrow?'

He kissed her cold little nose and then her cheeks and then her mouth.

'I don't know about dining, Arabella Huntingdon, but you're welcome to take your dinner with us.'

And in full view of the disapproving windows he kissed her again.

Chapter Twenty-Four

The Estate was being sold. Mairi could not believe it. It had been in the hands of the Grey and then the Grey-Watson families for nearly three hundred years. It was rumoured that an Insurance Company was prepared to make a sizeable offer as was one of the Ammunitions barons who had found himself, on the cessation of hostilities, with both a fortune and a title.

'Well, let's hope we don't have to work for him,' was Ian's comment when he read this item in the local news.

'Didn't Bella say *anything*?' Bella's letters, since she had returned to London in late January, were if anything more frequent than before.

'She hasn't seen too much of her family, Mairi. It only leads to argument and distress for everyone.'

Mairi sighed but said nothing. Ian had returned from the Big House on Christmas Eve, a little shaken, but he had said nothing except that Bella would be coming for Christmas dinner. That news, as he had expected, had thrown both Mairi and Milly into a panic and they had swept and dusted the already swept and dusted house and threatened the children with all manner of horrible penalties, should they drop a crumb anywhere. Ian wisely stayed away until Mairi herself decided that 'Bella can lump it or like it.' Still, when the children were in bed, she returned to the scullery to make one more baking of shortbread to add to the already heavily overburdened table.

Bella arrived wearing her silver fur coat. She had not

considered not wearing it. If Mairi was to be her sister-in-law she would have to take her as she was, fur coat and all. And if Ian was to be her husband, and she was determined that he was, then it would, in all probability, be her last fur coat.

She ate a hearty dinner, insisted on helping Mairi clear the table and so Ian felt that he too had to offer to help. In the end everyone helped and each got in the other's way and they had a delightful time.

Then, delicately, Arabella asked about hygiene arrangements and so Mairi took her to the outside privy which she had made as comfortable as she could, although nothing could prevent it from being cold. Bella judged it 'lovely fun' whilst silently vowing never again to enter the door, no matter how desperate she found herself.

She helped Jean and Milly dry the dishes and only dropped one cup. Bert and Angus fell madly in love with her and fought desperately to sit close to her by the fire. She foiled them by sitting the wool-clad Jean on her satin lap and Mairi watched and tried not to feel jealous of the beautiful girl's ability to win over everyone. But at last Christmas Day was over and Sir Humphrey's motor arrived to convey the silver princess back to her palace. Ian went with her and returned two hours later to tell the waiting Mairi that Rupert Grey-Watson had asked him in to take a glass of brandy with him.

'He was as nice as ninepence, Mairi, and very civil, but he thinks it won't work.'

'Perhaps he wants Bella for himself?'

'I must admit I thought that might be it. The Grey-Watsons lost money during the war while Bella's fortune seemed to multiply, but to Rupert she is merely a young cousin. He's fond of her, as you are of wee Jean, no more.'

For several days Bella seemed to be in the farmhouse more often than she was at her uncle's home and, on one auspicious day, Ian went into Dundee to hire an evening suit, shirt, tie and shoes. He had been bidden to dinner.

Mairi thought he looked magnificent. So too did Milly.

They watched him enter the Grey-Watson motor which had been sent for him and then drive off to the manor house.

'He'll easy be the best-looking laddie there,' said Milly proudly. 'That Rupert seems like a nice enough young man but he's no a patch on oor Ian. Well, I mean tae say, he's cried Rupert.'

'I think Rupert is very handsome,' teased Mairi as she shepherded Milly back indoors for their very last evening together, 'and I think Rupert is a lovely name.'

'Ach, you're Ian's sister right enough when you say daft things like that. Men should be cried Jim, or Angus, or Bert. You know where you are with a Jim.'

'Steak,' said Mairi softly.

'Aye, lassie, steak. Now come on and help me with my case. Noo that the Dominie's away tae see off Robin, I'll need tae get in there and take care of the dirt. I'll hae it readied up for him when he gets back.'

Mairi helped Milly with the family's accumulated belongings and tried to keep her mind off Ian's visit to the Big House and Robin's retreat to Italy. She would not allow herself to think about Robin, she would not. She would not remember that night before he went back, for the last time, to a war zone. She would not permit herself to think of the sweetness of being held against him while she listened to his heart.

Our hearts are beating together, Mairi. Can you hear them? Lub dub, lub dub. What can lub dub, lub dub mean?

But she had not been able to answer or to hear him tell her because the Dominie had come out and although he had pretended not to see and had hurried back into the Schoolhouse, the spell of the moment had been broken.

They had laughed, a little shamefacedly, a little resentfully – they had had so little time together – and they had gone back into the house so that Robin could share his last moments of leave with his father.

His last moments of leave. Were they, had they been, his last moments of sanity? But he was well, well enough to be released from the asylum. And instead of coming to her, he was running to Italy, the country where some of his best and his worst memories were buried. No, she would not think of it. She would think only of folding Jean's little nightdresses, her Sunday smock.

'Goodness, would you look at the size my laddies have grown here in the country, Mairi. If their daddy could just see them. Good country air, good country food.'

Mairi put the jumper Milly handed her into the box labelled 'Salvation Army'. 'The country is no paradise, Milly. There's some here as stunted as bairns in the towns. Look at that wee lassie Jean plays with.'

And they chattered on because neither could bear to talk about the future or the past. At last the cases were packed and they had no excuses left.

'How did I manage to gather all these things, Mairi, and still fill a box for the Sally Army? How can I ever thank you?'

'Please, Milly. If you talk like that it will feel as if you are going away for ever instead of just down the road.'

'Aye, and we've you to thank for that and all. The Dominie says my Angus has a brain.'

Mairi blew out the lamp and led the way downstairs to the kitchen. 'Your troubles will really start when he tells you Jean has a brain.'

Milly snorted with laughter. 'A lassie that's in love with Jack Black's old horse, a brain?'

They laughed together as they made a last pot of tea.

'Och, I'll miss having you to laugh with, Mairi. You've kept me sane these last few years.' Milly stopped, aware of what she had just said. 'Och, lassie. He'll come home to you, safe and well.'

Mairi stood up. 'We'd best go to bed, Milly. I don't want Ian to think we're waiting up for him as if he was a bairn.'

Milly moved as if to touch her and she shied away from the gesture. 'Don't say any more, Milly dear; we've been good for one another. I shall miss you so much but you'll only be in the village. Heavens, you could be going sixteen miles away to Dundee. Then I really would have something to be miserable about. Come on, off to bed, and we won't say goodbye the morn's morn, just cheerio.'

Milly said goodnight and went quietly off upstairs and Mairi fussed with the fire and the fire guard for a few minutes.

'Robin gone, now Milly and the children, and, if this dinner party has gone well, and how could it not, when they see Ian properly, Ian will be going soon too. If I have the farm I'll manage. Let them leave me the farm.'

She put out the light and followed Milly upstairs but she did not sleep. She lay wide awake, long after she heard Ian come back and climb the wooden stairs. She could tell nothing from his step. It sounded just as it always did.

She was, as usual, the first one up in the morning, and only someone who looked very closely at her face could tell that she had not slept at all.

Jean was excited about going to a new home but she was unhappy too and only the promise that Ian was going to walk with them to the Schoolhouse carrying their cases calmed her down.

'And you can come back as often as you like, wee Jean,' he said. 'Especially since Mairi only makes crumble when you're there to eat it.'

'And why not, since Jean's always willing to go out and pull rhubarb, unlike some I could mention.'

232

That remark, of course, set Milly off. 'Mairi McGloughlin, you cannae expect a man that's working all the hours God gives him to come hame and dig up his dinner afore he eats it.'

'And why not? There's maybe cause for saying a man should learn to cook. Mind you,' she added, as she noted joyfully the appalled expression on Milly's honest face, 'if anybody at the Schoolhouse had learned to boil an egg, there's you would be out of a job.'

Milly looked at her. 'Well, I'm off then. I have every afternoon off. Give me a few days to clean the place properly and I'll come back tae see you.'

'Fine,' said Mairi lightly. She did not want Milly and the children to go. They had known each other such a short time but, so much grief and happiness had been woven into their time together, it was as if they had always been friends. She hugged Jean and went back into the farmhouse as if this morning was just one of many mornings and she did not watch them walk off over the hill and down the school road.

Another step. Another stage. When Ian returned perhaps he would share his memories of the evening with her. Right now she had work to do. She would take the bedding from the big bed and soak it; too cold today for washing it and hanging it out to dry. She would have to wait for a dry day with a bit of wind.

Ian came back when she was turning the big mattress. 'Here, I'll give you a hand,' he laughed. 'And then I'll tell you about my grand dinner afore you burst.'

'Milly and I didn't give you a thought, Ian McGloughlin. We had far too many other things to discuss last night.'

'That's better, more your feisty wee self. Come on. The world won't end if you sit down before the sun sets. Now what do you want to know? Not the ladies' frocks, I hope, because apart from Arabella who was wearing a sort of blue thing, I haven't the smallest notion. I near died of fright when

233

I went into the dining room. First I had to take in, that's what they say, take in some old auntie who put her hand on my arm so gingerly for fear she would catch something, and I was seated miles away from Bella. The table would have filled the big barn and come out the other end and never in my life have I imagined so many dishes and glasses and bits of silver. Bella had shown me place settings – that's what it's called, a place setting, the right number of spoons and forks and knives for this, that and the next and a glass for this wine and another for that wine and a special one for water – but everything she had told me went right out of my head and up the chimney.

'"Not to your taste, young man?" asked this old lady on my right but she was smiling and holding her fork almost in front of my nose so I smiled back at her and picked up my matching fork and then ate what she ate and used the same fork or spoon she was using. And don't ask me about the food although there was chicken, I think, but I couldn't see it for sauce, and there was fish before the chicken, and they take a kind of frozen icecream between courses and different wine with fish and even a wine with the pudding, but not a dish a patch on your game pie . . .'

'And I suppose you told them so,' said Mairi, since he appeared to have run out of breath.

'I was too scared, Mairi,' he confessed. 'There were so many people and it was so hot and then the wine . . . I'm not used to drink. Sir Humphrey kept introducing me as "Bella's protégé, you know: damn good young war poet". But I let him talk. It was his house, after all, and I listened and tried to answer questions. At these affairs, it's like people are on strings. You talk to the person on one side and then everybody's string gets tweaked and you turn and talk to the person on the other. I got to talk to Bella after dinner in this huge room with two fire places and more wood burning than we've used all winter and she said it was going well.'

'And what did you think, Ian?'

He got up and put another log defiantly on the fire. 'I don't know. Rupert's a decent bloke and he thinks it would be wrong for me to marry Bella.' Ian laughed, but it was not a pleasant sound. 'It's me he's thinking of; he thinks Bella will make me miserable, even if I let her keep me, which I will not do. His mother is a different story. No matter how much she smiles and seems polite, I can tell that Lady Grey-Watson can't stomach the thought of me at her table. One or two of the other elderly ones seemed all right, interested in the war and in my poetry, but at least one of the old ladies thought I was a shirker and therefore ought to have been shot. They let Bella come back with me in the motor. She wanted to come in with me, force them, if you know what I mean, and it nearly killed me to send her away but everything has got to be right, above board, honourable, if you want to use such a word. She leaves today and I must get this book out and it has to do well, give me some kind of reputation.' He fell silent and they sat for several minutes looking into the fire.

'Will she come to say goodbye?' asked Mairi after a while.

'No. I don't think I could let her go again, Mairi. It's easy to be noble when she's not in my arms. Ach, damn it.' He jumped up. 'I shouldn't be talking like this to you.'

'I understand, Ian, of course I do. Goodness, war has an awful lot to answer for, doesn't it, or at least the people that cause the wars. Can you remember when we were wee, running to the school, scared to be late? If anyone had asked we would have said that by this time we'd be married with families of our own, and here's Dad dead and not even enough bits of him to bury, you, with your experiences, and Robin, my gentle Robin with his silly old Romans, marked so badly and cruelly that no one can even see the marks. Write your poems, Ian, and maybe even a book about the nature of pacifism, and write them so well that people will read and understand and vow that nothing like this will ever happen again.' She stopped, embarrassed, and, as usual, took refuge in mock anger. 'Now, will you get your great feet out of my kitchen and let me get on with my work. There's a farm to run, in case you had forgotten, and only you to run it.'

He went to the door, put on his coat and cap, and went out without a word, but she knew he was not hurt or angry. He would do his work and when he came in, his dinner, piping hot, nourishing, and recognizable, would be on the table, and things would be back to how they were before the war, except for the empty seat by the fire and the empty spaces in their hearts.

Chapter Twenty-Five

The postman, Davie Wishart, who had had a fairly good break from cycling all the way to Windydykes farm, was back on his rounds by February.

'Could you no consider gettin one of thay fancy telephone machines in, Ian, tae save my auld legs?'

Ian brought him in to the warmth of the fire. 'I would but we won't be here that long. I doubt the next farmer of Windydykes will have use for a telephone.'

'Unless I'm the next farmer,' said Mairi lightly as she handed the postman a steaming mug of strong sweet tea. 'I've decided to apply, Ian. They can only say no.'

Ian looked at her in astonishment but he would say nothing in front of old Davie.

He was eloquent enough when the man had gone, free-wheeling down the hill and then struggling up the other side.

'Talk to me, Mairi.'

'What would you like to talk about?'

Ian looked at her bowed head in exasperation. 'Mairi, was that a joke, a female emancipation thing, now that you're nearly eligible to vote?'

All men over twenty-one and all women over thirty had become eligible to vote in 1918. Ian had happily availed himself of the opportunity to participate in the government of his country but Mairi, of course, had still over a year to wait.

She looked up from her mending. 'Possibly, but I hadn't meant to say it until it popped out.'

'You are going to apply for the tenancy?'

'Ian, I don't want to live with you and Bella, if you ever swallow your pride and marry her, and frankly I want to be here if Robin comes home. The new owners of the Estate will put a tenant in the Big House and so you and Bella won't come back.'

'Yes, we will . . . I mean we would if it was necessary.'

'Ian, you can hardly wait to leave this farm, and I don't mind, really I don't. I think you and Bella should start somewhere else, probably not in her house either, but that's up to you.'

Mairi had done a great deal of thinking since Christmas. A marriage between Ian and Arabella would not be welcomed by the Grey-Watson family but it would happen and Arabella Huntingdon-McGloughlin would not fit in at Windydykes farm. Neither would Mairi McGloughlin fit her sister-in-law's life style. Ian would. He would adapt. He had never liked the farm; a cuckoo, perhaps, in another bird's nest.

'We will marry this year, but nothing will be done before I see how this first book is received.'

Mairi looked at him shrewdly. He was so strong when his beloved Bella was hundreds of miles away. His love and desire for her shone from his eyes when she was with him. Which would be stronger, his principles or his longing?

She smiled. 'Ian, does it really matter who is paying the rent? Don't waste your life or Bella's. Marry her and don't think about me. Maybe the new owners will be enlightened men and will allow me to take on the tenancy.'

Ian stood up. It was winter and there was nothing growing in his fields but there was still work to be done. 'If I could see you settled, Mairi. You're my sister and it's my duty . . .'

Mairi rounded on him and her eyes were full of anger. 'Duty? You owe me nothing, Ian. You have more than done your duty. If the Estate throws me out then of course I will stay with you and Bella until . . . until some other arrangement can be made, but for God's sake, put Bella

238

and her happiness first. Don't have her growing old and wrinkled and frustrated too.'

Ian laughed and got slapped for his sense of humour. 'Och, Mairi,' he said, still laughing, 'if you could see yourself. Anything less old and wrinkled I have yet to see.'

She went to slap him again and then started to laugh too. 'Well, give me frustrated at least. Away and tend to your beasts and I'll take my frustrations out on a batch of dough. And when are you going to look at the post after old Davie cycling out here and him two minutes from retirement?'

He had forgotten the letters and she watched him flip through them, smiling as he saw the usual thick missive from Bella. She turned away. No, once again there was nothing, not even a picture card from Robin. She was wrong to keep hoping. To leave the farm and follow Ian south was probably the most dignified way to handle the situation. He had known that he was going to leave her, that last day when she had visited him, and she had known but neither had had the courage to speak of what was really in their hearts.

She had met him in the greenhouse, a greenhouse bigger even than the one belonging to the Big House.

Robin had smiled shyly when she had come in.

'It's snowing, Mairi,' he had said.

'Yes, but it was exciting watching the snow from the train, Robin. And the train was warm.'

She had moved closer to him and immediately he had picked up two of his little pots. 'Seedlings. I shall give you one, Mairi.'

She moved back towards the bench on the other side of the room and he had relaxed again. 'Is Dad with you?' He had looked round as if expecting his father to materialize before him.

'He's talking to the doctor. He'll join us for tea.'

'You're good to come here, Mairi, but it's such a long way and . . .' He stopped and very carefully, as if it were the most important thing he would ever do, he measured soil into a pot. 'There must be other things to do, I mean, other . . . friends . . .'

'No one more important than you, Robin.'

At that he had turned and taken a quick step towards her and then he had stopped again and turned back to his bench. He had put his pots down and his hands gripped the edge of the bench so that she could see his knuckles standing out against the dirt on his skin. She ached to run and hold him, to turn him against her breast, to show him that he was safe, but she dared not. He was too fragile.

'I've brought my last pot of raspberry jam,' she said instead.

His voice was low. 'I love your jam, Mairi.'

'April! April,' yelled Ian behind her and she was propelled back into the present. She turned to see his face suffused by joy. 'April,' he yelled again. It seemed to be all he was capable of saying.

'April what?'

'Publication, Mairi. My poems are to be published in April.'

Immediately she forgot Robin. 'Oh, Ian, how wonderful! Come on, don't leave me in suspense. Tell me everything.'

He handed her the letter from his publisher. 'There's to be a launch, like for a ship. I'll have to go to London. You'll come with me, Mairi, on the train.' He grabbed his bonnet. 'I want to write to Bella but the cattle . . .'

'I'll feed them.'

'No you won't. Half an hour won't make any difference; I'm still farmer here. You stay in the kitchen, wee sister, where you belong.'

He laughed, kissed the envelope from Bella and put it back on the table to read later, jammed his bonnet on his head and went out, and Mairi was left with the letter that surely, surely would change her brother's life.

Ian, a published poet. She had never actually believed

240

that she would see the day. It seemed the kind of thing that happened to other people but here it stated that his first author's copy would be with him shortly.

London? She would go to London with him. She would stand proudly beside him . . . Mairi stopped in exultant mid-glow. No, she would not. Arabella Huntingdon, in silver furs and sparkling diamonds, would stand beside him.

'Not in April surely,' she tried to laugh and the laugh caught on a sob. She was not crying because Arabella would be there, but because Colin would not. How proud he would have been.

She told Ian so as they ate their dinner later, after he had done his chores, read his letter, and answered both the letter from the publisher and the letter from Arabella.

Ian's face, which had been so full of life, became cold. 'Would he? I'm not sure that his feelings might have been more embarrassment, but we'll never know.'

'Ian, he did not join up because he was ashamed of you. He wanted to do his share so that it would be over for you and the boy he saved and all the other boys, sooner.'

Ian put down his spoon and stood up. He pushed his chair in to the table. 'Please, Mairi. I just don't want to think about Dad. I want to think about Bella and April and nothing else.'

She watched him as he left the room and then listened to the sound of his boots as he walked up the stairs and across the landing into his room. The door closed and she could imagine him going to his table and taking refuge in his books or his writing. Wearily she too got up and began to clear away the unfinished meal, shaking her head a little at the waste and at the thought of Ian without food.

'He's a big lad and knows where the pantry is. I'm not going to worry about him.'

After she had washed up and prepared the table for breakfast she went to her father's desk where all the papers relating to the farm were kept and reread the letters about

241

the take-over. All existing tenancy agreements would be honoured. That meant that she was safe until September. But by the autumn, if Ian married and left the farm, she would be homeless unless she was awarded the tenancy. And, she decided, she would fight for her right to stay.

The next few weeks were busy. Usually, in the cold months, a farmer could relax a little, take care of repairs to his house or his steading or his equipment, even go curling on the ponds with other farmers, but Ian seemed forever to be at his desk answering the letters from London and Surrey.

Bella had insisted on paying for a launch party at an exclusive London hotel and she wanted Ian and Mairi to take rooms in the hotel while she stayed with the Grey-Watsons at their London home.

'And I want you to get some new clothes, Mairi,' said Ian. 'The money from the book is earmarked for a ring for Bella but I want you to take this to buy yourself something nice. You haven't had anything since before the war.'

Mairi looked at the heavy purse he had given her and remembered the thrill she had had all those years ago when Colin had given her money to buy a dress. 'I don't need this, Ian. I'm not coming with you.' He made to interrupt and she put her hands up as if physically to stop him. 'It's not that I don't want to be come but Bella will be there . . .'

'Of course she'll be there but *you* have to be there too. You *must* share it with me, Mairi.'

'I can share just as well up here. Och, Ian, take the money and get yourself a suit made. I want all those smart people in London to see that you're every bit as good as the Grey-Watsons.'

'That's got nothing to do with fancy clothes.'

'Damn it, Ian. Are you still so naive? Of course to decent people the cost of your clothes doesn't matter . . .'

'Decent people, like you and Bella, are the only people who matter to me, Mairi. I know Bella pays more for her

242

clothes than we could ever imagine but she's sensitive.' He saw from the look on his sister's face that he had said the wrong thing. Damn it, but women were difficult.

'You have discussed me with Bella?' She was furious.

'Yes. No. Of course. Not discuss, Mairi, but naturally we talk about you. You're my family as the Grey-Watsons are Bella's. We *discuss* all of you. Mairi, it would break my heart if you weren't with me at the launch. And Bella's too. She doesn't want to come between us.'

'That's daft. She's to be your wife. Of course she has come between us' – she saw his face and changed what she had been about to say – 'that's only right, Ian. Bella must come first – always.'

'You're my wee sister, Mairi. We are the same blood. That's a different tie from the one I want to have with Bella. Don't hurt me by not sharing my big moment with me.'

'Who will look after the farm?'

'Mairi McGloughlin? You know fine well any one of our neighbours will help out willingly. We can ask Jack now that his wife has decided that he's not still in love with you.'

Jack had married just before the end of the war, a marriage of necessity it was rumoured, and their first baby had arrived rather precipitately after the wedding, but they seemed to be quite happy and Jack's father-in-law, an Arbroath grocer, had been seen to smile, occasionally, at his son-in-law.

'I don't know that Jack ever was in love with me and I certainly was never in love with him.'

She turned and smiled at her brother. 'I'll come to your launch, Ian, and I'll stay at Bella's nice hotel. How could I miss your big day?'

He looked at her and he was perplexed. One moment she said one thing and immediately she said another. But she would come and his happiness would be all the sweeter because his wee sister was sharing with him.

'And will you buy something nice?'

She nodded and he should have remembered from their

childhood that Mairi nodded when she did not mean what she was saying. She would buy new material but she would not waste their hard-earned money on store-bought clothes.

As soon as she could she went off to see Milly. Jean opened the door of the Schoolhouse and threw herself into Mairi's arms. Oh, the sweetness and innocence of Jean who was not afraid or ashamed to show where she loved.

'Your mum busy, Jean?'

Jean rolled her eyes heavenwards as if for Divine guidance. 'You know Mum, Mairi. She's having a wonderful time finding things to do.'

Milly had heard their voices and came bustling out of the kitchen, her face rosy from her ovens.

'When did I ever have to look for something to do, you cheeky wee madam. Mairi, love, how good to see you. Come on in and tell me what you think.'

'Mrs Morrison used to call me a *pert wee madam*. Cheeky must be the same thing.'

Mairi looked around. Milly had been back to the farm several times since she had started working for the Dominie but this was the first time that Mairi had visited the Schoolhouse.

'Goodness what a transformation!' There were new curtains, new cushions, a rag rug in front of the fire.

Milly saw Mairi looking at it and beamed with pride. 'Would you believe the Dominie and Angus made that? My Jim showed me how to do it and I showed Mr Morrison that time we had the snow too deep for the school to open. They're making you one but you're not supposed to know. Gin they find enough old rags, there'll be everybody in the county with one of their rugs. Even Bert's had a try but he hasnae the patience. Come on, lass, come on, come away ben and tell what's up, or is this just a social call?'

'You're happy, Milly.' Mairi sat down in the old chair

244

with its new plump cushion. It was a statement, not a question. Milly was blooming.

'Och, he's the easiest man in the world tae work for. That besom took real advantage of him and I'm sure she was skimming off the housekeeping because could we no live like kings on what he gives me for foodstuffs and the farmers that generous with what they have. Mr Morrison is tutoring Angus for a scholarship to the High School in Dundee and he says he'll win it. Says he hasn't had a brain like this to work with since Ian and Robin were bairns. Bert's behaving; a stroke or two with the tawse has done him the world of good and Jean's that happy between her wee friends at school and that dopey auld horse, but come on, tell me all. Has Ian set the day? Is that it? Are there wedding bells about to peal?'

'I don't know about wedding bells but Ian has the date for the publication of his first book of poetry and they want more and even the novel he's going to write. Would you believe some manny in a big firm in London wants that from just talking to Ian and reading his poems?'

Milly sat back and basked in the reflected glow from Ian's success. 'A published writer. Well, I hope he'll never get so grand we can't talk to him – but not oor Ian. Even when he wins this noble prize that people talk about, he'll jist be Ian.'

Mairi knew exactly what Ian would say about his chances of winning a Nobel prize but she kept it to herself.

'It's about the day the book gets printed that I wanted to talk to you, Milly. It's going to be in London and Ian wants me there. But that means staying in a posh hotel that Bella has picked out. Clothes, Milly. Nightwear, underwear. I can't go into a splendid hotel in London wearing my own sewing. Ian has given me money for a new dress for the big day, a lot of money, but he doesn't realize about things like stockings and gloves and petticoats . . .'

'Trimmed with lace,' put in Milly. 'And hats and gloves.

And here's Miss Arabella with her silks and satins and you don't want to let Ian down.'

'I'm sure Bella won't care what I wear. She only ever sees Ian when he's in the room. It's not Bella so much as . . .'

'The maids,' agreed Milly, nodding her head vigorously. 'Now, how much time do we have?'

'Oh, Milly, you're a dear, but you're so busy here. I didn't realize you were doing so much.'

'Because there is nothing else to do, with Angus and Mr Morrison with their heads in books all evening and Bert doing his homework and bringing in the coal the way I hear Robin did when he was a lad. We'll go into Dundee on Saturday and we'll buy material and then I'll take you to meet Jim's sister, Jeanette, that has a stall at the market and we'll get trimmings from her and a decent dinner. Isn't she grateful for everything you did for Jim's bairns.'

Mairi tried hard to suppress them but in spite of her best efforts, the tears stared to fall. 'Oh, Milly, I took you in for me, not for you.'

'Ach, at first, lassie, and of course it was to help out, but God alone knows what would have happened to us if you hadn't needed me. If we were lucky it would have been ten in one room up a stair in Dundee, and my Angus would have been in some kind of trouble before he was fifteen. My boy's got a life ahead of him, thanks to you, and a few evenings sewing pretty things instead of cushion covers will be a joy. Now stop greeting. God, you're worse than Jean with your greet, greet, greet. But with her it's aye for a horse.'

'I've never wept over a horse.'

'Good. Now when's the big day, because weather'll make a difference.'

'April.'

'Is that not one of the nicest months of the year? We'll probably be able to use a nice linen and do you know what, Mairi? We'll make a silk nightgown and I'll embroider roses on it. I haven't done roses in a long time. It'll be perfect, white silk with wee pink roses, and when you get back from London, you can put it away for your honeymoon. For heaven's sake, lassie, don't start again. Hasn't the Dominie had a letter all the way from Italy saying that Robin's feeling better every single day?'

Chapter Twenty-Six

Ian's book *Quietus* was published in April to impressive reviews and, whether because of its subject matter or his military history or possibly because of Bella – maybe even a combination of all three – he soon found himself courted and honoured. He thoroughly enjoyed himself – for about a week – and then told Bella he would have to head north. The farm and his pen were both waiting and the publishers were pressuring him to produce more work. But it was becoming harder and harder to leave Bella behind.

'Talk to him, Mairi,' begged Bella as they sat in the foyer of the elegant London hotel. 'He won't listen to me. Doesn't he realize that every mother with an unmarried daughter will be throwing their offspring at his feet? I don't want him to find someone prettier than me – or younger.'

Ian laughed but Mairi did not. Bella had loved Ian for a long time. She deserved her prize.

'Bella's right,' said Mairi as she looked down at her silk-stockinged ankles peeping out demurely from under her lilac silk skirts. Oh, Milly was a treasure beyond all treasures. During this week of exciting happenings more than one young man had made Miss McGloughlin realize that she was not a dried-up old maid. Fine feathers make fine birds, she told herself with a smile. 'I must return to Windydykes' – for one thing she had no more lovely new clothes in which to show herself off and had in fact worn this dress to dinner the night they had arrived – 'but, Ian, you need not. Why don't you marry now in London, by special licence or whatever.'

Ian was scandalized. 'Mairi McGloughlin, what a thing to say.'

'Are you sure you want to marry such an old fuddy duddy?' Mairi asked Bella. She was amazed at herself. New clothes, the admiration of young men who had not grown up with her and who had not, thank Heaven, seen her in Ian's old dungarees and her rubber boots, had been, she felt, good for her morale. She could never have spoken like this before Bella even a year ago. 'Take your pride in hand, Ian, before it ruins the best thing that ever happened to you. Get married now. You're on your way. What more do you want?'

'I want nothing more than Arabella Huntingdon,' said Ian and it was at Bella that he was looking.

'Shall I come to you in my shift, like maidens of old, my lovely poet? Is that what you want?'

Mairi got up but they did not notice her going; their eyes were only for one another. She would go out, one last walk along the capital's exciting streets. Tomorrow she would return to Windydykes farm and she would put her lovely clothes away with a prayer that she might soon need them again.

Ian was not in the hotel when she returned and eventually she ordered a light meal from room service. She checked Ian's room again before she got ready for bed but still he had not returned.

He knocked on her door just before she went down for breakfast the next morning.

'I should have got a message to you,' he said and he was blushing with embarrassment. 'I took Bella home.' Then he looked at her directly. 'I stayed with her.'

'Have you had breakfast?' asked Mairi demurely.

Ian looked at his wee sister and the hot colour came and went in his face and then he laughed. 'You're a wicked girl, Mairi McGloughlin,' he said. 'Come on. We'll have breakfast and then get that train home. I'll need to get a

249

second book out faster than ever now.' He steered her away from the lift to the staircase where there was more privacy. 'We have decided. I'm going home but I *will* get a special licence and as soon as it's granted she'll come north. Maybe there'll be time for Milly to make you a bridesmaid's dress.'

Mairi threw her arms around him. 'Oh, Ian, I am so happy for you and Bella, so happy. Bella doesn't mind not having a big wedding?'

'Mind? Can you picture the eyes of the villagers if she turned up in her petticoat, and I wouldn't put it past her, especially after last night,' he finished quietly, enjoying his memories. 'She is so wonderful, Mairi, and I don't deserve her but I'll try to make her happy. Come on, are you hungry? One last big breakfast you don't have to cook.'

They went downstairs into the magnificent dining room which always filled Mairi with awe. Ian seemed not to notice his surroundings, to take for granted the elegant furnishings, the linen and china, the dutiful but not servile waiters. Oh, yes, he would fit very easily into Bella's world. But Mairi, though she could enjoy this life for a few days now and again, would only really be happy among her fields. She would only be really happy when . . . no, *O, that way madness lies* . . . she would not think of Robin.

'Are you going to ask Robin to stand up with you?' The words blurted themselves out.

'That would be wonderful but I doubt there'll be time. It shouldn't take too long to get the licence, and by the time even a cable got to Rome and Robin got leave – if it's the middle of a school term – we'll be married. Married, Mairi, can you believe it? Married, to the most wonderful woman in the entire world.'

His infatuation did not get between the lover and an enormous breakfast. Mairi, on the other hand, ordered tea and toast and had trouble forcing the toast down. Robin loved Ian and with Ian gone there would be one fewer reason for Robin to return to the village.

Her lovely new clothes were packed into her suitcase. It was a new suitcase and had looked so exciting in the farm kitchen but in the opulence of the hotel bedroom it seemed shabby.

'Never mind, little suitcase,' she consoled it. 'I think you're marvellous and I will use you every time I travel.'

She sat back on her heels as a picture of a nine-year-old Mairi in a flannel nightgown sitting at a window waving to the London train came into her head.

'What did I tell you I would wear?' she asked the long-ago train. 'I think I used to have a passion for red gloves but I don't remember. That wee Mairi no longer exists. And this Mairi has grown out of thinking brilliant red is a colour for redheads.'

Ian took out his jotter and his pen when they were settled in the carriage and Mairi tried to lose herself in a book but she was still too excited by train travel and so, until the conductor came to call the first sitting for lunch, she looked out of the window at the wonder that was England, that green and pleasant land.

Faster than fairies, faster than witches . . . The poem from childhood came back, word for word. Robin had recited it so well at his Dux prize giving. She would tell . . . no, she would not.

The words ran through her head as they raced through the countryside and halted for a moment when the conductor dragged Ian from the depths of Creation.

'Did you no order lunch, sir, the first sitting?'

Ian blinked at him several times and then smiled. 'Lunch, of course. My sister must be hungry.'

He was beginning to speak like Bella, if not to sound like her. His accent was Scottish but his language was different.

251

'I like it,' thought Mairi. 'My brother the poet. I wish, I wish that Dad had lived to see him acknowledged, to read these beautiful words.'

Colin was not alive to read his son's words but hundreds of others were. The small leather-covered book sold out within a few weeks of publication and was reprinted. Then letters with foreign stamps arrived and yet more letters from Ian's publisher: the book was to be translated into French, into German, into Russian. Ian was asked to contribute to literary journals and even to be an after-dinner speaker.

He took it all in his farmer's stride. 'Goodness, Mairi,' he said. 'It's an awesome thing that a man can put money in a bank just by sitting at his own fireside. If I did everything these people are asking me to do I'd never have time to write. And as for being an entertainment after too many well-fed people have eaten too much food . . .'

The wedding was to be at the beginning of May and Arabella arrived, together with her maid and her chauffeur and several suitcases, and installed herself in Arbroath's best hotel. The Big House stood empty waiting for its new tenant and they drove up one day so that Arabella could say goodbye to it.

'I loved this house, Mairi,' she said. 'The best games of my childhood were played here, and here I saw Ian for the first time, my knight in shining armour. I would like to have been married from here.'

'Why did they sell?' There, it was out. It was none of her business but Mairi wanted to know.

Bella seemed to understand her worry. She smiled as she turned away from the house and walked towards the car. 'Oh, nothing so melodramatic as trying to thwart us. It's retrenchment, nothing more. Not everyone made money out of this ghastly war, and poor Uncle Humphrey was harder hit than many. He needed to raise some money and it was a simple choice between Scotland and England. No one really

252

looked on this place as home, just really a little place to come to for shooting.'

Mairi looked at the 'little place'. The farmhouse of Windydykes plus the steading would no doubt fit nicely into the Ballroom.

'And your home, Bella, in Surrey?'

Bella looked at Ian who was contributing nothing. 'Well, I suppose it's a bit grander, would you say, Ian. It's older, Mairi, Elizabethan. When you come we'll go round. I don't believe I have been in every room; should be quite fun, Ian. We might find some ghosts or some treasure. He won't be able to say he has nowhere quiet to write, Mairi, and there's plenty of room for you. I shall enjoy having a sister, if you'll let me enjoy it, that is.'

Mairi had the terrifying notion that Bella's idea of having a sister was to spend as much money on said sister as possible. She abhorred the idea but she rightly interpreted Ian's warning look and said nothing. There would be plenty of opportunity to avoid Bella's well-meaning generosity. They would be married on Saturday, a simple ceremony with Mairi as maid of honour and young Angus as proud groomsman. Milly and Mairi would serve a wedding breakfast at the farm and the newlyweds, with Bella's maid, would drive off on their new life together straight from there.

Ian had asked Robin's father to act as Bella's father since Sir Humphrey had refused to participate in something he could not approve, but at the very beginning of the ceremony, just as they stood quietly waiting for the arrival of the bride, there was an interruption. A second car hurtled to a stop at the door and there was Rupert.

'I couldn't *not* be here, Bella my sweet. I don't approve, think you'll make one another miserable in a month, but here I am to give you to the poor poetic blighter, if you want me to. Maybe that's some kind of blessing that will bring you both luck.'

Bella started to cry and threw herself into her cousin's

arms but as Mairi began to wonder if a weeping bride would be welcomed by her groom, Rupert stopped her.

'Come on, old thing. If he sees you with great red-rimmed eyes he might well throw you back at me and I'll have driven five hundred miles on devilish roads for nothing.'

Bella sniffed, breathed deeply, and blew her nose delicately on a piece, it seemed, of gossamer. Then she awarded Rupert a tremulous smile and took his arm. 'You don't mind, Mr Morrison,' and, preceded by the Dominie and followed by Mairi, began her walk down the aisle.

It is doubtful if Ian even saw Rupert. His eyes were on Bella's beautiful face. She had chosen to wear not white but a dress in her favourite salmon pink and a small pink hat with a tiny veil that just covered her eyes. Mairi's new dress was in pale green and she too looked lovely.

She stood behind Ian and Bella as they made their vows in strong, clear voices and she tried hard to think only of them. This was their day and it would be as happy as the small family group could make it.

There, it was over, they were man and wife. Mairi heard a burst of glorious music and looked round and only then realized that the music was in her head. There was no one in the church but the small party.

'There should have been music.'

Bella had certainly given up a great deal to wed the man of her choice. Had she married Rupert or someone like him, there would have been organ music and banks of exotic flowers, rich, well-dressed guests, bridesmaids in beautiful designer gowns, but Bella seemed to be perfectly content with her simple wedding. She threw her bouquet which Bert caught and dropped as if it were red hot.

With Rupert's car there was plenty of room for the entire party and the Minister to be driven back to the farm and if Rupert winced at the paucity of his cousin's reception he gave no sign but danced with Mairi and then with Milly to the tunes played by Mr Morrison's ancient gramophone. Bella and Ian had eyes only for each other and they had to be reminded to eat and to cut their cake, made three weeks before by Mairi, and decorated with roses by Milly.

Then it was time for them to go and Rupert helped his cousin into her fur coat, since the day had grown chilly and they had a long drive ahead of them.

'You'll come and see us soon, Mairi,' begged Ian, 'and you'll keep in touch about . . . everything, the farm and everything,' he finished lamely.

'Of course, I'll keep in touch. Bella's postie will get as tired of me as old Davie got of Bella.'

'This is the worst time for me to leave you in the lurch . . .'

She stopped his worries with her hand. 'Ian, haven't I three men coming for interviews tomorrow and I have Angus and Bert as soon as the school is out? You have a whole new life ahead of you . . .'

'Which I can't enjoy to the full if I have a wee sister to worry about.' He turned her around so that they were both facing the little house where they had been born and brought up. 'It's not so easy to leave now as I thought it would be, Mairi. Part of me stays here.'

'Aye, but it's time for you to leave, Ian. I'll come to visit you both as soon as I can and I'll write to you every week. There, I can say no fairer than that.'

'After our honeymoon trip . . .' he began but she turned him again to the car where his wife was waiting.

'I know there's room and I know Bella really wants me . . .'

'And if you don't get a better offer,' he interrupted her and they both laughed.

'Bella waited for you and the look on her face says you were worth it, but this is her wedding day and you have kept her waiting long enough.'

She walked with him to the beautiful sleek motor car

where Rupert was standing talking to his cousin through the open window.

'Bye, Bella, be happy,' she said sincerely as she kissed her sister-in-law.

Ian turned to Rupert and saw the outstretched hand. 'Welcome to the family, cousin,' said Rupert and Ian could say nothing but only shake the hand that had once been withheld from him.

He hugged Mairi and then slipped in beside his wife; the chauffeur started the engine and the motor car, with Bella and Ian almost hanging out of the window waving, drew away from the farm.

Mairi was left with Rupert but there was no shyness now. 'Well, that's that,' he said. 'They make a handsome couple.' He gestured to his own car. 'Must be off,' he said. 'Staying with friends in the area.'

'Goodnight then, Captain Grey-Watson,' said Mairi.

He laughed. 'Goodnight, *Rupert*,' he said. 'Are we not family now? It's a strange new world, Mairi, and perhaps it will be a better place for us all. Make some sense of four years of carnage, I do hope,' and to Mairi's surprise and even greater embarrassment he bent and kissed her very lightly before he climbed into his motor car and drove away.

It was a lovely evening and Mairi stood for a while just reliving the last few hours – Bella's beauty, Ian's obvious happiness, Rupert's generosity of spirit.

'It's a strange new world,' she repeated to Milly who had come out with a shawl for her, 'and a better place for us all.'

Chapter Twenty-Seven

On 21 June 1920, Mid-summer's day, Mairi woke up feeling, for some unaccountable reason, serene and at peace. She was, as far as she knew, about to lose the home where she had been born and where she had laboured, lived and loved, laughed and cried, mourned and rejoiced, during all those years. There was no reason, except that it was a perfect morning, for her to feel so happy.

The sky was a deep blue, and the fields stretched out in all directions from the farmhouse like the spokes of a particularly verdant green wheel. She could hear the hens clucking happily just outside her window as they searched in the dust for crumbs or seeds.

And then she heard the sound of the postman's bicycle bell and she ran downstairs without bothering to tie back her hair. A letter. It had to be a letter from Ian. But he was on his honeymoon and had promised postcards. Who else would write? Robin?

It had to be Robin.

She threw the door open. 'Hello, Davie, you'll have a cup of tea and a bap?'

'I won't say no,' he said, which was what he always said.

He handed her the letter. She looked at the writing and the bright day dulled. It was not from Robin. Neither was it from Ian. She looked at it as if she stared hard enough she might see through the cheap envelope to the ill-written signature. The envelope was flimsy and her name, Miss

McGloughlin, was written in block letters in a poorly educated and laborious hand.

'Are you no going to open it, Mairi?'

Mairi looked from the envelope to the old postman's honest craggy face. 'I can't think who it could possibly be from. There's an old friend writes to me sometimes when she's needing something but even her writing is better than this.'

Davie Wishart sighed and flexed his bunions inside his comfortable old shoes. 'Have you got the kettle on, lass?'

Flustered, Mairi looked up again from the letter. 'Sorry, Davie. I hoped it was from . . . my brother.'

'On his honeymoon? You'll be lucky. What a bonnie bride she must have made. You'll have a likeness somewhere.'

'The beautiful bride and, Davie Wishart, her very handsome groom had a likeness taken in London. When it arrives I'll show it to you.'

Davie made himself comfortable at the table and began to spread butter on a soft, fresh morning roll. 'A fairy story, my missus calls it, except it's the poor boy marrying the princess.'

'The princess married an up-and-coming poet,' Mairi reminded him as she poured the boiling water into the teapot.

'Aye, imagine a farm laddie writing poems. It's the war has changed everything for the better.'

Mairi decided not to remind him of the legion of farm laddies who had written poetry before Ian McGloughlin and whose poems had not stopped the worst war the world had ever seen. But it was going to be better. It would never happen again. At last the world had learned a salutary lesson. She smiled at Davie, poured the tea, and turned again to her letter. It had been written from an Arbroath address but it was not one with which she was familiar. She turned the lined piece of grubby paper over but the signature meant nothing to her and she turned back to the beginning of the letter.

Dear Miss McGloughlin,
   I saw in the paper about your bruther.

Oh, no, thought Mairi, a begging letter. Many of those had come among the letters of congratulations.

I had been sorry not to have rote before but I was woonded and in the hospital in Rooong thats in France, 25 Stayshonary. Your father was my sargint the best ever and I'm here becos he got killt for me. I wantit to say thanks but also to tell his son that the sarge was riting till him when he got it. I give him my unvilope and he was saying as how his boy was the best and he loved him and ment to say and he was proud that his boy was rite all the time and the grenade came and he yelled not him, you bastard, xcuse my french, and flung hissel on me and sometimes I wundered maybe he dun it for his boy too.
   Anyways, hope this finds you well and I will never forget the sarge and my mam too.
      Chay Maxwell

'No more bad news, lassie?' The old postman was looking at her and she became aware that tears were streaming down her cheeks.

She smiled at him, a glorious, glowing smile. 'Wonderful news, Davie. I knew this was going to be a very special day. Here, read it. It's from the boy my father saved when he won his Victoria Cross.'

Davie solemnly put down his bap, took out his glasses and fixed them on his nose before he took the sheet of paper. He struggled to decipher it. 'Well, he never spent much time at the school, did he?'

259

'Who cares? I'll write to him, no, I won't. I'll go into Arbroath and take him and his mam my best boiling fowl. This will mean more to Ian than all his valuable wedding presents put together.'

She would go in the afternoon when all her chores were done until it was time to feed the animals in the evening. First she would wring the hen's neck and the carcass could cool while she was working. She gave Davie another bap and a second cup of tea and tried not to be impatient while he sat savouring them. He was, after all, her life-line to the outside world.

But, at last he was gone, freewheeling as usual down the hill beyond the house to gather strength for the steep hill that led to the main road, and she put on her apron and went out to the coop to choose the hen.

No matter how often she had had to do this unpleasant task, it got no easier. But, people had to eat, and a nice plump hen would be an excellent gift for Chay Maxwell and his mother. She wanted desperately to see the boy for whom her father had given up his life.

She did what had to be done and left the rest of the, no doubt, relieved chickens to commiserate with one another and took the unfortunate hen back to the kitchen. The postman was out of sight but someone else was on the farm road, someone walking.

'Good gracious, another visitor. Who can it be today?'

She looked again at the small dark dot on the hill. Was there something familiar? No, she was desperately trying to find something recognizable but she thrust the wish away. It was a salesman, merely a salesman. But he was so thin, tall, not so tall as Ian but thinner, so much thinner even than someone who had spent over a year in a prison camp. She stood, the dead hen in her hand, and refused to hope, but she could not move from the path.

The dark speck came nearer and got larger. Dark longish hair flopping over a too-pale face. He had seen her. He stopped. He looked and then he began to walk again, a gait she recognized, a stride that she had followed from the time, oh so long ago, when she had begun to follow her beloved brother and his friend, his friend.

'Robin,' she called and then she began to run and to cry at one and the same time and he began to run and when she reached him and was gathered up into his arms she had time to notice that he was crying too, before he bent to kiss her.

He pushed her away, his face flushing with embarrassment. 'I'm sorry,' he said and his voice was hesitant and unsure. 'I have no right . . .'

She put her fingers up to his lips. 'Oh, Robin,' she began.

'Let me speak, Mairi; for so long I have been unable to tell you. I was terrified, you see. Everything had been so clear when we were small. I was clever. I would go to the university, get a good degree, become a teacher, the seasons, everything in its place, following one another as the moon follows the sun. And you? You were just wee Mairi, an infernal nuisance, to be tolerated because of Ian. And then you stopped being a pest.' He was looking away from her towards the sea as if the story was written there on the waves for him to read. 'Then the war came and that was easy too, Mairi. I had to do my duty but Ian spoiled it because, next to my parents, I respected him most, loved him most, and he wouldn't fight and I knew he could lick us all. So the questions started and I went to the Front and I shot people, Mairi, I know I did, day after day, but it was my duty, wasn't it? And it was madness but you were there and I knew you were important to me, to my sanity, but that went too. Everything was so muddled, mixed up, like wire fencing that's got all tangled. The noise, that unbelievable, insupportable noise, never stopped. Even when I was in the hospital or here in my bed at the Schoolhouse, I could hear the noise and so I could hear nothing else, not Dad's voice or yours or the doctors'. I had dreams.' He looked away from her again, ashamed of his nightmares. 'The dreams made me afraid and I'm afraid again, Mairi, that it took too long. I wasted time when we were young, so much wasted time.' He looked down at her. How long had he known that he loved her? How long *had* he loved her? All his life? Since the dance at the Kirk Hall? What did it matter? She was so beautiful. Surely someone who was not afraid had come during those wasted years to tell her what a treasure she was.

Mairi put her hands up and touched his shoulders. She looked into his face, so brown from his months in the sun. His body felt strong, although it was still too thin.

'What is time, Robin? I read one of your books, one the Dominie loaned Ian. It's still here. "We live . . . in feelings, not in figures on a dial. We should count time by heart throbs . . ." A nice poem, don't you think?'

He did not move. She kept her hands where they rested but looked deep into his troubled eyes and at last he spoke.

'I know my feelings, Mairi, but I have no right to hope I know yours. I gave you nothing . . .'

'You give me everything, Robin,' she said and kissed him gently on his dry lips.

And then he moved. His arms imprisoned her and he bent his head to kiss her more deeply.

Still he could not allow the exultation to flow like warm wine through his blood. 'Mairi? I can't believe . . . surely . . .'

This time her lips and not her fingers stopped his words. 'Well?' she asked when at last they drew apart. 'Does that answer your question, Robin Morrison?'

The tears started in his eyes and, embarrassed, he dashed them away. 'I hoped, I prayed, but, heavens, Mairi, are all the men in Forfarshire blind?'

'Could I see anyone else with my heart full of you?' she said and kissed him again.

'My dinner?' he asked when they stopped for breath,

glancing then at the poor old hen lying abandoned on the grass and they laughed again as she explained about the letter.

They were walking now back to the farmhouse and her hand was in his, naturally, happily, where it had always belonged.

'I still owe it to you to tell you everything, Mairi. Perhaps I should have written but I didn't because I had to test myself, not my love for you. That has been strong and secure for a long time now, but my self, my head, I suppose. At Easter I went back to Rome and I got a job in the school where I taught before. They've asked me to sign a contract.'

He turned to her and the delight on his face sent a chill of fear through her. He was so happy. He was well and he was wanted by people whom he respected.

'That's wonderful, Robin,' she said and tried with all her heart to sound excited and happy for him.

'It is, isn't it? I'm well, Mairi. Now I can come to you with something to offer.' He took the hen which she was still holding and this time it was he who laid it on the grass. 'We'll take that into Arbroath later. Right now . . . Oh, Mairi, I do love you so.' And he kissed her again and this time as she responded she knew that she was offering him her heart, her future to do with as he chose. He understood and exulted.

'What would the village say?' he asked laughingly. '*What a hoyden that Mairi McGloughlin turned out to be.* Come on, let's get this poor old hen – hasn't it gone through enough this morning – to its new home and then we'll write to Ian and tell him we're going to be married. You will marry me, Mairi, won't you?'

Mairi looked at the little house where she had grown up. She saw the roses clambering over the doorway, the old dog asleep in the sun. She saw the fields and she photographed them in their summer dresses onto her heart and she said goodbye. For Robin she would go anywhere.

'Yes,' she said simply.

He turned to the hedgerow where the wild roses were blooming and he broke off one perfect little white briar rose.

'Roses, Mairi. I promised you roses, and maybe for a year or two wild roses are all there will be. Schoolmasters don't make a great deal of money. You won't have a home like the magnificent one Ian now owns.'

She put her hand to his lips and stopped him. 'I won't mind where we live, just as long as we are together. I'm sure I'll like Italy.'

'Italy? Well, it would be nice for a honeymoon, but I have no money left. We'd have to wait until next year and I want us to be well married by then; we've wasted so much time, Mairi, too much time.'

'But of course, Robin. We'll marry as soon as Ian gets back, before the harvest, so that you can be back in Italy by the start of the new term.'

He looked at her and then realization dawned and he hugged her to him and laughed and kissed her and kissed her and laughed again.

'What a brave woman! You thought I took the job in Italy? No, no, Mairi mine. I like Italy but I love you and . . . Mairi, I've taken a job teaching Latin and Greek in Dundee. We could live at the Schoolhouse with my father but, oh, Mairi, couldn't we live here?'

Live here? To live on the farm with its memories of Colin and Ian, the child Mairi, Milly, Angus, Jean, and even Bert. With a husband she could become a tenant. And Robin had loved occasional days of harvest; he had loved lambs and calves and, most of all, he had loved sitting under trees with Ian while they read, or wrote, poetry. He had grown flowers to help him in his therapy; she could teach him how to grow other things. A farm would be a grand place for a teacher to relax, a grand place to bring up children, a grand place for a poet and his wife to bring their children. She looked at her rose, already drooping. She would take it home and press it between the pages of Ian's first pamphlet of war poems, maybe between the pages with the poems called 'Friend' and 'Mairi'.

'This poor hen,' she said, holding it up for inspection.

'Let's take it down to Arbroath,' said Robin. 'And then we'll come back and we'll talk, Mairi McGloughlin, about changing your name.'